Advance praise for *Winterwood*:

"Swashbuckling action, folklore, and characters to care about: this is an authentic English take on historical fantasy, magic, and class."

—Kari Sperring, author of *The Grass King's Concubine*

"A fabulous and fun action-packed story, with an engaging heroine." —Liz Williams, author of *The Ghost Sister*

"I should read my outside my comfort zone more often: this book proves it. *Winterwood* is an easy, compelling read which ticks loads of boxes—pirates, fae, adventure, angst, ghosts, wild magic—whilst managing to surprise you with unexpected plot developments and delight you with its beautifully paced story and believably strange world. A delicious page-turner."

—Jaine Fenn, author of the Hidden Empire novels

Praise for the novels of Jacey Bedford:

"Well-defined and intriguing.... Everything is undeniably creative and colorful. Author Bedford's worldbuilding feels very complete and believable, with excellent descriptions bringing it all to life." —*RT Book Reviews*

"Bedford mixes romance and intrigue in this promising debut.... Readers who crave high adventure and tense plots will enjoy this voyage." —*Publishers Weekly*

"I'm very, very excited to see where this series goes next. The foundation that Bedford has laid has so much potential and promise. This is an author I will watch."

—Bookworm Blues

DAW Books proudly presents the novels of Jacey Bedford:

Rowankind

WINTERWOOD
SILVERWOLF*

The Psi-Tech Universe

EMPIRE OF DUST
CROSSWAYS

*Coming soon from DAW

Rowankind: Book One

JACEY BEDFORD

DAW BOOKS, INC.
DONALD A. WOLLHEIM, FOUNDER
375 Hudson Street, New York, NY 10014
ELIZABETH R. WOLLHEIM
SHEILA E. GILBERT
PUBLISHERS
www.dawbooks.com

Cover art by Larry Rostant.

Cover design by G-Force Design.

DAW Book Collectors No. 1717.

Published by DAW Books, Inc.
375 Hudson Street, New York, NY 10014

First Printing, February 2016
1 2 3 4 5 6 7 8 9

Acknowledgments

Novels are rarely the work of one individual.

Thanks to: my editor at DAW, Sheila Gilbert, for guidance and insightful comments, and for having faith in my writing; Josh Starr and all the DAW staff who work so hard behind the scenes; my agent Amy Boggs at Donald Maass Literary Agency; Larry Rostant for the fantastic cover illustration; Beth Fleisher who pushed me to make this better and better long before it was sold; my first readers: N. M. Browne, Kari Sperring, Carl Allery, Bill Swears; Liz Williams and all the participating writers from the Milford SF Writers' Conference who critiqued sections in the early stages; Northwrite members, Tina Anghelatos, John Moran (and Sara), Terry Jackman and Liz Sourbutt, who acted as beta readers on the final version; Hilary Spencer for proofreading skills, and to Jaine Fenn for the tiny, model, cross-dressing, female pirate, who sat on my desk and threatened me with a flintlock pistol if I shirked my writing duties.

As ever my love and thanks to my husband, Brian Bedford; kids Ghillan and Joe, and my mother Joan Lockyer. I probably owe them sincere apologies, too, for my obsessive writing habits.

And my thanks to you for reading. You can catch up with me and my books at www.jaceybedford.co.uk, on Facebook at www.facebook.com/jacey.bedford.writer, and on Twitter @jaceybedford.

Jacey Bedford
Yorkshire, England

1

A Bitter Farewell

April 1800, Plymouth, England

THE STUFFY BEDROOM STANK OF SICKNESS, with an underlying taint of old lady, stale urine, and unwashed clothes, poorly disguised with attar of roses. I'd never thought to return to Plymouth, to the house I'd once called home; a house with memories so bitter that I'd tried to scour them from my mind with saltwater and blood.

Had something in my own magic drawn me back? I didn't know why it should, though it still had the capacity to surprise me. I could control it at sea, but on land it gnawed at my insides. Even here, less than a mile from the harbor, power pulsed through my veins, heating my blood. I needed to take ship soon, before I lost control.

Little wonder that I'd felt no need to return home since eloping with Will.

My ears adjusted to the muffled street sounds, my eyes to the curtained gloom. I began to pick out familiar shapes in the shadows, each one bringing back a memory, all of them painful. The dressing table with its monstrously carved lion mask and paw feet where I had once sat and experimented with my mother's face powder and patches, earning a beating with the back of a hairbrush for the mess. The tall bed—a mountain to a small child—upon which I had first seen the tiny, shawl-wrapped form of my brother, Philip, the new son and heir, pride and joy, in my mother's arms.

And there was the ornate screen I'd once hidden behind, trapped accidentally in some small mischief, to witness a larger mischief when my mother took Larien, our rowankind bondsman, to her lonely bed. I hadn't understood, then, what was happening beneath the covers, but I'd instinctively known that I should not be there, so I'd swallowed my puzzlement and kept silent.

Now, the heaped covers on that same bed stirred and shifted.

"Philip?" Her voice trembled and her hand fluttered to her breast. "Am I dreaming?"

My stomach churned and my magic flared. I swallowed hard, pushed it down and did my best to keep my voice low and level. "No, Mother, it's me."

"Rossalinde? Good God! Dressed like a man! You never had a sense of decorum."

It wasn't a question of decorum. It was my armor. I wore the persona as well as the clothes.

"Don't just stand there, come closer." My mother beckoned me into the gloom. "Help me up."

She had no expectation that I would disobey, so I didn't. I put my right arm under hers and my left arm around her frail shoulders and eased her into a sitting position, hearing her sharp indrawn gasp as I moved her. I plumped up pillows, stepped back and turned away, needing the distance.

I twitched the curtain back from the sash window an inch or two to check that the street outside was still empty, listening hard for any sound of disturbance in the normality of Twiling Avenue—a disturbance that might indicate a hue and cry heading in my direction. I'd crept into the house via a back entrance through the next-door neighbor's shrubbery. The hedge surrounding the house across the street rippled as if a bird had fled its shelter. I waited to see if there was any further movement, but there wasn't. So far there was nothing beyond the faint cries of the vendors in the market two streets over and the raucous clamor of the wheeling gulls overhead.

Satisfied that I was safe for now, I turned back to find my mother had closed her eyes for a moment. She snatched a series of shallow breaths before she gave one long sigh. Opening her eyes again, she regarded me long and steady. "Life as a pirate's whore certainly seems to suit you."

"Yes, Mother." *Pirate's whore!* I pressed my lips together. It wasn't worth arguing. She was wrong on both counts, pirate and whore. As privateers, we cruised under letters of marque from Mad King George for prizes of French merchantmen, Bonaparte's supply vessels. As to the whore part, Will and I had married almost seven years ago.

"So you finally risked your neck to come and say goodbye. I wondered how long it would take. You're almost too late."

I didn't answer.

"Oh, come on, girl, don't beat about the bush. My belly's swollen tight as a football. This damn growth is sucking the life out of me. Does it make you happy to see me like this? Do you think I deserve it?"

I shook my head, only half-sure I meant it. Damn her! She still had me where it hurt. I'd come to dance on her grave and found it empty.

"What's the matter?"

I waited for "Cat got your tongue?" but it didn't come.

"Give me some light, girl."

I went to open the curtains.

"No, keep the day away. Lamplight's kinder."

I could have brightened the room with magic, but magic—specifically my use of it—had driven a wedge between us. She had wanted a world of safety and comfort with the only serious concerns being those of fashion and taste, acceptable manners and suitable suitors. Instead she'd been faced with my unacceptable talents.

I struck a phosphor match from the inlaid silver box on the table, lifted the lamp glass and lit the wick. It guttered and smoked like cheap penny whale oil. My mother's standards were slipping.

I took a deep breath; then, to show that she didn't have complete control of the proceedings, I flopped down into the chair beside the bed, trying to look more casual than I felt.

Her iron-gray hair was not many shades lighter than when I'd last seen her seven years ago. Her skin was pale and translucent, but still unblemished. She'd always had good skin, my mother: still tight at fifty, as mine would probably be if the wind and the salt didn't ruin it, or if the Mysterium didn't hang me for a witch first.

She caught me studying her. "You really didn't expect to see me alive, did you?"

I shrugged. I hadn't known what to expect.

"But you came all the same."

"I had to." I still wasn't sure why.

"Yes, you did." She smirked. "Did you think to pick over my bones and see what I'd left you in my will?"

No, old woman, to confront you one last time and see if you still had the same effect on me. I cleared my throat. "I don't want your money."

"Good, because I have none." She pushed herself forward off her pillows with one elbow. "Every last penny from your father's investments has gone to pay the bills. I've had to sell the plate and my jewelry, such as it was. All that's left is show. This disease has saved me from the workhouse." She sank back. "Don't say you're sorry."

"I won't because I'm not."

Leaving had been the best thing I'd ever done.

Life with Will had been infinitely more tender than it had ever been at home. I didn't regret a minute of it. I wished there had been more.

The harridan regarded me through half-closed eyes. "And have I got any by-blow grandchildren I should know about?"

"No." There had been one, born early, but the little mite had not lasted beyond his second day. She didn't need to know that.

"Not up to it, is he, this Redbeard of yours? Or have you unmanned him with your witchcraft?"

I ignored her taunts. "What do you want, forgiveness? Reconciliation?"

"What do I want?" She screwed her face up in the semblance of a laugh, but it turned to a grimace.

"You nearly got us killed, Mother, or have you conveniently forgotten?"

"That murdering thief took all I had in the world."

All she had in the world? Ha! That would be the ship she was talking about, not me.

"That murdering thief, as you put it, saved my life."

And my soul and my sanity, but I didn't tell her that. He'd taught me to be a man by day and a woman by night, to use a sword and pistol, and to captain a ship. He'd been my love, my strength and my mentor. Since his death I'd been Captain Redbeard Tremayne in his stead—three years a privateer captain in my own right.

"Is he with you now?"

"He's always with me."

That wasn't a lie. Will showed up at the most unlikely times, sometimes as nothing more than a whisper on the wind.

"So you only came to gloat and to see what was left."

"I don't want anything of yours. I never did."

"Oh, don't worry, what's coming to you is not mine. I'm only passing it on—one final obligation to the past." Her voice, still sharp, caught in her throat and she coughed.

"Do you want a drink?" I asked, suddenly seeing her as a lonely and sick old woman.

"I want nothing from you." She screwed up her eyes. Her hand went to her belly. I could only stand by while she struggled against whatever pain wracked her body.

Finally she spoke again. "In the chest at the foot of the bed, below the sheet."

I knelt and ran my fingers across it. It had been my father's first sea chest, oak with a tarnished brass binding. I let my fingers linger over his initials burnt into the top. He'd been an absentee father, always away on one long voyage after the other, but I'd loved his homecomings, the feel of his scratchy beard on my cheek as he hugged me to him, the smell of the salt sea and pipe tobacco, the presents, small but thoughtful: a tortoiseshell comb, a silken scarf, a bracelet of bright beads from far-off Africa.

I pulled open the catch and lifted the lid.

"Don't disturb things. Feel beneath the left-hand edge."

I slid my hand under the folded linen. My fingers touched something smooth and cool. I felt the snap and fizz of magic and jerked back, but it was too late, the thing, whatever it was, had already tasted me. Damn my mother. What had she done?

I drew the object out to look and found it to be a small, polished wooden box, not much deeper than my thumb. I'd never seen its like before, but I'd heard winterwood described and knew full well what it was. The grain held a rainbow, from the gold of oak to the rich red of mahogany, shot through with ebony hues. It sat comfortably in the palm of my hand, so finely crafted that it was almost seamless. My magic rose up to meet it.

I tried the lid. "It's locked."

She had an odd expression on her face.

"Is this some kind of riddle?" I asked.

"Your inheritance."

"How does it open? What's inside it?"

"That's for you to find out. I never wanted any of it."

My head was full of questions. My mother hated magic, even the sleight-of-hand tricks of street illusionists. How could this be any inheritance of mine?

Yet I could feel that it was.

I turned the box around in my hands. There was something trapped inside that wanted its freedom. No point in asking if anyone had tried to saw it open. You don't work ensorcelled winterwood with human tools.

Wrapping both hands around the box, I could feel it was alive with promise. It didn't seem to have a taint of the black about it, but it didn't have to be dark magic to be dangerous.

I shuddered. "I don't want it."

"It's yours now. You've touched it. I've never handled it without gloves."

"Where did it come from?"

She shook her head. "Family."

"Neither you nor Father ever mentioned family, not even my grandparents."

"Long gone, all of them. Gone and forgotten."

"I don't even know their names."

"And better that way. We left all that behind us. We started afresh, Teague and I, making our own place in society. It wasn't easy even in this tarry-trousers town. Your ancestors companied with royalty, you know, though much good it did them in the end. You're a lady, Rossalinde, not a hoyden." She winced, but whether from the memories or the pain I couldn't tell. "That blasted thing is all that's left of the past. It followed me, but it's too much to . . ." Her voice trailed off, but then she rallied. "I wasn't having any of it. It's your responsibility now. I meant to give it to you when you came of age." She narrowed her eyes and glared at me. "How old are you, anyway?"

I was lean and hard from life at sea. You didn't go soft in my line of work. "I'm not yet five and twenty, Mother." I held up the box and stared at it. "What if I can't open it?"

"I suppose you'll have to pass it on to the next generation."

"There won't be a next generation."

She shrugged and waved me away with one hand.

"Give it to Philip." I held it out to her, but she shrank back from it and her eyes moistened at my brother's name. What had he been up to now? Likely he was the one who'd spent all her money. I hadn't seen Philip for seven years, but I doubted he'd reformed in that time. He'd been a sweet babe, but had grown into a spoilt brat, manipulative and selfish, and last I saw he was carrying his boyhood traits into adolescence, turning into an opportunist with a slippery tongue.

"Always to the firstborn. But you're behind the times, girl. Philip's dead. Dead these last seven months." Her voice broke on the last words.

"Dead?" I must have sounded stupid, but an early death was the last thing I'd envisioned for Philip. The grievances

I'd held against him for years melted away in an instant. All I could think of was the child who'd followed me around, begging that I give him a horsey ride or tell him a story.

"How?"

"A duel. In London. A matter of honor was the way it was written to me."

"Oh." It was such an ineffectual thing to say, but right at that moment I didn't really know how I felt. Had Philip actually developed a sense of honor as he grew? Was there a better side to my brother that I'd never seen? I hoped so.

"Is that all you can say? You didn't deserve a brother. You never had any love for him."

I let that go. It wasn't true.

"I thought you might have changed." My mother's words startled me and I realized my mind had wandered into the past. Stay sharp. This might yet be a trap, some petty revenge for the wrongs she perceived that I heaped on her: loss of wealth, loss of station, now loss of son. Next she'd be blaming me for the loss of my father, though only the sea was to blame for that.

"That's all I've got for you." She turned away from me. "It's done. Now, get out."

"Mother, I—"

"I'm ready for my medicine."

I knew it would be the last time I'd see her. I wanted to say how sorry I was. Sorry for ruining her life, sorry for Philip's death. I wanted to take her frail body in my arms and hold her like I could never remember her holding me, but there was nothing between us except bitterness. Even dying, there was no forgiveness.

I turned and walked out, not looking back.

2

Departure

THE DAMP APRIL DAY had faded to an early dusk, a good time to slip between shadows. I left Twiling Avenue behind me and turned downhill, toward the sea and through the market into the Old Town.

Philip, dead. I still couldn't quite believe it.

Any ill will I'd harbored was already receding, though I could summon it if I recalled the times he'd caused me to be blamed for his own petty misdemeanors.

"I forgive you, Philip." I muttered the words quietly and tried to recall the good times: games in the nursery with Ruth, our rowankind nurse; making up stories to send him to sleep at night; our shared dislike of the governess Mother appointed to look after us the year she went traveling.

Cobbled East Street burrowed between crazily crooked houses where the licensed witchkind lived and did their business, constrained by the town's bylaws and the Mysterium to practice only small magics.

I was not like them.

The Mysterium was afraid of my kind of magic. Natural magic couldn't be constrained by their rules.

A shadow moved ahead of me.

"Cap'n."

"Hookey?"

"Aye." A lean figure, face like a walnut above a bushy brown beard, emerged from a gloomy alley between two shops. "Been waiting here nigh on an hour. Best not go down to Sutton Pool. One of the sailors from the *Dormir* let slip there was a woman in breeches an' a bearded man on board. There's a few rumors flying 'bout Redbeard being back in town, and there's a troop of marines sniffing their way from tavern to tavern on the quay."

"Goddammit!" We'd lost our planned exit route back to the *Heart*. My mother might be the death of me yet. "Are you certain they know who we are?"

"They ain't takin' no chances. Redbeard's still wanted for murder and you for—"

"I know. Any other ships getting ready to sail?"

"Nothing we can take passage on. There's a navy ship heading off to Dover and a merchantman taking on cargo for Boston, but she ain't due to leave until three days hence."

The winterwood box sat solid in my pouch, giving off a low-level magic tingle that I could feel in my bones. I couldn't take time to think about it now. My head was spinning. Damn my brother's mortality and my mother's deliberate obfuscation!

We were going to have to go cross-country to the northern coast. That would tax my control of magic to the limit. If I had a better choice I'd take it, but I hadn't. Since we couldn't safely leave by sea from here, we were out of options.

I weighed the danger of going against the danger of staying, and decided I didn't want to risk dancing the hempen jig anytime soon.

"We'll have to go across the peninsula and take a ship from Bideford."

"Go inland?" Hookey's tone indicated that I'd asked him to do something unthinkable.

"Yes."

"What, walk?"

"No, we'll take horses."

"Oh, no, Cap'n. 'Tain't right to put a seaman upon a horse. Sink me, it ain't."

"It's fifty miles. Would you prefer to go on foot?"

"I'd rather lay low here and take a ship later. You know me and horses. My arse don't much like saddle leather."

I had different reasons for not wanting to pass close to the Okewood. That haunted woodland still had power to drive good men mad, even in this enlightened age. Magic may have been sanitized in our towns, confined to licensed, "safe" practitioners controlled by the Mysterium, but it still gathered in the wild woods, pooling in the hollows, twining with the roots, and dripping from the branches of the great trees. The last thing I wanted, or needed, was to go near any of those places. I hoped to skirt the Okewood rather than go through it. I'd grown up with my mother's stories and her warnings to stay away from the forests where evil lurks.

I shuddered. It wouldn't take much to dissuade me from going inland, and Hookey knew that. He looked at me from under heavy-lidded eyes. "Or you could call the *Heart*."

It's a part of my magic that works without my knowing how or why. Deep inside me, I know where the *Heart* is at any given time. When I need her, she comes to me. Mr. Sharpner, my sailing master, was skeptical at first, but he long ago stopped worrying about it. When the *Heart* turns her bow and runs counter to her course, he's learned to follow.

I let my senses rove to the *Heart* and found her sailing off the coast of France, probably cruising for a prize, preferably one of Bonaparte's supply ships. I shook my head. "She's six or seven days away, Hookey, and besides, I'd not risk her in Plymouth waters under the Citadel's guns. She's too well known around this coast as Redbeard's ship, even with letters of marque."

I could tell that Hookey had his eye on a whorehouse down by Sutton Pool for a hideout, and that stiffened my resolve as it stiffened other parts of my very able seaman.

Even if we could keep away from the redcoats, I was damned if I was going to spend a week or more imprisoned in some garret, whiling away my hours by darning my stockings, whilst Hookey took a blithesome holiday endeavoring to catch seven different doses of the pox.

I grinned at him. "Besides, what possible attraction could a week in a whorehouse have for a sailor?"

"Aww, Cap'n."

"And with that thick bush on your chin it's likely they'll hang you for Redbeard Tremayne without asking too many questions."

He sniffed. "Where are we going to get horses from?"

"My mother has a pair of carriage horses. She's not likely to be needing them again."

Side by side, Hookey and I strolled back to Twiling Avenue, trying not to look furtive. As dusk deepened, people about us hurried home, hunched against the weather.

A pair of rowankind, one middle-aged and one young, struggled to push a large barrel up the short ramp to an inn door. One glanced at me, and for a moment I saw a look of barely concealed hostility before he blinked, and that vague rowankind expression smoothed out the lines on his face.

"Have you ever wondered," I asked Hookey, "why the abolitionists press the cause of the Africa trade so fervently, yet never make mention of our own rowankind?"

Rowankind were bonded to one family, usually for life. They couldn't be sold like cattle, but their bond-papers could be transferred if circumstances required it.

"They don't see it," he answered gruffly. "Or maybe they don't want to see it. It ain't like rowankind are whipped or beaten or starved or frozen to death in the winter."

Was he right? Could it be that few perceived the rowankind's bondage as slavery? It was never named as such. Just because the fetters were paper rather than iron didn't mean the rowankind had freedom, though.

"Did you have rowankind—before you went to sea, I mean?"

Hookey had never offered to tell of his background and I'd never asked. He'd been a pirate, I knew that much.

He made a dismissive noise and shook his head. "There were times I'd have signed away my freedom like the rowankind for a hot meal and a place to sleep out of the rain. I was so scrawny when I was twelve that I practically had to beg the press-gang to take me. That's how I went to sea, courtesy of His Majesty." He held up his hook. "Until this. I was put off in Portsmouth with five shillings and what I wore on my back."

"How old were you?"

"Seventeen—eighteen, maybe, but I'd grown some by that time, even on navy vittles, and I'd learned the seafaring life. Managed to talk my way aboard a barquentine. Sloppy ship, she was. Got attacked by pirates. I was happy to take up the pirating trade. Couldn't be any worse than the bilges of a barquentine, and it was a good alternative to being thrown overboard." We walked in silence for a minute or two, until Hookey said, "Rowankind don't fare well on the sea, though. When I sailed with Rogers on the *Black Dog* we took a Scottish schooner on its way to the Americas with a family trying to transport their rowankind. Three of the poor bastards had died already and two more were belowdecks puking their lives away. Too far gone to save, so the first mate made an end of them. A kindness."

I didn't ask what had happened to the family or the ship's crew.

"Have you ever seen rowankind or their like anywhere else in the world?"

Hookey shook his head.

"Neither have I. When I lived in Plymouth I never questioned their presence—our own rowankind were part of my family—but have you ever wondered why rowankind bondservants are unique to Britain? It's only coming back that I see the strangeness of it. If the abolitionists achieve their aims for the Africans, will they then turn their attention to the rowankind, do you think?"

No one sailed aboard my ship as a slave. They were all

free and equal, regardless of their origins, hue, or even their gender.

Hookey just shrugged. "There's a lot wrong with the world. The do-gooders can only tackle a small part of it."

The hill took our breath away as we climbed toward Twiling Avenue and ended our conversation.

My mother's house stood behind a high wall in a quarter-acre of overgrown greenery. It was an elegantly proportioned residence, built some years ago in the time of the first King George. The facade had once been gracious, but now patches of stucco crumbled away from the brickwork, and ivy rampaged up the side wall and over the hipped roof. There were no lamps burning that I could see, but that didn't signify. My mother's thick curtains would effectively smother any light at birth.

As we turned down the alley toward the back of the house we walked into evening shadows solid enough to make an undertaker's hat. Hookey cursed as he tripped over something. I risked a tiny witchlight, no bigger than a single candle flame, and sent it ahead of us, low down to the ground, to guide our way via the back gate to the yard.

The gate stood wide open. Next to it was a stable attached to a cottage where, in my father's time, our rowankind groom and gardener had lived.

My mother had retained just four rowankind after my father's death. Larien and a stable lad had lived in the cottage while Ruth and Evy had had the attic rooms above the main house. I hadn't seen any on this visit, but I wondered whether Mother still had rowankind. Larien, perhaps, though a rowankind who's seen the underside of his mistress's bed sheets is an embarrassing liability.

I motioned to Hookey to follow me, and we slipped into the stable. I took the risk of making another witchlight. The magic sprang from deep within, tingled down my right arm and rushed into my fingertips faster than ever it did at sea. I molded it and tossed a glowing ball of energy up into the rafters.

A pair of round bay rumps faced me from wooden-walled stalls. She might have been near destitution, but my mother had kept up appearances. Selling the carriage and pair would have been an admission of defeat.

The stable was neat. Someone must be looking after the horses.

"Saddles, over there." I nodded Hookey toward the harness room.

I slapped the rump of the nearest gelding and clicked my tongue. "Move over," I told him. He obligingly sidestepped in his stall to leave enough room for me to walk to his head. I patted his neck and spoke softly, and he flicked his ears, listening. I'd missed horses more than almost anything during my years on the sea. As if he knew, the big bay dropped his velvet muzzle into my hand and blew warm hay-breath over my fingers.

Hookey came back with the first saddle. "They look a bit old, but they've been looked after."

"As long as they fit." I saved the horses from Hookey's tender ministrations and saddled them myself while Hookey hacked off the reins of the driving bridles and tied them into a knot. I was always amazed at how dexterous he was with only a hook for a left hand.

"Shh!" Hookey hissed.

I let the witchlight blink out, leaving both of us at a disadvantage. If someone was outside, their eyes would already be used to the dark.

"Who's there?" It was a young voice.

The door creaked open and a shadow passed across it. I held my breath. A scuffle in the darkness and a choked off cry made me snap on the witchlight again.

"Hookey, no!"

Hookey's left arm froze in mid plunge. The lethal steel hook glittered an inch away from a young rowankind's throat. The boy gulped, his brown eyes wide with terror.

"Who are you?" I asked.

He didn't reply.

"Well, boy? Cat got your tongue?" I heard my mother's phrase and repressed an overwhelming urge to spit to clear my mouth.

"D-David." His voice broke. Having Hookey's hook

poised above their larynx will often have that effect on people.

"Work at the house, D-David?"

He nodded.

"Been looking after . . ." I almost said *my mother*, but I stopped myself in time. "Mrs. Goodliffe?"

"No one else left to do it."

I nodded to Hookey to back off, but the boy still watched him warily. To his credit, he didn't try and bolt.

"What about Larien?"

"I don't even remember him. He was my father."

I didn't remember Larien fathering children with any of our rowankind.

"Who was your mother?"

"Ruth."

"Ruth never had children. You're lying, boy."

"I wasn't born here. Ruth was the missis's maid when she went traveling. I was born in Dover and Missis didn't want the bother of a baby, so I was left with a Kentish family. Missis sent for me when I was ten."

I remembered my mother traveling one year while my father was away on a long sea voyage.

So Ruth had presented her with a baby, legally belonging to the Goodliffe household, but too much of a bother to travel with. What a terrible separation. It's a wonder she never said anything. And how like my mother to reclaim what she still considered to be hers as soon as he was old enough to have some usefulness.

"I never knew my momma. She died before I was brought here."

Ruth had nursed me as a baby and had raised me just as much, if not more, than my mother. She had soothed my hurts and calmed my fears, given me sweet treats from the kitchen. She'd explained what was happening to my body when I'd started my courses and shown me how to deal with it. She'd stood by me when I developed magic, when my mother had rejected me, never showing fear or offering recrimination. She'd always been there for me. I'd taken her for granted, taken her love for granted as if she'd been a mother to me. In a way she had been. I'd last seen her just before I'd run away with Will. She'd held me in her comfortable embrace and had kissed my hair and wished me well. I'd thanked her and told her that I loved her. I was glad I'd said it at last.

"I'm sorry about Ruth. I didn't know," I said, swallowing a lump in my throat. "She was . . . kindly."

"That's what Evy said."

The horses began to stomp uneasily from side to side and one let out a shrill whinny.

"So you saw the witchlight and came to investigate."

He shook his head. "I came to get the horses out before the roof goes up."

I must have been a little slow on the uptake, because it took Hookey's warning to make me look at the crack around the open door. Across the yard, flames were leaping behind the lower windows of the house. As I watched, glass shattered, and a cloud of acrid smoke billowed across the cobbles. My eyes began to water even as my heart began to thump.

"Mother!" I started toward the door, but Hookey shot his arm out to bar my way. The house was consuming itself from the inside out.

"It's all right, Miss Rossalinde, she's already gone." David knew who I was. "Gone on, I mean. Passed."

"She's dead?"

"Called for her medicine right after you left. Took the whole bottle like it was the finest wine. Told me to wait until she stopped breathing, then set the fire and get out. I . . ." He swallowed. "I sat with her until the end."

Tears threatened to flood my eyes. It was the smoke, I told myself, just the smoke. I swallowed hard to ease the lump in my throat and took a steadying breath. How like my mother: if she couldn't take it with her, no one else was going to have it. The house and all it contained was going up in flames, including any debts on it.

Sparks flew. Both horses began to fuss uneasily in their stalls as the smell of burning roiled around us. Luckily the wind wasn't blowing directly this way.

"Get the horses out."

The order was for Hookey, but David patted the rump of the nearest gelding, moved it over, and took hold of its reins, talking nonsense to it in a low voice. I took the second horse, trying to keep calm so as not to spook it. Trying not to think of my mother.

In the yard, my horse snorted and danced away from the flames. My eyes streamed and my throat clenched against the smoke. It was already hot enough to scorch my skin. My ready-magic, that which comes easiest to me, is with wind and weather, so I reached into the atmosphere and conjured a breeze to push back the smoke and heat. The power rose from the small of my back and flowed out of my shoulders. A fresh wind blew in from the north, stronger than I expected. It fanned the flames licking up the eaves of the house, but gave us grace to clear the yard.

Messing with the weather is a difficult magic to balance. With the wind came the first splashes of sleety rain, drops as large as shillings plopping onto exposed flesh.

Hookey got behind my horse and gave it a slap with the side of his hook. It shot forward, half-dragging me into the lane behind the house. I clutched the reins with both hands and leaned into its shoulder, pulling its head down to steady it, then scrambled into the saddle. I used to be a fair rider, but with seven years at sea I was out of practice. The saddle felt stiff and cold between my thighs, and the horse pokey, more used to a collar than a saddle.

Even above the roar of the flames and the crackling of burning timber I could hear shouts in the street at the front of the house. We needed to get out fast.

Hookey heaved himself on to the other horse with little style and much determination. "What about the kid?"

"What about me?"

Hookey and David spoke almost together.

"What about you?" I looked down at a pale, frightened face illuminated by flickering flames.

"Where do I go?"

"Grab your freedom and run, or go find another master."

From his scowl, finding another master hadn't been part of his plan. "I was going to take the horses and go inland."

Hookey spat. "Well, you ain't taking 'em now."

I could hear running feet in the alley and a curse as someone tripped. David could identify me. I should kill him—or let Hookey do it if I didn't have the stomach.

I kicked my foot out of the stirrup, shoved my leg forward and reached down to grab the boy's wet hand with mine. Quick as a cat he jammed his foot in the stirrup and leaped up behind me.

Five men emerged from the alley. Hookey wheeled his horse away from them, but I knew the lane ended at a neighbor's wall. One shouted, "Hold!" and the others crouched. I heard the unmistakable clank of powder flasks tipping against musket muzzles. Redcoats. Damn!

"Let's go." I clapped my heels into my horse's sides and with a grunt it sprang forward, knocking down the first man and clattering his musket to the ground. Hands grabbed at my leg as we barged past. A musket ball whistled over my left shoulder and David ducked his head into my back. A volley of shots and curses followed us into the black night.

Damn! Someone had obviously already tied together rumors of Tremayne on the dockside and the Goodliffe house going up in flames. The whole town knew about the business between Margery Goodliffe and Redbeard Tremayne. She'd tried to have him charged with stealing her precious ship. Even though the charge had been erroneous, what had happened in the resulting fight and flight had left Will with a death to answer for. They'd think Redbeard had taken his revenge at last and burned the Widow Goodliffe in her bed.

I pointed my horse's nose toward the Tavistock road and with the rain lashing our faces we clattered north through Plymouth town. They'd doubtless send soldiers after us, even into the depths of the Okewood if they had to. We'd be lucky if it was a troop of redcoats. It would more likely be Kingsmen, mounted on fast horses.

We had no choice but to go north. Bideford, with its

history of smuggling and known dislike of the Excise men, was our best option. Fifty miles as the crow flies, almost seventy if we didn't go through the Okewood. I turned my mind from the old stories. We might not have the luxury of skirting the forest. If the Kingsmen braved it and we did not, they'd get in front of us and cut us off. Not a happy prospect.

3

The Tavistock Road

ICY RAIN DRIPPED FROM MY HAIR and eyelashes. Lightning flashed and a pale figure materialized, his arms open wide. Thunder rolled. My horse gave a half-rear then stood quivering. Hookey's mount stopped completely, goggling at the apparition. Horses have the sight. I doubted Hookey or David could see him.

"Hello, love." I mouthed the words. He didn't need to hear me out loud, he always knew what I was saying.

You're going the wrong way, he said.

"We're going the only way that makes sense."

Inland.

"Well done, Will. Being dead hasn't impaired your sense of direction."

You know how you are when you're away from the sea.

"I'll manage."

You can't go to the forest.

"You don't think I'm scared of ghosts, do you, Will?"

You should be scared of the things that scare ghosts.

"And what might that be?"

He shook his head and put his ghostly hand on my rein.

My horse swung his haunches sideways, but was unable to pull out of Will's grip. Ah, if only I could feel that hand on my own skin. I looked down into his blue eyes and my resolve softened. I reached to touch his cheek, but my hand passed through him. He faded to nothing.

My gut twisted. All I wanted to do was hold him again. Having him appear and disappear on a whim was so frustrating. Sometimes—rarely—his breath whispered on the back of my neck and once, just once, I swore I felt his arms around me, but mostly I had to be satisfied with a cryptic comment here, a terse instruction there. Sometimes it was good advice, but sometimes it was contrary and it seemed that he was sailing an altogether different ocean.

Behind me I heard David clear his throat as if to speak, so I touched my heels to the horse's side and we pressed on. Hookey gave me a sideways look but kept silent.

We made good time along the Tavistock Road, almost deserted except for an overloaded wagon limping for Plymouth and a smart curricle traveling much too fast for the moonlit road, even with carriage lamps aglow. We only had to scurry off the main highway once when the mail coach came through, Plymouth-bound at a spanking pace, horn a-blowing. We ran out of the downpour as we crested a low bank near Crownhill, a few miles out of the town, but by that time all of me, except for the part of my back that David leaned against and what I sat on, was soaked through. Water trickled inside my clothes in uncomfortable places. Even the binding on my breasts was damp and beginning to chafe.

Worse, my magic had begun to burn inside me as though I'd swallowed a ladleful of too-hot soup. I must have been more keyed up than I thought to infuse my bones with so much magical energy so quickly. I needed to bleed off some of the heat before it became unmanageable. I didn't want to make us into any more of a target than we already were, though. I judged the horses could see well enough by the moon, so I didn't bother with a witchlight. My ears have always been unnaturally sharp—one of my witch skills, I think—and so I concentrated on blocking out the sound of our horses' hooves clattering on the rough road and listened instead for sounds of pursuit with what my mother used to call my unnatural senses.

Just after we passed a milestone telling us that Plymouth lay four miles behind us and Tavistock eleven miles ahead, the roughly surfaced road dipped steeply down into a river valley and snaked through a small village, hardly more than a cluster of thatched cob cottages. It hadn't rained here at all. The tavern porch was decked out with wedding ribbons. Young men and women had spilt out on to the lantern-lit steps where they laughed and teased in easy courtship. In the open space by the side of the inn a bonfire burned, and a knot of dancers clasped hands and circled to a lively reel played by two fiddlers whose timekeeping was better than their intonation.

"Cap'n?" Hookey turned back in his saddle to glance at me. He knew full well that I wasn't good at cloaking. His look asked if it was worth expending the energy. If only he knew. I was desperate to shed it.

We slowed our horses to a walk. Some magic comes easy to me, some is difficult, and some is downright impossible. Hiding something big from plain sight, like two horses and three riders, usually comes in the damned difficult category, but this time I had energy to spare.

I called up that reservoir within me where my magic lies. At sea it remained barely half-full, little more than a brackish puddle. Today it churned and eddied to the brim, in danger of spilling over. I imagined that I knelt by it and plunged my hands in to the wrists, scooping out that very essence of magic and bringing it to my lips to sup and sup until I could sup no more.

Then, sated and infused, I imagined us as little more than shadows in the darkness, not invisible, but not worth noticing or remembering. In the imagining I made it so. The tingle that tells me when magic is working, mine or other people's, coursed through my body from inside to out, and despite the fact that we were no more than a few strides from the nearest reveler, no heads turned in our direction. We walked quietly through the village and onward into the night.

Not until the inn was safely behind us did I feel David breathe out and relax. "What did you do?" he asked.

I shook my head. The buzz of power had drained now. My mouth felt dry and doughy and I didn't want to try speaking until I had a reasonable chance of forming words without slurring.

"Back there—what happened?" David put a hand on my shoulder as if he thought I hadn't heard, but Hookey, in an unusual show of sensitivity for someone who purports to be a hard-as-nails, barely reformed pirate, reached out and tapped his fingers.

"Leave her be."

"She did magic, didn't she?" There was more than a touch of excitement in his voice. "She's a witch."

"That kind of talk costs lives." Hookey's voice was low and full of menace. "If your tongue flaps loose I swear I'll rive it from your head."

"Who am I going to tell? The Mysterium? I swear I'll not blab, only I *sensed* something."

"She hid us from the villagers." Hookey agreed.

"Made us invisible?"

"Not really." I sucked on the inside of my cheeks to coax saliva to flow. "Made them not see us. There's a difference. Invisibility is higher magic. Much more difficult."

I heard Hookey suppress a grunt.

David had been able to feel my magic working. "What else can you do?" he asked, excitement in his voice.

"Not much." I wasn't used to anyone asking me directly. I played it down, as usual, but he wouldn't let it go.

"Can you call fire?"

"No."

"What about the invisibility thing?"

"That doesn't come as easy, nor does finding lost things."

"You can find lost things?"

"Not easily."

"Can you do spells?"

"I'm not really that kind of witch."

"You don't have a spell book?"

"I told you, I'm not that kind of witch."

"You could, though, if you wanted to?"

I just shook my head. I'd never tried.

"I said, leave her be." Hookey nudged his horse closer, threat implicit in his tone. "She ain't never been comfortable wi' landlubber magicking."

"Sorry," David mumbled. "It's just . . ."

A growl from Hookey silenced him and I felt a weight lift. In truth I'd never explored the limits of my magic.

As soon as we were far enough from the village we nudged our horses into a steady trot, not wishing to tire them but needing to put as many miles as possible between us and pursuit. Intermittent moonlight from between the scudding clouds lit our path once more as we left farms behind and neared the forest. Tended fields gave way to rough grassland, broken up by gorse. The locals obviously left the common land around the Okewood well alone. Especially after dark.

My *hard listening* alerted me to the fast beat of hooves: a full troop of Kingsmen at least, but still a distance behind us. Neither Hookey nor David had heard them yet. They must have thrashed their mounts to catch up with us so soon, but we'd saved our horses' strength. I nudged mine into a steady, ground-eating canter, taking the lead from Hookey.

"They're behind us. We have to go through the Okewood!"

It was our best chance. We'd be safe there—from the Kingsmen at least. There were no guarantees. The rumors of ghosts and enchantment might be true. They might even be understated.

"Can't you hide us again?" David's voice came close in my ear as he pressed against my back and wrapped his arms around my waist for security.

"Not like I did before. It doesn't work on someone who's actually looking for you, only on people who don't need to notice. Truly hiding us from them for five minutes would use me up for a week." I reined my horse in. "You can get off now and disappear if you wish. The Kingsmen are after Redbeard Tremayne, not you. Go make a new life for yourself."

"You have a ship. Where else can I go? I set the fire. If they don't find you they'll come looking for me."

"Can they prove anything?"

"I'm rowankind, do they need to?"

He had a point. Rowankind were not usually lawbreakers, but any who did cross the line had no voice unless their masters spoke up for them.

"The Okewood's dangerous."

"And the Kingsmen aren't?"

I nodded. "All right."

We pushed on as fast as we dared in the moonlight until the road dropped down a long hill and turned to skirt the Okewood, a black presence in the darkness. The back of my neck prickled, and, as if to add to my apprehension, the moon fled behind a fat cloud. I pulled up my horse and stared. All the stories of my childhood came plunging back into my brain. The forest . . . the evil forest . . . full of goblins and boggarts, relics of dark magic from England's deep past when the Fae were lords of all and God help anyone who crossed them. Even kings had respected the Fae.

But that was a long time ago.

I heard David catch his breath behind me. He could feel it, too. The forest had a personality of its own, and approaching it felt like tiptoeing toward the chair of some ancient and irascible uncle, never knowing whether you'd be met with a sweet treat and a story or a sharp crack with a cane. Hookey seemed oblivious, but I found that with every stride the air itself seemed to weigh more. My chest felt cramped as if by too-tight stays and I had to force myself to breathe.

"Have you been here before?" David's voice was barely more than a whisper as we approached the tree line and reined in our horses.

"Never."

"Want me to go first, Cap'n?" Hookey asked.

I pulled up and looked at the darkness of the trees now towering above us, hearing their voices rustling in the breeze.

"Cap'n! Behind us."

"The Kingsmen. Dammit!" I'd been on the point of balking, but now I had no choice, "Dismount. Follow me."

By feel alone I found a path through the trees, thankful that the horse followed without a fuss. My spine felt as if spiders were marching up and down it, and my palms were wet enough to slip on the leather reins. I hoped no one else could hear my breath rasping in my chest.

When it felt as though we were far enough from the road I stopped.

"Keep the horses quiet," I said.

I let David take the reins of both our mounts. Cautiously I crept back the way we'd come. The ting of metal on metal behind me caused me to pause. "Hookey, if you're coming with me, stop your damned sword hilt from clanking against your hook."

"Sorry, Cap'n."

There were no more sounds behind me. For a heavy man in seaboots, Hookey could walk like a cat when he needed to. We squatted down in a tangle of bushes. Briefly I considered that they may have brought one of the witches from the town, but the Kingsmen were, even more than most, against the use of magic. One of their jobs was to detain anyone suspected of magical crimes and to deliver them to the Mysterium for trial, and that included unlicensed practitioners of magic—any who had not registered with the Mysterium by their eighteenth birthday.

The Kingsmen sounded like an army as they clattered down the road. The moon had emerged from her cloud and gave them light. They pulled up not twenty yards from where we crouched.

The man at the front of the column was a northerner by his voice. "Sergeant, take six men and search the forest. If you find them, fire three pistol rounds and take them back to Plymouth on this road."

"Begging your pardon, Lieutenant, but this is the Okewood."

"I have studied a map of the area. I know perfectly well where we are."

"I was born in Tavistock, sir. There are stories—"

"Superstitious nonsense."

"But—"

"Lieutenant, your sergeant is correct. There are many local stories about the Okewood, some of them very strange."

My eyes snapped wide open at the sound of another voice. I couldn't be sure. It was seven years after all, but . . . My mother had thought him dead, had grieved for him, no doubt much more than she would ever have grieved for me.

"Philip."

I barely whispered his name, but the figure who rode close to the front of the column whipped his head in my direction. I held my breath and kept very still. Could it be? Was my brother alive after all?

My hope was tempered by the company he kept.

"What say you, Mr. Walsingham?" The lieutenant deferred to another dark-coated man riding alongside Philip.

"Mr. Goodliffe knows the area." The voice was deep and commanding. "But if you feel you can spare the men, then I would be obliged." He couched his request in the politest of terms, but it was clear that he intended to be obeyed.

"Very well, sir, I was told to follow your instructions in this matter. You can always rely on the cooperation of the Kingsmen, sir, and mine in partic'lar." He turned to the hapless sergeant. "You heard, Sergeant."

"Yes, sir. I'll take local men, sir, if it's all the same to you." There was a shake in the sergeant's voice as he called six men, and more than one muffled curse from those chosen.

"Lieutenant . . ." The man called Walsingham leaned toward the young officer.

"Yes, sir?"

"The fugitives must be caught. You understand how important this is?"

"I do, sir."

"Your men failed me once at the Goodliffe house. I'll not countenance failure again."

He said it quietly, but my keen hearing picked up not only the words, but the tone of both his voice and the lieutenant's. Whoever he was, this Walsingham held enough sway to make the lieutenant very unhappy about failure.

The unlucky sergeant and his men dismounted as the rest of the troop clattered off down the road. They led their horses into the shadow of the trees, as we had done. I heard Hookey draw his knife.

"Lads!" The sergeant called his men to a halt and waited until the sound of hooves on the road had dwindled. "You all know this place and what's said about it." He waited for an answer.

"It's dark, lads, don't just nod."

"Yes, Sergeant." They spoke almost in unison.

The sergeant made a noncommittal grunt, but he sounded satisfied. "Good. Once Lieutenant Buckram-Britches and his mystery men from London are out of sight, we'll clear out of this devil-cursed place and wait for the dawn up on yonder hill. And then we'll all go back to barracks. If anyone asks, as surely they will, we thrashed around in these little old trees for hours and found nothing. Understood?"

There was a chorus of agreement.

Hookey and I waited as they departed with never a backward glance.

I heard Hookey let out a sigh of relief.

"Don't let your guard down yet, Hookey. Everything that frightened them is still in here," I said.

"Ghosts don't frighten me," Hookey said.

"There was one ghost right there I never thought to see."

"Huh? I never saw no ghost, Cap'n."

"Ghost?" David asked as we came upon him and the horses waiting just where we'd left him.

"One of the two gentlemen riding with the Kingsmen was my supposedly deceased brother, Philip."

"Master Philip?"

"I would say I'm glad of it, but he seemed to be helping the Kingsmen. There was another man with him, a Mr. Walsingham. He was obviously in charge."

"I ain't never seen no civilians riding with the Kingsmen before, Cap'n."

"No, me neither, Hookey. Curious, isn't it?"

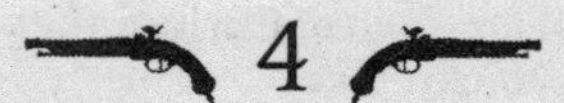

4

The Okewood

I SENT A WITCHLIGHT IN FRONT OF US, low to the ground at first, but raising it up once we were far enough inside the trees that neither the sergeant nor his men would see it if they looked back. We needed to make our way through these woods and beat the Kingsmen to Bideford.

"Is this wise?" David jerked his chin toward the light.

"Whatever is in this wood doesn't need to see a light to know we're here, and I'd rather not lame a horse or sprain my ankle over a tree root." Besides, the light gave me courage to continue through this strange place, even though it threw the nearest tree trunks into sharp relief and made them seem like giants of their species, with leering faces carved into their gnarled bark.

We hadn't walked far when the forest turned unnaturally quiet, not a rustle of leaves on the breeze or the usual creature sounds of the night. The air clustered around my head and seemed so thick I had trouble sucking it into my lungs. Right then I'd have been thankful for the eerie screech of an owl or the last, terrified squeak of its prey. I shivered and rubbed my arms. Though the temperature had not dropped I was aching with cold inside.

My light flickered and died. The thread of magic snapped as total darkness descended.

A heavy dread filled my bones.

"Cap'n." It was the first time I'd ever heard Hookey's voice quaver. "Can 'ee make another light, Cap'n?" Hookey asked. "Quickly-like."

"I can, but I think we should wait a while. See what's here and what it wants."

"Or we could just run," Hookey said.

A wolf's howl cut the night somewhere behind us and sent shivers up my spine. David jumped like a startled deer. Despite the cold in my bones, my palms were clammy with sweat.

Another howl answered the first, closer now.

"On the horses," I said. There was no sense in taking chances.

I heard rather than saw Hookey scrambling into the saddle. I mounted my horse and David swung up lightly behind me.

I heard Hookey curse his horse as it fussed at the bit. Mine stood poised ready for flight, held only by the reins and my hand soothing its trembling shoulder.

A third howl, still behind us, but to our left now.

My nerve broke.

"Come on." I flung a new witchlight into the air and sent my horse crashing through the trees, leaning low to avoid branches whipping across my face.

Yet another howl, more to our right, drove us on.

My horse stumbled on a tree root. I pitched forward, grabbed a handful of mane as he recovered, and pushed myself back into the saddle. David's face crunched into my spine and I heard a muffled *oww*. Hookey, close behind, launched a stream of colorful invective at his horse, but whether it helped or not, I didn't know. The ground opened up in front of us and we plunged down a steep bank, splashed across a rill and up the other side again. Hookey's horse arrived at the top, riderless, and David leaned sideways to grab its rein.

"Hookey?" I shouted.

"All right, Cap'n." He spat. "Though I ain't been this wet on dry land since I don't know when." He hauled himself up the bank, grabbing exposed tree roots as he came, then clambered aboard the horse again.

A wolf yip, closer now, drove us forward again, and then one on our right flank drove us left before another on our left drove us right.

"Whoa." I pulled up. The trees here grew farther apart, and ahead was a small clearing. "We're not being hunted, we're being driven. If they were that close they'd have tried to pull Hookey down when he fell in the water."

A silver tinkle of laughter arrived on a breeze.

"What do you want of us?" I shouted.

A tiny pinpoint of light ahead grew to the size of a child, then the size of a man, and bigger still until it was like the opening of a tunnel of bright silver. I heard David gasp and my blood seemed to clog my veins. A primal urge told me to turn and run again, but my horse's feet were rooted to the forest floor, and though I nudged him with my heels, gently first, then stronger, he didn't move.

A procession came toward us down that tunnel of light, bathed in an unearthly glow. To the fore a couple, human in shape, but at once both larger and smaller than real flesh-and-blood people. He was dressed in buckskin with the antlers of a stag upon his head. He carried a longbow; the hunter, not the hunted. She was the doe to his buck. I looked at them both. It wasn't buckskin: they were naked, with furred hide instead of human skin. The antlers grew from the forest lord's head as if from a stag's, and though the rest of him was purely human in form, his gender was in no doubt, his fertility rampant. By her generously rounded belly and full breasts, the lady was with child.

On her wrist she held a yellow-beaked blackbird.

My first thought said *Fae*, but the Fae had not been seen in this country for more than two hundred years, to my knowledge. There were stories about them, of course, but nothing that tied in with this vision now before us. Something inside me, a race memory maybe, told me I knew this couple in both this and other forms. I was in no doubt that they were the essence of the land. The Green Man and his Lady of the Forests. By all the legends, guardians of this island's wild places, elemental spirits who rarely showed themselves to mortals.

Behind the couple came a procession of woodland animals: buck, doe, badger, rabbits, an unruly gang of red squirrels, a fox and a vixen, and a lone silver wolf, a gorgeous specimen standing almost as big as a pony. His tongue lolled out as though he had been running.

"God's ballocks! Bandits! That's all we need." I heard Hookey loosen his sword.

"Huh?" David obviously didn't share Hookey's illusion. He seemed to have some awareness of magic, which was highly unusual in a rowankind.

"No weapons, Hookey."

"Aye, Cap'n." The snick of steel betrayed his sword settling back into his scabbard.

"Stay back. David, hold the horses."

I swung my right leg over my horse's neck, slid to the ground and bowed low before the royal couple.

"Rossalinde." The Lady spoke in the tones of a cool woodland stream. "I know you. It was foretold that you would come."

She *knew* me? My scalp prickled.

"You come at last to our realm." The Green Man's voice held the dark sounds of creaking tree trunks and the slow movement of roots through earth.

"My apologies for the intrusion. I beg passage through the forest for myself and my companions."

I looked over my shoulder instinctively, but I could neither hear nor see any pursuit.

The Lady released the blackbird from her wrist with a little upward motion and watched him fly up into the canopy of leaves. She stepped forward and peered into my eyes. I couldn't look away while she stripped my soul bare from the inside out. A tremor passed through me, starting in my toes and running up my body to the roots of my hair. I shook with the force of it and only with considerable effort managed to blink.

She released my gaze. "I see you. You have ever been ruled by your heart. Yet that which is your downfall may also be your salvation."

She held up her wrist and the bird flew back to it. She turned to me again. "See, the creature who is truly free returns out of choice. You are a child of the land, Rossalinde. Why have you chosen the sea?"

I probably stood with my mouth open trying to find an answer to a question I had not suspected needed asking.

"Circumstances led me to the sea, and my heart kept me there."

The Green Man frowned. "She did it for love." He rolled the last word around his mouth as if tasting it.

"Yes, I loved Will." *And I still do.* "What of it?"

"His spirit is wind and water and yet you shackle him to the earth. Let him go. Soon." He was used to being obeyed.

I could only nod meekly, though my heart screamed out that I'd never let Will go.

"Something else," the Lady said. "An inheritance recently received, but not looked for. Show me!"

I reached into my pouch and offered her the box. She didn't touch it, but a frown wrinkled her forehead. I put it on the palm of my hand and held it up for her to examine with her eyes. David dismounted behind me and stepped closer, staring at it, mesmerized.

"A family thing. I don't know any more than that. My father's, possibly."

She shook her head. "No. From your mother's family, of course."

"My mother had no magic."

"How little you know." The Lady pursed her lips. "Your mother could have been the greatest witch of her generation, but she rejected her obligations out of fear. Now the task is certainly yours, but it's not for you alone."

A task? What task? My head swam, though I didn't know if it was from her power or from the casual words that turned my world and all I knew of my mother on its head. *My mother could have been the greatest witch of her generation?* The small phrase, slipped between the rest, suddenly impinged on my consciousness.

"Why was she afraid, Lady?"

"The Mad King's hounds would stop at nothing to rid the country of your family for what they did, and for what *you* might yet do. They almost had you in their net tonight."

"You must not let them prevent you from doing that which your ancestor could not." The Green Man's voice was a rough creak. "It is time."

I took a breath to ask more questions, but the Lady held up her hand to silence me and closed her eyes as if searching for something inside her head. At length she looked at me with piercing green eyes that I could have sworn were brown a second ago. "You stand on the brink between the old world and the new, Rossalinde. Between Magic and Reason. You hold the key to that which is all but lost and have within your grasp the chance to right a great and terrible wrong. You hold a new future in your hands, if you are brave enough to take up the challenge. But know that the hounds are out and they have your scent." She turned to David. "And his. Search, Rossalinde. Find your family. Gather together that which was sundered."

"Besides my brother Philip, if that was truly him and not some illusion, I don't have any family."

"Yes, you do." She turned to look at David. "Starting with this one."

"He's my brother?" I felt dizzy.

I looked at David. Rowankind were generally smaller and slighter than us, with refined, delicate features, upswept eyebrows, and pale gray skin like polished rowan wood that showed faint grain lines. David had the features, but his skin was less gray, creamy and more translucent, and he was taller than most rowankind, though just as slender. At this age he was as beautiful as a girl without being feminine in any way. I thought that, given a few years, he would make a handsome young man. I searched his face for any hint of my mother. Maybe he had her mouth.

I swallowed hard. To lose one brother and find another all in the same day, well, shock hardly described the emotion. I had come close to seeing Hookey tear David's throat out. My scalp prickled. I felt slightly light-headed. Everything clicked into place. His age, my mother's dalliance with Larien, her long absence one year. It would have been a dreadful scandal, of course, so she'd covered it up, even from family.

I wondered if she'd told Larien.

And the consequence?

David was both rowankind and witchkind.

"But . . ." David's face had turned moon-pale.

I didn't know whether I could ever grow to love this strange half-rowankind child, but I felt sorry for him. This was as big a shock for him as it was for me. I could see the confusion written on his face.

I turned and put my hand on his arm. "My mother—our mother—took your father to her bed while my father was away at sea. He made her happy, I believe, as she had not been in a long time."

"Ruth?"

"A scapegoat to hide her infidelity."

The Lady reached out and touched all the fingers of her right hand to the center of David's chest. "He is strangely dark with old magic, and that should not be. You say his father was rowankind? You're sure?"

I nodded. "Our bondservant."

"Where is he now?"

"I don't know. Long gone."

She pursed her lips. "We shall see. All is not as it seems."

David focused on her face. He would have spoken, but the Lady shook her head and dropped her hand to her side. "All will be made clear in the fullness of time, young man. For now, remain with your sister."

She turned back to me, her intensity making my scalp prickle. "Search for your family, Rossalinde—your mother's family—all of them. Open the box. But remember the Mad King's hounds. Always remember the hounds."

A tremor ran through me. Not just the Kingsmen, but

the king himself. Why should Mad King George be interested in me?

"It is time and past time. The world turns. If this thing is to be done, it's best done now while the world of men can still bear it. That which was and which should have been might yet be again."

I blinked, wishing she'd not talk in mystic riddles. Why should I take up some quest that wasn't mine? If my mother successfully hid her magic all her life, couldn't I do the same? I was quite happy as captain of the *Heart*, and it was much more difficult for anyone to sneak up on me on the open ocean. As far as I was concerned, the winterwood box could go to the bottom of my sea chest, or even to the bottom of the sea itself.

She leaned slightly forward, and her gaze locked with mine. The force of it chilled me to the bone. I found myself choking on frosted air.

Then she was speaking again, and I could breathe freely. "You lose your magic on the sea. You must come to the land, to the forest, to gain your full power." She stepped back and her shoulders rose in the smallest of shrugs. "And you must come to this quest, by yourself. Or not—as your conscience dictates—for you retain your free will in all things." Free will. I held on to that thought. "But one thing I will lay on you: you must keep your half-brother with you, for he is part of this."

"What's in the box?" I asked.

She shook her head as if unsure. "The mistake of a foolish man. The sin of a nation," she replied. "The fate of the world. Everything, and nothing. The contents are yours to discover."

More riddles. Did magic folk always speak in frustrating riddles?

"If you would beat the soldiers on the road, you need to be swift." The Green Man said. "I feel their hooves shaking my land."

"Are they the hounds you speak of?" I asked.

The Lady shook her head and gave me a look that said plainly I was asking stupid questions. "Go now. Take your brother and your pirate. I will send Silverwolf as your watch-wolf and guide."

She called the huge wolf to her and rested her hand on his head, speaking in tones so low that I couldn't catch them.

He nodded his head, a curious gesture for a wolf.

"Be swift." She turned back to me. "He will not wait for stragglers. When you need me again, you will find me here."

The wolf, silver-coated and gray-eyed, stood a little way ahead of us. As we turned, he put his head on one side and regarded us with a steady gaze, almost human in its intensity and understanding. Then he turned and loped into the forest.

I needed no excuse to flee the royal couple and their entourage. My mind churned so much that I was thankful to lose myself in action. I flung myself into the saddle again and David scrambled up behind. Now that I knew he was my brother the burden felt different—more personal. With Hookey behind us, we followed the wolf at a lumbering canter. The carriage horses were neither fleet nor flexible, and whipping around trees and crashing through undergrowth was hard on them.

"Slow down, wolf," I called.

On the next rise he paused, seeming to smile at me through sharp white fangs, then loped away again.

I swore under my breath. "He's making sport of us."

My horse pounded on, and David clung to my waist for dear life as we cleared a fallen tree trunk and slithered down a steep hill, across a shallow river strewn with boulders and up the other side.

A yell behind me and a riderless horse galloping alongside announced that Hookey's rough horsemanship had failed him again. Damn the wolf. I'd rather lose the wolf than Hookey. I pulled up sharp and we slithered to a stop. The other horse stopped with us and David caught its bridle.

"Coming, Cap'n. Damn horse!" Hookey's language trailed off into a line of seamanlike expletives. I smiled. I'd seen Hookey seriously hurt. He didn't talk or yell. He limped up beside us, took the horse's reins and gave it a mouthful of verbal abuse before flinging himself back aboard with grim determination.

"Have we lost yon wolf?" Hookey asked.

I looked around, surprised to find that he did wait for stragglers. "No, he's still here."

The wolf sat watching Hookey's horsemanship. I swear he was laughing.

"Mind your manners," I told him. "It's no good escaping the Kingsmen if we all end up with our necks broken."

He gave a little yip and set off once again, this time at a slightly steadier pace. We followed him as the sky lightened past dawn. At the edge of the forest he melted away into the undergrowth and was gone, but I could see the Bideford road down in the valley and no Kingsmen either behind or before us.

"I think we're in the clear." I'd been listening hard for sounds of pursuit along the road and heard nothing.

"You're sure?" David asked.

Hookey laughed. "He hasn't got your hearing, Cap'n."

"He knows I'm your brother?" David looked from me to Hookey and back again.

"It weren't exactly difficult to guess." Hookey bunched his reins up in one hand and scratched his beard. "Besides, you're already taller than most rowankind, though you got the looks, I'll grant you that. But you and she got a resemblance—something around the mouth—an' I know you got magic, 'cos you could feel hers working an' I never can."

"About that," David said.

"All in good time. Hush," I hissed between my teeth.

We dismounted, slipped out the bits, and let the horses graze on roadside grass for an hour that we could ill afford, but better to have them refreshed in case of pursuit. When we set off again, we did so at a sedate pace, alternating walking and steady jog-trotting, so as not to lather them unnecessarily. All the time I listened for pursuers, but the early morning remained peaceful. The road rolled across farmland. A lone ploughman turning winter-worn fields to straight dark lines pulled up his horse at the end of a furrow and looked in our direction. I gathered my magic and he gazed through us. In similar fashion I hid us from a shepherd and his dog.

David was obviously wrestling with questions. In truth, I didn't know what I could say. To be brought up disenfranchised and then to discover you're the mistress's bastard son is one thing, but to also discover that you've inherited magic that has the potential to be dark and dangerous added a new twist.

I had my own questions, but there was no one to answer. *Oh, Will, how I miss your wise counsel.*

"The Lady . . ." David said at last. "She wants you to go to the forest. She says your magic is stronger there."

"It's true I always feel its heat inland. It's cooling now the sea's in sight." It was easier to talk to him when he was behind me. I didn't have to look into his eyes.

"So you won't take up the quest or return to the forest?"

"The Lady's not even human. How can I begin to guess at her motives? Besides, if people hunt me on land, what better place to be than the ocean?"

"What about Philip?"

"It's been seven years. We were close once, but in later years . . ." I shook my head. "We grew apart. I hardly know him now. Besides, I have a life. People depend on me. A crew, a ship."

"A husband?"

"Life doesn't always turn out the way you expect it to." I spoke almost to myself. "I hadn't expected to be a widow so soon."

"That was Redbeard Tremayne—the spirit back on the road?"

"Yes, that was Will. After he died, I, well, let's just say I took his place."

He was silent for a while and then he said, "You never went back to see your mother."

Anger flushed through me. "After the circumstances of our final parting? Why should I?"

"She's your mother. Was your mother, I mean."

"I'll bet she never spoke my name."

His silence was answer enough.

"See."

"Once, a few days ago. She said you'd be here soon. I thought her mind was wandering."

"Too much laudanum." I didn't speculate further. How could I begin to say what I felt about the woman who gave me life? I didn't even know myself. Right now all I wanted to do was to get back to the safety of the *Heart*.

"Was it magic that parted you from your mother?"

"Yes, in a way it was, though other disagreements as well. Philip, you see, was her shining boy. A girl will always be a drain on family finances, and Father had mentioned more than once that when I married one of the ships would be my dowry."

"Did your father know—about your magic, I mean?"

"It was one of the things my parents argued about. My father said Mother should not worry, that I could suppress it. I—"

Words failed me as I remembered my father's exact words. *She can learn to suppress it. You can help her.*

5

Bideford

BY THE TIME WE GOT TO BIDEFORD we were close enough to the sea that my magic sank safely back to its usual manageable levels. While Hookey went down to the docks to look for a likely ship I sold the poor tired horses on the outskirts of town, for far less than they were worth, but the dealer asked no questions and required no provenance. I regretted abandoning the beasts, but the dealer's yard was clean and orderly, his horses well cared for.

As we walked down the hill into the town I offered David the proceeds from the sale. It seemed only fair.

He looked at the small pouch of guineas in my hand.

"Take it," I said. "The horses were your only inheritance."

His hand twitched toward the pouch and then he pulled back.

"What's the matter? You've handled money before."

"The household money, yes. Never my own."

"Not even a few shillings at Christmas?" There had always been silver for the rowankind at Christmas.

"That's what Evy said, but Missis—our mother—" He

corrected himself awkwardly. "She sent what she could to London, to Master Philip, and there wasn't much left after that. That's why she let the rest of the rowankind go. Evy was the last, then there was only me. When she took to her bed, I managed what there was as well as I could, but we've left a debt behind us at the butcher's."

"Don't think of paying off our mother's debts with this." I pushed the money into his hand. "Whatever you decide to do, it's yours. It's little enough. I fancy Philip had the best of her fortune. I wonder what he spent it on."

"I heard mention of gambling debts."

"Why am I not surprised?"

Philip had always had a way of wheedling what he wanted, even as a boy. The thought of Philip troubled me again.

Lord knows we had not been close as children, yet we had shared a sibling bond.

When Mother had taken it into her head to travel alone, Philip and I had shared a sense of abandonment that brought us closer together. If only we could have retained the camaraderie that we felt in those few short months, but Mother's return reminded us both that Philip was her firm favorite. I can't blame Philip for taking advantage of her indulgence, though I don't know what hurt more, my obvious second place in her regard, or Philip's defection from our little cabal of two.

Dwelling on the past? Will floated in the air by my side, keeping pace as we walked. *Hookey's on the dockside, eyeing up a barquentine.*

Bideford town was a collection of twisting, narrow streets lined with pastel-colored cottages clinging to the hillside above the wide river Torridge, only recently contained by a new embankment.

Once a major port in the area, handling cargoes of cotton and tobacco from the New World, Bideford had lost much of its trade to Bristol and had had the rest curtailed by the war with France. The ships that docked here were mostly coastal vessels carrying ball clay out and lime in, but there was still a fishing fleet. And if you knew where to look or who to talk to there were those captains who specialized in the import of certain goods, mostly French, under the noses of the Excise men.

As we walked the length of the quay, Hookey was waiting by a barquentine, the *Alessandra*, a neat, three-masted vessel, square rigged on the foremast and fore-and-aft rigged on the main and mizzenmasts. She'd just taken on cargo and looked almost ready to sail.

Hookey scowled at me. He'd never liked barquentines: said they were a poor compromise between a barque and a ship.

"She's a bastard vessel, Cap'n, but she's seaworthy. The word on the dock is that her master is canny but fair. He might charge you through the nose, but his word's good."

Barque, barquentine, or fishing smack, I didn't mind what we sailed on—I'd probably be spending the next few days heaving up my insides and wanting to die. Why, oh why, did I have to be the only captain on the ocean who was thoroughly and miserably seasick?

Hookey professed that he could gut a quart pot, so he took David in search of a hospitable tavern while I went aboard to negotiate passage. For a guinea apiece, the captain, Joshua Haggerty, a tough old cove with a face that looked as though it had been carved out of a slab of mahogany, agreed to take us around the coast to Harper's Inlet. It was an extortionate price, but we didn't have much choice and the captain knew it. I found Hookey and David in a likely looking drinking hole and directed them to be on the dock within two hours.

I had a bit of business to attend to in the meantime.

The Kingsmen couldn't be far behind us. I had a couple of hours before the *Alessandra* sailed, and with luck it might be long enough to check on what Philip was up to. Or had my mind been playing tricks? Was it really Philip? And if it was, were he and the dark-coated Mr. Walsingham both working for the Mysterium?

Bideford was famous for being the place where the

Mysterium had been founded following a notorious witch trial and burning. By the licensing of approved witches, the Mysterium, now run from London, had established itself as the single authority on magic in the land. Those who knew no better supported them, believing that a regulated witch was a safe witch.

More fool them.

Even so, the Mysterium would have me swinging on a rope if they ever caught me, just for the crime of being an unregistered witch. They'd have to catch me first, of course. The less contact I had with the Mysterium, the better, but I needed to know whether Philip worked for them. If I waited to see the Kingsmen arrive I might find out whether the Mysterium was their first port of call. I had nothing better to do with my time.

The Mysterium's regional office on the junction of Bridgeland Street and the Quay was in an elegant old building which had once been one of Bideford's merchant's houses, part residence, part place of business. I needed someplace that would let me see it without being seen, so I settled upon an inn opposite, which boasted a coffee room that was all smoke-darkened paneling and dingy leaded windows. I ordered coffee from a sullen rowankind girl—you could see the resentment if you were looking for it, though I suspect most people didn't look—and settled on a bench close to the window, hidden from full view by the height of the bench back.

I'd finished my coffee, a bitter brew and not much to my liking, when the clatter of hooves on cobbles made me duck instinctively. Lucky I did. The Kingsmen rode straight down the street, their horses lathered with sweat and the riders' jackets, green with red facings, dusty from the road. They ignored the Mysterium office. That answered my primary question.

At their head rode a lieutenant, and immediately behind him were two dark-coated men, one older and broader than the other, but hard, without an inch of flab on him. His face was pockmarked; otherwise it might have been brutishly handsome, with a straight jab of a nose and strong, dark brows. Walsingham. The younger man was Philip, seven years older than the last time I'd seen him, but unmistakably my baby brother. I could see why my mother had mistaken me for him. He was as slender as a woman, his features still boyish and unmarked at twenty-one.

As I studied him he looked in my direction, and our eyes met through the glass. I jerked my head back behind the stout mullion of the window and heard hooves break the regular pattern of the troop. The Kingsmen didn't stop, but I heard another horse join Philip's right outside the window.

"What's the matter, boy?" The voice was deep and resonant.

"My horse is going uneven, Mr. Walsingham. I think he's picked up a stone in his shoe."

Walsingham gave a disapproving grunt. "Come straight to the White Hart as soon as you've cleaned it out."

"Yes, sir."

"Remember you are still on parole. I have your poppet with me at all times. Don't play me false, Mr. Goodliffe, or you'll regret it."

The back of my neck prickled with the menace held in his words.

"I won't forget, sir. How could I?"

I heard Walsingham's horse clatter off after the troop at a trot, and Philip jerked his head toward the alley by the inn.

I left my coffee cup and made my way casually outside.

Philip stood fumbling with his horse's rein in both hands. He glanced over his shoulder so many times it almost looked like a tic.

I wanted to rush and hug him, but he stepped back, his attitude a cold slap.

"Goddamn, Ross, it's true then, you are a counterfeit man. I'd heard rumors, but I hardly believed them. You were always such a girly-girl."

If that was the way he wanted it between us, I could play at that game. "Except when I fought a duel against Josh Clemmow to save you from a thrashing."

"I'd almost forgotten that. You used sticks for swords. You won but you got the hem of your dress so muddy that Ruth made you change it quickly and took it for washing so Mother wouldn't throw a fit, but Mother realized you weren't in the same dress and got the truth from you. You were always such a bad liar, Ross." He managed a rueful smile. "You were sent to bed without supper."

"You sneaked a slice of bread and jam out of the kitchen for me."

He laughed. "I wheedled it out of Ruth. Didn't take much wheedling, actually. Ruth had it ready prepared."

"Ruth always looked out for me. But how about you? You look quite lively for a corpse. This is a reunion I hadn't expected."

"Listen, reunion be damned. I don't have much time." He was suddenly serious again.

"What are you doing here, Philip? Are you working for the Mysterium?"

Philip shook his head. "The Mysterium dances to Walsingham's tune if he needs it to. He takes his orders from much higher up. As high as you can go without talking to God in His Heaven."

"The king?"

Had the Lady of the Forests been right?

"Or one of his ministers."

"I've never wronged the king."

"It's not for what you've done, but for what you might yet do." He glanced over his shoulder again and snapped the reins in his fingers. "Walsingham is single-minded. A dedicated man. His job is to fight against magical threats to the realm. He's looking for a winterwood box that our mother may have had. It's old and it's dangerous. Have you got it?"

There was something in the way he asked that question that warned me off the truth. "A box? No." I barely stopped myself from touching my pocket. Old and dangerous according to Walsingham. The hope of the future and the instrument of righting a great wrong according to the Lady. Which one did I believe?

Which one was trying to kill me?

"It could turn the whole world on its head," Philip said. "Walsingham is searching for Sumners and the key to the box, by all accounts. Do you know anything of them?"

I shook my head. "Sumner? I've never even heard the name before."

"Our mother's family." He gave me a long look as if waiting for my reaction. When I gave none, he shook his head. "No matter. We go to Totnes next, and thence to Chard."

"Why have you thrown in your lot with Walsingham? Aren't you in danger, too?"

He gave a short sharp grunt that might have been meant as a laugh, but it stuck in his throat. "I have no choice. I dabbled in magic. Careless of me, I know. I should have taken the advice of the old harridan and left it well alone. I registered with the Mysterium. Walsingham found me soon after. He has magic of his own. Magic like I've never seen before." He glanced up at the loud cry of a gull directly overhead.

"He keeps me with him, night and day." Philip's voice faltered as he saw my expression. "Oh, not like that. He's no shirt-lifter. Single-minded, I tell you. He's fashioned a poppet, a tiny model of me with a strand of my hair stuffed into it and stained with my blood. All he has to do is squeeze it and he can break my leg, or my arm, or my head. Or he can stop my lungs or even my heart. He doesn't even have to be near me." He threw up his hands, causing his horse to start.

"Walsingham has magic? He's a registered witch?"

Philip's laugh was hollow. "He uses spells, but he's as far above a registered witch as that seagull is above the street."

Much more than a witch? How scared should I be of this man?

"Can you get free of him?"

"The poppet never leaves his person. Believe me, I've been waiting for an opportunity." His face twisted. "I know you never loved me, but—"

"How can you say that? You're my brother. We may have had our differences, but we are family."

"Then, that should count for something, Ross. For pity's sake, if you know where the box is, tell me."

I didn't want the damn box, so why didn't I just give it to him? It seemed so straightforward. Give him the box then flee the country, and let that be an end to it. But my stomach clenched when I thought about handing it over. It tugged at me. The Lady had said it was important. Even if I didn't want to deal with it, I wasn't sure Philip could be trusted. Family he may be, but I hardly knew the young man he'd become. And this Walsingham was an unknown quantity, but I disliked everything I knew of him so far.

"Maybe it was in the house and has gone up in flames." I schooled my face. I was a better liar now than I used to be.

"I suggested that to Walsingham. He doubts that fire would destroy it."

"I don't know, then. If I should think of where the box might be, how do I find you again?"

"In London. We never stay in the same lodgings for long, but we're always somewhere close to the river. When you get there, summon me. I'll find you."

"Summon you?"

"With magic, Ross." He glanced to Heaven and clicked his tongue as though I should have instantly known what he was talking about.

"Are you safe, for now?"

"I've made myself compliant. While he has the poppet he knows I can't go against him."

I put my hand up to his face and turned his head to look in my eyes. The years stripped away and I saw the small boy I had fought a duel for. "Are you treated well?"

"Well enough."

He turned to go.

"You didn't ask, but she's dead, you know—our mother."

He shrugged and raised an eyebrow at my clothing. "You want me to wear black?"

I wouldn't be wearing black for my mother. I hadn't even worn black for Will. Anywhere the *Heart* was known it had suited me better to suppress news of his death. Will might be dead, but Captain Tremayne wasn't. His legend still lived on.

"They say Tremayne did it," Philip said. "Is that true?"

"She was sick and in pain, and wanted to leave the world. She went by her own hand with the help of a bottle of laudanum. The house in flames was her funeral pyre, not her death."

He nodded. "Walsingham left her alone so she might lead him to you. I got that much of a concession from him. I didn't think you were so stupid as to come." He grinned, a flash of the old, malicious Philip. "The box, Ross. If you ever loved me, don't let me down."

He mounted his horse and trotted off without a backward glance.

I waited until he'd ridden to the far end of the street then made a smart dash for the *Alessandra*. Hookey and David waited on board, crouching by the deck rail where they would not be easily seen from the quayside.

Hookey raised an eyebrow.

"It's all right. They didn't see me," I reassured him. "We need to cast off now. Where's Captain Haggerty?"

"In his cabin."

I sighed. "This is going to cost me deep in the purse."

The captain's cooperation and our swift departure from port drained me of another three gold guineas, but it was worth it to get away cleanly. The three of us hunkered down as our sails blossomed in the wind, lest anyone on shore had a keen eye or a good glass.

The *Alessandra* hugged the coast of the Cornubian Peninsula, southwestward, past St. Ives. Even with the wind against us, we made Harper's Inlet in two gut-emptying days, during which I was genuinely sorry to have David as my companion in misery, heaving over the rail or groaning in the adjacent hammock.

At Harper's Inlet, the captain had us rowed into the bay in the ship's boat. David kissed his fingers and picked up a fistful of shingle as we waded out of the shallows.

"Tell me my stomach will get used to the motion," he said as we watched the boat crew row back out to sea.

"Mine never has."

"But the sickness goes away, right?"

"I'm always all right on the *Heart*. Hopefully you will be, too."

He scowled. In his place I'd have done the same.

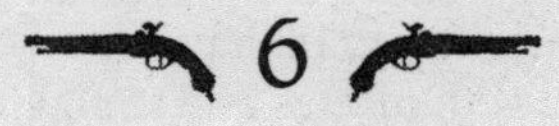

6

Harper's Inlet

HARPER'S INLET WAS NOTHING but a sheltered rocky cove with a shingle beach and a sloping track up to a couple of rows of squat cob cottages. Besides the inevitable tavern, more a meeting place than an inn, there was not one business evident anywhere save for a shop in the front room of a cottage, and a carter's yard which, by its stink, carried the catch inland to market over the narrow track across the moor.

There were a few individuals mending nets, others unloading and gutting a recent herring catch, letting the tide and the swarm of gulls take the innards away, and a group of four young children at play. On the beach, a handful of crab and lobster boats were drawn up on the sand.

Hookey sauntered over to talk to a weather-beaten woman dressed in canvas trousers and an oiled wool jumper. She straightened up from stacking lobster pots and flashed him the kind of welcoming smile reserved for an old friend or a lover.

"I thought you said boats sailed from here to the Dark Islands," David said.

"They do."

"Carrying what, crabs and mud? There are no warehouses here, not even a decent-sized shed."

"But there are caves. Very useful for incoming cargoes under the noses of the Excise men. They deal in brandy, wines, and lace—probably from France. The war doesn't stop ordinary men trading."

"You associate with pirates and smugglers?"

"His Majesty doesn't pay me to police the high seas. We follow a mutually beneficial policy of ignoring each other."

"Why are there no rowankind here?"

"Too poor."

"They're staring at me."

"Just curious."

I set off into the village, gesturing to Hookey so that he knew where we were going, but not really expecting him to follow. A few elderly men idled outside the tavern, sitting along the low stone wall, nursing tankards and sucking on ill-smelling pipes.

"Cap'n!" One of the drinkers put down his ale and reached for a crutch trying to struggle up with one leg of his cotton trousers hanging empty below the knee.

"Stay at anchor, Walter. How are you doing?"

He flopped back on to the bench, relief evident. "Oh, you know, all right for a sailor becalmed. I ain't gotten used to the jury leg, yet, but I do all right on the crutch."

"Tell 'er 'bout Emily." One of his companions dug him in the ribs.

"Oh, aye. We're tying the knot next week. Me and the Widow Heath."

"Good job he only lost his leg. Not his yard-arm." One of the other drinkers winked at me and it seemed likely he was testing to see if I could be shocked. I didn't shock easily.

"Good, for you, Walter. You'll be a family man. Hasn't the Widow Heath got seven children?"

"Eight. Three of 'em's grown enough to take out Heath's old fishing boat and I thought I might do a bit of fair-weather herring fishing, you know, to keep my sea-legs . . . sea-leg . . . in trim, not that I need the money, of course."

"Mind how you go, Walter. There's pirates about."

"Oh, aye." He laughed and winked.

"Who was that?" David asked as we ducked under the low doorway of the tavern into the closeness of the dark interior.

"An old crewman. Retired with a payoff when he lost half a leg in a skirmish last year."

"Payoff?"

"It's tradition with the pirates and it makes sense. Walter's set for the rest of his life as long as he's not stupid with his money. You've got to give a man an incentive for facing the danger. Hookey lost his hand courtesy of His Majesty's Navy. No compensation there."

"Isn't Walter worried that the people here know who he is?"

"Harper's Inlet is a long way from the Citadel at Plymouth. Besides, the people here do good business with pirates—they wouldn't risk their livelihood."

"Cap'n Tremayne!" The young man behind the bar sounded genuinely pleased to see us. "What can I get you?" He was reaching for a tankard, but I shook my head.

"Food first, Jack. I need to put something inside me now the horizon's stopped rolling. Has your mother got her eternal stewpot on the fire?"

"Two bowls is it?"

I looked at David. "It is, and two mugs of spiced cider if you please, not that rotgut you dissolved a dead dog in."

David nodded. "I'm beginning to feel as though I own my stomach again."

"Line it while you can. I'm sorry about the seasickness. Maybe you'll get over it."

"And if I don't?"

I shrugged and ushered him into a booth in the far corner of the empty room, sitting with my back into the corner out of habit. "I don't know. Rowankind don't make good sailors, but you're half-blood so you may be all right. I'm making this up as I go along. I thought my life was settled, but now, it seems, it isn't."

I told him quickly about meeting with Philip, trying to

articulate why I hadn't handed over the box, but his questions were interrupted by Jack's mother bustling over with a board on which balanced two bowls of thick mutton stew, a loaf of soda bread and a block of pale yellow butter.

"Later," I whispered.

She plonked the board down in the middle of our table with more relish than grace and fished spoons and knives out of her apron pocket. "You just missed the *Anna Claire* outward bound for the Dark Islands."

"Your spare room available?"

"Aye." She looked at David. "Want to put your rowankind in the stable?"

"David's k—" I nearly said kin. "Crew."

Her eyes clearly said, *But he's still rowankind.*

"He can have the spare room and I'll take the stable," I said.

Her mouth compressed into a line.

"Or you could get him a good blanket and let him sleep down here by the fire."

She stared me down, but I'm good at staring, and she blinked first, then nodded tightly.

"Thank you," I said. "I take it as a kindness."

"What about Hookey?" David ignored the slight.

"Didn't you see him talking to that woman on the quay?"

"That was a woman?"

It was easy to forget how young David was sometimes.

"Maria. She washes up well. I'll guess Hookey has somewhere a lot more comfortable than an inn's hearth to lay his head this week."

Once I'd eaten, I needed to sleep, even though I'd been horizontal most of the way from Bideford. Unfortunately it followed that I was wide awake by the time the first cock crowed in the early dawn. I rolled out of the creaky box-bed, stretching my back to get rid of the knots caused by the lumps in the mattress. At least it was clean and dry and the blankets smelled of carbolic rather than seawater. I dressed quickly and went to use the privy.

On my way back inside I met David with an arm full of logs.

"What are you doing?" As if it wasn't obvious.

"Making up the fire."

I took the logs from him, carried them into the large inglenook fireplace, and set them down in the hearth.

"You don't have to do that. I'm paying for your place by the fire and your breakfast. You're not her servant. Did that old besom . . . ?"

"No. No one asked me to do it. I thought I'd help."

I stared into his face and found nothing there but innocence. I sighed. "Come walk with me outside before breakfast. We've got things to talk about."

We climbed the narrow track and walked along the salt-lashed cliff top. At a solitary oak, the path broadened out and divided. The wind off the water carried the smell of fish, salt, tar, and mud.

A fallen stone way-marker had made a bench and I perched on the edge. My magic sat easy on my shoulders today, calmed by the sea. I imagined pale light, gentle and soft, and felt power shiver through my body and down my right arm. I directed my thoughts, and a ball of light appeared at my fingertips. I tossed it gently into the oak tree, where it hovered in the lower branches until I blinked it out.

"Can you teach me how to do that?" David asked. "Is it a spell?"

"Can I teach you? Maybe. Lord knows I've been a poor one for learning more than I need to get by, but I'll try. Is it a spell? Well, it is and it isn't. There are two ways to use magic, natural and ritual. That is, some people simply are magic, and others use magic by way of spells."

"Two magics?"

"One magic—only one—but there are two ways of approaching it." I thought of the Green Man and his Lady. "Maybe more than two."

He looked puzzled. "And your magic is—what?"

"The natural kind. The Mysterium doesn't know what to do with people like me. We can't be regulated or defined.

And if they can't define us, they can't control us. That's what scares them. So they pretend we don't exist, though if they catch us they'll trump up a charge and hang us quickly enough, or likely kill us some other way if they can."

"What about the other kind? Can anyone do magic with a spell book?"

I shook my head. "No, you've got to have a talent for it. If you have it, then you must register and use the spell book. It's the law. They say that Mad King George himself is a registered witch—though they say lots of things about the monarch and I'm not sure I believe half of them. But if he does have magic, that might explain the madness. I've heard it can affect people that way."

"The Lady said our mother was a witch, or could have been. Does it run in families?"

"Maybe. I don't know enough about it. To be honest I've always been reluctant to find out. I can call wind and manipulate weather. My hearing is very acute, more so than might be called normal, and I have a small talent for finding lost things—if I focus very hard, things I thought were lost reveal themselves to me."

"And you can make light."

"That's about the extent of it, except for the *Heart*. I can call her to me."

"How did you find out about it all?"

"When things first started happening around me, I didn't realize I was causing them. I thought I was being haunted. Things would move. Articles that I knew had been on the table when I went to sleep at night were on the floor when I woke in the morning. Clothes in my cupboard would be wet for no reason. I know now that I was calling tiny wind and rainstorms, but until I learned to do it consciously I must have been doing it unconsciously, maybe in my sleep. I sometimes had the strangest dreams. I learned things gradually. There's no primer to teach a person that kind of thing. Or if there is, the Mysterium keeps it close."

"Your—our mother found out."

"There was an incident. The magic I thought I'd kept hidden manifested in such an obvious way. Luckily it happened at home and not in public, but it changed everything in an instant. I realize why, now. If she was hiding her own magic."

"What did she do?"

"She tried to beat it out of me and pray it out of me. And when that didn't work she made me promise to keep it hidden. That was good advice in retrospect."

"And am I like you?"

I shrugged. "I don't know. Show me your magic."

"I can't do anything."

"Don't tell me you've never tried to use it."

At length he said, "I've made fire. Twice."

"That's natural magic. How did you know you could do it?"

"I felt it."

"And what happened?"

"The first time I nearly burnt the house down."

"And the second time?"

"I did burn the house down."

Christ on a pig! Was I planning to take a firestarter on to a wooden ship? My skin went clammy at the thought. I tried to keep my voice even.

I stood up and moved away from the overhanging branches of the oak tree. "All right. Show me a small flame."

"Now?"

"Right now."

He held out his right hand, palm upward and looked at it.

Nothing happened.

"Well?" I asked.

"I . . . I might hurt you."

I moved over and stood right behind him, figuring it was the safest place to be. With my hands on his shoulders I said, "Clear your mind and think about where your magic comes from and what brings it closer to the surface."

"No spell words, then?"

"It's thoughts that count, or at least it always has been for me. Did you need words before?"

"Not really, I thought hard about fire, and—"

A sharp blast spun us both around. The world canted over crazily, and I hit the grass hard. A fireball the size of a house flared overhead and vanished. I felt the searing heat for a split second and heard an intense roar and crackle that died away in an instant, leaving only a smell like burning metal, charcoal, and blood.

My cheeks stung as if I'd been out in the sun all day. Green spots danced in front of my eyes. David lay sprawled across my legs on his back. The light was somehow different. I rolled David to one side and sat up cautiously.

The oak tree had gone.

Completely.

Where it had been there was now only a circle of scorched earth and a mound of fine, gray ash already beginning to blow away on the westerly breeze.

"God's ballocks!" I took a deep breath. "As a demonstration that was . . . very effective, but less than ideal." I got unsteadily to my feet and held out my hand to David. "Come on."

He sat there, eyes wide open and blowing out his cheeks.

"David!" I dusted down the backside of my breeches and held out my hand again. "You've got to give it another try. There's no way I'm taking you on board the *Heart* unless you can control this."

"What? Again? After that?"

"You've got to get rid of some of that excess power and learn to control what's left, otherwise I walk away from you right now. I learned to tame mine, and so must you." I could hear my voice shaking. I hoped David couldn't.

Reluctantly he reached out, and I hauled him to his feet. His hand trembled.

"I can't teach you what to do," I said. "Magic isn't a precise science."

"You said Philip dabbled in magic," David said. "Did you mean dabbled, or is he good at it?"

"I didn't have time to ask for details."

"Did you tell him about me?"

"I didn't tell him anything. What he doesn't know he

can't tell under duress." I tried to push away the idea of Philip's poppet being tortured by Walsingham. My brother might die tomorrow and I would never know.

"I expected that real magic would be like 'eye of toad and blood of bat,'" David said.

He looked so glum I couldn't help but laugh. "In fairy tales."

"What if the Lady was right about dark magic? What if I can't control it? What if I hurt somebody?"

Sometimes David seemed very young, and at other times when I looked at him there was an old soul looking out from behind his eyes.

"You won't. I won't let you." If all else failed I had my blade at my hip, and, brother or not, I would use it, presuming I wasn't a little pile of gray ash. "First of all, let's bleed off that energy." I walked him to the edge of the cliff and pointed him to the empty air. "All right, do that again."

"Stand behind me," he said. "No, right behind me. Don't let me get turned around."

I wasn't going to argue with him. He took several deep breaths and pointed out to sea. I thought for a moment that he wasn't going to succeed, but suddenly a fireball even bigger than the first erupted from his fingertips. This time I was ready for it and held him steady so we neither spun nor fell.

"Again," I said.

He took three quick breaths and shot another gout of flame out from the cliff edge. This time I fancied it wasn't so huge.

"Again."

The next flame he produced was much smaller, but I still had him make another three fireballs before I was satisfied that he'd drained his energy to a manageable level.

"Try a small flame now."

He pointed his hand out toward the cliff edge, but nothing happened.

"I can't," he said. "It's completely gone."

"Yes, you can. Think about how you called it before. Do the same again, but more gently. Put a limit on the size of the flame you want to produce. Visualize it, soft like a candle instead of roaring like a bonfire. How did you do it before?"

"I thought of fire and what fire feels like: the heat and the flames and the sound."

"You need to focus on something small. Like when I'm making a witchlight. I have to imagine how much light I need and focus on what I'm trying to create." I made another softly glowing light ball and held it on the tip of my index finger for a few moments before I let it fade. "Try again and this time don't think about fire, think about a single flame."

"All right, but stand behind me again."

I stood behind him with both hands on his shoulders. "Don't try too hard. It shouldn't take an enormous effort. Just a little willpower."

He held out his arm and pointed his finger upward. I could feel the tension in him as he concentrated . . . and concentrated.

Nothing.

His shoulders slumped. "I'll never get the hang of this."

"You will. Try again."

This time there was a shimmer, and a tiny flame burned steadily from the end of his finger.

"Well done." I called up a stiff breeze to blow away the last of the oak ash. "Come on, it's probably well past breakfast time. Let's go back down to the village and find out if anyone knows what's happened to the old tree." I raised one eyebrow. "It looks like it got struck by a bolt of lightning."

In the afternoon David and I walked along the cliff path to the south of the village, talking about anything and everything, touching on his life and mine. He was eager to know more details of how and when my magic emerged. Some of the memories were painful, almost too painful for me to deal with. I'd locked them away a long time ago and didn't want to bring them out again now, but maybe he needed to know that it wasn't easy for me either.

"I was fourteen. It all started with an argument. You never knew my father. He was away such a lot I hardly knew him myself, but I loved him blindly. I was his little sweeting when he was at home, and I missed him so terribly when he was at sea. He and our mother were a cold couple. Maybe living apart so much meant they didn't really know each other anymore. My father was a visitor in his own house, welcomed like a hero when he returned from a voyage, but within a day or two the arguments started. Mother would save up grievances and trot them out. I never heard Father raise his voice to any servant, and he was always gentle with me and Philip, but behind closed doors he and Mother would rage at each other. This particular time, he'd lost a cargo of rum brought from the Americas. His ship had run onto a sandbar off the Lizard in a storm. He got every single sailor safe ashore, but by morning the ship was in two halves and the cargo was gone. Lloyds of London paid out insurance for the ship, but on a technicality, not for the cargo. Mother berated him constantly for his fecklessness, but he only said he'd rather lose a ship than her crew."

I'm fourteen again and watching it all unfold. My skin goes clammy and my heart seems to pound every time the two of them argue. She digs at him at every opportunity. He puts up with just so much before he finally snaps back at her and slams the drawing room door, taking himself off to his study and pouring a large glass of brandy, not his first. She leaves him alone for a couple of hours then finds a reason to go in and it all starts again.

I sit halfway up the staircase, listening, my face pressed between the turned baluster rails. There's nothing new, the same arguments over and over.

Philip hurtles out of the kitchen with a huge lump of fruitcake in his fingers, laughing and stuffing it into his mouth, trailing crumbs along the hallway. Evy shrieks after him and he calls her a name I'm not supposed to know, but I've been down to the harbor with Father and sailors don't mind their language for anybody. I know Philip's bad behavior is entirely down to Mother's overindulgence. Someone should say no to that boy, but every time I try she overrules me, and Father is so rarely home to see the way of it.

I hear voices raised still further. I've always had good hearing, but even if I were deaf I'd hear Mother's voice scream, "Privateering? That's not for a gentleman."

Father drops his voice and I can hear how tired he is. "We're close to the edge. With only three ships now, and all the trouble with France, I can hardly keep us afloat. There's prize money to be had."

"Our reputation will be ruined!" My mother's voice rises to a shriek again. "I'll not be sneered at. Think of your children. How will I ever find a suitable match for Rossalinde if her father's little better than a pirate?"

"I'm going to be a pirate when I grow up." Philip comes down and crouches on the stair above me. He's big for his age, having had a recent growth spurt.

"Father's not a pirate, he's going to be a privateer. It's different. Privateers are gentlemen. Pirates are scum."

"It's attacking ships for the prize money, and taking their treasure, and cutting the throats of the crew, or maybe casting them adrift in an open boat without oars or compass. How's that different from being a pirate?"

"A privateer has letters of marque from the king and he only attacks the king's enemies. In this case France and Spain. It's respectable, whatever Mother says."

"Is there fighting and killing?"

"Some."

"I heard how pirates tie their prisoners to the mast and make a little slit in their belly here." He points to his own belly. "And they hook out a man's guts." He does the actions in graphic detail. "All rubbery and shiny like a string of wet sausages. Next they tie a cannonball to the end and roll it along the deck so that his guts unravel right out of his belly. Did you know there's more than twenty feet of guts in a man?"

"No I didn't," I say, looking away.

"When his guts are all unraveled one of 'em will kick the cannonball clean over the side. I wonder how long a man can live with the guts ripped out of his belly."

I turn my head back and see he's grinning. Horrible child. He's made all that up to disgust me.

Mother's voice is raised again. She's almost incoherent with rage. The study door opens and Father storms out.

"Don't you dare walk out on me, Teague Goodliffe," she screams.

"Madam, this conversation is over. I have made my decision." Father's voice is icily polite. I don't think I've ever seen him so angry. She doesn't even realize. Mother's shrieking is almost normal, but Father's cold anger terrifies me. I feel myself trembling and tingling inside, my heart is fluttering like a bird.

"Don't!" I want to shout it, but it comes out close to a whine.

Father looks up at the sound of my voice. From out of the study door a vase comes flying. It crashes at Father's feet. She's actually thrown something at him.

"Mother, don't!" I'm yelling too, now. I pick up my skirts, cursing them, and run down the curving staircase. Father takes two steps toward me and is felled by another object flying out of the study, an oil lamp this time. Father and the lamp crash to the ground. The spilt oil ignites upon him, insidiously small flames across the thick woolen cloth of his jacket. I don't know what to do. I need something to smother the flames with. I feel the fear fizzing through me, as if I'm in the middle of a whirlwind.

I'm moving the air, swirling it around the hall, sucking it away from the flames so they're dying. I shake my father's shoulder and I don't stop until he shudders and comes around, dislodging me as he turns over. He looks pained and groggy; blood trickles from a scalp wound.

Suddenly it goes quiet.

Mother's standing by the study door, an expression of horror on her face. I assume it's horror at what she did, but she's looking at me. I see her mouth move, and the word she doesn't say out loud is: witch.

Up above on the stairs I hear a chuckle. It's Philip.

"And was your father all right?" David asked.

"Eventually. He called for Larien to harness the carriage, went down to the quay and spent the night on the *Heart*."

"And what about you? Your father didn't take you with him?"

"He hadn't seen what I'd done. I'm not sure if he even realized his coat had been on fire. Not right then, anyway. He was still confused from the bash on the head. Mother went into a swoon as though she was the one who'd been injured. I was left to puzzle it out for myself."

"No one helped you?"

"Ruth. Later that night she came up to my room. She didn't seem to mind about the magic, just said there were things in the world that we'd never be able to understand, so we just had to accept them as part of God's will. Ruth was always like a mother to me. I guess I took her love for granted, but it wasn't her love I craved. I cried myself to sleep in Ruth's arms because I knew Mother would never love me now."

7

Heart of Oak

THAT EVENING THE TAVERN FILLED with locals, including Walter with the Widow Heath, and Hookey with his Maria, now dressed in a respectable skirt and a low-cut blouse. With her hair hanging loose rather than jammed under a canvas cap, her face looked tanned and handsome rather than hard and weather-beaten.

"Is it true what they say about a sailor having a girl in every port?" David sounded hopeful.

"If it is it's because the girls have a sailor on every ship." I laughed as he worked out the implications.

As the ale flowed and the air in the room thickened, one of the villagers brought out a roughhewn fiddle and started scraping a tune. Within minutes tables had been pushed back and a space cleared for dancing, with the men vying with the women for fancy stepping. Hookey had enough ale inside him to volunteer a hornpipe, and not too much ale that he couldn't manage it quite creditably.

The night dragged on past midnight and though some of the fishermen who were sailing on the morning tide took themselves home to sleep, a few stalwarts hung on for the pleasure of good company. After my early start that morning I was tired, so I made my excuses and went to my room, leaving David to fend for himself. If he got tired, no one would mind him curling up and sleeping in a corner.

The following morning I came down early to find one of last night's revelers lying straight and stiff on a settle, arms folded across his chest and snoring fit to waken the dead. David was sitting cross-legged, straight-backed, almost in the hearth, staring into the glowing embers of the fire.

"David?"

"Ross, quick, put another log on, I can't hold it for much longer."

I did as he asked and the flames began to lick up around the wood. I heard him breathe out and saw his body relax. "What did you do?"

"I needed to understand fire, so I watched it all night. When it started to go out I took it and held it and kept it burning, even though there was nothing left to burn. By the time you came down it was my fire in the hearth." He smiled sheepishly at me. "And now I'd like to sleep."

His eyes were already closing. I walked him up the stairs as if he was in a daze, and rolled him into the bed I'd so recently vacated. He'd kept the fire alight and not burned the inn around our ears. Well, it was a start.

I'd called the *Heart* as soon as we'd set sail from Bideford, and on the fourth day a sail appeared around the headland and a cry went up. Sailing sweetly into view, as pretty as a picture, came the *Heart of Oak*, and I flushed with pride. She's beautiful: a two-masted topsail schooner with a deck length of only ninety-three feet and a bow that cuts the waves like a hot knife through butter.

"Oh." I heard David catch his breath beside me.

"Isn't she beautiful?" I couldn't help it, the pride always showed in my voice.

"I expected her to be bigger, and armed to the teeth with cannon. She's tiny."

"She's fast and maneuverable, and she can beat to weather better than any vessel afloat."

"In the stories she sounds so *fearsome*."

I heard Hookey come up beside us and choke back a laugh. "Fearsome is as fearsome does, Davy boy. There's many a Frenchie skipper who's wet hisself when he's seen her on the horizon, for though she only carries eight guns it's the speed of her closing and the mettle of her crew that frights 'em the most. She can make a good four knots faster than the best ship in the Frenchie fleet, which is a good thing, all considered."

I stood on the shore to watch the *Heart*'s boat gliding into the bay with Simeon Fairlow at the tiller and eight oarsmen.

"Cap'n." Sim grinned up at me, nodded to Hookey and looked at David with frank curiosity. "Mr. Sharpner's compliments. We took *La Grenouille* three days ago."

"Nice work, Sim." We splashed through the shallows and settled into the boat.

"Gentlemen." Hookey ruffled David's hair. "This is our new crewmate, Davy."

The *Heart* had a small crew for a privateer vessel, only sixty men, but even that stretched the available space to the limit and meant that watches had to be staggered to give the sleeping men enough room to sling their hammocks. Almost every man was on deck as we came aboard, having little to do while she lay at anchor. Daniel Rafiq, our quartermaster, waited patiently to offer me a hand as we climbed the rope ladder from the boat to the deck. He was an impressive man, statuesque with blue-black skin, white teeth, and a cap of short, black, curly hair. I've never been a high-handed captain, but there was something about Mr. Rafiq that oozed formality. It wasn't that he stood to attention for me to come on deck—his posture was always that upright.

"Captain Tremayne." He was also the only member of my crew who never shortened captain to cap'n. He enunciated every syllable in a rich, deep baritone and the slightly flattened vowels of Africa.

"Mr. Rafiq, good to see you, and you, too, Mr. Cruikshanks." I grinned past Mr. Rafiq to Abel Cruikshanks, Mr. Rafiq's assistant and one of only three men ever to have tunneled out of the king's gaol on Darkmoor.

"Cap'n." Mr. Cruikshanks beamed back at me.

"Cap'n Tremayne." Mr. Sharpner, my sailing master, came across to greet us with his rolling gait more used to the rise and fall of a ship's deck than to dry land.

"Mr. Sharpner, that was a very timely arrival. I hear you've been busy while I've been away."

"We took *La Grenouille*. With a name like that she presented too good an opportunity to miss."

I glanced along the *Heart*'s deck. She looked immaculate. "An easy prize, I take it."

"One shot across her bow and she surrendered to us." He grinned. "They should all be so easy."

"A good catch?"

"A cargo of wool plus a little silver, and in her stores brandy, rum, and petty tally, mostly almonds and raisins. We put all hands into their jolly boat and set them on a course back to France. Mr. Effingham and a skeleton crew are sailing the vessel into Bristol for the prize money. Mr. Rafiq took the liberty of retaining the silver and the spirits."

"Excellent." The ship was worth more than the cargo, and His Majesty wouldn't mind the brandy and rum. What he didn't know about the silver wouldn't hurt. We were privateers, not angels.

"I put a small sack of raisins and nuts in your cabin, Cap'n," Lazy Billy grinned a lopsided grin at me. He'd lost all the teeth on the right-hand side of his mouth to a belaying pin in a skirmish.

"Thanks, Billy. Does that mean you drank all the rum yourself?"

He hung his head. "Only a very little bit."

Mr. Sharpner turned and looked at David, a polite way of asking who he was and what he was doing aboard the *Heart*. I'd give him his explanation soon.

"Let's get her underway, Mr. Sharpner. I'll join you on deck later."

"Aye-aye, Cap'n. Heading?"

I turned to the crew. "What say we close haul and beat to weather, lads? We'll head southwest into the French shipping lanes and see what prize we might find there."

There was a general chorus of ayes and I nodded. "She's all yours, Sailing Master."

"Aye, aye, Cap'n."

I heard the instructions being passed down through the crew and saw men start to go aloft as I beckoned David down to my cabin.

The captain's cabin in a schooner is neither large nor grand, and even I had to bend my head to duck beneath her beams, but it was my home. I had a bed, wide enough for two, just. It was an extravagance left over from when Will was alive. I'd never been able to bring myself to change it for a single cot even though it would have given me considerably more floor space. A chart table and a stool took up most of the rest of the room, and my sea chest slid under the bed alongside my modesty-saving commode, which spared me from going for'ard and hanging my arse over the bowsprit with the crew. There was a narrow strip of tiny windows in the stern with glass as thick as a man's thumb, scoured opaque by wind and salt.

My one luxury was an easy chair, threadbare now, but still comfortable. I'd liberated it from the captain's cabin of a barque we'd plundered off the coast of the West Indies the year after Will died. That was the year I'd felt as though I'd never be warm again.

David stared around at my home.

"Sit down, David." I waved him to the stool and dropped into my armchair. "You've got some decisions to make. We both have."

"Hookey said . . ."

"Never mind Hookey. We've flowed with the currents up to now, but I have to decide what to do about that damn box, and you have to decide what to do with the rest of your life." I rubbed my eyes, feeling them gritty from the salt spray.

"Am I bonded to you?"

"What?"

"Am I yours?"

"Of course not. I don't own anyone."

"Everyone on board this ship is a free man?"

"Free to come and go, to stay or leave as they please."

He took a deep breath. "Do you like the life?"

The breath whooshed out of my body. What a question! My first impulse was to say yes, but did I? I'd never had any great ambition to sail the oceans. Chance led me to the quay, love drew my feet onto the deck, and circumstances had barred me from returning home.

I'd certainly been happy while Will lived.

"I like it well enough. The question is: will you like it?"

"If I don't, can I leave?"

I nodded. "If your rowankind half is stronger than your human half, you'll not take to the sea at all, and then we'll have to think again. I'll not lie to you, it's hard work. Long days of routine interspersed with bouts of high excitement. Occasionally it's dirty, bloody, and dangerous. By the time we get to the middle of a winter voyage, the meat in the barrels is as high as the mainmast and the bilgewater stinks as though something's died in it. You'll think the height of luxury is to crawl into your hammock with a damp blanket wrapped around you."

"You make it sound as if no one could like it."

I sighed. "We're our own masters, and that's worth a lot."

"If I stay, will you teach me more magic?"

"I can't teach you, I can only guide you to finding your own way. But I'll do what I can."

He thought for perhaps half a minute. "Where do I sign?"

"On deck, at the next change of watch, in front of all the crew."

When David walked out of my cabin to report to Mr. Sharpner as the newest member of my crew, I sat for a while longer, resisting the idea, and then came to a decision. I took the winterwood box and held it firmly in my fist, letting my fingers find where the cleverly hidden seams might be. I willed that box open, concentrating my mind on the image of a soft click and the lid flying back to reveal . . .

To reveal what? That's where my imagination failed me. If I could but picture the contents of the box, maybe I could do this. As it was, the mind-game gave me the beginnings of a headache. I relaxed for a moment and let my thoughts idly wander, the box still clasped in my hands.

Was it really evil, or did it, as the Lady said, hold a way to right an ancient wrong? I couldn't even begin to think what that wrong might be.

Oh, Will, I need your guidance now.

Three years a widow and it didn't get any easier.

I felt a presence.

"I think you love this ship more than you love me, Will Tremayne. Where were you when I was in the forest?"

You went where I couldn't follow. In my head his voice sounded empty. *I hate that place.*

"You hate everywhere that's not the ocean."

Will's ghost often exhibited a capriciousness and a petulance that Will himself had never shown in life, but I put up with it because the ghost was all I had left. My dashing savior, brave, intelligent, and kind, had been ripped from me by a falling spar in a storm. One minute we had everything to look forward to, and the next he was gone and I was a widow, picking up the pieces of a life I'd never thought to have. I'd stitched his corpse into a sail myself, suitably weighting it to send him to the depths to join our son. I'd not been able to speak, not even to say the words as we consigned his body to the ocean. Mr. Rafiq had said them for me.

Three days later I had cried so much that it was a wonder I had not turned my eyeballs inside out. Then, alone in my cabin, I had wished so hard that I had wished Will's ghost into existence.

A ghost only, but anything of my Will was better than nothing.

I turned, but the shadowy figure faded, leaving me alone with my thoughts. Was it my need for him that drove him away?

I had a decision to make. I stared at the winterwood box on the corner of my chart table. The back of my neck prickled as though it was staring back. At last, I decided to do what I'd been doing since I left the forest—procrastinate. I packed the damn thing at the bottom of my sea chest, hoping to forget about it again.

And I did—for about three days.

On the fourth day, I reached into my chest for a clean shirt and my hand closed around the box. How had it come to the surface when I'd packed it so deep down? The tingle in my fingers told me it was still mine, but I'd teach it that it didn't own me. I'd defy it. I put it on the chart table and vowed to ignore it steadfastly.

"Hello, Will." A presence hovered behind me. I didn't turn, just tried to catch sight of him out of the corner of my eye.

Ghostly lips brushed the back of my neck. I shivered. My nipples, tight inside the bindings beneath my shirt, began to tingle. I swallowed hard and fought down the urge to rip off my clothes and hide beneath the blankets alone to find comfort.

I tried to distract myself. "What about this?" I pointed to the winterwood box. "What am I supposed to do about it?"

It's dangerous. Do nothing. It's not your quest.

"I'm inclined to agree. Will, I . . ." I turned to face him but there was no one and nothing there. The presence had vanished. Once more I was left empty and alone.

Oh, Will!

Watching David settle to life aboard the *Heart* reminded me painfully of my first weeks aboard, when I didn't know a bowsprit from a belaying pin. I'd been brought up to be a prim miss. In those early days, loving Will had almost not been enough.

The *Heart*'s cruise took us southward down the coast of France, across the Bay of Biscay and to the coast of Portugal. We took a Spanish barque without a fight and sailed in tandem with her around to Gibraltar for the prize money for the vessel, and to sell her cargo of olives, olive oil, and sherry wine. Freshly supplied, we cruised back up the coast toward England, but our luck had run out, and despite haunting the shipping lanes and sighting an American, two Dutch and several Royal Navy third-rate ships of the line, we came across no more potential prizes.

At length we decided to turn for the mid-Atlantic island of Bacalao and our home port of Elizabethtown, some fourteen days away. Our dwindling supplies were not enough to keep us sitting doing nothing if Boney's ships didn't want to come out to play.

I was tempted to ease the *Heart*'s passage by calling a favorable wind. Having a captain who can call the wind is an obvious advantage for any sailing vessel, but Mr. Sharpner rarely asked me to do it unless the situation was desperate. It's a tricky procedure to deliver exactly the right wind for exactly the right length of time without starting a cycle that will lead to a summer blizzard in the Sahara.

I stood in the bows with David, explaining all that to him—yet another of our mixed magic and sailing lessons. "If there's one fault with the *Heart* it's that she's a little light in the front end. She's got the speed because her bows are sharp and shallow. With nearly eight hundred square yards of sail she can make thirteen-and-a-half knots, that's a good five knots faster than many of His Majesty's naval ships or a ship-rigged merchantman. What drives a ship forward through the water isn't only the wind in her sails, it's the additional action of water on the hull. If I give her a little magic push with the wind and don't apply it evenly, she might pitchpole, literally drive herself down into the sea, nose-first and—"

"Sail ho off the starboard bow!"

A call from the lookout in the tops ended our discussion prematurely. All that waiting and it seemed we'd been looking in the wrong place.

"Go stand by for Mr. Sharpner, David. It looks like we may have business to conduct."

I kicked off my shoes and peeled off my fine cotton socks. I felt much safer in the rigging in my bare feet, though my toes were not as tough as they used to be, when I'd crewed for Will alongside the rest of the lads. I climbed to the tiny platform that hardly deserved the name crow's nest. Nick Padder, a young lad with sharp eyes, sat tied on to a safety line.

"There, Cap'n." He pointed with his glass. My own was a good glass, made better with a bit of magical help. On the horizon a three-masted merchant vessel, ship-rigged, rode low in the water. French built. She carried six guns, probably no more than eight-pounders. *We're in business!* Then I checked her flag. English. Damn! Not in business.

"Stand down," I hollered to the deck below.

I didn't think she'd seen us yet. I checked the glass again.

If it hadn't been enhanced with magic I wouldn't have seen the two larger ships of the line beyond the merchant vessel, and I doubt if I'd have seen her change her flag from English to French.

"What is it, Cap'n?" Hookey called up.

"I don't know. Looks like a fishing expedition to me. Two ships of the line as an escort, neither flying a flag of any kind. Both third-raters, but too rich for our blood, whether they're French or English."

But were they English fishing for French or French fishing for English?

Or are they fishing for me? The thought sat cold in my gut.

"Best stay out of it for now." Hookey folded his arms and tapped his foot on the deck.

"My thoughts entirely."

Leaving Nick back on his lonely watch, I climbed down and nodded to Mr. Sharpner. "Set a course for Bacalao if you will, Mr. Sharpner. There's some game afoot that I don't want any part of."

"Aye-aye, Cap'n."

8
The *Lydia*

WE ALTERED COURSE TWICE, but they stayed with us through our irrational twists and turns. Four hours later I was sure we were their target. Did those ships sail at the behest of Walsingham? Had finding us been a stroke of luck, or had they a witch on board who could track by magic?

If so, were they tracking me, or the box?

I needed to know.

The sea had always been my haven. If trouble was following me here, nowhere on earth was safe anymore.

Under cover of darkness we changed course again, and I filled our sails with a favorable wind. The merchantman had running lights, but the ships of the line were in darkness. Useful that I could call light into my spyglass lens. I could even see the officers on deck.

"English officers. Damn!"

Of course there was always the possibility that they were simply cruising for the kind of Frenchie likely to attack an English merchant ship, but the more I thought about it, the more likely it seemed that they were chasing something more specific and that magic was involved. The back of my neck prickled. Was it my intuition or my overactive imagination?

It was suicide to tackle the British Navy, but I dearly wanted to find out what they were about. That meant I had to talk to the captain of the merchantman. My glass showed me that she was named the *Lydia*.

"What's to do, Cap'n?" Mr. Sharpner asked.

"We'll cut the *Lydia* out like a prize cow from the herd."

"But what if she is English?" Mr. Rafiq asked.

"No matter. She's flying a French flag. That's all the excuse we need. I'll give her a breeze. By first light we'll be well over the horizon from her guardians. And I can give them a stiff gale in the opposite direction."

"She's carrying six guns on her main deck. She's fully loaded with something. Could be guano of course."

"It could be gold!" Mr. Rafiq said with a glint in his eye.

Information was more precious to me than gold, but I didn't disillusion him. There would certainly be something on the *Lydia* to cheer my crew. And she was flying a French flag, so she was fair game.

"Let's take a look then." I grinned.

"Aye-aye, Cap'n." Mr. Sharpner turned to give orders to the helmsman.

"Gunners, make ready. Mr. Rafiq, the powder and the side arms locker."

"Aye-aye, Captain."

"Lads, get yourselves into fighting trim ready for first light. Mr. Rafiq will issue rum for breakfast."

There was a general cheer, but as everybody started to move around me I saw the expression on David's face. I took him on one side. "Don't look so worried. We always prepare for the worst, but in truth most of our marks give up without a fight."

"Why do they do that?"

"Reputation. The owners of the goods are rarely aboard the vessels themselves. Both the masters and common sailors know that if they give up without a fight they'll live to sail again another day. If they fight and lose then it will go badly for them."

"You'll butcher them."

"Only if they resist us. Only if we have to."

"I've heard stories. Men being bled to death with a thousand small cuts or keelhauled until the bones showed through their back."

"Luckily they've heard the same stories. They've also heard of crews being let go with no harm if they offer no resistance."

"Have you done those things?"

He'd find out sometime. The crew might have told him some stories already. There was the time, before Will's death, when we'd taken a slaver. Will had not been kind to the crew. There had been fourteen dead Africans below-decks, still chained to their living companions in conditions no decent human being would have kept a dog in. Will had chained a slaver to each sad corpse and tossed them overboard before sailing back to the African coast and freeing the survivors along with the gift of the captain and the remaining crew. As we sailed away, I could hear screams from the shore.

I patted David on the shoulder. "I want you to help Mr. Rafiq bag the powder for the gun charges. You'll be powder monkey tomorrow with Tommy Jelks. That means you keep the guns supplied as they need it. When we close to board her, you'll need something to defend yourself with—try a marlinspike and see how it feels in your hand. Don't stick close to me or Hookey, we'll be in the thick of it. Stay with Mr. Sharpner. We can't afford to lose him, he knows to hang back."

"I don't want you to do me any favors or try and mollycoddle me."

"I'm not. Mr. Sharpner needs protecting. I expect you to get between him and trouble."

I didn't tell him that Mr. Sharpner was a veteran of a hundred such engagements and could take care of himself very nicely, and take care of David too, if I asked him to.

"And when it's issued, take a double tot of rum. If you do get a scratch or two you'll not notice so much."

I kept the wind steady throughout the night, and with neither lights nor sound on board we ran at a fair ten knots. Our quarry carried lights and even in the dead of night was easy to track. By the dark hours just before dawn I estimated she was within range of our guns, so in total silence, save for the creaking of our timbers, masked by the creaking of their own, we close-hauled and ran alongside.

It was time. I slipped away to my cabin and dressed in my most intimidating raiding garb: breeches, soft leather knee boots (a stiletto holstered in each) with soles designed to grip in slippery conditions, silk open-necked shirt and frock coat cut for action. All black, save for the silk shirt in blood red. I tied a black kerchief around my hair and jammed my tricorn hat (it had been Will's) on top. At my side I had a short sword, not as elegant as a cutlass but better suited to my strength and size. I had three flintlocks, loaded, primed, and ready to fire, tucked into a red sash at my waist.

I could smell the rum as I came back up on deck, but under orders not to break silence, it was gulped down quietly with some smacking of lips, but no toasts to the venture except for silent ones. I saw David throw back his head and down a tot and Hookey clap him on the back when he started to choke on the strong spirit. He looked like he was about to throw up. The worm churned in my own gut, but I pushed it down.

At first light their lookout probably pissed himself. I was standing by our number one port gun as the shout went up.

"Run up the black flag," I shouted, and our plain black symbol unfurled from the rigging along with our Privateer Jack, the Union flag as a large canton on a red field. Though my objective was information, this had to look like a privateer raid. I nodded to Jeb Huddlestone, who kissed his burning rope-end to the touchhole and fired a clean round across the *Lydia*'s bow. His team swabbed out and reloaded with chain shot.

Sixty drunken, ugly, leering, jeering privateers shouted obscenities and gestured.

Mr. Rafiq used the hailing trumpet. "Surrender and you go free with your lives." He repeated it in French for good measure. In answer there was a flurry of activity on board as they primed their guns.

"Fire as your guns bear," I yelled. The last thing I wanted was an artillery battle; the *Heart* wasn't built to take a pounding, and I didn't want to hole the *Lydia* and lose her, cargo, crew, information and all. Apart from the first shot, I'd had all the guns load with chain shot designed to take out sail, rigging and masts. Before she could even run out her guns, three of our four had discharged chain. One had torn clean through the mainsail, its shreds flapping, and another had clipped the foremast.

"She's pissing wind, Cap'n. We got 'er!" Nick Padder yelled from aloft.

Lydia's canvas flapped like a petticoat, but her captain fought on.

"Starboard gun crews, make ready!" I yelled and ran aft to Mr. Sharpner. "Come about, Mr. Sharpner, let's get behind her. I'll give you a breeze."

Our canvas snapped as wind filled the sails and the *Heart* surged like a willing horse into its bridle.

The *Lydia* got off one broadside, but it screamed over our topmasts, too high to do any damage. I began to count. We had maybe three minutes before she was ready to give us all her guns again. Two minutes. One and a half. One! When we came about there was that heart-stopping moment as we presented our vulnerable stern for the *Lydia*'s second broadside, giving her the opportunity to rake us, an opportunity I suspected she was waiting for. Damn her, why hadn't she surrendered? We'd have her anyway, eventually, barring the worst of incidents. Her captain must know that.

At the crucial moment, when we were at our most vulnerable, I sent a rogue wind to catch what was left of the *Lydia*'s sails and cause her to roll. Her broadside went high and one ball punched a neat hole in our main tops'l. I heard a yell above the flapping of canvas and looked up to see

Nick Padder swinging from his safety line, indignant but unhurt.

Then we were around and racing to the *Lydia*'s stern, out of reach of her guns and in a position to do to her exactly what she had hoped to do to us.

"That's it, Cap'n. Fuck her up the arse," Lazy Billy called out with relish.

The gun crews readied the starboard guns.

"Chain shot," I yelled. "Take out her masts."

My gunners may not be Royal Navy-trained, but they're steady and true. Four guns discharged chain into the *Lydia*'s rigging simultaneously and her mainmast splintered like matchwood about halfway down. The lookout who had allowed us to creep up in the dead of night went with it. I fancied I heard a scream, but it was probably the wind.

"That's it, she's ours. Let's close and board her before she comes about. Get ready lads."

I had six marksmen go aloft with two rifles apiece, the new type designed by Ezekiel Baker for the British infantry. Hookey had acquired them from a navy connection, a supply officer with a gambling debt. I hadn't asked for details, just accepted them gratefully. They were slower to load than muskets, but in the hands of a sharpshooter much more accurate. The *Lydia*'s captain tried to bring her around to present her guns again, but, with her mainmast gone and fouling the rest of his sail, he'd lost way. We nudged in neatly, our bow kissing the *Lydia*'s stern. My heart pounded as if trying to break out of my chest. I wiped my hand on my coat and took my sword with a dry palm.

By my left elbow, Hookey growled a string of obscenities. By my right elbow, Daniel Rafiq seemed as composed as if he were out for a Sunday stroll.

A deafening, primal roar came from the throats of the men.

"Now!" I shouted. We all rushed forward together, yelling fit to bust a gut.

Will was ahead of me, ghostly cutlass in one hand, knife in the other.

Too late, I saw the swivel gun mounted on the aft rail.

Too small to be effective at long range, they were bloody murderers close up.

I yelled, "Get down!"

I flung myself sideways. Someone landed on top of me. I heard the gun discharge. Someone—more than one voice—started screaming and my nostrils were full of the stench of blood, gore and shit.

"Up and on before the bastard reloads." I pushed a corpse off me and scrambled to my feet. I daren't stop to count the maimed or help the living. If their gunners reloaded that swivel gun we could all be dead or screaming within the next minute.

We swarmed over the rails, and as soon as my feet touched the *Lydia*'s deck I had my sword in my right hand and the first of my flintlocks in my left. I pulled the doghead all the way back and aimed randomly into the press of *Lydia*'s sailors.

Red-coated marines boiled up from the two companionways. The *Lydia* was certainly not an ordinary merchant ship. Our English Privateer Jack was plain enough. They knew we were for King George and still they fought. Counting heads was impossible, but I estimated we had them outnumbered. Their muskets would be useless once we were amongst them. There was no room for fear. Rifles cracked out from our tops as we swarmed over the rails. Some of the marines fell, others hesitated.

Thoughts gave way to instinct as we hacked, slashed and shot our way around the smashed rigging and into a general mêlée. If there was another swivel gun aboard we were fighting too closely for them to use it without killing their own. I saw Hookey to my right facing off against two marines and David to my left with a belaying pin in one hand and a marlinspike in the other. So much for hanging back with Mr. Sharpner.

A sailor ran at me with a club, and I discharged my second flintlock into his face then used it to beat his body out of my way while he was still falling. My sword, seemingly working by itself, bit into the soft flesh of a marine who'd come at me from the right. I twisted and pulled the blade free of the sucking flesh and turned to find Simeon had his long knife at the captain's throat and all but half a dozen of the marines dead or wounded.

It was over, but we'd taken some severe losses ourselves.

I looked around. Will floated up to the rigging, laughing silently. Hookey stood, chest heaving, flecked with blood that was not his own. David sat on a fallen spar, eyes glazed but otherwise uninjured. Mr. Rafiq looked as cool as he had before. I had the *Lydia*'s survivors herded together, stripped of their weapons with enough of my men surrounding them as to allow no rebellion. I set my gunners gathering the wounded. From the blood on the deck, the butcher's bill would be high, I heard David choke back a sob.

"David, go with Lazy Billy, see what you can do for the injured."

He didn't move.

"Go!"

With a start he gathered his legs under him and tottered unsteadily back to the *Heart*.

"Mr. Rafiq, inventory."

"Yes, Captain."

"Hookey, take men and scour belowdecks for stragglers. See if you can find the logbook. That might help us make sense of this."

9
Information

NAVIGATING DEBRIS AND BODIES, Nick Padder trotted across the deck, apparently none the worse for being dangled eighty feet in the air on a safety line. He obviously didn't want what he had to say to be heard generally, so I turned away to let him speak softly.

"Mr. Sharpner asks if you can come belowdecks, Cap'n. That damn swivel gun was loaded with scrap iron. We've six dead already and more wounded. Mr. Cruikshanks is very bad."

There were some of ours dead on the deck, too.

"Tell Mr. Sharpner I'll come as soon as I can."

There was a commotion on the companionway and Hookey and his men returned to the deck pushing two men in front of them. One was in his forties, the other barely out of his teens and wearing an apron covered in blood.

As soon as he had line of sight, Hookey yelled, "They got a sawbones aboard, Cap'n. Damn me if he weren't hiding away in his cabin wi' his 'prentice doin' all the work."

"I'll take the sawbones to the *Heart*. Guard the prisoners,

Hookey. No games." I stared hard at the captain. "Not yet, anyway."

That would get the captain thinking hard about cooperation.

"You." I pointed at the surgeon and his lad. "Both of you come with me."

"If you think I'm going to lay a finger on that unsanitary rabble—" the doctor started.

"You're a surgeon, there are men hurt."

"Scum!"

I turned and cracked him across the jaw with the pommel of my sword. "Let's have some respect. A man's a man."

He reeled backward as if he'd never been hit in his life before and sat down hard on his arse, clutching his bleeding mouth and looking dazed.

"You, boy, got a name?" I glared at the apprentice.

"Louis, sir."

"How do you feel about treating scum?"

"A man's a man, sir."

"Good answer." The boy would do. I wouldn't trust the surgeon not to snip an artery and call it an accident.

I turned to go, but he put a hand on my arm. It was almost the last thing he did. I saw Hookey start forward and I only just stopped myself from bringing my sword up into the boy's guts. He knew immediately that he'd made a big mistake, but he just kept his eyes on my face.

"S-sorry, sir, but if you want me to be useful there's things I'll need down in the cabin."

I nodded. "Simeon and Jake, take Louis down to the surgeon's cabin and bring back whatever he needs. If it's sharp and made of metal, you carry it. Watch him for tricks. Bring him to the *Heart*."

I clambered across the ships' rails, now securely lashed together and bridged by a plank and safety line. I tried to ignore the bodies of men I'd known, spread-eagled in death where they'd fallen, and I headed belowdecks.

The stench was overwhelming. I'm used to the perfumes of shipboard life. They'd make most landsmen gag on a good day, but this was something else: blood, coppery and pungent, mixed with sweat, gore, and shit from ruptured guts. It was the smell of death.

Someone had rigged up a table in the open space beneath the cargo hatch, and there was a pale, half-naked body on it surrounded by four men.

In the middle of so much blood and pain, Mr. Cruikshanks was just one more casualty, yet I'd sailed with this man for seven years, shared laughter and tears. I swallowed hard to try and relieve the burning sensation at the back of my throat, and blinked tears out of my eyes.

David stood at his head and had a firm grasp of his hand while Lazy Billy, unofficial sawbones to the whole ship's company, stood over him shaking his head. The daylight fell across the scene in squares from the grating above. I sent up a witchlight to even out the shadows, and by it I could see what was left of Mr. Cruikshanks' belly. By rights he should have been dead already, but somehow he was not only alive but conscious and not screaming.

"I've given him laudanum, Cap'n," Billy said. "Damn near the whole bottle, but I don't know whether it'll help."

"There's a surgeon coming over from the *Lydia*." I didn't tell them: an apprentice. A groan drew my attention to another body slumped against the bulkhead. Edmund Morrow was covered in blood, with his hand clutched to his chest. By him lay two more men, variously bloodied. Two others were obviously beyond help.

"How goes it, Mr. Cruikshanks?" I gulped down rising gorge and tried to school my expression to hide the horror. David hung on to Mr. Cruikshanks' hand as if offering a lifeline, but no magic in the world could put this right.

"I'm dead, Captain."

"We have a surgeon coming."

"I hope he's a miracle worker." His words were cut short as a wave of pain overtook him.

I heard footsteps on the companionway and extinguished the witchlight quickly. Louis appeared at my elbow. He took one look at Mr. Cruikshanks' belly and shook his head.

"Can you do anything?" I asked.

"I can stitch and patch and bandage and maybe he'll die in two hours instead of one, and that fellow over there with the blood pouring out of his arm will bleed out while I'm doing it. Then you'll have two corpses where there need only be one."

It was hard, but it was fair.

"We'll move him to my cabin," I said.

"No. Leave him be while he's in no pain. Set me up another table over there where there's light to work by."

So commanding for such a youngster. I liked this Louis already. The men jumped to while David and I stayed with Mr. Cruikshanks.

When David started to weave on his feet I brought a barrel and sat him down on it. I could see Mr. Cruikshanks' pain building. David's hand was white from the man's grip.

"My thanks to you, Davy." Mr. Cruikshanks' voice was very quiet now. "I think you won't have to lend me your hand for much longer. Cap'n . . ." He turned to me.

"Don't try to talk. Save your strength."

"For what? I'll talk while I can."

I smiled. "Fair enough."

"Simeon Fairlow is a very capable young man . . . Make a good quartermaster's mate."

"He's young."

"Brought up in a dockside tavern." Mr. Cruikshanks' voice was harder to hear, his breathing labored. What words he uttered were between harsh breaths. "He understands business. Understands sailors."

"Simeon Fairlow, right. I'll see to it."

"And that bloody swivel gun . . ."

"I'll send it to the bottom of the ocean."

"Send the ship down, instead."

"I will."

"A favor."

"Anything."

"Put a ball in my brain. I won't die screaming."

I still had my third flintlock. I took it from my belt and pulled the doghead all the way back with a heavy click.

"Ross!" David gaped at me when he saw the flintlock.

"S'all right, Master David. My thanks. You can let go now." Mr. Cruikshanks' eyes closed. Before he could take another breath I put the muzzle of the flintlock to the center of his forehead and pulled the trigger. Then I threw it down and staggered out up on to the deck, my ears ringing and my eyes stinging and running with powder smoke. I got as far as the ship's side before I heaved my insides up into the sea.

"Cap'n."

I opened my eyes to find Simeon Fairlow standing over me. I'd slithered down on to the deck for a moment and my eyes had blurred with tears. That was no way for a captain to behave.

"Aye, Mr. Fairlow."

I saw recognition of his promotion dawn with my use of his formal name. The crew would have to ratify it, of course, but there would be no problem. Abel Cruikshanks had been popular. They'd give his chosen successor a fair chance.

I got to my feet, conscious of the rancid taste in my mouth and the burning ache in my bladder, which had been there for some time though I'd chosen to ignore it. I couldn't ignore it for much longer.

I wiped my face on my sleeve. "Give me a few minutes and I'll come back aboard the *Lydia*."

In my cabin I made use of my commode, wiped my face with a wet rag and swallowed a full pint of water, then I straightened my clothes, blood-spattered as they were, and made my way back on deck. Someone had moved the fallen and laid them out neatly amidships. I looked at the faces: Henry Tyler; Rob and Willie Fletcher, twins who did everything together, even die it seems; Yates, a muscular woman who'd forgotten her gender a long time ago and who never used her given name; Billy Sims; Harry Fitz; Henry Evans; Nathaniel Mansour; Jeb Huddlestone; and Abel Cruikshanks.

"Good-bye, Mr. Cruikshanks," I whispered.

"You liked him, didn't you?" David came up behind me.

"Yes. He was a good man—a friend. Treated shabbily by the law for nothing more than poaching. How are the injured?"

"I think the rest will live. That young surgeon, Lewis, he's good."

"Louis. Shall we keep him? It's fair plunder. They've robbed us of some good men today when no lives need have been lost."

"They've lost some, too."

"Yes. The butcher's bill is high on both sides."

"Are you going to sink the *Lydia* for Mr. Cruikshanks?"

"I always keep my promises."

"What about her crew?"

"We'll see about them."

I would allow myself time for shakes and nightmares later. Right now I needed information, and I needed it before the *Lydia*'s escort caught up with us. I straightened my coat and took several deep breaths before clambering over to the *Lydia* once more.

First things first. I had spare barrels of powder transferred to the *Heart* and the rest positioned where they would be most effective when they blew.

All the *Lydia*'s survivors sat in a group. The captain and the doctor had tried to sit a little apart from the sailors, but the marines had somehow contrived to remain close together. I didn't like that. Four nursed minor hurts while one was all but out of it from a head wound. Another two were likely to die, though the surgeon had been allowed to tend them. Six were uninjured. Seasoned troops, I thought, and their lieutenant looked as though he could take care of himself in a difficult situation. This was about as difficult as it could get. Desperate men try desperate measures.

"Marines, one man at a time, stand up, step forward, and strip."

They looked at me as though I was mad, but Hookey knew what I was about. Nothing demoralizes a captive more than being stripped down to their bare skin—even without knowing that I'm female.

They did as they were told, one by one. The wounded I let be.

"Gentlemen, if you would be so good as to sit with your backs to the ship's rail over there. One at a time. Take care not to get splinters in your arses."

My men tied them, one by one, making sure to take a hitch around the rail. They wouldn't get out of those knots easily.

I dealt with the sailors next.

"Honest seafaring men like yourselves have nothing to fear if you mind your manners. Let just one man try anything and you'll all be sorry. Do I make myself clear?"

One or two nodded.

"I said: Do I make myself clear?"

"Yes, Cap'n."

"Good. Now get over there. Don't make a move and you might live to see another dawn." I wouldn't trust them, of course, but my crew was good at this.

"Captain." Mr. Rafiq emerged from the *Lydia*'s companionway. "We've found a strong box filled with coin."

I frowned. We might not have long before the two ships of the line found us. I turned my attention to the captain.

"Captain, you're flying false colors. Can you tell me any reason why I shouldn't slit your throat and take your vessel? I'll have the reason for your actions, if you please."

"You'll get nothing from me." He spoke English with a heavy Welsh accent.

"Oh, I think we will, even if it's only blood. The lads are very unhappy about the swivel gun."

"Bosun says his name's Searle," Hookey said. "Sailed out of Chatham."

"Captain Searle, it would save me time, and you not a little pain, if you would kindly tell us the meaning of your false colors. What are you about? You've been paid handsomely for something."

Searle stared at me. Dumb insolence written in every line of his face.

I tried again. "If I am convinced by your reason I may let you live."

Still no answer. Every minute we wasted gave the escort ships chance to catch up. Time for harsh measures. "Bring a fuse, Hookey. Let's see if we can encourage him to be a little more cooperative."

Crayfish Jake and a giant of a man only known as Windward held the captain tight.

"We wind this fuse around your fingers," Hookey said as he did it. "You have less than a minute to start talking once it's lit."

I'd never yet seen a man hold out past thirty seconds, but there was a mad look in the Welshman's eye.

"I'll lay he doesn't go beyond halfway," Jake said.

"A shilling that he burns." Windward grinned.

"We could tie it round his prick, Cap'n." Hookey sounded hopeful.

"Maybe next time. Light the fuse."

Simeon stood by with a closed lantern and couple of buckets of seawater. Hookey lit a knot of rope and touched it to the end of the fuse.

The captain stared as the flame inched toward his right hand.

Fifteen seconds.

He tried to drag away.

Thirty seconds.

He squirmed and fought.

Forty-five seconds

Any second now.

But he didn't give in.

The fire touched his fingers. He screamed and writhed. I didn't let it get beyond the first knuckle before I nodded to Sim to pour on water.

David came at a run, drawn by the noise. He broke through the circle of spectators.

"What are you doing?" he yelled.

"My job. There are two ships of the line out there somewhere close and they're hunting for something. If it's us, I need to know. All our lives depend upon it."

I saw a quick flicker in the captain's eyes, which confirmed my suspicions.

"David, go back to the *Heart* and stay there." I looked at him hard, and he knew he'd overstepped the mark.

The captain nursed his burned finger. "Right, what shall it be, Captain Searle? Information or your other hand? I hardly like to deprive a man of both. Perhaps Hookey's suggestion is more to your liking. Off with his breeches, lads."

Windward and Jake pinned the captain while Hookey carved his buttons off with a knife and quickly yanked off his breeches and pulled up his shirttails, leaving him exposed. Inda and Jelks took an ankle each so Searle's kicking was to no avail.

"Seen the size of that, Cap'n? He's hardly going to miss it." Hookey grasped the man's flaccid tackle, not gently, and began to wind a length of fuse spiral-wise. "What do you think? Just his prick or his ballocks as well? Shall we have him singing like a girl?"

Searle was already shaking from head to toe, but now he started to whimper as Hookey ran the fuse down from his groin between his spread legs and cut it off at his ankles.

"Stop. Stop! I'll tell you."

Searle broke, but Hookey lit the fuse anyway while the man begged and yelped. The flame was already scorching the inside of the man's thighs before Hookey's boot came down hard, just inches away from tender flesh, and stamped out the sputtering flame.

"Right, Captain Searle," I said. "What's an English ship doing flying French colors, and why are two ships of the line hanging back over the horizon? What are you fishing for?"

He didn't answer.

Hookey leaned down as if to touch his slow match to the fuse again.

"No! Wait!" Beads of sweat trickled down Searle's face. "They paid me to bait a trap. Promised they'd protect me."

"What are they after? Get on with it, man, if you want to stay a man, that is."

"Tremayne's w-witch whore."

Hookey saved me from hiding my feelings by back-handing Searle across the jaw. "Show some respect for Mrs. Tremayne."

"Who wants her?" It took an effort of will to keep my voice steady and low.

He shook his head. "I don't know."

Hookey leaned forward to touch the slow match to the fuse again.

"I don't know!" Searle screamed. "They only told me that it was a matter of national importance, and . . ."

"And what?"

"They have a witch on board who can search by magic. They're looking for an artifact that lately passed into M-Mrs. Tremayne's hands. I overheard them say it had lain dormant and was recently awoken. I d-don't know what they meant."

I did. Something had happened when that winterwood box tasted me, something that a witch with seeking skills could follow.

"Is there a man aboard with a pockmarked face and a deep voice? Walsingham, his name is."

"N-not that I know."

Hookey leaned toward the fuse.

"No! I've seen no one on board except the crew and the witch."

"Pah!" I stepped back. "I want none of these intrigues. I'm out here to take French shipping for the king, not to play games of hide-and-go-seek with His Majesty's Navy. When you get back home tell them it was Captain Tremayne who gave you your life and your prick. Hookey, set the survivors adrift in the ship's boats."

"But you are English. Taking the *Lydia* is an act of piracy."

"But who could blame me for sinking a Frenchman?"

"Sink?"

"Well, I can hardly sell your ship back to the navy, can I? And if you fly a French flag you must expect to be treated like the enemy."

"Please . . ."

"You may have one pair of oars for each boat. If you try very hard you can pull far enough away before the *Lydia*'s powder magazine goes up. You'll note Hookey is a good man with a fuse. Louis," I called to the young apprentice surgeon who had come back on board, having finished his grisly business. "You're a handy lad to have around, do you want a promotion? We can use a good sawbones."

"Do I have a choice?"

"All men have choices."

He glanced at the surgeon, then shook his head reluctantly. "I've got family back in Chatham."

"Good luck to you, then."

"Row for your lives, boys," Hookey called to *Lydia*'s survivors as my lads loosed the boats.

They took me at my word and began to pull away.

"Sail astern, Cap'n!" Nick was back on watch up aloft.

We didn't have much time. "Right. Let's do this quickly and leave. Hookey, set the fuses. Mr. Sharpner, I'll give us a favorable wind to take us well clear."

The *Lydia* blew with a satisfying boom that the two escort ships could not fail to hear. Let them make of it what they would. I wanted sleep and I wanted a bath, probably in that order, but there were things to take care of and, besides, there was never enough fresh water on board for more than a sponge-down. Before I could look to my own needs I had to see to the crew: bury the dead, and do what could be done for the living.

The haul of coins would go a long way toward making up for the survivors' injuries. Blood, pain, and death were part of life when you signed on a fighting ship. Many of the crew had joined the *Heart* in Bacalao, and Will had not asked their history, though I knew some of them had been pirates. In their minds they still were, even though we flew the Privateer Jack for King George. To balance the expectations of sudden horror were the hopes of sudden wealth, and this time we'd struck lucky.

Mr. Rafiq had the wealth under control in the tiny cubby that was our strong room and his office. Like a dragon in his lair, he guarded our treasure by sleeping over it.

Our wounded rested below, watched by Lazy Billy.

Edmund Morrow had lost his left arm below the elbow, so if it didn't fester and kill him he'd be pensioned off back in Elizabethtown with his share plus a thousand for his injury. He'd be a rich man if he didn't drink and whore it all away. Chas Kennedy might yet die of his injuries. He had a shoulder full of scrap iron and Louis hadn't been able to remove all of it. If the iron didn't move and cut through a major blood vessel and if it didn't poison his blood he might survive, but he might never have full use of that arm again.

On deck, ten bodies lay wrapped in their own canvas hammocks, hastily stitched up the front into shrouds and each one weighted. We all gathered around. There were those amongst the crew who held to a Christian God, some who prayed to Allah, and others who held to no gods at all, but at times like this we didn't stand on ceremony for long. It did us no good to ponder the fact that any of us might be next. But something had to be said, so I had to be the one to say it.

"These were our crewmates. They knew the dangers. They took the risks and they paid the price. We are sorry to lose them. We send them to the deep. May they find their god in Heaven or the peace of oblivion, each to his or her own beliefs."

As each one was tipped into the ocean I called out their names. "Jeb Huddlestone. Henry Tyler. Martha Yates. Rob Fletcher. Willie Fletcher. Billy Sims. Harry Fitz. Nathaniel Mansour. Henry Evans." And as the last corpse slid into the water, "Abel Cruikshanks."

Even as all this was happening, we were escaping from the scene of our crime. The *Heart* can show any ship, especially a cumbersome ship of the fleet, a clean pair of heels. With Mr. Sharpner on watch I didn't have to worry. Our present course was *anywhere but here*.

10

The Storm

WE RAN WITH THE WIND in our sails.

If their witch was one who specialized in finding what was lost, he, or most likely she, might not be able to work weather like I could. I didn't know how close she needed to be to sense the winterwood box, for that's surely what she was following.

We couldn't set a direct course for Bacalao until we'd lost the English ships. So we sailed toward Jamaica, hoping to draw the ships of the line from our intended course.

I would have to leave the *Heart*. I couldn't stay. Too many of my crew were already dead or sorely injured. Life at sea was dangerous enough without carrying a jinx on board, especially if that jinx was me.

I dropped my clothes on the floor and collapsed onto my bed. Sleep wouldn't come. I fretted all night. I must have slept, eventually, because I awoke to gray dawn, but I didn't feel refreshed.

The familiar creak of timbers and the heave and surge of the *Heart* plunging like a horse in the freshening breeze comforted me in a way I couldn't begin to understand. I could almost imagine Will was here beside me, warm and alive.

I'm here, my love.

"I'm rich."

Yes you are. He sounded faintly amused.

"I've never known what to do with money."

Spend it.

"Wine, women and song?"

Find yourself a boy whore.

"Not my style, Will."

I wanted to feel him next to me one more time. I wanted it so badly. To feel his hands on my body, his lips on mine, his weight between my thighs.

Is this your style?

His breath tickled my ear, his hand lightly touching the side of my neck, traveling down. Could it really be happening? Had I willed him corporeal? I closed my eyes. If I tried too hard to see him or to touch him he always vanished, and I was left with my heart thumping, unfulfilled. This time I wasn't going to let him go, so I resisted running my palms down his flank. Instead I put my hand above his hand and felt the warmth of it as it traveled over my breasts, stroking, caressing, until I hissed at him through my teeth, impatient for more. His mouth hovered over mine, whispering love words that meant nothing and everything until I parted my lips, tasting a faint hint of rum.

His hand explored the taut skin of my belly and moved still further down, rubbing, circling, kneading until I drew up my knees and opened for him. He teased my pearl from no more than a seed until it felt like a ripe berry, ready to burst, and left me gasping and wordless. It had been so long.

I longed to see the look on his face, but daren't even open my eyes in case he vanished, leaving me halfway between Heaven and Hell. His body lay strangely weightless between my thighs. I moaned with need, rocking with each thrust until I tumbled into the final maelstrom, infinite, endless . . .

I shuddered, utterly spent. The world held its breath. Sighing, I relaxed, boneless, back on to the rumpled sheets.

"Ah, Will . . ."

But he wasn't there.

I don't know how long I lay abed. I let time stretch out inside me and slip away like water beneath the hull. Eventually I stirred and sat up. All the aches and pains from the fighting returned. I'd developed a huge purple bruise on my hip, though for the life of me I didn't remember what specific knock caused it.

Will's breath ruffled my hair.

"I thought you'd gone."

I heard him laugh softly. He made no comment about the bruise or our lovemaking. It might never have happened for him. I blinked back tears.

"What shall I do, Will? I could retire in the Americas and live in luxury, hand over the role of Redbeard Tremayne to someone else."

Will's dismay was palpable. *It's the box and your brother Philip. You want to take the quest.*

"No. I'd rather stay here, but I'm a danger to the *Heart*. My staying could kill us all."

The box is still on the table.

It was, and it was time to do something about that. It was too dangerous to keep, whatever its potential. Well, no more procrastinating. In two strides I crossed over to the box, picked it up, ignoring the tingle of magic in my fingers, and took it to the window. I opened the catch and stood there with the salt spray stinging my face and blowing my loose hair into a halo around my naked shoulders.

Do it. Will's voice whispered in my ear. *Let it go.*

I thrust my hand through the narrow opening and held the box, half-tempted to bring it back in. I forced my fingers to open. For the longest moment the box didn't fall, as if giving me the opportunity to change my mind, then it dropped away. I didn't even hear the splash or see where it landed in our wake. There! That was an end to it. Let the navy's witch follow that.

"Happy now?" I asked. But Will had really gone this time.

Without the box on board I felt altogether lighter. I gave the order and we changed course again, this time heading for Bacalao. The whole day passed in routine, all the more welcome for being completely uneventful.

Lazy Billy had liberated hams, pickled cauliflower, and preserved peaches from the *Lydia*'s store before we blew her to high Heaven, and dinner had been a wonderful concoction, sweet, sharp and salty, all at the same time. My belly was full and I was at peace with the world, which made me almost cheery as I took over the middle watch from Mr. Sharpner. A sensible lad called Abe Bennett stood at the helm alongside me and I checked our heading. There was a steady wind from the north-northwest, 340 degrees, at about ten knots, and the sky was patchy with a slow-moving bank of cloud sitting half over an almost-full moon. A sprinkling of stars was visible in the east. It looked as though this weather would hold until morning at least, so it would be a quiet night.

Most of the crewmen were already snoring their heads off in their hammocks. They deserved a break. We'd anchor up in Elizabethtown, let everyone blow off a little steam and get used to being wealthy—at least for as long as it took for them to become poor again. Then I'd depart and let them take on extra men to replace dead shipmates and sail out for new adventures.

And then what? a little worm in the back of my brain asked.

I realized, as I stood in the gathering gloom, that I had not seen David all day, except at a distance. I left Abe to hold our course while I went in search of him. As if I'd called his name, David walked slowly toward me down the length of the deck from his favorite place by the foremast.

"Am I David or Davy tonight?" His face looked pale, his eyes haunted. He extinguished my witchlight with a wave of his hand, so I let it be, content that the soft glow from the deck lantern was enough.

It took me a moment to get his meaning. "I can be your sister for a while instead of your captain."

"Yesterday. Mr. Cruikshanks." He swallowed. "He was kind to me. All those men, dead."

An errant wind played with my hair and teased out a strand from the manly black ribbon that held it at the nape of my neck. I hooked it out of the corner of my mouth with my fingers.

"Dead for our sake," he said.

"Only for me. I don't think Walsingham knows about you, yet. You could start a new life on your own and be safe."

"You tortured that man."

I didn't want to think about it.

"What if he had a wife at home, and a daughter called Rossalinde?"

A cold slap of driven spray and a crack of canvas above my head suddenly made me notice that the breeze had changed. I looked up at the tops'ls.

"All that blood. I wanted to answer it with fire. I drew it into myself. It's still here, churning in my gut, trying to burn its way out of my skin."

The wind rose to meet David's voice and kept on rising. A sharp stab and buzz in my spine told me there was magic at work, but it wasn't mine. Lightning flashed overhead and thunder rolled. From out of nowhere rain sliced down like knives. I stared at David.

"What have you done?"

"I don't know what you mean."

But I was already turning toward the helm and yelling, "All hands on deck."

We carried too much canvas for a storm, it would drive her under. We needed to shorten sail and ride it out.

"You there, get up aloft." Mr. Sharpner bellowed at two seamen as he ran up beside me on deck. "And you, you bastards, bring in the tops'ls. Billy! Where are you, you lazy bugger? Jelks, Windward, Inda, and Jake, reef the mainsail."

Half-dressed sailors, blinking away dreams, tumbled up the companionway on to the deck, cursing and calling to each other in the black night.

A thick bank of nothing had swallowed the moon and the *Heart* pitched and rolled as she climbed each watery hill only to have the sea fall away from underneath her and slap at her flank as she landed. Waves crashed over her bow and washed across the deck. I grabbed Mr. Sharpner's arm, solid as a rock.

"This isn't a normal storm," I yelled above the tumult, then had to repeat myself as he pushed his ear close to my mouth.

"Of course it's not. See what you can do. Leave the *Heart* to me. And tie on a line. We're close to the wind, she may buck a bit."

I grabbed David by the hand and dragged him to the bow of the *Heart*, throwing him to the floor in my haste and winding a line around the both of us.

"What did you do?" I screamed at him above the wind.

"I didn't . . ."

"This storm is magic and I didn't make it."

"I didn't even know . . ."

"You were angry and upset. You let your feelings set this in motion. Now help me to bring it under control."

Lightning cracked above our heads. Rain like razor-blades lashed our faces. The *Heart* heeled over with a blast from the north. Following hard on that an easterly buffeted her sideways. She wasn't built for these unnatural stresses, and for the first time ever I feared she might tear herself apart.

There's always a price to pay for magic. That's doubly true of wind-and-weather-working, and this wasn't even a working by any recognized definition, simply a reaction to a very strong feeling by a boy who'd been dragged from the safe life he'd known and christened in blood.

The *Heart* lifted and plunged again and again. Her timbers groaned, not the comforting creak of a living ship, but the loud protest of timber under extreme stress. Her bowsprit dipped beneath the waves and drenched us, only the lines saving us from being washed overboard. We struggled back and sat cross-legged, knees touching. I grasped David's two icy hands in mine. The deck beneath us heaved and a stray shred of canvas smacked into my back like a fist.

"See if you can feel what you did," I yelled. "It may not be too late."

He looked at me blankly, so I reached into the storm and I found a whirlwind of anger, fear, indecision and indignation twisting round like a tornado.

"Can you feel the thunderhead?" It was there, a huge, heavy anvil-shaped cloud. Dear Lord, there were two, merging together from opposite directions.

Lightning flashed again and the *Heart* leaped out of the water and spun, tossed high and caught again like a child's toy.

Our words whipped away on the wind.

I felt David, fumbling at the corners of the maelstrom, but the underlying terrors still drove him. He was only a frightened boy. I pulled him into my arms and hugged him fiercely and put my lips to his ear. "I know it's a terrible life. I fell into it by accident, pulled by the love of a man and pushed by the vindictiveness of a woman. But it's all I can do, now, all I know."

"You're better than this, Ross." David's voice faltered. "Come back to the land. Let's take the winterwood box and follow where it leads."

"The box is gone. It's too late for me, but we'll take you to port. Boston if you like, or Upper Canada where a rowankind might be a free man. I should never have brought you on board."

"But I don't want to lose you."

He began to sob, great howling, shuddering, wrenching cries that blended with the wind and weather until I didn't know where the noise was coming from and all I could do was to hold on to him for fear that he would slip away from me and be lost in his own storm.

A heart-stopping crash jarred the whole ship from stem to stern, louder even than the gale. Rigging smashed to the deck between the masts. I willed myself up into the storm and reached out my hands to smooth the thunderhead, even out the pressure, divert the lightning to crack harmlessly in our wake, but all I could do was lessen the effects. It was too late to stop it. We'd have to do like generations of sailors had done before us and ride it out.

I'm not sure how long we huddled together, but when the seas ran calm again, David was fast asleep in my arms.

We were in a bad way, our main topmast gone and our mainsail gaff cracked clean in two, but worse than that, we'd sprung a leak in timbers below the water line. We were taking in water faster than we could pump it out, inexorably losing our fight with the sea. We'd been blown off course to the south, closer to the Dark Islands than to Bacalao.

There was nothing for it. We'd have to head for the nearest refuge.

Our first welcome sighting of land was of the windward shore of Auvienne, the most easterly of the Dark Islands. With gold in our strong room, it was the last place I wanted to be. No one ever explained the concept of honor amongst thieves to Gentleman Jim Mayo. His stronghold, Ravenscraig, sat on the southern tip of the island. Thankfully we fetched up on her northern shore. If we'd been in any condition to turn and run for Elizabethtown I'd have done it, but it was Auvienne or Davy Jones. We put into a shallow, sheltered bay.

We'd have to patch her up and get out again as fast as we could.

I hoped.

A horseshoe of steep wooded hills rising to a treeless rocky ridge cradled our sandy bay. Dark birds wheeled above the trees and there were tracks in the sand that might have been made by turtles, but there was no sign of human presence. So far, so good.

We dropped anchor offshore where one broadside of guns could cover the beach—offering some protection to our shore party.

I set three lookouts along the ridge and sent Lazy Billy inland with ten men to hunt for suitable timber for a thirty-foot spar to replace the main gaff. I'd take anything that looked like I could hang a sail from it. We could manage without a topmast, at least as far as Elizabethtown.

Teams continued working the pumps in short energetic shifts, trying to keep the sea out. Hookey set a vat of pitch to boil to coat a sail. Swimmers would drag one end under the keel, lashing it securely to the stay mountings to wrap the hull. The sea's own pressure would temporarily waterproof the timbers. We'd have to limp home slowly, so that water didn't get under the leading edge, but providing we didn't hit rough seas we could make it back to Elizabethtown in a few days.

It would be dangerous work, diving beneath the hull, dragging rope and a mountain of unbiddable sodden cloth through seawater that still held more than a memory of winter. The *Heart* had been recently careened, but there would still be barnacles clinging to the keel to snag canvas. The bay was so shallow that we'd have only a few feet of water beneath us at low tide, but waiting for the next high would be foolish. We needed to get away from Auvienne before Gentleman Jim came to deliver his calling card. David thought I was bloodthirsty, but Mayo's propensity for violence made the *Heart*'s crew look like gentle Quakers.

I asked for volunteers to swim the sail under.

The Greek, who had lungs on him like a forge bellows and had been a sponge diver on his home island, took the lead, together with Nick Padder, Abe Bennett, Sim Fairlow and Crayfish Jake.

Hookey shuddered. I'm always surprised how few sailors learn to swim, using the excuse that it takes longer to drown.

"Right lads, over the side," I said. "Take care you don't die down there or I'll dock your pay for malingering."

They all dropped their sailors' slops and pulled off their shirts, jumping into the sea mother-naked.

Hookey's lads fed the pitch-covered canvas over the side for the swimmers. The Greek plunged in first with a single line. I watched him disappear beneath the hull with a flick of his heels and crossed the deck to see him emerge at the other side barely panting. He held his hands apart to indicate that we had only three feet of clearance beneath the keel.

The next swimmer came through successfully and the swim crew started to haul the canvas, some at one side, some at the other, going down in pairs whenever the canvas snagged.

It was almost dark by the time Lazy Billy arrived back with the trunk of a pine long enough to fashion a gaff and I began to breathe easier. I gave them a witchlight when darkness fell and we all worked through the night in shifts, some pumping the bilges, the carpenters on shore stripping bark from our soon-to-be gaff. I stayed ashore with an armed picket, getting about four hours sleep, but only after the first light began to filter up from the eastern horizon.

Soon after true dawn a shout from David woke me and brought me running. He was kneeling in the sand. In front of him, nestling in a small pile of flotsam left by the retreating tide, was the winterwood box.

David looked up at me. "You can't say it's not your quest now. It's followed you."

"Leave it where it is. That's how the navy's witch found us before."

"I don't care. It's important. Remember what the Lady said. It can right a great wrong. It's the key to a new future. If you don't take it, I will." His eyes narrowed and his mouth set in a thin line.

Dammit, he would, too. I bent over and snatched the box out of the pile, feeling the familiar tingle as I touched it. "Happy now?" I asked him.

"Only if you do something about it."

He was going to be very disappointed. It would be back in the ocean as soon as we sailed. I hoped the two ships of the line were far enough behind that we could finish our repairs and get off the island free and clear before they caught up with us.

“Cap’n!” I looked up to see Hookey pointing toward the number one lookout on the easternmost hill.

It was inevitable. Very little happened on Auvienne without Mayo hearing about it.

“Get ready, lads,” I said. “It looks likely that we’re going to have company.”

11

Ravenscraig

PIRATES!

And not just any old pirates: Gentleman Jim Mayo, my own personal nemesis. No, I considered. Nemesis was not quite the word. Things were much more complicated between Jim and me.

I ran to where the carpenters were working. "Get the spar on board. Tow it behind the boat."

"It's almost ready, Cap'n. We can finish her as we sail if we have to."

"Hookey, bring the lookouts in and arm every spare hand." I waved at Mr. Sharpner. "Run out the guns!" I shouted.

I'd hoped to avoid seeing Gentleman Jim at all, but given that that was now impossible, I hoped to avoid a confrontation neither of us could back away from. He'd propositioned me more than once since Will died, and after the last time I wasn't sure I could hold him off without getting nasty about it.

Besides, there was always the thought at the back of my mind that I might not want to hold him off. Despite his reputation, both personal and piratical, James Mayo cut a striking figure, and there were many women who would fall in a swoon at his feet if he even looked in their direction.

I wasn't one of those, I really wasn't. Really.

I needed to keep telling myself that. Jim Mayo had a certain personal charm, and I was not immune.

As I loaded the last of my three pistols I heard hoof beats. A forty-strong force of horsemen cleaved through the undergrowth and streamed down the hill. Maybe not horsemen. A pirate on top of a horse is no more a horseman than a cavalryman stuck on a ship is a sailor.

Our full ship's company outnumbered them, but not by much. There would be heavy losses if it came to a skirmish. Leaving my pistols at the ready but still firmly tucked into my sash, I stepped forward as the riders pulled to a sloppy stop on the beach not thirty feet away from where the carpenters had launched the boat barely a minute before, towing the new gaff. Hookey stood a pace back from me and a little to my left. Mr. Sharpner had returned to the *Heart* with enough of a crew to sail her into deeper water if things came to a head. Gentleman Jim Mayo would have neither my ship nor our booty today.

Mayo cocked a leg carelessly across his horse's neck and slid down to the sand, resplendent in a rakish hat and ruffled shirt beneath a blue velvet waistcoat.

"Captain Tremayne, as I live and breathe." His Virginia drawl and his low, warm voice made it sound like an invitation, which, in truth, it was. He grinned at me lasciviously and my treacherous heart began to pound with more than the threat of imminent violence.

"Still dressing to impress, I see, Captain Mayo." I kept my voice light and inclined my head—the closest I was prepared to get to deference.

"Which is more than you are, dear lady." He tossed the reins to the closest rider, stepped forward, reached for my hand and kissed it soundly. "I have a bolt of very fine Spanish lace. I would be delighted to offer it to you if you would only have it made into something a little more feminine and wear it at my table."

"You have a large escort to deliver a dinner invitation. Besides, my mantua maker is not aboard on this voyage, and I fear Mr. Sharpner's sewing skills are not up to the task."

"You have a considerable escort yourself." He glanced over my left shoulder. "Hello, Hookey."

"Cap'n Mayo." I heard the wary note in Hookey's voice and remembered that he'd sailed with Jim in the past and that they'd not parted on the best of terms.

"Besides," Jim turned his attention back to me. "I don't wish to risk getting the little end of the horn."

"I'm poor company, Captain."

"I'll take that chance." He smiled and I blushed, which is something I almost never do, but somehow Jim could always call roses into my cheeks. Bastard! My mouth twitched in a returned smile that I had not intended to bestow.

"Another time, perhaps. We're somewhat occupied at present with repairs."

"So I see. Had your rigging shot away?"

"A squall caught us out."

He raised one eyebrow.

I shrugged. Our storm, rough as it had been, was probably localized enough that it hadn't touched the island.

"And using my trees to make repairs."

"You don't own the whole island."

"I doubt anyone else would lay claim." He stepped up close. "So it only remains to see what lay you'll make in return."

Hookey tensed behind me, the explicit choice of Jim's slang word for payment not being lost on him.

Jim whispered, "Are you sure you won't accept that invitation to dinner?" He put one arm behind my back and pulled me toward him. My crew were only a whisker away from starting a rumpus, so I didn't show any temper, merely put one hand up between us and pushed him away calmly, but I'd forgotten the winterwood box. As I moved I caught it against the bare skin of his hand and he jumped as if stung. I hadn't known, until that moment, that Gentleman

Jim was sensitive to magic. His eyes fixed on the box. He looked hungry for it.

"Booty?"

As far as I was aware he didn't know I was a magic user either. It wasn't something I flaunted or encouraged my crew to talk about.

"A trifle, nothing important. Some tropical wood, I think. The lid's jammed."

"But it's so very pretty. Such workmanship. May I?" He held out his hand for it and having no reason to deny it to him I gave it up. This time he didn't flinch. He looked at it from all angles, tried to open it and failed. He handed it back to me, and I could tell he didn't really want to let it go.

"I'm feeling generous, let's trade wood for wood."

I raised my eyebrow as a question.

He laughed. "I meant your pretty geegaw for my pine trees."

I know what sort of wood he wants to trade. Will's ghost stood between me and Jim. *Don't trust him!*

Out of my face, Will. You wanted me to get rid of the box, leave me alone to do it.

I tried to ignore the scowling ghost and to look doubtful, whilst inside I wanted to jump at Jim's offer. Let the navy chase after him for a change. Losing the box would make my life simple again. It wouldn't even really be my fault.

I shrugged, trying to judge how much nonchalance to display. I needed Jim to think the box valuable. It almost was; in its own way it was both without price and worthless at the same time.

"Come on, my lovely, what do you say?"

You are not his lovely! Will's ghost scowled.

Get lost, Will!

I let resignation creep into my eyes and looked at Jim from beneath my lashes. "You have a quick eye for an unusual trinket."

He laughed. "I have indeed. If we're agreed on it, let's fix our flint."

I spat on the palm of my hand and held it out. He spat

on his own, took my hand and shook it—a bargain sealed—but instead of letting it drop again he pulled me to him and planted his wet mouth full on mine.

"A bargain sealed with a kiss!" He grinned at me, and I swear the bastard smacked his lips as if he found me tasty.

I told you not to trust him, Will's ghost said.

I'll deal with you later, I promised him.

I slapped the grin right off Jim's mouth.

"Fair enough." Jim laughed and held out his hand for the box.

I passed it over, glad to see the back of it, but the second I let go I felt a peculiar pang of loss.

"You can't!" David's shout interrupted us.

Luckily Hookey caught him before he ran right between us and onto the point of Jim's knife, pulled in an eyeblink.

"What's it to you, boy?" Jim glanced at David and his eyes opened wide in surprise. "You're keeping rowankind now? On the ocean?"

"He's free."

"If he's free, he's free to come with me. He looks a likely enough lad and seems to know something of this trinket. How about it, boy?"

"Full crew, full belly, full share?" David adopted the gutter accent used by half the crew. He learned fast.

"You're in no position to bargain."

"If'n I'se free an' I crew for you. I gets three squares a day an' a full share, elsewise I stick here."

"What do you know of this?" Jim held up the box.

"Somethin'. Enough. Full share?"

"Yes, full share. Come on."

David scampered over to Jim's side without catching my eye. What was he playing at? It was the box, of course. Tempted as I was to let him stew in his own juice, I couldn't turn around and sail away.

He knew that, damn him.

"Well, now that's settled, and since there's no element of coercion involved . . ." I turned to Gentleman Jim and gave him my most dazzling smile. "Is your dinner invitation still open?"

Hookey flashed me a look of disbelief, and Jim momentarily looked wary before he grinned at me. "I would be honored, my dear Captain Tremayne. Would you share my horse?"

I shook my head. "I'd like to change first. I may not have Spanish lace in my sea chest, but I can manage something better than my working shirt. Perhaps you could leave me a horse and I'll join you later in the afternoon."

"As you wish, Captain." He motioned to one of his men who gave me his horse and scrambled up to ride double behind another man. Jim waved for David to double up, too, and they rode off, David clinging on behind a burly seaman.

"Will? Will? Dammit, Will, where are you when I need you?"

I think you've already shown me what you need.

"Please. Don't be vexed with me. Can you follow Mayo? Keep an eye on David?"

Will made a disparaging noise, but faded from my sight.

I turned to the crew. "Make ready to get underway. I want the *Heart* seaworthy by noon."

Hookey scowled at me. "You're not going, Cap'n, are you?"

"He's got David, what do you think?"

"I'll come with you."

I shook my head. "I might need to make a fast getaway on horseback, Hookey."

"I'll manage."

"I need you here in case Mayo sends a crew back while I'm otherwise occupied. Put out into deep water, but bring the boat back into the bay under cover of darkness with eight good men at the oars." By that I meant eight good men in a scrap. Hookey would know that.

"Aye-aye, Cap'n!" Hookey grinned at me, happy that I seemed to have a plan.

I'd once spent almost two weeks in Ravenscraig, with Will, under a flag of truce at the Pirate Council, setting the lines to be drawn between those of us who carried letters of marque and those who didn't. Privateers versus pirates, and there was little to choose between us except for the nicety of a paper from our respective governments.

Mayo had been no less attentive to me then, despite the fact that Will had warned him off. It was not long after the loss of our firstborn, and, thinking back, my emotions had been barely under control. I admit to an attraction, possibly stronger for not being acted upon. I would never have acted upon it. I might have felt a buzz in Jim's presence, but I was Will's wife.

Though, I admit, I might have flirted a little.

Jim thought he could take liberties now that I was a free woman again.

Well, liberties were one thing, but he wasn't going to take my brother, even though it would serve David right if I sailed back to Elizabethtown and left him to his own salvation.

Going down to my cabin to change my working clothes I found myself in a quandary. Should I rescue the one dress I had in the bottom of my sea chest? I'd spent the last three years dressing and acting as a man. I'd bound my breasts and sewed a roll of cloth into my breeches to make my clothes hang properly. I'd even taught myself to piss standing up—a not inconsiderable feat. No wonder my mother had been horrified to see me in breeches—it wasn't just the garment, it was the whole touch-me-at-your-peril persona I'd cultivated.

I pulled off the black ribbon and let my hair hang down to my shoulders. My own face looked back at me from the small glass. I couldn't judge it. Will had often told me I was beautiful, but I doubted that. My father used to say I was on the pleasing side of plain. I think he'd meant it as a compliment. I shrugged. The dress could stay where it was. I pulled on my stockings and best breeches. On a whim I left off my breast bindings as I pulled on my cleanest white shirt, feeling the well-washed linen slip over my skin and settle comfortably. My velvet frock coat and a pair of buckled shoes finished the outfit. I checked the mirror again. There! Dressed for action, not the kind that James Mayo had in mind, of course. Though . . . would that be so bad?

I was a widow, not a nun, and still young enough to have feelings and needs. Needs my ghostly husband could not meet. I swallowed hard, feeling my face flush at my own thoughts. Mayo's rakish smile and devil-may-care attitude was not entirely unattractive, and three years of celibacy was a long time.

Yes. I felt the faintest whisper of breath on my cheek. *It would be very bad.*

"And what are you going to do about it?" I asked Will's ghost. "You said I should find a boy whore. What's the difference between that and James Mayo? Anyway, aren't you supposed to be looking out for David?"

The air turned to frost as he melted away.

The mare Mayo had left me had a mouth like iron. Once I turned her head for home she almost pulled my arms out of their sockets in an effort to get there as fast as she could. My shoulders ached by the time I reached Ravenscraig, and I had to practically saw at her mouth to get her to stand while I answered the guard's questions at the town gate.

Town? No, Ravenscraig was more like a fortress with a stout wooden stockade landward and a deep-water harbor. Most of the town perched on the cliff top while a single street, known as the Stair, ran steeply down to the sea.

A promontory outside the walls contained gun emplacements, three batteries of carronade, and a mixture of twenty-four and thirty-two pounders. There was no way in Hell I'd let the *Heart* come under those guns. Slipping in and out across the land was the only way I'd engage Gentleman Jim.

As I got close to the top of the Stair, I could see five ships in the harbor, including Mayo's own *Black Hawk*, bristling with armaments.

Mayo's landward home was the Golden Compass, the

largest of Ravenscraig's many whorehouses and taverns. A doll-faced girl, hardly more than a child, dressed in a fine chemise and lace corset, shimmied up to me as I entered. I saw in her eyes the moment she realized I was female, but she was a real pro, and it made no difference to her come-on. I flipped her a copper and asked her to take me to Captain Mayo. With a toss of her head that said *you don't fool me, but I'm playing along,* she led me up a wooden staircase and along a landing to a door guarded by two tall henchmen. One of them opened the door for me, and the little whore bobbed back out of sight.

"Come in, Captain Tremayne." James Mayo's face lit into an easy smile. He beckoned me into a room that was much more comfortable than I expected. "Will you take a drink with me?" He held out a large glass of brandy.

"I will, but wine if you please. Brandy doesn't agree with my stomach." My stomach was fine, but that amount of brandy certainly wouldn't agree with my head, or my rational thinking.

"You disappoint, Captain." He looked me up and down critically. "I had thought you might be dressing for dinner in more appropriate manner."

I twirled around and held out my hands, taking in as much of the room as I could with a quick glance. Glazed long windows leading onto a balcony. A smaller window on the west wall through which the last rays of the setting sun blazed briefly. Door on the left in an alcove by an elaborate mahogany fireplace leading to another room—a bedroom, maybe? Fire lit. Set of fire irons by the log basket. Nice brass-handled poker—it looked to have a good heft to it. A small table laid for an intimate dinner for two, and back to Mayo himself, immaculate in white silk shirt and plum-colored breeches. No sword, not even a knife. Cocky bastard was sure of himself.

I kept my voice light, maybe a little teasing. "Is this not appropriate garb for two shipmasters dining together, Captain Mayo?"

"Is that all this is? You disappoint me again. Please, call me Jim. We've been friends for a long time."

"I'd hardly have called us friends." Though in truth there had been a brief time when we might have been.

"You misremember, my lady. Friends we were, and I hope we might become more than that."

"With guards on the door it certainly doesn't appear to be a romantic assignation."

"Ah." He crossed to the door, opened it, and dismissed the men. "I've told them we are not to be disturbed for any reason short of all the demons of Hell boiling up out of the kitchen cook pot. Better?"

"Much." I slipped off my jacket, draped it over one arm of his plush sofa, and unbuttoned my shirt neck, one button lower than was wise. I felt undressed already with my breasts bobbing against the linen of my shirt.

"Thank you." I accepted the glass of dark red liquid and sipped. It was sweet, with a kick of cinnamon and cloves. "Spiced wine, nice. How did you know?"

"It was all you drank when you were last here."

"You have a long memory."

"I remember everything."

"If I gave you any reason to . . ."

"Shh." He touched his finger to my lips and his mouth curved up in a smile. A shiver of warmth washed over me. "Food first." He rang a bell by the side of the fireplace. "You should have sailed into Ravenscraig to do your repairs. How did you take so much damage anyway?"

"I told you, storm at sea."

"I've sailed these waters for twenty years. There was no storm, not a natural one anyway."

"I didn't say it was natural."

"That box. It had something to do with it, didn't it? Tell me."

"What did Davy tell you?" I didn't care about the box, but I did care about David.

"Not much. He's nothing more than a blowfish. I doubt he knows anything."

I took Jim's meaning. "The chap's sometimes prone to a little exaggeration." I tried not to smirk. "But he's still very young."

"Old enough to see action, I'll warrant."

"One skirmish, that's all. I'm not sure the lad's suited to it. He's a bit soft hearted, to be honest, or maybe a little soft in the head."

Jim shrugged and crossed to a chest of drawers, opened the top one and took out the box. He offered it to me, but I declined to touch it.

"So what do you know?" He placed it on the mantel above the fire.

"It's a weird thing," I said. "It's magic, did you know that?" Of course he did, that's why he wanted it. "It seems to have a mind of its own. Don't blame me if it causes you trouble or tries to leave you."

He looked thoughtful. "How did you come by it?"

I looked at him. "I got it from a dying woman." That wasn't a lie.

"I don't suppose its previous owner gave you any information to go with it."

"She wasn't exactly cooperative." That much was also true. "So, why the interest? You must see some profit."

"I've heard that someone is looking for such an item and willing to pay well for it. I've already sent a messenger."

"Oh." I tried to suppress my curiosity. I wanted rid of the box—of course I did. I was only here for David. "Who might that be?"

He shrugged. "A gentleman from London. It may not even be the correct article, of course. You're sure it's magic?"

"That's what I've been told. Of course, I know nothing of such matters."

"Of course." By the tone of his voice he knew that I had some magical abilities, but that didn't matter as long as he kept up the pretense. If he was magic-sensitive that might explain why he'd been so fascinated by me for such a long time. I hardly thought it was my feminine wiles, for, truth to tell, I'd never displayed them for anyone but Will.

We were interrupted by a stream of four servants carrying in a variety of hot and cold dishes. The last in line raised his head and caught my eye. David!

A rowankind butler stayed behind to light the lanterns and candles with a taper. He placed two candelabra on the table, to either side of where the places were set. It meant I had a good view of Jim's face, as he had of mine, while we sat over our meal.

"You keep rowankind?" I asked as the butler left.

"He's free to come or go as he wishes, though since leaving means a sea voyage I doubt he'll ever go. He was brought here in misery by a Portuguese who didn't understand that rowankind can't survive on the sea. Your Davy didn't take sick?"

"A little, but I suspect he's not full-blood."

"You may be right, though you don't get many of those. Rowankind make lackluster lemen, as I understand it. I've never tried one. I had a China girl once. They say the French are good lovers, but I've always fancied a cool-cheeked English rose."

He looked at me sideways as if trying to judge my reaction. I looked away in some confusion, my earlier thoughts returning to make me blush. I was not altogether immune to the glint in his eye. He was a handsome devil with near-black tousled curls, a strong, weather-browned face with a straight spear of a nose and dark-lashed eyes. Beneath his shirt, the width of his shoulders indicated a wiry strength.

I felt a certain stirring.

Well, it had been three years . . .

The candle flames guttered. *Three years, Will!* I muttered under my breath. *Should I remain a nun forever?*

12

Gentleman Jim

JIM MAYO WAS SMART AND CHARMING, if untrustworthy. I began to tremble at the thoughts that surfaced. I hadn't come here for this, had I? Now I knew David wasn't hanging by his thumbs over a tar pit I could relax a little. I certainly wasn't afraid of Mayo, black though his piratical reputation may have been. He'd been a civilized and sophisticated host five years ago. I'd never asked about his background, but he was obviously educated, maybe even from a good family before some misdemeanor had sent him to sea.

"If we are to know each other better, tell me about yourself," I said. "How did you come to piracy?"

He smiled a lazy smile. "Only if you'll return the confidence. Tremayne was a wanted man in Plymouth, I understand."

"Mine's a simple tale." Simple enough if I left the magic out of it. "My father had four ships. He was lost at sea while my brother was too young to step into his shoes. My mother tried to manage his fleet, but had little aptitude for it, never having taken any interest before being widowed. Will and I already had an understanding, and Father had promised the *Heart* as my dowry, but my mother had other ideas. We decided to elope. My mother set the redcoats on us. One was killed, and Will blamed for it."

He made conciliatory tsk-tsk kind of sounds, leaned forward and pushed back a stray lock of my hair, just as Will used to do. "And you had so little time to enjoy each other."

"Four years."

"I don't believe I ever had occasion to offer my condolences. Tremayne was a fair man with a level head on him. Twice during our talks here he turned a bad situation around. He talked Black Jock Booth down from calling out Alexander Armstrong over an affair of the heart with one of my girls, and he pushed through an equitable agreement when Henry Crook would have set pirate against privateer in a war that would have done no good to anyone."

I nodded. "Will always had a powerful helping of common sense. What about you, though? You've had my story, now it's your turn."

"My family had—still has, I expect—a plantation in Virginia. With three older brothers, I was never in line to inherit much, so my father determined I should have a profession. He sent me to be educated at the College of William and Mary in Virginia, to study divinity, can you believe?" He laughed. "Unfortunately that was very shortly before my country and yours had a serious argument over taxation and I absconded to join a militia. If I have one very serious piece of advice it's never to get roaring drunk with your comrades in a seaport while the fleet is recruiting. Portsmouth, Virginia was my downfall. When I came to my senses the ground was rolling beneath me in a somewhat unfamiliar manner and I perceived myself to be at sea. To make matters worse, it was a French ship of the line, a third-rater called the *Jason* in the fleet of Rear Admiral Destouches."

He shook his head. "I had a few disagreements with my sudden transfer from the militia to the navy, but to my surprise, and to that of my captain, a fine sailor by the name of Jean de la Clocheterie, I took to the ocean. In recognition of my education I was elevated to the grand position of his cabin steward, where, I may say, I prospered. It's surprising what you can learn once you've acquired a position of trust. I survived the battle of the Chesapeake in 1781, was on board the *Jason* at the Battle of Mona Passage a year later when she was captured by the British. I had no liking for the idea of being at the mercy of King George, who had a tendency to insist that Americans were subjects of the Crown and therefore eligible to become cannon fodder in the Royal Navy, so along with a few compatriots I contrived to escape in a ship's jolly boat, and we made the shores of Hispaniola, where there are many opportunities open to a young man of keen intelligence and fighting spirit."

"You became a pirate?"

He bowed his head in acquiescence.

"It took another few years before I was in a position to captain my own ship, but I'm a fast learner and I didn't waste much time."

"And your family?"

"They didn't need me. Otherwise they'd never have sent me away to college. As long as I don't enquire, they are safe and well and living in my head just as they always did."

"Twenty years and you never once enquired?"

He shrugged. "Not once. I have a new family." He waved expansively toward the inn and to Ravenscraig. "Your own family . . ."

"Yes, it's complicated," I sighed. "And I, too, have a new family."

"Ah, madam, I would be happy to welcome you into my family. We could be allies."

"Piracy? I think not."

"And what is it that you do now? Legalized piracy, is it not?"

I wasn't sure I wanted to discuss ethics with a man of the reputation of Gentleman James Mayo.

He laughed again. An easy laugh. "Don't fear, my dear Captain. I shall not force anything upon you tonight." He emphasized the word: anything. "You are entirely safe in my hands. You can trust me on that."

Trust. Strangely I did trust that my person was safe with him, though I might not trust him with my money or my ship.

He reached across the table and took my hand in his, running his strong thumb across my knuckles, still bruised from the action on the *Lydia*. He tsk-tsked again and raised my hand to his lips. A little shiver of pleasure ran down my spine.

"Just what are you offering, Captain Mayo?"

"A respite, a gentle dalliance, a night of passion, a lifetime of protection. What is it that you seek, madam?"

I felt a quivering in the pit of my belly. Did I really need to justify this to myself? Isn't this what I'd intended all along? Quick, before I lost my nerve.

"I don't know if I qualify as a cool-cheeked English rose." I ignored the remainder of the dinner and stood up.

Gentleman Jim was on his feet and around that table so quickly that I didn't actually remember him moving until his lips were crushing the life out of mine. I'd had better kisses, but not recently. I pressed up close. I could feel him, ramrod stiff, thrust against my belly. With his left hand firmly in the center of my back holding me tight to his hips, he leaned me back and hastily pulled my shirt out of the grip of my sash, groping for my breasts. As love-play went, it wasn't subtle.

He groaned. "Lord, if I don't get out of these breeches soon, I'll burst the buttons."

My belly churned. Fight or flight. Not quite the reaction I was looking for, but close enough. I could do this. It was time.

The candle flames flickered again. *It's not adultery. You're dead, Will.*

I remembered Will's lips on mine, the way his beard tickled; his scent—man, honest sweat, tar, salt and a hint of rum; the way I always felt between my legs, hollow until he was inside me. *Oh, Will.*

There'd never been anyone else but Will.

I took a deep breath.

This would be on my terms.

"Slow down, Captain Mayo. I'm not a tuppenny whore."

The window crashed open as if pounded by a sudden gust of wind. Both candelabra toppled sideways, extinguishing the candles. Despite what he occasionally said, Will was a jealous ghost.

Jim pushed up my shirt and kissed my breasts. "One moment, dear lady." He closed the window and relit the candles with a taper from the fire.

"That's enough, Will," I muttered softly. "Let me have this."

Jim turned back to me, window safely latched. "Where were we?"

I took his right hand and placed it beneath my shirt, on my breast. "Here."

There was no empty ache between my legs, only a slight tremble in my stomach. *I can do this.* It was too late to change my mind.

Jim's thumbs made free with my nipples and they responded.

"Tell me what you like." His voice was soft and low in my ear.

I hadn't expected anything more than cooperating with what Jim liked.

"I want you to take it slowly. It's been a long time for me." *With a living man, anyway.*

"There's been no one since Tremayne?"

"No."

"Dear lady, I'm honored."

He swept me against him and almost danced us into the adjoining bedroom, the bed freshly made and turned down and a couple of lanterns burning softly. He'd been expecting this, or at least hoping for it. Damn him!

"May I?" He drew my shirt off up and over my head, his fingers tracing warm lines up my ribs as he gathered the folds of cloth in his capable fists. He gazed at my breasts in the soft lamplight and twirled me round as if in a dance then divested me of breeches and hose, his gaze hungry. In one smooth movement he reached behind my head to untie my ribbon and let my hair swirl about my shoulders.

"Enough dallying, lady." He lifted me on to the bed. "It's time to give you what you deserve."

My emotions were all over the place. While I wanted him, I almost hated him for his consideration. If he'd shoved himself between my legs and fucked me like a whore I could have kept my image of Will as the perfect lover. What Will and I had was special. How could another man make me feel like that?

I closed my eyes tight. *He's NOT Will. Not Will.*

Jim proceeded to attend to me with fingers, lips, tongue and teeth until—I confess—I was a jelly with no brain, giving back as good as I got. Tremors roiled through me. He swept me right over the edge. The moment stretched. My heart slowed to a steady rhythm. A dangerous lethargy swept over me. If I kept my eyes closed I could imagine . . .

He settled his weight between my thighs and his lips pressed down on mine. His tongue forced my teeth apart and invaded my mouth until I feared I would choke. I slapped my hand twice against his shoulder and he eased back. Resting his weight on one elbow, he brushed my hair back from my face, and finally I opened my eyes and I looked up at him. Dark and angular, fierce and intense, instead of copper-brown and smiling. Could I abandon myself to him? He was strong. He would protect me. With everything that had happened, the idea of relinquishing responsibility was tempting.

He's not Will. Had I almost fooled myself for a moment? His weight pinned me at the hips.

"Ross. Rossalinde." His voice was throaty and low and there was a catch in it.

Please don't spoil it. Please don't say you love me. I couldn't bear it. Filling my body doesn't fill my heart.

"Shh," I said, taking his face between my two hands and staring into his eyes. "Just do it."

With a groan he parted me quickly and thrust himself inside.

I threw my head back and gasped, opening my eyes—

And there was Will staring at us from the ceiling. The

look on his face killed my passion stone dead, not that Jim noticed, caught in the rhythm of the oldest dance of all.

It was as if it was happening to someone else, and though I tilted to meet him I'd lost the moment. I felt curiously uninvolved. *Please let it be over soon.*

Jim groaned in his final spasm and then, like a puppet bereft of strings, he collapsed down on to me. Tears trickled down my cheeks.

"Let me breathe." I pushed him sideways.

Now I truly felt like that tuppenny whore. *I'm sorry, Will.*

The lantern flames guttered. *Don't be angry. There were no boy whores. This was the best I could manage. I thought I was ready. It was a mistake.*

"Oh, you beauty. My lovely, lovely girl." At length Jim raised himself on one elbow, bent his head and kissed my breasts. "Tears? Should I be flattered?"

He wiped them away with his thumb and I tried to smile, but my lower lip trembled. He'd been as gentlemanly as his nickname. It had been my mistake, not his, but now I wanted to run screaming from the room.

"You set my belly on fire," he whispered. "Give me but a minute and we'll go again and I'll pleasure you any way you like it. Every way you like it."

"No!"

I wriggled sideways and swung my legs over the edge of the bed, drying myself on a corner of his sheet, thankful that it was early in my monthly cycle and I was safe from conceiving. That would be too ironic after taking so much care not to let myself get with child again.

"What?"

"Enough's enough, Jim. I'll hardly be able to waddle tomorrow as it is."

I reached for my breeches and dragged them on to my sweaty body, ignoring my hose and shoving my feet straight into my shoes. I dragged my shirt over my head, not caring that I left it loose.

"Was it something I said? Something I did?" He leaped off the bed to stand in front of me and stop me from running out of the bedroom.

"No, you were—" I looked up at him and tried to be honest. "You were . . . I didn't expect . . . I'm just overwhelmed. I need to leave."

"You can't go now. You have to stay. Stay with me, Rossalinde. Forever. Please."

"What? No!" It came out a little louder than I'd intended. I ducked around him and ran into the main room, remembering the poker in the fireplace. I hoped it wouldn't come to that.

The candle flames guttered and died, and the window crashed open once again. I could feel Will's agitation and it fed mine.

Get out now, Ross. Get out! Will was in my head again, though I couldn't see him.

"I'm trying to," I muttered under my breath.

Jim turned quickly to the window and then away from it and back to me. "I can't lose you. Not now!"

Ross, get down. Away from the window! Move!

With Jim the more obvious threat, I didn't register the urgency of Will's words quickly enough.

"You can't lose what you never had, Jim. That was nice, truly, but it wasn't a commitment."

Jim grabbed me in a fierce embrace and held me, burying my face in his naked chest.

The window exploded inwards, shards of glass flying across the room. I heard Jim gasp and then swear. He leaped back and turned to the window. His back and buttocks ran with blood from glass cuts.

You've gone too far this time, Will, I thought, but then a second explosion, bigger than the first, shook the building to its foundations, and I realized it wasn't Will.

"Is this your doing?" Jim turned on me.

Hellish flames blossomed in the town, lighting his face and his blood-slick bare body.

"Hardly. Your back is full of glass. That could have been my face."

A third explosion shook the air. Jim cursed, hopped around on one foot getting into his breeches, and ran for the door.

I counted to five and then followed. On the landing outside I met David coming up the front stairs at a dead run. "The box! Have you got it? Let's go."

"Box?" I hadn't even thought about it. "It's on the mantel."

He dashed into the room and out again, shoving the box into the long pocket on his waistcoat front. Then he grabbed my hand and pulled me toward a door and on to a narrow landing above the servants' stairs.

I followed him down into the chaos of the kitchen.

Two gunboats off the harbor bar, a voice yelled. Then *four*. Then *ten. The Royal Navy! Barbary pirates! The American fleet!* All took the blame in swift succession. Another explosion. Debris flew. Flames flared outside. Somebody screamed for water, and miraculously the chaos ordered itself into a bucket chain.

I heard the order to close the harbor gate.

"Let's get going before they close the landward gates as well," I said.

"This way. Quick." David dragged my sleeve.

We ran out of the yard, toward the nearest gate, and through it while the guard was busy. Another explosion to my left stung my face with flying earth. On the headland I could see Jim's gun crews loading to return fire.

"Wait!" I ran to the nearest gun battery.

Jim's gun crews worked together like a good team, but targeting in pitch darkness was next to impossible. Jim had his glass to his eye and was calling out distances, but until the ships fired a broadside he couldn't pinpoint them.

I could help.

"Give me your glass." I held out my hand. When he ignored me I snatched it from him. As I put it up to my own eye I called light into the paired lenses. Below the town, maybe a third of a mile outside the harbor, two English ships of the line cruised like sharks.

"Two," I said. "English. This should help."

I handed him the glass back. The magic would last for

less than an hour but it would be enough to let him target the warships more effectively. He didn't even thank me, but began to direct his gunners, all business. I ran back to David.

"What did you do that for?" David asked.

"Because I owe him, and because if Jim sinks those bastards they won't be on my conscience. And we'll have a breathing space. Come on, back to the *Heart*."

It was a full three miles in the dark over a murderously rough track. I couldn't risk a witchlight until we were far enough away from Ravenscraig for it not to be seen. In daylight we could have covered the ground quickly, but in the pitch dark it was better to feel our way slowly rather than risk a turned ankle or worse.

We'd not gone more than a mile when a huge explosion lit the night sky, roaring like the belching of hellfire. The magazine of one of the ships. I hoped it was the one with the witch.

Would the second ship press the attack alone? Unlikely, but even if it did, Mayo's guns had proved surprisingly accurate—with my help. That might mean Mayo would finish the fight and discover our escape sooner than I'd hoped.

Jim's carronade ceased firing. I waited to see if it would recommence, but it didn't. How long would it take him to discover he'd been robbed? Not long enough.

"Run!" I risked a small witchlight close to the ground.

We scrambled over clumps of vegetation and around rocky outcrops, slithering down steep valley sides and splashing through streams. Because I daren't send a light high enough to illuminate a broad sweep of the land ahead everything came out of the darkness as a surprise. I'd ridden this way only a few hours before, but none of it looked familiar from this new perspective.

"Hookey's waiting on the beach." I saved the rest of my breath for running. If Jim found David and I both missing and the box as well, he'd be after us as soon as he could get enough men together.

The sound of horses crashing through the brush behind us didn't surprise me, but it spurred me to run faster.

Damn! I doubted he was coming to say thank you for the magic spyglass.

I doused my witchlight, grabbed David's hand, and we charged into the undergrowth, stumbling over rough grass and loose stones. Will's ghost popped into being and guided us past the worst obstructions. He drew me to one side or the other and I followed him instinctively. Run—walk—run—walk—run, punctuated by a few stumbles, the occasional fall and the smart between my legs, a reminder of something I'd rather forget. At last we crested the ridge, almost tumbling down the hill to the beach. Hookey whistled, and I waved David toward where the boat bobbed in the shallows by an outcrop of boulders.

A loud report, and a pistol ball kicked up sand to the side of us.

I could see Hookey and his lads deployed by the boat, unsure of whether to grab oars or pistols. I mimed oars at them and they pushed the boat into the shallows. Legs pounding in the soft sand, we sprinted hard, but it wasn't good enough.

I heard Jim's voice call out. "Ross! Rossalinde! Bring my damn box back!"

Hookey drew pistols and fired over our heads to slow down our pursuers.

Desperately wishing for the power I could command in the forest, I began to build a working to hide us all, feeling my stomach twinge and my heart pound fit to burst as I put everything I had into it. The horsemen were looking for me and looking for a boat. This was going to take more than simply cloaking. I added illusion to distraction and poured all my strength into it.

Hookey reached me as I fell. David hesitated, then his form wavered and blinked out of sight. As the horsemen charged across the beach, I wove the last thread into place and my vision started to cloud.

I heard Hookey grab David and whisper, "Move slowly. Keep quiet." Then he lifted me like a child, his hook cold against my arm.

I closed my eyes and concentrated on keeping up the

illusion of an empty beach. The rhythm of Hookey's stride changed as he left the sand and waded through knee-deep water. He handed me into the boat, and David held me as the lads rowed for safety. Before we reached the *Heart* I was asleep.

13

Bacalao

I CAME TO IN MY CABIN tucked up safe beneath warm blankets. Someone had stripped me of my outer garments and left me in just my shirt. From the gentle creaking of her timbers and the scant movement of water beneath us, the *Heart* was in dock. Either something had gone terribly wrong and we were in Ravenscraig or we were already in Elizabethtown and I'd been unconscious for—how long?

"Elizabethtown." David stood up from where he'd been sitting in my chair, reading.

I nodded and it felt like a knife had sliced though my head. I winced and put one hand to my eyes.

"How long?"

"You've been out for four days. We've been in port for one. And Hookey's almost been camping outside your door. You and he aren't . . . ? No, of course not, sorry."

"I need to get dressed."

He left me alone to dress, which was much more difficult than I expected. My legs felt wobbly and by the time I finished, my blood was pumping through my head, pounding in my ears. I tied my sash, then had to sit down for a few minutes.

David came back in and put the winterwood box on my knee.

"What about the English warships?" I asked.

"One sunk at Ravenscraig with all hands, including the witch, apparently. The second turned tail and headed back to England. It buys us time to decide what to do."

"I knew you'd gone for the box." I let my fingertip trail across its smooth surface, felt the familiar tingle. "Why can't you let it go?"

"Three times it's come to you."

"You can hardly call that little escapade the box's doing. What did you do?"

"Took advantage. I guessed with a witch on board, the English ships would assume you were at Ravenscraig once the box went there, so I was ready when they came."

Smart boy, I thought.

"This quest's yours, Ross, whether you want it or not." David closed my hand over the box.

"I don't."

"That's not an option."

"Isn't it?" My head was starting to ache again from the tension in my jaw. "I've always made my own choices in life!"

"Have you? You chose Will Tremayne, but it seems to me that all the choices after that were his. He's still making choices for you, and he's been dead three years."

Leave the box, Ross. Let it go. Will's ghost whispered in my ear.

I looked David in the eyes. "I don't have to be ruled by some stupid box. I can't stay here, but I can go to the Americas. Start over." I picked up the offending article and hurled it across the room. It cracked against the bulkhead and rebounded, landing at my feet, undamaged.

David looked at me with one eyebrow raised.

Will's ghost glowered.

I sighed and stood up, leaving the box where it had fallen. "Mayo said that someone had put the word out after it."

"Walsingham?" David picked it up and put it on the corner of my chart table. "He's still got our brother. Lord above knows that Master Philip was never particularly kind to me, but if he's my blood kin then how can I stand back and do nothing?"

Did I owe Philip anything? I hardly knew him anymore, but he was my brother. I didn't want to see him hurt either by my action or inaction.

"Philip wanted me to bring the box to him. Maybe I should."

"Walsingham doesn't just want the box. He wants you dead. How long are you going to be able to keep running if he's got witches who can track you?"

He was right, but I didn't want to admit it. My head ached. I couldn't reach a sensible decision. Whichever avenue my thoughts took I found disaster at the end. The box had lain undisturbed for years—maybe for more years than we knew—why should it suddenly be so important now? What had changed and what might that change mean?

Get rid of it, Ross. Stay on the Heart. *Stay with me.* Will's ghost breathed down my neck. His ghostly arm was around my shoulders, drawing me to him. *How dare that little toad try and take you away?*

"Get off me, Will. This is my decision, not his, not yours!"

With a swirl, Will's ghost took himself off to the farthest corner of my tiny cabin. I flopped back into my sagging armchair.

All my adult life had been spent here within these few frail planks upon this churning ocean. These rough men were my companions, comrades, my only friends, my family. Walsingham or whoever was after me would find another witch, maybe a weather witch this time, and the *Heart* would be done for, and so would the crew.

It seemed that my choice was between leaving the box in the ocean, if it would stay there quietly, which I doubted, and maybe hiding in the Americas, or following the quest into whatever dangers were waiting. I was tempted by the Americas, so tempted, but the box was important. Deep down, I knew that. Dammit. Philip still weighed on my conscience, and I might have other family that I didn't even know about yet.

The box sat on my chart table. Even without touching it, I could feel the magic rolling off it in waves. No wonder it could be tracked. Something was changing. The tides of magic were turning in a different direction.

I took a deep breath. "Sorry, Will. I'll be away for a while. I've got business to attend to."

David looked pleased. Will simply vanished in a huff.

The freeport of Elizabethtown was a British enclave on the neutral island of Bacalao, that mid-Atlantic refuge for all sailors. While Elizabethtown looked east toward Sou' Spain, the American enclave, New Martha, sat on the western seaboard, facing toward Boston. Despite occasional saber-rattling and fist-shaking, the Revolutionary War hadn't touched Bacalao. I suspect because neither one side nor the other wished to threaten such a valuable trading hub.

Bacalao was also free of the Mysterium. If any magic happened here it was discreet. I'd always been careful to respect the status quo. There were no practicing witches here, which was a pity because right now I would have cheerfully paid one to cast a spell to hide the damned box from whoever was searching for it. That was a talent that was in neither my magical repertoire nor David's. I'd have to find someone who could do it back in England, for that's where I was heading.

Once my decision had been made I felt obliged to move quickly, but I was still weak from expending so much magic on hiding us on the beach, and so it was a full day before I ventured up into the town. It was time to spend some of my earnings and prepare for the journey.

I deposited most of my booty from the *Lydia* with Mr. Plunkett of Hillman and Plunkett's bank, and took time there to review my finances. I was indeed rich, due to Mr. Plunkett's wise investment advice and my rarely needing to draw from accumulating funds. I took a very small part of my fortune in coin and headed toward a mantua maker on Yates Street that catered for ladies of good taste. If I was going to move freely about England, whether Plymouth or London, I was going to have to dress properly and look as though I fitted in. I couldn't go as a man to Plymouth again after nearly being caught last time. I'd changed enough in seven years that I hoped not to be recognized as the Goodliffe girl. Mannerisms and carriage had as much to do with disguise as facial features and hair coloring. Even so, I bought enough henna to give my brown hair a reddish cast and took note of the way women of fashion were winding their hair on top of their head. What a pity wigs were out of fashion, especially for someone of my age.

The mantua maker, the venerable Mrs. Simpson, had adapted her art to the new, more natural styles, though she still had a pattern book, beautifully hand drawn, depicting stiffly corseted figures in stomachers and caged skirts or sack-back gowns. A second book showed nothing but the classical styles, and I listened carefully to what was in fashion in London and Paris and trusted that she knew her business. The visit left me poorer by nearly twenty guineas, but I came away having ordered a traveling dress of dark green linsey-woolsey, a walking dress of the palest violet muslin with a deep rose spencer for warmth, and a day dress of gray linen as well as a redingote of deep burgundy wool to protect against the English autumn, all high-waisted and draped in the current fashion.

Mrs. Simpson understood immediately when I asked for hidden pockets for my pistols, a pair of flintlocks by Mr. Bunney of London with embossed mock ivory grips and gold-tone barrels. They were only six inches in length and weighed less than a pound each, but they were accurate at close range, and I had a steady hand.

Gowns and accessories ordered, I returned to the *Heart* to find Mr. Sharpner on deck in consultation with Emmanuel Taylor from Taylor, Taylor, and Steerforth, the only shipwrights I'd trust to refit the *Heart* properly. She'd needed some maintenance work doing for the last few months and the storm had precipitated a rest from the ocean for maybe as long as a month or six weeks, depending on when Mr. Taylor could schedule our repairs.

"He can't make a start on her for at least a fortnight, Cap'n." Mr. Sharpner sounded as though he'd been trying to negotiate this down to a shorter time lapse, but that suited me well. I didn't know how long I'd be away.

"I told him Robbins can take her in three days."

"And I told him Robbins would botch the job at best," Taylor pushed his spectacles up his nose with one finger and glared at Mr. Sharpner.

I sighed and smiled at Mr. Taylor, a balding gent whom I knew to be the best shipwright on Bacalao. "You have us there, Mr. Taylor. We know the *Heart* is in safe hands in your yard." I turned to Mr. Sharpner. "A word?"

We walked for'ard out of earshot of Mr. Taylor. "I'd rather have them do the work, Mr. Sharpner. Do we have anywhere pressing to be?"

"No, Cap'n. I didn't want to let him think he could take half a year over her refit, but I agree, I wouldn't touch Robbins' yard with a boat hook."

"Good. I'll let you settle the details then. I'm not sure how long I'll be away."

If they gave their best efforts, it would probably take at least nine or ten days once the *Heart* went into refit, maybe more. I brought the ship's log up on deck and handed it over to my sailing master for him to take to his lodgings for safekeeping. "I'm sure I can leave everything in your capable hands while I'm away, Mr. Sharpner." I didn't add that I might never be coming back. It was easier this way.

"Will you be taking Hookey?"

I shook my head. Hookey wouldn't like being left behind, but I had limited ways to disguise him in polite society. It was going to be difficult enough remembering my own finer manners. This wasn't seafaring business, and Hookey had no taste for magic. Besides, the *Heart* needed him more than I did.

"With your permission, Mr. Sharpner, and with Mr. Rafiq's blessing, I'd like to propose Hookey for captain while I'm gone. I know he's not your match in seamanship, or Mr. Rafiq's in bookwork, but he's got a rare fighting edge. The three of you together will be unbeatable."

He nodded. "I never thought you'd make anything of him, surly as he was, and a hot temper on him, too, but now I'd be right glad to serve with him."

"Thank you." I breathed out a sigh of relief. "I'll see you later, as we planned."

"Count on it."

I had three days to wait for my gowns to be delivered, so I went below to begin preparations for the journey, resigned to what was to come. Between Elizabethtown and Plymouth, David and I had several bouts of seasickness to look forward to.

It's only temporary, I told myself as David and I stepped off the *Heart*'s gangplank and onto the dock three days later. *I'll be home again soon.* But something inside me said that this choice might lead to other choices and those choices would draw me further away from the sea—and from Will.

As I looked back at the *Heart* I saw two figures standing in the bows watching us leave. Hookey and Will, side by side, though Hookey wasn't aware of his companion. Both looked sad.

I raised my hand, but neither of them returned the wave.

Over the course of the next fifteen days, on a brig called the *Bonaventure* sailing direct to Plymouth, David and I heaved up our guts into the ocean until we had nothing left to heave and then settled into an uneasy truce with the sea. At least there were no more ships of the line following in our wake, though I didn't know how long it would take for them to get another witch who could search us out over long distances. If we sat still for long enough, it would draw our unknown enemies like a lodestone. My first task on reaching Plymouth would be to visit the street of witches in the artisan quarter and see if anything might be done to conceal the box.

David grabbed my bags as we finally disembarked onto New Quay and took them to the shipping office for temporary safekeeping. Disguised as my rowankind bondservant, he would be able to move freely about the town, but he hated the subterfuge with a passion. "You don't know what it's like," he said as he looked at toiling groups of rowankind on the dockside.

"No, I don't." I glanced around to make sure there were no familiar faces I needed to avoid. "I've never understood why the rowankind continue in our service. It's obvious some of them hate us for what we've done to them. Why don't they run off?"

"Where would they go?"

I shook my head. "Some of them seethe beneath the surface, but others have no drive to be free—unlike you. Why is that?"

"I don't know." He turned away as a squad of rowankind began to unload the *Bonaventure*'s cargo, overseen by the quartermaster. "Evy always talked about how lucky she was to be in such an easy household."

We began our steady walk up the hill toward the artisan quarter where the registered witches clustered in one street. I needed to hide the box, and quickly.

"What do you know about the rowankind—their history?" I asked.

"Nothing."

"No stories or fairy tales? No myths or songs? Not even a nursery rhyme whispered for rowankind ears alone?"

He shook his head. "No."

Even though I'd rejected them completely, at the back of my mind I still harbored platitudes drummed into me by my parents: we're saving them from themselves; they're like children; they want to be looked after, and—probably worst of all—they're well treated, so they have nothing to complain about.

A knot of anger burned in my belly, anger at myself for never questioning the situation. I was an educated woman, so why could I name every king and queen of England, recite the course of the Spanish Armada and why it failed, and explain the economic development of Bacalao Island since Columbus without knowing the history of the rowankind? Had we always had them? Where did they come from before they were ours to command?

Saving them from themselves resurfaced in my mind and I pushed it away. It wasn't true. Might there be free rowankind tucked somewhere between the folds of the world?

That thought came from the part of my brain that pulled the blankets over its head at night and prayed that there was nothing under the bed. What would they think of us for the way we treated their race? I'd seen the subtle looks the rowankind saved for when they thought we were not watching. If they did have somewhere to go, some of them would slit our throats and be away as quick as blinking.

I shuddered. I had more research to do than I had at first anticipated. I wasn't only looking for family history, I was looking for hidden history.

14

Plymouth

WE NEEDED A WAY to mask the box from any seekers, though it might be that Walsingham already had a witch on our trail. Since I intended to journey to London next in pursuit of more intelligence on Walsingham and to rescue Philip if I could, I wanted the box's trail to go cold in Plymouth, where I might have a number of possibilities for escape, either to the Okewood or straight out to sea again on any number of vessels traveling to all parts of the world.

I could find lost things by magic, though it wasn't something that came easily, but I didn't know how to hide them. So first we had to risk a licensed witch. We tramped the slick cobbles of Old Town to East Street, which looked shabbier than I remembered it. Five establishments displayed brass plaques proclaiming their residents to be licensed by the Mysterium. I knocked on the first door I came to. A scrawny girl of about fourteen answered, her straw-blonde hair escaping the ribbons tying it back from her face.

"You here for business?" she asked. Her voice cracked as if her throat was sore.

I nodded and she held the door open. David and I entered the narrow hallway and followed her to the front room.

"Please be seated. I'll get my ma." She glanced at David. "He can wait out by the door."

I shot him a look, trying to warn him not to react, but I needn't have worried. David's face was impassive.

"I'd rather he stayed where I could keep an eye on him."

"Suit yourself."

David took up his position behind the chair I settled into.

It didn't take long before a tired-looking woman entered the room, an older version of the girl, with hair fading from blonde to silver. Her dress had once been fashionable, before high waists. The red band of her profession had been attached around one sleeve with large, uneven stitches.

She bobbed an awkward curtsey. "Mrs. Haldane, madam. I'm obliged by law to tell you I'm registered with the Mysterium."

"Thank you, Mrs. Haldane." I didn't offer my own name, and she didn't seem to expect it.

"How may I assist you?" Her accent was pure Cornubian and her airs and graces were acquired, not natural to her upbringing.

David and I had agreed on our story on the way to East Street. "I have an item, a trinket belonging to my late husband, which his mother disputes the ownership of. A family matter. It's my understanding that she's likely to employ a witch to seek it out and I wish to have it remain hidden from any magical seeking. Is that possible?"

She pursed her mouth and sucked in air through her teeth. She was going to try to drive the price up. I waved my hand. "Just tell me how much it will cost. I'm not going to bargain with you."

Her eyes narrowed. "A guinea, ma'am."

I nodded and took two from my reticule. "The first is for your trouble and the second is to make sure that I was never here and you never worked magic for me."

She took the coins with undue haste. "Of course, ma'am. You were never here."

I took a block of wood I had prepared, the size of the box, and held it out for her. "This is the size of the piece. I want it hidden from prying magics as though it didn't exist, and I want to watch you working the spell."

"There's not much to see, ma'am." She set the block of wood down on a low table in front of my chair together with parchment, pen and ink. Then she stepped out into the hallway for a moment and brought back a hatbox. This she placed by the table and knelt facing me to take up the pen and dip it in the ink. With deliberate strokes of her crow-feather quill she made fine lines in strange shapes that I gathered were specific runes or magical symbols, concentrating hard on each one as she did it, sounding out letters then muttering whole words in some unrecognizable language, and finally full phrases, as if she was reading what she was writing over and over again from the beginning, each time adding what she'd written since the last recitation.

The tingle of magic built up and the back of my hands began to itch unbearably. David, who had leaned forward for a better view, rubbed his nose.

As Mrs. Haldane worked, her face, quite florid at the beginning, paled significantly until her lips drained of all color. I could almost see energy flowing from her into the spell on the parchment. When she'd finished, she sanded the ink to dry it and, still reading over and over again, she reached down to the hatbox. As she flipped the lid off and quickly grabbed what was inside I heard a squawk. She pulled out a white hen and, still muttering to herself, expertly tucked it under her left arm and with one pull and a twist broke the creature's neck.

There was a silent pop as the magic came together and my itches vanished between one breath and the next. Mrs. Haldane's face flushed from bloodless to healthy pink once more.

David rocked back on his heels at the sudden and unexpected slaughter. No doubt he'd snapped enough chickens' necks for the pot, but though dead chickens were commonplace enough by the kitchen door, they were less so in the parlor.

"Ellie!" Mrs. Haldane barely had to raise her voice. The scrawny girl must have been standing outside the door. She took the dead chicken by the feet and held it with its neck dangling down.

"Pluck it and draw it, child, then hang it in the larder. And don't make a mess in the yard."

Ellie nodded and scuttled out.

She turned to me. "You are surprised?"

"I thought blood magic—death magic—was not allowed."

She laughed. "Blood magic? That wasn't what you saw, my dear. It was merely a fat hen, bought for the pot, who aided in our endeavors. Waste not, want not."

Mrs. Haldane wrapped the inscribed parchment around the block of wood. "There, no one will find anything you wrap in that now."

I took the parchment covered block without comment. "Thank you. Is that it?"

"Aye, ma'am."

"Does it only protect the bauble while it's inside the parchment?"

"Aye, ma'am, but you can take it out and put it back in again as many times as you like and the spell won't break as long as the parchment stays whole."

"How long is it good for?"

"Until you burn the parchment, or leave it empty for a year and a day, thanks to our good fat hen. And a tasty supper she'll make."

I nodded. "Understood. Thank you, Mrs. Haldane."

"You're welcome, ma'am."

We ducked into a dim alleyway and I hastily wrapped the box in the parchment. Feeling safer by the minute, we returned to the shipping office for my bags and walked back up the hill, passing by the monstrous new Guildhall that had opened a few months earlier. We found lodgings at the Twisted Skein just off Frankfort Place. The inn had a decent reputation, and had the advantage that I'd never visited as either Rossalinde or Tremayne. It was a comfortable old half-timbered building with a stone lower story and black and white upper walls cantilevered twice, so the front leaned precipitously above the lower floors. A typical inn, built over and around its own arched entryway from the street into a stable yard big enough to accommodate at least three carriages and a stable.

In the yard a smart chaise stood empty, its horses already unharnessed, while next to it a boy was busy harnessing a fat dapple gray pony to a dog cart while a woman in a floral bonnet, equally rotund as her pony, directed a rowankind servant to place packages in the back. She looked like the wife of a reasonably prosperous farmer or country gentleman, and I stiffened to make a bow, only just recalling in time that I was wearing skirts. She looked up, smiled, and then, as if unsure, dipped a polite curtsey. I returned it.

The innkeeper, a thick-necked man in his fifties with a port wine-drinker's nose and a beer-drinker's gut, met us at the door, polite and welcoming as his position demanded, but not obsequious. I enquired about the availability of one of the three rooms in the courtyard. I liked the notion of being somewhere that was easy to enter and exit without attracting attention.

I was lucky, the man said, Mrs. Tregorran of Pendowna—did I know the family? No, well, no matter. She always patronized the Twisted Skein when she came to town, and she'd just vacated the end room of three. He'd get Annie to bring fresh sheets. There was a place in the communal sleeping loft with the ostlers for the boy. He jerked his chin toward David. The landlord showed me the way, leaving David to walk behind with my bag.

David played his part to perfection, obeying my every order quietly and calmly, his eyes dead and disinterested, even when I could see he was angry. Once inside our room with the door safely locked behind us, David dropped my traveling trunk and leaned back against the wall, screwing up his eyes and banging his head a couple of times gently against the lime-washed plaster. I made to put my arms around him but he shrugged me off.

"I know," I sighed. "I don't know what it's like."

David would have to retreat to the ostler's loft for the sake of propriety later tonight, but in the meantime, the bed was plenty big enough for two. We slept for a few hours, curled back-to-back, and then followed our noses into the inn's dining room. We were either late for breakfast or early for nooning because all the other tables were empty. We were offered thick roast ham, hard-boiled eggs, cheeses, bread, butter, and glutinous dark coffee to help it down. It was served by the same fresh-faced rowankind girl who had brought our sheets. She couldn't have been more than twelve or thirteen years old. She looked askance at David, sitting at the table with his mistress, then her eyes slid downward and she bobbed a curtsey.

"What's your name?" I asked her.

She answered that it was Annie if it pleased me and curtseyed again, all the time looking anywhere but my eyes, though she glanced sideways at David and he returned her look with a reassuring smile which seemed to put her at her ease.

"She hates me," I whispered when she'd gone.

"Not you in particular, just the masters and mistresses in general, always snapping out orders and expecting instant obedience."

I swallowed. I'd been guilty of that myself once upon a time. "Why didn't I ever see it before?"

"Because you weren't looking," he replied.

Halfway through our meal, our solitude was ended by the arrival of a newcomer. Silver-haired and wearing a long greatcoat, he strode into the dining room as if he owned the place, peeled off his coat and threw it across a chair.

"Ma'am." He nodded politely to me and I caught a flash of cool gray eyes. "I regret that we haven't been introduced, but polite company seems scant at the moment." He glanced around the empty room. "Corwen's the name, at your service."

"Mr. Corwen. I'm Mrs. Webster, and this is David." I'd pulled my alias out of nowhere when the landlord had asked me earlier. I was the widow of a sea captain recently killed in action against the French.

Mr. Corwen half-bowed. Then he endeared himself to me immediately by nodding politely to David as well before taking himself off to a corner booth. I noticed little Annie smiled as she left his table with his order, and I immediately felt better that there was at least one other person in Plymouth who didn't treat rowankind as if they didn't exist.

With the box safely wrapped, David and I walked through the town toward the ruin of our former home on Twiling Avenue. Philip had given me a family name, Sumner, but the only clue as to their whereabouts was his passing remark that Walsingham had spoken of going to both Totnes and Chard.

If I was going to seek out Philip and the rest of our family I hoped to find something which might enable a magical search for them, essentially doing to them what Walsingham's witches had been doing to me via the box. Searching didn't come naturally to me like weather-working did, but I had had some small success in the past. The remains of the house were as good a starting point as any, though I couldn't be sure that there was not some watch set upon it, magical or otherwise. Walsingham could well have a whole coven of witches at his command in addition to the one lost at sea.

"It's a pity Mrs. Haldane couldn't wrap us up in a piece of her magicked paper." David was obviously thinking along the same lines.

"I suspect it can be done, but it's probably bigger magic than a Mysterium witch is licensed to use. Magic that affects living things is a lot harder than magic that works on inanimate objects."

We walked on in silence for a while.

"What happens to the ones who can magic living things?" David asked.

"Hmm?" I'd been lost in my own thoughts, somewhere between my childhood memories of the town and my relationship with my mother.

David paused as if collecting his thoughts. "The Mysterium witches are like dogs with their teeth pulled. They can snap but they can't bite. They're licensed only to do small magics. What happens to the ones with the real power? There must be some. Do they just promise never to use it and live their lives pretending to conjure ninepenny spells? Or are they locked up in prison, or put away in Bedlam, or worse? Or does the Mysterium have another use for them?"

I shook my head, unsure of the inner workings of the Mysterium, but knowing that just talking about that arcane organization gave me chills in my spine. No one really knew how they worked. They had powers from the Crown to investigate witchcraft and could condemn without public trial. Philip had registered, and Walsingham had found him soon after. Coincidence? I thought not. Was Philip one of those witches with greater power? Was I?

"Only . . ." David continued, "It would be terribly difficult to live your life being less than you could be. There would always be the temptation to do bigger magic. Bigger and bigger still, if you had the power."

I thought about the difference between David's fireballs and the small candle flame he had eventually mastered. The candle flame had been more difficult than the fireball for him.

"Maybe that's where Walsingham gets his witches from. Maybe the ones the Mysterium daren't let loose in public are given special jobs for the government, whether they like it or not. Imagine if you could stand on the deck of a ship of the line in a sea battle and with a thought and a wave of your hand turn an enemy ship into a blazing bonfire."

He shuddered. "I could, but I wouldn't. There's hundreds

of people on a ship of the line. Even if they're enemies, they're still people."

Sometimes I felt a rush of affection for my little brother. This was one of those times.

"What about you, Ross? Would you use your magic against people?"

"I have. But weather magic isn't like being able to burn somebody to a crisp. I've used my magic to catch a ship's sails just as they were about to blast us to matchwood with a broadside."

"That's defense. I bet you've never used it to drive a ship on to the rocks."

I thought. "No, I haven't."

Should I tell him my guilty secret? Would he think less of me? I glanced sideways. He was giving me one of his curious looks. I huffed out a breath. "The day Will and I ran away, Mother sent a message to the Citadel to say that Will planned to steal her ship. They knew him, of course, by sight and by reputation; he'd sailed out of Plymouth since he was a cabin boy. Redcoats surrounded us as we made our way down toward Sutton Pool. I realized what must have happened and cursed myself for a fool. I should have waited until dark and crept out to join Will quietly instead of having a blazing row and then taking time to pack a valise. I was angry and terrified. I'd never had a pistol pointed at me before. When Will put himself between me and the muzzle of the captain's flintlock, I lost any good sense I may have had. I called a sudden wind, so violent that it blew the captain right off his feet without so much as a hair on Will's head being ruffled. Startled, I let the wind drop. The captain rolled to his feet, grabbing the pistol from where it had dropped, but Will was ready for him this time. He drew his sword and stuck him through the belly. Then we both took off and ran as if the devil was after us. He might have been, of course. Will's name is on the warrant for the captain's death, but I'm equally to blame."

David didn't try to fob me off with platitudes.

"What do you think of your sister now?"

"Our mother told it slightly differently."

"All my fault, I expect."

He shook his head. "She said Will shot the captain in cold blood."

I shook my head. "Will was the one in danger of being shot. Mother made us both murderers that day."

"I'm sure she didn't me—"

"Mean it? Yes, she did. Or at least she meant to have Will charged with stealing her ship and that would have been a hanging offense. My father had always told me that the *Heart* was my dowry. He knew Will and I had intentions, and we had his blessing even though it had never been formally announced."

"You hated her, didn't you?"

"Hated? That's too strong a word. When I was younger I never wanted anything but her love and approval. I could have been a dutiful daughter, the one she wanted, but magic put an end to that. Why didn't she tell me? All this time I thought she hated magic, but she was scared of it."

"Scared of what it meant, I think," David said.

"Hush, we're getting close." I put my hand up to end the conversation. "Be wary."

Due to my weather-working, it had rained torrents on the night of the fire, so there should be plenty of smoke-damaged remains. With Mother's will leaving everything to Philip, and Philip being officially deceased, the estate should be tied up in enough red tape to mean that little had been done other than seal off the property.

Had whatever remained of our mother gone into a pauper's grave? I didn't like to think about that.

As we approached along the tree-lined avenue, it was obvious that instead of the expected charred and blackened ruin there was a neat space where the house had been. I heard David's gasp of surprise as he realized that the garden wall enclosed emptiness.

Not quite emptiness.

The soot-stained stones from the house were now stacked in many neat piles some five feet high, wide and long. The cellars had been opened to the light, their vaulting demolished completely, and even the stable had been pulled down brick by brick. Of the contents of the house and all the rubble and debris, there was no sign.

The back of my neck prickled. "I think someone's watching," I said.

So we walked straight past, took a turn along the avenue itself and then walked back. I glanced across the street. The opposite house stood still and quiet, no activity behind the high hedge, but plenty of cover for someone to watch from. We kept walking casually. We needed to come back after dark to be safe.

15

Dark Magic

IF WE WERE GOING TO VENTURE back to Twiling Avenue in the dark, we would need a way to be able to see and examine the wreckage. Putting up a witchlight would be foolish in the extreme, so I had to think of a better way. I had seen a well-stocked apothecary's shop just a few hundred yards from the Twisted Skein and hoped to find what I was looking for there.

The apothecary didn't have what I needed, but said I was in luck and handed me a handbill which read:

Mr. Reginald Gorton
Optician
Respectfully informs the Good People of
Plymouth that he is Arrived in the Town with a
large Assortment of Spectacles to suit any Age or
Sight. Reading Glasses, Opera Glasses,
Telescopes and Microscopes and being well
versed in the science of optics
he trusts he will give Satisfaction.
He will be in Plymouth for a Fortnight at
the Three Tuns Inn, Market Street.

I thanked the apothecary and David and I went in search of the Three Tuns. Mr. Gorton had reserved a private room and had installed, on a sturdy table, a glass-fronted mahogany display case containing several pairs of eyeglasses of various designs. I wondered how he'd managed to transport it without breaking the glass if he moved from venue to venue every couple of weeks, but there was not a crack to be seen, and the glass was polished to perfection. I dismissed the lorgnettes and a pair of highly decorated eyeglasses which opened up like scissors and needed to be held in front of the face with one hand. I thought that spectacles with wire rims and side pieces that gripped the wearer's head might be more practical.

"Missis had a pair just like those," David said with a catch in his voice, pointing to a pair in the style known as *pince-nez*. They were little more than two round lenses in brass frames, held in place with a precarious nose clip. "For reading. She was forever going to sleep in them at night and losing them in the blankets."

I looked at the nose clip. Not very practical for anything other than a very sedentary reading experience.

Mr. Gorton was very attentive, showing me pair after pair of eyeglasses, some in metal frames, both silver and brass, some in tortoiseshell

"Dear Lady, I need to examine your eyes, if you would be so kind." Mr. Gorton indicated a chair and seized upon his own magnifying glass.

"My eyes are excellent, but I would like a pair of spectacles for my sister. She has a little trouble reading by candlelight."

"But how can I give you the correct lenses without seeing the lady in question?"

"Something of low magnification will be suitable. It's not a great affliction."

"Perhaps these?" He selected a pair with tortoiseshell rims and handed them to me. I slipped them on, blinking at the distortion caused by the lenses.

"Something less strong, I think."

"Try these." This time he handed me a pair with brass rims.

"Perfect." I slipped them on and took them off again. "And a second pair the same."

"Two pairs?" He seemed surprised.

"My sister is forever putting things down and forgetting where they are. It seems prudent to have another pair, does it not?"

"Perhaps I might suggest the same lens in a different frame. Silver, perhaps?"

He'd obviously decided that if I could afford two pairs of eyeglasses, I might be persuaded to the extra expense of silver frames.

"Brass will be fine," I said, "or tortoiseshell."

We settled on one pair of brass frames and one of tortoiseshell with the weakest lenses available. I suspected they were little more than clear glass, but that suited me well. We agreed on a price, and Mr. Gorton asked the address for delivery.

"We'll take them with us," I said, forgetting for a moment that I was no longer dressed as a man. When I saw Mr. Gorton's eyes widen I nodded toward David. "You may entrust them to my boy. He'll wait while you pack them."

Having recovered from my small breach of etiquette, I left the consulting room without a backward glance.

"Spectacles?" David asked when he brought the package back to our room.

"You'll thank me tonight."

I'd been hoping to have an early meal before the dining room filled up, but we were out of luck. The landlord apologized as we entered.

"There's no private table free, Mrs. Webster, very sorry. Would you care to share or would you rather wait?"

I started to say I'd wait, but then spotted Mr. Corwen across the busy dining room, sitting alone in the corner nook. He looked up and smiled, and seeing the situation waved invitingly to the empty space opposite him. "Well, perhaps I could share."

"I'll eat at the kitchen door, ma'am." David cleared his throat deferentially, and a horrible pang of guilt consumed me. There was no way, in such a crowded place, that the landlord would allow a rowankind table space. I guessed Mr. Corwen wouldn't mind, and there was room for both of us to squeeze on to the bench, but we couldn't risk attracting attention by making a fuss.

"Yes, David, run along."

"Will you be needing me this evening, madam?"

He gave me a meaningful look. I gave him a tiny shake of the head to tell him I'd understood, and he bowed and stepped away like any well-trained servant. I didn't dare spare him another glance as I joined Mr. Corwen, who stood politely until I sat and then left his meal uneaten on his plate.

"Oh, please, don't let your dinner cool on my account," I said.

"It's no hardship. I find most cooked food too hot for my palate," he said. "I prefer it at blood heat."

I smiled back while somewhere in the back of my mind a little alarm bell rang. I knew this man from somewhere—but where? Surely I'd remember someone so striking. I tried to study him without being obvious while we made small talk: the weather, the price of fish, the state of the cobbles in the market square, the French, and the sinking of the *Lydia* by Redbeard Tremayne due to a terrible misunderstanding about nationalities. Apparently that incident had been reported in the *Times* and had been the talk of Plymouth, since Tremayne was considered something of a local celebrity, a certain section of the population seeing nothing wrong in defending self and property from marauding redcoats who were altogether unpopular down by the port where innocent vessels were often searched on behalf of the Excise.

As we talked, I tried to recall where I might have seen those cool gray eyes and that thick pelt of elegant silver hair. The hair had almost fooled me at first; I'd thought him older, but Mr. Corwen was not old enough to have grayed with age. Silver-gray was his natural color. The skin around his eyes and on his neck and hands proclaimed him to be in his late twenties, or thirtyish at most. He was certainly not quite what he seemed on the surface. Charming as he was, I began to prickle with unease. That pleasant exterior didn't mean he was harmless.

Was that a little frisson of magic that I picked up?

Without seeming impolite, I made my excuses as soon as I could and retreated to my room.

I dressed in the breeches and jacket at the bottom of my traveling valise then waited, and worried, until just after midnight, when a scratching at my door told me that David had successfully crept out of the ostler's sleeping loft.

"Any trouble?" I asked him.

He shook his head. "The head ostler snores like a pig and the two stable lads were almost asleep facedown in their supper. They are dead to the world until dawn."

We waited for ten more minutes to be safe, and then David and I soft-footed down the steps and out through the inn yard, heading toward our old home. The gibbous moon gave us a little light along the back lane behind Twiling Avenue as woolly clouds scudded across the face of it.

We paused at the back gate to the yard.

"Spectacles," I whispered.

"Huh?"

I called light into the spectacles and handed them to him. He put them on, and I was pleased to note that from the outside they were completely normal, that is, I couldn't see them glowing in the dark.

"Ho!" David gasped. "It's not like daylight, but I can see. What did you do?"

"More or less the same as I did to Mayo's glass at Ravenscraig. The light should last for an hour or more, but let me know if the effect begins to fade."

I surveyed the scene through the tortoiseshell pair, seeing things before me clearly outlined. Through the spectacles the night was brighter than in the brightest full moon, showing me washed-out colors and details.

In the natural moonlight I saw the eerie bulk of the

stone stacks. Through the spectacles I saw sharp detail: the blackened stones, the care with which they had been lined up, the darker pits of the now-open cellars, the relief of the lines of grubbed-out trenches where walls had once spread their toes deep into the earth.

"Who could have done this?" David raised the spectacles, looked beneath them and then settled them firmly on his nose again.

"I don't know, but if I had to guess—Walsingham."

"Who owns it now?" David asked.

"I guess it belongs to the Crown if Philip's registered dead or doesn't come forward to claim it. Even if I might inherit it officially, I could never show my face."

The town, tied up by its usual inefficient bureaucracy and petty corruption, should have been squabbling over what to do with the ruin for years, but instead someone had moved quickly to clear the site. Not only to clear it, but to *clean* it, a large-scale operation that must have taken a whole gang of careful workers. Not a cinder crunched underfoot. Every last scrap of ash and charcoal had been swept and brushed away and all that remained were these piles of neatly stacked stones. What had happened to the rubble and the charred remains of the house's contents?

My spine tingled.

I knelt and brushed the floor with gloved fingers. There was a dark patch, dried now, blood, perhaps, from some spellworking.

David shuddered. "Someone's been looking for something," he said.

I nodded. "Very thoroughly." I could feel the echo of a spellworked magical *search*. "Walsingham's witch, maybe? Or Walsingham himself?" I frowned. "How many witches might he have at his command?"

"Maybe it's not Walsingham." David sounded hopeful.

I shook my head. "I'd bet my pretty captain's hat that Walsingham is the one Jim Mayo was planning to sell the box to."

Will's ghost rose from the stones. *You should have done more talking and less—*

I rounded on him. *You had no right to invade my privacy that night.*

He scowled.

I'm a free woman. What I do is my own affair. I was going to continue my tirade, but the look on Will's face was heartbreaking. I sighed. *All right. Forget it.*

Will wouldn't, and neither would I. Think about something else.

I walked over to the nearest bank of stones, almost as tall as I was. If I touched it with my bare skin, would it leave an imprint by which Walsingham could track me? I put my right hand flat against it. My kid-leather glove was fine enough to let me feel the roughness beneath my fingers. I leaned my cheek toward it, not quite connecting. There was a slight tingle, nothing more.

David wiped the palms of his hands down his trousers, rubbed them together, and flicked his fingers away from him as if flicking off water droplets. Then he touched the back of his knuckles to the stone.

"David! Where are your gloves? If Walsingham . . ."

Too late.

He shrugged, wincing slightly as his flesh connected. I watched his face as his expression changed from wary, to interested, and then to dreamy as he turned his hand to touch the stone with fingertips, then palm. His other hand came up and reached for the stones, too, and I saw hunger in his face and a dark glint in his eye. He sucked in a sharp breath and his elbows bent as his whole body leaned toward the stones.

I grabbed him around his waist and pulled, feeling him anchored surprisingly firmly. A darkness shot through my head, like a reverse lightning bolt, sharp, black, and charged with intent. I gasped at the pain and then saw things in my own mind illuminated by black light, things I never wanted to see again. I gagged on a hot rush of acid into my mouth and swallowed hard.

Instead of pulling I pushed sideways, and David's grip sundered. We both crashed to the ground, and my spectacles flew off. He struggled, and growled at me, an inhuman rasping of vocal chords. His body spasmed and shook. I cradled his head as best I could and clung tightly to his shoulders until his threshing stopped and he stilled.

"All right now?" I asked. "Can I let go?"

"Ye . . . yes." He cleared his throat between attempts to speak, and the second try came out sounding closer to normal.

"David, what was that?"

He shook his head. "I don't know, but I do know that whoever—whatever—searched here was powerful and . . . and . . . more than just a simple witch. Death was involved in their seeking. A human death for a powerful spell."

"Death magic!" I felt sick.

"Ross, let's leave this place."

Even without the spectacles I could tell his face was pale. I didn't need him to ask twice. If Walsingham had set a magical watch there might be searchers converging on us any moment. I listened as hard as I could: street sounds in the distance; the soughing of leaves on the neighbor's trees, stirred by a light breeze; the cry of an owl in the darkness; a barking dog, far enough away to be of no importance, and yet . . . and yet . . . I started to shiver.

"I've lost the spectacles," David said.

"Me, too." We groped around until we found the brass-rimmed ones, and then David used them to find the tortoiseshell pair.

"Let's go." I took David's hand and, rather than leave by Twiling Avenue or by the back lane, we pushed through the hedge into the neighbor's garden. It wasn't as easy as it had been when I was eight and had trespassed to see Lucy Clemmow's new kittens, or, later, to challenge Josh Clemmow to a childish duel for his bullying of Philip. The Clemmow children were long gone, both carried off by the quinsy in the winter of eighty-seven. I didn't know who lived there now, but the house was in darkness. We ran around the side of it and exited along a narrow alley that led through to Whinmoor Avenue.

"Do you think . . . ?" David whispered when we were far enough away for the sound of our voices not to carry back.

"I don't know, but I'm not going back to find out."

We took a very roundabout route to get back to the Twisted Skein. All the time I was listening hard for sounds of pursuit, but if anyone had been trying to apprehend us, we'd got out in time.

This time.

But we needed to be more careful. There were things here that neither of us understood.

There was still the question of what had happened to the remains of the furniture and items from the house. More than stone should have survived the fire. If someone was looking for something so important, then surely they wouldn't have disposed of anything. They'd want to check thoroughly. The burnt remains of the interior had probably been taken somewhere more private. But if dark magic, blood magic, was involved, we were out of our depth.

Not only that but I was scared out of my wits. Blood magic wasn't sanctioned by the Mysterium any more than natural magic was. I'd heard rumors. It was a type of ritual magic often practiced in the Caribbean, most frequently on the island of Hispaniola. Details were scarce, but most sources said it was powerful and dark, calling on ancient gods and wild spirits, strengthened by the power of fear and death. I thought of Mrs. Haldane killing the chicken. Maybe blood magic was an extension of the Mysterium-sanctioned spell-magic.

"Are you sure you're all right?" I asked David, when our room door closed behind us, not sure that I was.

"I will be," he said. "What next?" He rubbed his face with both hands and sat heavily on the edge of the bed.

I was tempted to tell him to pack up and flee back to the *Heart*, but that could be even more dangerous. I wished I knew more about magic—not just my magic, but how it fitted in with other magics. I'd been a fool to try and ignore it. I vowed that when all this was over I would seek out more information, but in the meantime I could only go with my gut instinct.

"I want to find out who gave the order for the remains of my—of our mother's house to be so thoroughly searched."

"How do you hope to find that?"

"Mother owned the property outright. If it's been seized by the city, the records should be in the new Guildhall."

"The new Guildhall also houses the town's Watch House and gaol."

"It does? Damn!" I was out of touch with Plymouth's changes.

I shuddered. The Mysterium's regulations are strict. Step outside the acceptable boundaries and the hangman's noose awaits. Unfortunately when I'd bolted with Will I'd charged headlong and irrevocably across those boundaries.

The dead marine captain still weighed on my conscience.

It wasn't my fault.

But by a single vengeful act my mother had turned us both into fugitives.

Telling David about that day had resurrected memories I'd tried to bury. Terror rose inside me again. My mother screaming that we should not take her ship. *Her* ship, she called it, even though my father had promised it as my dowry. The marines surrounding us. Will stepping in front of me. I couldn't think beyond the barrel of the captain's pistol pointing at his heart and his sweaty finger on the trigger. Calling a whirlwind. Red-coated men bowled over like ninepins. The captain staggering to his feet, pistol in hand. Will reacting to protect me.

There was no way I could go anywhere near that Guildhall. For all I knew, my crude likeness may still be pinned to the Watch House wall.

". . . go out and about."

"What?" I realized David had been speaking while I was lost in my own thoughts.

"I said," David repeated slowly, "there are one or two places a rowankind might go to hear things that might not be heard elsewhere."

"Is it safe? Will anyone recognize you?"

"One more rowankind bondservant in streets so full of them?"

I nodded. "All right. Do what you need to do. In the meantime we still need to get information from the Guildhall." I took a deep breath. "We'll have to get a proxy. Tomorrow we go to the Ratcatchers."

The following morning, after breakfast, David nodded to me meaningfully and slipped away in the direction of the market. He didn't show up at noon, and I was beginning to worry about him when I heard voices in the yard below, looked out, and saw him with Annie. They were laughing together as if they hadn't a care in the world. Anger rose inside me. How dare he scare me like that!

As he came in he had such a look of gentle peace on his face that I swallowed my harsh words, and "Where have you been?" came out a little softer than I'd intended.

"For a walk. Taking the temperature of the town."

"With Annie?"

He shook his head. "An inn servant doesn't get time off for strolling, though I did steal a few minutes with her when I returned. It's not what you think." He smiled. "But she's pretty, is she not?"

"How do you know what I think?"

Was it my business anyway? I think my mouth opened and closed a few times. How old was he? How old was Annie?

"I wanted to talk to her about how she felt, how her friends felt about being bonded. I also wanted to know if she'd ever heard of any rowankind with magic. A girl like her in a place like this hears a lot of things."

"And?"

"She has some connections who talk of rebellion, but she wouldn't give me details. She says it's all talk, but thinks if they had the opportunity to run away they'd take it. Some are angry. Annie isn't. She likes the missis here and gets fair treatment and half a guinea every Christmas. She thinks the idea of any rowankind with magic is impossible."

"You didn't . . ."

"Tell her about me? No." He shook his head. "I saw Mr. Corwen on the way in. He seems decent." He looked to see my reaction.

Despite the incident with Gentleman Jim, something I bitterly regretted now, surely David didn't think I popped my buttons for every halfway-handsome man that came along? Did he think I had a yen for Mr. Corwen? True the man was attractive, very attractive even, but . . .

I didn't know whether to slap some sense into David, in a sisterly way, or laugh. In the end I did neither.

"I don't trust that man," I said, recalling the cool gray eyes. "There's something about him. I think I've seen him before, but I can't figure out where. We came here to solve one riddle and find ourselves with two."

"Family business. Maybe they're both connected."

"I doubt it. I don't know why Mother never spoke of our kin unless she wanted to stay hidden from them. Perhaps there was a monumental argument and she flounced off with her lover. Maybe it runs in the family."

16

The Ratcatchers

DAN FAIRLOW, landlord of The Ratcatchers, looked at me without a glimmer of recognition until I gave him the sign, touching my right eyebrow with my left index finger, a casual enough movement to most observers. His eyes widened, and he ushered David and me straight through into the back kitchen, which was also his own cozy living room, furnished with a scrubbed table. He waved me to a Windsor chair and set a three-legged stool for David.

"It's not our Simeon is it, Cap'n?" he asked as soon as the door closed behind us.

"No, nothing like that. In fact, he's been made assistant quartermaster."

"Has he? My boy Sim?"

"Not such a boy, now."

"I expect not. Tell him I'm proud."

"Of course I will."

"But you didn't come here to tell me that. Can I offer you refreshment? I've a keg of best broached. Or if it's a bit early in the day I've tea?"

"Tea would be lovely, thanks."

Dan looked at David.

"This is Davy, a shipmate."

"Any shipmate of Sim's is welcome here. Tea, Davy?"

David nodded.

I grinned at Dan. "And he's also my brother, so I'd appreciate it if you would give him any assistance he needs."

Dan's eyebrows went up a notch, but he recovered quickly. "O' course, Cap'n. Goes without sayin'."

"Right now I need help with two matters. Firstly, someone who can run an errand to the town clerk's office in the Guildhall for information, but I want my identity kept clean out of it."

"So you'll be looking for a man of letters then?"

"Someone with a decent head on his shoulders who knows how to keep his mouth shut. There's payment, of course."

Dan nodded. "You want me to engage him on your behalf?"

"That's the idea. This is what I want him to find out . . ."

I gave Dan the details of the house in Twiling Avenue and told him to make sure the man thought he was enquiring on behalf of a gentleman who wanted to buy the plot for building, so needed to trace the ownership of it. If he could find out anything about where the remains from the fire had been taken, so much the better.

"I know just the man," Dan said. "Zachary Coe. Used to be a lawyer's clerk, but a familiarity with strong drink lost him his place." He saw my doubtful expression. "Catch him before three of the clock and he's sober as a judge."

"What about after three?"

"He's too blathered to remember his own name."

"Fair enough." I handed Dan five guineas. "Only one in advance. He can drink himself to death after he's done the job. Do you think you can procure his services quickly?"

"I'll try. I'll send word to your lodging when he's got your information."

"Thanks, Dan."

"And the second matter?"

"I wonder if you know where I might find Ezra Pargeter."

"Old Captain Cyclops?"

"The very same."

"Last I heard he was half-crazy. I've neither seen nor heard of him in years."

"Ask about, will you? If he's still living I have a question for him."

That evening I was once again forced by circumstances to share a table with Mr. Corwen. His conversation was light and pleasant, and once or twice he made me laugh with his wry humor. Even so, I gave my excuses as soon as I could and left him in the dining room.

I expected to find David in our room, but I couldn't even see any sign that he'd been there. I checked on Annie, wondering if he was hanging around the kitchen. He seemed to have taken a shine to her. She hadn't seen David since before dinner. She posited that he may have gone to bed, since the stable boys retired early.

I knew he wouldn't settle down for the night without checking in with me. He'd indicated that he would be going out again. I told myself to stop worrying; David knew his way around Plymouth well enough. So only slightly worried, I lay down and dozed.

I hadn't meant to fall deeply asleep. I dreamed the *Heart* sailed upon an ocean of cold fire, her sails blazing without being consumed. I awoke with a start, the dream already half-forgotten. The room was dark save for a few glowing embers in the grate. The candle I'd left alight had burned out. It had to be after midnight, and still no David.

Now I had just cause to be worried.

Where was he?

I groped for a new candle in the dark and poked the wick into the embers of the fire, trying to tease it alight before the wax softened too badly. Setting it in the simple wooden candlestick, I held it up and checked the room, hoping he'd come in while I was asleep and, not wishing to wake me, had settled down on the room's only chair.

I was out of luck. The room was empty except for shadows.

There was only one course of action. Lying down on the

bed and wrapping a blanket around myself, I began to weave a seeking. I wove it with words and with intent and with urgency and with love. I'd actually come to love him. That thought almost surprised me.

This certainly wasn't my ready-magic, and I could feel my energy draining like water running out of a leaky bucket as tendrils of magic snaked their way across the city.

My thoughts traveled along the streets, alleyways, squares, courts and closes of the town. It was as if I was passing hundreds of locked doors with nothing behind them. If David was there I'd know it instantly. I called him to me, focused in the way that a mother might summon a single child from a crowded schoolyard.

There. Something! I almost slipped past a door that I needed to see behind, but it did not open for me. There was a presence behind it that was, at the same time, exploding with power and yet utterly still. But the stillness held a warning of violence to come.

David.

I called out to him, but there was no response. It was as if he was encased in ice.

So where was he? I had him on the metaphysical plane, but how did that translate into a geographical location within the city? I stepped back in my vision and looked at the door. It was oak with huge iron studs, like a castle door, or like a prison.

My heart sank. Either the Kingsmen or the Watch had him. If it was the Kingsmen, he was already in the Citadel and nothing less than an army could secure his freedom. If it was the Watch, I had a chance.

I pulled back all my magic, saving what energy I had. It could have been the end of the world and I wouldn't have been able to force myself to walk more than the three paces to the chamber pot and then back to the bed. Sleep now. Rescue tomorrow.

I slept.

Little Annie was making up the great fire when I tottered into the kitchen early the following morning. She bobbed a curtsey at me, her hands black with ashes and coal. "I'm sorry, ma'am, there's only me here. Can I get you something?" She jumped up and put her bucket of coals down.

"I have to go out, Annie. Can I help myself to some bread and ham?"

"I'll get it, ma'am."

"No, honestly, don't trouble yourself. Finish what you're doing. I don't want to interrupt your routine." I found the larder by intuition and cut a slab of yesterday's bread, a thick slice of ham and, wrapping the two together, tore into them ravenously. The energy gap left after doing magic like that couldn't be filled by sleep alone.

Still munching on my breakfast, somewhat indelicately, I crossed the yard to the steps up to my room only to find Mr. Corwen coming in the opposite direction.

"Mrs. Webster, up early I see."

"Business to attend, Mr. Corwen. Urgent business."

"Your boy, David. I wonder if I might have a word."

"Later, maybe. He's out. On an errand." I didn't try to be polite, just swept around him and ran back up the steps and into my room.

Instinct told me to dress for action—trousers, shirt, knife and sword—but if I did that, then I'd lose the advantage of my disguise. So instead I decided on my lilac muslin walking dress with my rose-colored spencer.

If David was in custody he'd either be at the Citadel or the Watch House in the Guildhall, somewhere I'd been avoiding. The Guildhall was closest.

As I walked past the building then turned and walked back again I could sense that some huge, pent-up magical force was almost on the point of unraveling completely. I dithered by the side of the building, wondering how best to approach this.

"Can I help?" It was Mr. Corwen. He'd come up close behind me without me even hearing his footsteps. Was I losing my edge?

My hand immediately snaked to the knife in the small

of my back, concealed beneath my dress lest anyone spot it and become suspicious.

He held both hands up so that I could see he wasn't armed. "I know right now you don't know whether to trust me or not, but I won't ask any questions. If you need my help, it's yours."

I glared at him, not knowing whether to fillet him or just send him packing.

"I swear by the Lady that I'm not your enemy," he said.

"The what?" My heart started to thump in my chest. Who was this man? What was he? I swallowed the lump in my throat that was constricting my breathing. "Mr. Corwen I don't know what you're talking about. Excuse me."

I brushed past him and in through the doors.

The Watch House smelt of rum and despair, and that was just the office. I catalogued the potential dangers and the possible escape routes, not liking my conclusion. The counter was to my left and a heavy oak door, probably to the holding cells, straight ahead of me. With five people already waiting, the place was crowded; obviously the sergeant in charge was supposed to deal with petitioners and miscreants swiftly and not let them hang about for long.

And so it proved. One unfortunate woman was taken to the cells, another led into a small side room to have her statement taken by a pimple-faced clerk. The rest, two men and a wizened-cheeked woman, were shooed out of the door like a flock of hens.

This didn't look like somewhere the niceties were observed. No place for a lady. Good thing I wasn't, but I had to remember my manners if I wanted to be taken for one.

The sergeant at the desk was armed with a smoothly polished truncheon, suspiciously stained. There was only one shallow window, well above head height. On one wall was a board covered with wanted notices, at the center of which was Redbeard Tremayne. I wanted to laugh at the artist's impression, which looked like neither me nor Will, but instead had the countenance of a bearded demon with a merciless expression. Ridiculous as the drawing was, I did take notice of the fact that Redbeard was wanted for arson and the murder of the Widow Goodliffe.

The sergeant looked up as I coughed politely to remind him that I was still waiting. "No soliciting in—Oh, sorry, ma'am."

I drew myself up to my full height, in truth a little short for a privateer captain, but impressive for a well-to-do widow, and gave him as haughty a stare as I could manage.

"I'm looking for my rowankind boy, Sergeant. He doesn't know his way around the city and I fear he's lost or fallen into some danger."

"Runaway, ma'am?" the sergeant reached under the counter and pulled out a sheet of cheap wood-pulp paper and started to write with a stub of a pencil.

"Runaway? Of course not. The boy's completely devoted to me."

He crossed out what he'd already written.

"Name?"

"My name is Mrs. Webster. His name is David and he belongs to the Webster estate."

"Description?"

"He's rowankind, age fourteen, about my height. Damn me, Sergeant!" I allowed myself one unladylike expletive. "He looks like any rowankind: dark hair, dark eyes, fine features, pale gray complexion, the usual skin markings, slightly built. They all look the same except to an experienced eye, don't you think?"

"You might want to consider branding him, ma'am, or tattooing if you want to go to the extra expense."

I felt sick. "Sergeant, can you help me find my lost boy, or am I wasting my time and yours?"

He muttered something about waiting and took his paper into the back room. I heard voices, but I couldn't make out what they were saying. After a few minutes an officer, obviously one step up from the sergeant in rank, came out.

"You say your boy is called David?"

"Yes."

"We have a David in custody."

"In custody? Is he injured? Can I see him?" I tried to act flustered and surprised to cover up a deeper panic.

"You can identify him for us, ma'am. We got his name out of him, but he wouldn't say anything else."

I wondered if they'd beaten him for information.

The officer led me through the heavy wooden door to the cells. I could feel a buildup of magic under pressure and I shuddered at the potential. We stopped outside a door and the officer opened a small window in it. I didn't even need to look, I could sense David inside the cell, his power barely contained. I needed to get him out before someone got hurt. He could easily bring the whole building crashing down on himself and everyone in here.

When I looked through the window, he was sitting on the hard stone floor, back against the wall, knees drawn up and hands clasped tightly around them. He didn't look up at the scraping sound the window made and I could see a minute shake in his shoulders, no, in all of his body. He was wound up tight as a mainspring.

I tried to keep my voice calm and not let my panic show. "That's him, officer. Can I take him now?"

"Not so fast, ma'am. Can you prove he's yours? One of my lads identified him as an escapee, wanted in connection with a fire at the Goodliffe house some months back. The Goodliffe rowankind was a David, too."

I don't know what I'd been expecting. I thought they might have accused him of vagrancy. "It's a common enough name." I tried to keep my voice level and swallow the egg that seemed to have lodged itself deep in my throat. "I can assure you he's not the boy you think he is."

"You can prove it?"

"I don't have his papers on my person, but he's been in my family since his birth."

That wasn't even a lie.

17 Short Fuse

WE WALKED BACK ALONG THE CORRIDOR, each step taking me further away from where I needed to be. It was as if my legs thought for themselves—one foot in front of the other—while my brain was occupied.

"I'm sure we can settle this easily, officer." I tried again. "To be honest, David's not the shiniest apple in the barrel, and I think right now he's probably so confused you'll never get any sense out of him unless you let me speak to him. I'd be happy to do that."

When we arrived back in the main room I was surprised to see Mr. Corwen there, standing at the counter. For a moment I considered pretending I didn't know him, but he half-bowed to me. "Mrs. Webster."

"Mr. Corwen." I glared at him. Whatever he did had better not make this mess worse.

"You two know each other?" The desk sergeant asked.

"We're both staying at the same inn," Mr. Corwen said. "Can you believe it, ma'am, I lost five guineas to a cutpurse not three streets from here?"

"I'm sorry for it."

"Oh, I'll survive the loss. I do hope you haven't lost anything."

"These good officers seem to think my rowankind, David, is someone else entirely, someone wanted in connection with setting a fire."

"Oh, surely not. Why, you've not been in Plymouth more than a few days, ma'am, and I have heard of no fire since you arrived."

The desk sergeant coughed to interrupt us. "When did you lose your purse, sir?"

"Five minutes ago. I came straight here, of course, but my business can wait. Surely you can't believe this lady's rowankind is the one you seek. I myself can identify the lad if you wish."

"Thank you, Mr. Corwen." Maybe it would be as easy as that. I turned to the sergeant. "Will that be sufficient?"

"Your boy's been here since yesterday night, ma'am, I can't just release him without proof he's yours. I have the likeness of the Goodliffe boy here."

He snatched a drawing from the overcrowded noticeboard where paper was pinned on top of paper.

"Damn!" He swore as a sheaf of other papers, precariously pinned, fluttered to the floor like autumn leaves. "Begging your pardon, ma'am."

He bent to scoop up the papers from the floor. Cold shock ran through me. The falling papers had cleared a small oasis of space on the board and peeping from it was my likeness, brown and curling at the edges. It was a passable likeness, too, copied, I thought, from a drawing my mother had made of me when I was sixteen. She'd had a good eye for shape and form.

"Ah here it is." He straightened up and I tried to look anywhere but at his noticeboard. "You must admit, it looks like him."

I glanced at the paper. It did indeed, though not captured as well as the one my mother had drawn of me.

"It could be any one of a hundred boys who walk past your door every day." I glanced at the drawing and dismissed it airily.

"Maybe you have your boy's papers back at your lodgings?" the sergeant asked hopefully.

Damn, I should have thought to forge some papers for David. Too late now to regret the omission.

I had to get David out of there fast.

"Let me help with those, Sergeant," Mr. Corwen retrieved a wanted notice that had floated to the public side of the counter and, bold as brass, he walked around the desk and pinned it firmly on top of my likeness, then stepped back without catching my eye. "Mrs. Webster, isn't your boy branded?" he asked. "I swear I saw a brand on his arm."

I started to say no, but he carried on regardless.

"Surely that will settle the matter, Sergeant? Bring the boy out and check his mark."

My heart's pounding rose a level. This was stupid. David had no brand. I glared at Mr. Corwen, opening my mouth to say that he must be mistaken and that I did not believe in branding rowankind as if they were no more than cattle, but he stared into my eyes in a very pointed way and gave an almost imperceptible shake of his head.

Did he have some kind of plan? What was he up to? He'd deliberately covered up my likeness, but I didn't trust him. Unfortunately, for now, it seemed that I didn't have much choice. I'd play along.

The constable brought David up from the cells and sat him down on the bench. I perched next to him, horrified by how stiff and unresponsive he was. I took his hand and it felt like dough in mine, but the physical feel belied the magical energy. I heard Mr. Corwen gasp as if he too felt the potential crackling around David like a cat o' nine tails.

So the man did have some magic, or at least an understanding of it.

Mr. Corwen's mouth compressed to a straight line and a slight sheen broke out on his brow. As the sergeant reached for David's arm and pushed up his sleeve Mr. Corwen took a deep breath.

I felt something in the air. A low rumble, outside the hearing of most people, settled like a rock in the pit of my stomach. Magic was being worked, and it was neither mine nor David's.

I looked at Mr. Corwen. What was he? A registered magic user? An illegal witch? He'd mentioned the Lady and I'd shrugged off the reference, too preoccupied with David to give it much thought. Was he something else altogether? Surely I'd have remembered him if I'd seen him in the Okewood, but the only other human-shaped beings I'd seen were the Lady and her consort.

The sergeant's hiss of discovery drew my attention. The inside of David's forearm clearly showed an old burn scar that spelled out the name Webster.

I glanced at Mr. Corwen, whose eyes had gone glazed with strain.

He was working an illusion.

"Well, I'll be damned," the sergeant said, glaring at the constable. "Begging your pardon, ma'am."

The constable started to reach out with a finger to feel the cicatrices. I wasn't sure the illusion would pass the touch test, so I quickly cleared my throat, stood up and bent over David to yank his sleeve down while indelicately giving the watch house a view of the shape of my arse beneath the fine fabric of my dress. I hoped it would be enough of a distraction, though in truth I'm almost as slim-hipped as a boy.

Was that a relieved sigh from Mr. Corwen as he released whatever magics he had been holding together?

"I wonder how you missed that, gentlemen?" I turned to the two watchmen.

The sergeant scowled and the constable looked faintly embarrassed.

"I wonder, too," the sergeant said. "But it's plain that this isn't the Goodliffes' rowankind. That brand's old. You should have mentioned it straightaway, Mrs. Webster."

"I'm sorry, sergeant. I had forgotten. We don't brand our rowankind now and I'm not proud that my grandfather used to insist on branding the poor things. I feel it's cruel. I thought David was too young to have been branded. He must have been one of the last ones, born just before my grandfather died and my father abandoned the practice."

"Mrs. Webster, if you wouldn't mind waiting." The sergeant indicated a bench and pulled out a handful of papers from beneath his desk.

"I would mind terribly. I intend to leave Plymouth today and I can hardly do that without my property."

"I'll get the admissions book and then . . ." The rest of his words were lost as he went into a second office beyond a wooden door.

I sat back down again. Truth to tell I was more than a little light-headed. This close to David, I could feel the slight tremble in his thigh muscles, but it was the pent-up magic that set me on edge. David didn't seem to be following what was going on. He might still have been in his cell. Maybe in his mind, he still was.

The potential for violence rose another notch

"I'm sure we'll be able to go soon," I said quietly, hoping it would have a calming effect.

"Sergeant!" I heard Mr. Corwen roar at the desk and the sergeant came lumbering back. I was concentrating on David, so whatever Mr. Corwen and the sergeant discussed passed me by until Mr. Corwen came back and said, "It's all right, ma'am, you can go, now."

"What?" I felt fuddled.

"Just go," Mr. Corwen said.

"Are you—"

He jerked his head sideways toward the door. "I have a lost purse to report, I'm sure you don't wish to be detained any longer than necessary."

"Of course not. Thank you for your assistance, Mr. Corwen."

As I said it, I realized that I meant it. I might not trust him, but his intervention had saved the day.

I'm not sure how David and I got back to the Twisted Skein. I think we held each other upright. As we walked into the yard Annie came to meet us, a smile on her face.

"Annie. Thank goodness." I sat David down on the bottom of the steps, took Annie's hands and put David's into them. "He's not feeling very well, Annie. Just hold on to him for two minutes."

And with that I couldn't wait any longer. I couldn't even run. I walked very sedately to the privy, and heaved up the remains of the bread and ham. The privy at the Twisted Skein is not the worst I've ever had the misfortune to visit, but it's not the best either. At that moment, noxious odors notwithstanding, it was more welcome than any palace. But I knew by the ache in my guts that we'd come close to disaster.

When I got back to David, Annie was still sitting with both his hands in hers, looking into his eyes. "He's not at home, ma'am."

"Oh he's in there all right, Annie, we just have to persuade him to come out again."

"He's as cold as death." She looked at me wide-eyed. "What have you—? No, don't tell me. I don't want to know. I knew he was different. Special." She cleared her throat and seemed to make up her mind. "What can I do? He needs something to warm him. Shall I fetch a firebrick from the back of the hearth?"

"Good idea, and a pot of soup if you have one."

"Oh, aye, ma'am. There's always soup."

I got David up the stairs one step at a time, along the landing, and into my room, then I rolled him into the bed and pulled off his boots. Annie brought a hot clay brick whose job was to distribute the heat evenly from the great kitchen fire to the bread oven next to it.

I wrapped the brick in a blanket and slipped it under David's chilled feet. Annie was back with the soup before I'd finished settling him. I sat David up while Annie tried to coax some of the broth down him. He swallowed some, but let the rest dribble over the towel Annie had thought to bring with her. The cook's voice roaring for her from the kitchen doorway sent her scurrying with an apology and a promise to return when she could.

"She's a good girl, your Annie," I said to David as I tucked the blankets around him. "Pretty, too."

I felt his forehead, but rather than hot it was just like his fingers, doughy and unreal. He'd locked all his magic away, and it was eating him from the inside out.

I sat on the bed beside him and started to talk about endless trivia, saying anything in the hope of a response, but none came.

"Oh, David, listen to me. Talk to me. You're not the first to be locked up in that place and you won't be the last. I know it makes you feel like nothing, nobody."

I thought I got, if not an answer, at least a listening silence.

It seemed to stretch forever until, at last, he started to shake and I realized he was sobbing—great, dry, heaving sobs.

At length he spoke.

"I was so scared. I could feel this . . . power and I didn't know what to do. I wanted to lash out and smash the walls to pieces and . . . I felt I could do it, too. I felt I could blast the whole city apart just to be free. All I needed to do was unleash it. How's that for a rowankind?"

"Wanting to lash out seems natural to me. We don't miss what we've never had. You didn't know what freedom was until recently. Now that you know, you're not going to let it go again in a hurry. As for the blasting of the whole city—well—you didn't. It's as simple as that. You could have, but you didn't. That's the David I've come to know—and love. There's no darkness in you. I'm proud to call you brother."

He reached for my hand and squeezed my fingers. "Thank you."

David eventually slept, and I let him lie for the whole day. I ate early and quickly, refused coffee, and hurried to my room to avoid Mr. Corwen. Part of me wanted to thank him, the other part to confront him, but to do that I would need to admit my own talents.

David was still asleep.

A knock on the door proved to be one of the urchins

who hung about the market, working for scraps. He snatched off his cap. "Mrs. Webster?"

I nodded.

He held out a small package. "Gotta message from Mr. F. He says Jackson's stall on the western edge of the market has good apples today and they're selling 'em off right about now as the market's closing."

I gave him a penny for his trouble and he ran off.

Inside the package, four golden guineas winked at me. So Zachary Coe didn't want the remainder of his payment for some reason. What could have happened? I put on my burgundy redingote, as the weather had taken a downturn and a sharp autumnal wind slapped my cheeks. I'd be trimming canvas if I were at sea.

As I walked across the inn yard I spotted Mr. Corwen apparently just taking the air, though why he should choose the inn yard I had no idea. I opened my mouth to speak, failed to find anything to say, and shut it again with a snap. He nodded politely as he walked past me and I returned the gesture.

Apparently what happened at the Watch House was not to be spoken of.

The market was only a short walk, and as some of the stalls were packing up, there were indeed bargains to be had, though my nose told me that some of them were not as fresh as they might be. I might forgive a bruised apple, but a three-day-old mackerel was no joke. I made my way past a tinker with pans spread out on a threadbare blanket and an elderly woman selling ribbons and laces. There were two stalls selling apples, but a familiar stocky figure by one caused me to wander over. I stopped by Dan Fairlow on the pretext of examining a basket of ripe pippins. Dan turned quickly, bumping into me, spilling apples at my feet.

"My apologies, ma'am."

"The fault's all mine. Let me help you."

I bent to pick up apples and Dan crouched down, his whiskery chin close to my ear.

"What's up, Dan?"

"Zack Coe facedown in Sutton Pool is what's up."

"What?"

"Not five hours after he set off for the Guildhall."

"You think it was on account of the errand?"

"He's never been drowned in Sutton Pool afore."

"Fair point. Any witnesses?"

"That's what took me so long to bring the news. Rumor is he was pitched out of a warehouse window on Cockside."

"Which one?"

"Skinners. Know it?"

"I do."

"Go careful, Cap'n. Zack had been beaten afore he died. There's been bad words about Skinner's of late. Strange goings on. There's some as say it's haunted."

"Thanks, Dan."

I finished loading his basket with apples and stood up. Dan stepped back, tugged his forelock, thanked me politely, and walked away without looking back. I bought two apples from the stall and took them back to the Skein, pondering on what it might all mean.

David was still sleeping. I set one of the apples on the nightstand by the bed and bit into the other one, letting its tart sweetness wash over my palate.

He's here with me. Will coalesced, made as if to sit on the bed, saw David, and grasped the wooden bed foot instead, though I noticed his fingers sank into the wood a little.

"Who is?"

Don't you want to know?

"You seem to think I do." Will's teasing sense of humor was often sadly missing from his ghostly appearances, but I caught a twinkle in his eye that made the breath catch in the back of my throat. So many times his ghost was petulant and whiny as my Will had never been. This time he was all Will.

He chuckled.

"Zachary Coe," I said.

Will looked disappointed.

"I've just had the news that he was found floating face-down in Sutton Pool."

I was? Oh my! A skinny figure appeared floating facedown in the room at my shoulder height. He wasn't quite solid in appearance, yet not quite ghostly either. I almost felt I could touch him, but I'd tried that with Will and it never worked.

"Mr. Coe, kind of you to drop in. I wish we were meeting under better circumstances."

Am I—?

"Deceased. I'm afraid so. What do you remember?"

A man. Walking darkness with a pockmarked face. Not old, except for his eyes. Hard eyes.

"At the Guildhall?"

Lord love you, ma'am, no, not at the Guildhall.

"What happened at the Guildhall? Did you enquire about the deeds to the house?"

I did. As soon as I mentioned the address, the pen-pusher fetched another man and he invited me to step into another room. Asked me who my client was. I used to clerk for a lawyer, ma'am.

"Yes, I know, Mr. Coe. Do go on."

Told him about client confidentiality. That's when he called two more men.

"Watchmen?"

He shook his head and his whole body wobbled in midair.

"Are you quite comfortable like that, Mr. Coe?"

Tell the truth, ma'am. I can't feel no hurts anywhere, though I recall a pain in my chest. Terrible it was, but like it belonged to someone else.

"Try tucking your legs up under you, as if you were swimming, see if it sets you upright."

I can't swim, ma'am. Found facedown in Sutton Pool, you say?

I nodded.

He bent his knees and gradually his body rotated until it was upright, but he forgot to straighten his legs again and sank until he looked as though he was crouching on the floor.

Sorry, being dead takes a bit of getting used to.

"Take your time. There's no rush."

Will cleared his throat. *Actually there is. Mr. Coe has an appointment.*

I do? Zack Coe straightened his legs, shot up to the ceiling and settled back down to his feet.

"Where's he going?" I asked.

Will just looked at me. *I'm sorry, Ross, you know there are things I can't tell you, even if I wanted to, which I don't.*

I swallowed hard and then nodded.

Will turned to Coe. *So better hurry, Mr. Coe. Tell her what happened.* It was kindly said.

The new-made ghost drew himself up. *They took me to a place on Cockside. They blindfolded me, but I recognized the smell. That's where the man was. Dan'l Fairlow's a good man, gives me rum on the house when I'm empty in the pockets. I didn't want to give them his name.*

I huffed a sigh of relief. "Thank you."

Don't need to thank me. I'm not strong, I might have told them when they hurt me, but I couldn't speak for the pain of it. Like a fist through my chest, squeezing and squeezing. The darkness was a blessing. Found in Sutton Pool, you say?

His heart had given out before he could give them any information.

"Yes, Sutton Pool. I'm sorry for your pain."

It's over now.

Will stood up. *Time to go, Zack.* Will held out a hand for the ghost. *Don't worry, I'll see you safely there.*

Coming, Captain. He turned back to me. *Tell Dan'l thank you for the rum.*

"I will. Safe journey, Mr. Coe."

Ma'am. He touched his forelock as he faded from my sight.

The bed creaked and I turned to find David sitting up. "Your late husband's reluctance to move on is useful."

Sometimes it was, though there were obviously things he either couldn't or wouldn't tell me.

"You heard all that? How are you feeling?"

"I heard most of it, I think. Enough. And I'm all right, I

think. No more urges to blast my surroundings flat, at any rate."

"That's a mercy."

"So we're going to Skinner's Warehouse, right?"

"I'm going." I hesitated. David was so young.

"Not without me." His mouth set firmly and I recalled he was already the veteran of a skirmish at sea. "Let me go down to the fish dock now and watch the warehouse until you arrive, see if there's any unusual activity. I can find somewhere to hide myself."

It made sense. "Take a pair of eyeglasses. But you are only to watch. Don't get nabbed again." My voice caught in my throat. "No risks."

"No risks."

I'd have preferred Hookey at my back with his steel and his experience, but David would have to do.

18

Sutton Pool

MUCH LATER THAT NIGHT I dressed in sailor's clothes borrowed from Dan Fairlow. I strapped my knife around my waist. Pistols aren't weapons of secrecy, but in a tight corner a knife is worth gold. I threw a blanket around me, pulled it up over my shoulders and head, like a long cloak, and tiptoed down the wooden steps into the yard. There was the sound of revelry coming from inside the inn, but the yard was deserted, and the street beyond was quiet enough. I stepped into the archway a woman, shed my blanket behind a stack of barrels, and emerged on the other side a young man.

It didn't take long to weave my way through the shadows of the late-night streets. The few people still abroad either had their own business to take care of or they were too drunk to notice anyone but themselves. By the corner of the market square, I had to duck back into an alley to avoid a pair of watchmen, but otherwise the journey to Cockside was uneventful.

If the port was Plymouth's economic heart, and the New Town its brain, Cockside was its old soul. Some of the buildings here dated back to before the great fire and were built of stone, mortar weathered so much it almost looked like dry-stone walls. It smelled of mackerel and cod and lives intimately spent with tarry rope and buckets of fish guts. The fishing trade was less important to the city than it used to be, but a small fleet of fishing boats still sailed out under the watchful eye of the Boatmaster, a title passed down from father to son in the Skinner family. Their old warehouse, at the inconvenient end of the dock, had long since ceased to be the center of operations and for as long as I could remember had stood empty and more or less derelict.

It had once been a block shop, where the blocks and tackle for rigging had been manufactured by skilled craftsmen. I'd been inside its cavernous interior as a child, with my father, and he'd explained how they needed the height to run the lines and blocks for the tall ships, but I could barely imagine what it had been like in its heyday; its block shop history was long in its past, even then.

The dock was quiet, the fleet away, and as I checked the alleys for sleeping drunks and vagrants—sometimes the unexpected downfall of a well-planned robbery—I realized how little the place had changed since my childhood. My father's first business venture on his own account had rented the Skinner warehouse for storing empty sherry casks awaiting return to a vineyard in Portugal.

I wondered how my life would have turned out if my father had not been lost at sea. Would I have run off with Will or would I have tried to register as a witch? And what might have happened if I had? My magic wasn't like theirs. I would have exposed myself to Walsingham sooner, just as Philip had done.

No use pondering that. Stick to the business in hand.

I slipped on the spectacles, once more charged with light, and found David crouching down in the shadows opposite the remains of the old Friary Gate, once one of Plymouth's outer defenses, and now barely a ruin separating the west and east sides of Sutton Pool. Cockside, a jumble of dilapidated warehouses and tumbledown sheds, had seen better days.

Face suitably muddied to disguise his complexion, dressed in canvas work trousers, threadbare shirt, and sailor's jacket, kerchief around his head, David looked like any down-and-out sailor lad sleeping in a doorway.

"How goes it?" I whispered, crouching next to him.

"Very quiet." He slipped his eyeglasses into a pocket.

"Any comings and goings?"

He shook his head.

"Right. We'll search the warehouse as quick as we can."

"And?"

"Depends on what we find."

We slipped down an alleyway, following rusted iron wagon tracks where the mule train used to run.

David and I explored the warehouse's possible entrances. One side had its feet in the water. On the main thoroughfare, double doors big enough to drive a loaded wagon through were barred and locked. At the north end, I found a small solid door with a new lock.

Don't go in there. Will's ghost said. *It's a bad place.*

As David touched the door I heard his hiss of breath. "This has had magic used on it."

I told you not to go in.

David glanced at Will apprehensively.

"Shut up, Will. This is my business," I said.

"How are we going to get in?" David ducked into the shadows by the door. "Do you have any suitable magic?"

"I thought we'd do it the simple way." Tucked up my sleeve in a linen roll, I had a set of thieves' charms: lock-picks, with one long, flat-headed blade and an array of metal probes topped with different curves and hooks. "It's only a basic pin-and-tumbler lock." I knelt down. "I might even be able to rake it."

"What?"

"Like this." I inserted the flat blade to apply tension and slightly turned the barrel of the lock. Keeping the tension on with my left hand, I used a pick slightly broader than the rest and shoved it right to the back of the barrel then withdrew it sharply, feeling the pins bounce. The barrel turned and the bolt clicked back

"Where did you learn to pick locks?"

"Shhh, softly now. Some of the lads on board the *Heart* have useful skills to share. Ask Lazy Billy to show you sometime."

I brushed my knuckles against the now-unlocked door. "It's been warded, but I can clear it."

I put my hands flat to the door and pulled together threads of magic to unpick what was there already. Like using the lockpicks, but just as lockpicks were called *charms* in thieves' cant, this time I really was using the magical kind. The ward resisted and then dropped away.

"It's gone."

"That was too easy," David said.

"Maybe I'm just *that* good." I grinned. "Besides, it was only designed to keep out the dockside riff-raff, not someone magical."

"Are you sure?"

I shrugged.

"If Walsingham's already been looking for you in Plymouth," David said, "can whoever set this ward trace the breaking of it back to you?"

"I don't know. If they can it's too late now, so let's get this over with and get out of here. Tomorrow we definitely leave the Twisted Skein." I pushed open the door.

If you go in there I can't follow you, Will said.

Why not?

But he'd already gone.

We stepped inside, and I listened and *sensed* before putting up a witchlight. Now it was my turn to gasp. The middle of the cavernous building was completely clear except for a circle drawn on the floor in something dark and oily—possibly blood—with a five-pointed star inside it and symbols at the points. This was major work. The spell-caster would have had to offset the damage to himself with the life of something substantially bigger than a chicken.

Imagination provided me with a vision. A man, dangling by his heels, blood from slit wrists dripping into a bucket. A brush to inscribe the design on the floor, runes I couldn't begin to understand. A hard-eyed man with a pockmarked face, walking darkness, chanting a spell and then finishing it by slashing the throat of the already-dying man.

My vision gave the corpse Philip's face. Dear God, no! Please.

I gulped to push down rising gorge. Steady. It was my imagination. I had no evidence whatsoever.

But I knew Walsingham was at the heart of this.

In the center of the star, in a smaller circle, there was a dusting of fine white ash. If I looked toward it, the back of my eyeballs began to buzz and my spine crawled. This went beyond anything that a registered witch might be capable of.

David swayed toward it and I grabbed him by the arm, pinching his flesh until he shook himself and turned to look at me, eyes still a little glazed.

"I've never felt anything as dark as this before," I said. "Keep well clear."

David screwed up his eyes and gave a sharp little nod.

"That circle makes me feel sick to my stomach," he said, walking carefully around it. "What does it do?"

"I don't know. It's nothing I've ever seen before. Dark. It's dark and nasty."

The hairs on the back of my neck stood on end and I shivered involuntarily.

The remains of half-burnt floor joists and charred roof timbers were stacked neatly on one side of the room.

It had rained on the night my mother's home had burned, an unnatural rain prompted by my calling of the wind, so as I had guessed, not everything in the house had burned away as it might have. Someone had meticulously and methodically gone through the remains searching for the winterwood box, or clues to its whereabouts.

Stacked in tumbledown heaps on the other side of the space were the blackened remains of my childhood, some pieces quite recognizable: the mirror from my mother's dresser, cracked, splintered, bubbled; half the frame of the grand dining room table, its cabriole legs now charcoal, but still a distinctive shape. The massive library bookcase from my father's study remained surprisingly whole despite the blackened, blistered wood. The doorframes, now empty of glass, swung open, but the inner shelves looked almost untouched by flames, probably protected by tightly packed, leather-bound books, which must be . . . ah, yes.

My eyes were drawn to a rickety-looking stair. Up above, on a wooden gallery, there was a worktable, and on it piles of books. The steps creaked ominously as we climbed them. This whole ancient place needed demolishing before it fell to pieces and killed someone.

Some books lay scattered on the table, others were piled together, their leather spines blistered and blackened, but the pages oddly untouched in the center. Many of them were my father's. After his ship went down I used to sneak into his study and take out any one of them at random, thinking I could smell his pipe tobacco on its pages, though not in the least bit interested in *Naval Encounters in the New World* or *The Vintners' Register*.

My mother caught me one day and snatched up the book I was about to look at. "Never. Never. Never touch this bookcase again, young lady, or I'll thrash you black and blue." She'd delivered a hard slap to the back of my hand. Then she'd balanced on a chair and shoved the book high on a top shelf and locked the glass doors. Why didn't she want me to see that particular book? I tried to remember what it was, but I'd picked it off the shelf at random.

David stood across the other side of the table. "The missis taught me to read with these books. They were hers, too, not only your father's."

"They were?"

"She had me help her rearrange them one day so the ones she wanted were on the lower shelves. We put your father's company books up high."

"Was there anything she wouldn't let you see?"

"No, but it was before I could read very well, so it didn't really matter if I saw them or not, I suppose."

"There was something she didn't want me to see, but it's so long ago."

"Did you ever touch it?" he asked. "Can you search—with magic, I mean?"

"I did handle it, but only briefly, and all this fire damage . . ."

"Surely it's worth a try."

I wasn't great at searching by magic, but I thought back to the day when I'd handled the book. David reached across the table and I took his hands. As our fingers touched, power surged between us and I almost let him go, but he held on tight. A new world opened up in my mind. I sensed David and the presence of something sickly coming from the dark stain in the center of the circle. I could also sense another presence, two in fact. One was an echo of my mother, and the other one was unmistakably Philip.

Why was there no echo of Walsingham? Maybe he had learned how to conceal himself.

I shivered.

As if in reply the books on the table shuddered, and one of them, halfway down the main pile, seemed to be waiting for me. I let go of David. The magical buzz stopped so suddenly that the wrench rocked me back on my heels and I had to grab the table for balance. Carefully we lifted the scorched books away until the one I'd had snatched from me all those years ago sat atop the pile.

"The Secret Commonwealth of Elves, Fauns and Fairies." David read the title. "By the Reverend Robert Kirk."

Why had my mother kept this book when she'd rejected the magical world? I put my hand on it. The front board was completely loose, and it lifted away clear. The book beneath it was relatively untouched apart from a charred spine. It was old. The Reverend Robert Kirk, Minister of the Parish of Aberfoyle, Stirling, Scotland had written it in 1691. I turned a few pages and read:

"These Siths or Fairies they call Sleagh Maith or the Good People are said to be of middle nature between Man and Angel, as were Daemons thought to be of old; of intelligent fluidous Spirits, and light changeable bodies (lyke those called Astral) somewhat of the nature of a condensed cloud, and best seen in twilight. These bodies be so pliable through

the subtlety of Spirits that agitate them, that they can make them appear or disappear at pleasure."

David looked at it over my shoulder. "Fairies?"

"Fairies, Fae, Hobgoblins. The old beliefs. This book is over a hundred years old."

"You think people don't believe any more?"

"Not so much."

"What about the Green Man and his Lady?"

"I don't know. A remnant of what used to be, perhaps."

"Pretty powerful for a remnant."

When I'd been in their forest the whole world of magic had seemed so open to me. Since I'd returned to the sea, I'd let it fade.

I looked at the book again. There was nothing special about it. Maybe my mother had wanted to keep me away from anything even vaguely related to magic. I looked at David and shrugged.

"I can't see why she made such a fuss." But David's eyes were not on the book, they were on the inside of the cover where I'd placed it on the table. There was an inscription, faded into the heat-browned paper. I called the witchlight down from the rafters to shine brightly over our heads. The very top bit was burned away, but it looked like a date, and might have been the year before I was born. Below it was inscribed: *To M. I have tried and failed. Perhaps I was not firstborn. It's yours now. Be strong. Your loving sister, Rosie.*

My mother had a sister.

"We've got an Aunt Rosie." David's voice held wonder. "First a mother and now I've got an aunt. The Lady said the key was in family. Can we search, using the book?"

"After more than twenty years?"

"She must have touched it."

I put my hand flat on it, and David placed his next to mine, but as soon as our eyes met we both knew there was something wrong. It had already given up that secret to someone else.

"We'll get no more help from this," David said.

"So now all we have to do is find someone called Rosie Sumner who had a sister called Margery, and at the same time try to avoid people who want to kill us, or me at any rate, since I hope they don't know you're my brother."

He shrugged. "When you put it that way . . ."

A sound below made me snap off the witchlight. I grabbed David by the wrist and retreated against the wooden wall, crouching low, away from the edge of the stair, in the recess of a loading door above the dock. The main door downstairs creaked. Two sets of footsteps, some indistinct muttering, and the sound of steel striking flint preceded a low flare of light from somewhere beneath us.

I stretched out my hearing to catch what they were saying, but after the first mutterings they went about their business silently, but separately. I could hear one moving about below our gallery floor. The other stopped suddenly and cursed.

"Look at this, Figgis. It's witchery. I want none of it. This place was bad enough in the daytime wiv the old feller carkin' it as soon as he was asked a civil question."

"Shut yer trap, there'll be none of it left if yer do yer job. Noffink to 'ang us for. Make haste, fer gawd's sake. He's a-waitin' on the dockside, an' 'e ain't a man to be kept waiting."

Walsingham? Here? My heart was already trying to break out of my chest, but the thought of Walsingham out there, waiting, turned my blood to ice water.

There was a crash as one of the piles of neatly stacked timber was tipped, a sudden stink of whale oil. My gut sank, and I squeezed David's wrist tighter. There was a whoomp as the oil ignited and the low light from the men's lantern was overwhelmed by flames, not just from one area of the warehouse, but from several, including one right beneath the rickety open steps. I heard them call to each other, and then the main door rattled, and rattled louder, as if they'd found it bolted from the outside.

"Quick! Over 'ere!" Figgis shouted. He coughed and spat and I heard him push on the side door that we'd used earlier. That was also now locked. Whoever had sent Figgis and his partner in here to torch the place didn't intend for them to get out again. A perfect, self-cleaning operation.

Searing flames billowed up the stair, our only means of escape, and sparks roiled into the rafters. The boards beneath our feet began to smoke. It would be our shoes next. The fire's crackling roar and crack of timbers filled my ears. I wrapped my forearm across my nose and mouth to try to filter the choking air, but with little effect. My eyes streamed from the heat and the smoke until I could hardly see where I was.

Figgis and his friend hammered on the door below. Their shouts rose in both volume and pitch, pleas for aid that went unanswered. I stood and fumbled with the shutter on the window, but it was closed and barred.

One of them began to scream, not a cry for help but a throat-tearing, primal scream of agony. I clawed at the shutter again, redoubling my efforts, David adding his strength to mine.

"It's no good. Stand back," he yelled.

David's explosion of desperate energy turned the door and a good section of the wall to ash, both in front of us and below. Our gallery floor creaked ominously, some of its joists supported by nothing more than thin air and habit. Figgis and his mate had an opening below us. They were on their own. The timbers shifted. Collapse was imminent. I clutched David's hand. We ran and leaped off the splintering boards out into the night. All I could think was that I hoped there was water beneath us, and not a solid, moored-up coaling barge.

The icy shock of water knocked the air out of me. It closed over my head, drilled into my ears and nose. I clamped my mouth shut, trying not to gulp convulsively, and kicked for the surface. Somehow I still had hold of David's hand. I didn't even know whether he could swim. I came up under the edge of a barnacle-encrusted hull, grazed my shoulder, but had the sense to stick close to it, treading water. David's head broke the surface beside me. I heard him gasp.

"All right?" I asked.

"For now."

"Can you swim?"

"A bit."

I let him go and he leaned into the hull, too.

The timber warehouse blazed like a million torches. Sparks rained down into the water. Only the hull of the fishing boat protected us from the inferno, but it would soon be alight itself. And then the rest of the ships in Sutton Pool.

The boat rocked as if someone had jumped into it, maybe Figgis or his partner. It began to drift away from the dock, released from its mooring. We drifted with it, protected from the worst of the flaming debris. Not until we were well into the middle of Sutton Pool did I tap David on the shoulder and begin to swim away. He followed me, and we reached the shelter of the moored craft on the Foxhole side, working our way around to the slipway by New Quay, where we staggered out of the water, thoroughly exhausted and almost too heavy to walk.

A crowd had gathered, their attention on the fire. The tumbledown buildings on Cockside could all go up like so much dry tinder. No one would be sorry to see the end of Skinner's warehouse, but if it took the rest of Cockside with it, and the shipping in the pool, there'd be hell to pay. Men ran for buckets and a fire crew shoved off from Plymouth Steps in a barge with a water-pumping engine and hoses on it.

David overbalanced and fell, dragging me down with him.

"It's all right, I've got you," a familiar voice said in my ear. "I've got him, too."

Mr. Corwen!

"What—?"

"Don't try to talk. You're in no danger from me." His arm wrapped itself around my waist, and he almost picked up David with the other arm. He was stronger than he looked. Like three drunks we staggered back to the Twisted Skein. He even retrieved my blanket from where I'd dropped it behind barrels in the alley. By that time I could stand by myself, and so could David, though he still supported himself with one hand on the wall.

"Mr. Corwen—" I tried again.

"Mrs. Webster. No need for words right now. I'll bid you good night and urge you to get into some dry clothes as soon as you can. It's cool for September, and I wouldn't want you to catch your death of cold. Either of you."

He nodded to David, a short, sharp movement picked out by the light of a lantern burning at the far end of the inn yard, and then he was gone.

19

Moving On

EXHAUSTED, David and I both fell onto the bed in my room. I expected Will's ghost to pay a visit, but he didn't show up. Within minutes David's breathing was deep and regular, but I couldn't sleep for thoughts chasing themselves around in circles.

I should get up right now and drag David as far away from Mr. Corwen as I could get, but my legs wouldn't move. If Mr. Corwen had wanted to turn us in to the authorities, he'd have done it by now.

If only I knew more about Mr. Corwen, the box, Walsingham and Philip. Right now I knew just enough to lead me into danger and not enough to get me out of it.

Finding Philip and the rest of my family suddenly became important for all sorts of reasons, as did finding out more about the box. I couldn't walk away from something I didn't understand, at least not until I knew more.

But the Twisted Skein was definitely no longer safe for us.

At first light, I was up and washing the stink of Sutton Pool out of my hair and clothes in a bucket of cold water. The clothes I'd borrowed from Dan were pitted with burn holes from flying sparks and had a huge scorch mark on one sleeve. Examining them closely made me realize how close we'd come to a horrible end.

Having done the best I could for now, I dressed in my green linsey-woolsey and packed everything else neatly. Leaving David sleeping, I turned up for breakfast as early as I could, hoping to avoid Mr. Corwen, but he was already at his usual table. After last night I could hardly snub him when he stood and asked if I would join him.

He was one of those annoying people who looked as good in the morning as he did at night. After my adventures, I doubted that I was at my best. Maybe if he'd had to jump out of the upper floor of a burning building into the harbor he might look a little more haggard.

"I'm afraid I'm bad company at breakfast before my third cup of coffee, Mr. Corwen. You'll have to forgive my lack of scintillating conversation."

"In that case . . ." he got up from the table, crossed over to the kitchen and brought me a huge cup of coffee, black and sweetened exactly as I like it.

"Ahh." I couldn't help sighing as I tasted it. "Very observant. That's perfect."

He grinned at me. "Self-preservation, I assure you. I would hate to be the object of your anger. I make it a point of honor never to argue with a lady who wears a concealed knife at her waist, especially when she's in need of coffee."

I froze with my cup halfway to my lips. I did indeed wear my leather-sheathed knife strapped horizontally behind me in the small of my back, beneath the flounce of my dress. I had only to reach my right hand behind my waist to grasp it through a concealed opening beneath a pleat.

He smiled. "A very sensible precaution for a lady traveling alone."

"I'm not traveling alone."

"Your rowankind companion . . ." I was pleased he didn't say servant. "How old is he? Fifteen at most. Hardly a bodyguard. In fact I suspect if there's any guarding to be done, Mrs. Webster, that lot might fall to you." He smiled. "But where is the lad this morning?"

“Sleeping.”

I prepared to fend off more questions about why my servant was abed while I was up and about, but they didn’t come. Him finding us half-drowned and singed around the edges might never have happened. Instead, breakfast arrived, hot and savory. There was blood pudding, kippers, bacon, coddled eggs, and stewed plums, plus a hunk of freshly baked bread, some cool butter, and a little strong cheese, all of it washed down with more coffee.

“I’m sorry to be so hasty, Mr. Corwen.” I got up from the table almost before I’d finished the last mouthful, and I could tell I’d caught him by surprise.

“I was hoping to invite you to stroll along Plymouth Hoe later this morning. I hear that it’s bracing at this time of year with the sea breezes.”

“I’m afraid I have business to attend to. I’m leaving this morning.”

“I’m sorry to hear that. I live in hope that our paths may cross again.” He stood while I left the table, then sat down to finish his own coffee.

I still couldn’t shake the conviction that I’d met him before, and I determined that David and I would truly be out of Plymouth by tomorrow morning at the latest.

Then where to? Will’s ghost asked.

“I don’t know. To find Philip, or to find our aunt. Wherever the quest leads us.”

And if it doesn’t lead anywhere?

“Back to the *Heart* I suppose, now that I know how to shield the box.”

Good enough.

By the time I’d settled up for our board and lodging with the Twisted Skein’s landlord and arranged for my bags to be stored until I could send one of Dan Fairlow’s boys to collect them, David had charmed his way into breakfast in the kitchen with Annie. He took his leave of her with a sigh, then we walked down through Old Town, taking a detour to avoid Market Street, the Guildhall and the Watch office. We turned right toward Southside and the Ratcatchers.

Dan ushered us into his kitchen again. "Everything all right, Cap'n?"

I nodded. "For now, but we need a place to stay if you can accommodate us."

"Of course. I've got a room at the back, off the yard."

As we stepped out of the Ratcatchers' front door to go around to the yard, I almost bumped into a tall, silver-haired figure.

"Mrs. Webster, David." He gave us both a polite nod.

"Mr. Corwen. What a surprise."

And not a pleasant one either. This was surely more than coincidence.

"Indeed." He glanced at the street, as rough and as businesslike as you may find in any dockside neighborhood, with taverns, small shipping offices and two rival chandlers side by side. "I thought you'd left town. I wouldn't expect to find a lady on business down here."

"That shows that your expectations of ladies are sometimes misguided. Good morning."

I stepped around him and walked on quickly, knowing he couldn't follow me unless he deliberately turned around. I found myself shaking inside.

Once around the corner of the building, I stopped and leaned against the wall, took three deep breaths, and popped back to watch Mr. Corwen as he strode toward the New Quay.

"Is he bothering you, Cap'n?" Dan asked. "You want I should find someone to deal with him?"

I looked at him blankly for a moment, thinking of alternatives, but I had no proof against him, so Mr. Corwen was one innocent man too many. I shook my head. "No, leave him be—for now."

We might have ended our quest right then and gone home to the *Heart* having reached a dead end, but the enquiries I'd asked Dan to make to find Captain Ezra Pargeter, otherwise known as Captain Cyclops for his one eye, bore fruit the very next morning. When I came down into the kitchen, Dan was already making up the fire in the inglenook. He straightened up and handed me a scrap of paper with an address scribbled on it.

I ran up and changed swiftly from my gray morning dress into my breeches and jacket. The address Dan had given me was not more than a quarter-hour walk from the Ratcatchers, but it took me a little time to find the right door in the middle of the mean streets behind the market. I knocked and waited. I could hear movement inside and eventually the scraping of a heavy bolt being drawn back. The door opened a crack, and a wary face peered out at me from the gloom. She was rowankind, maybe sixtyish, with pinched cheeks and flyaway hair. She seemed disinclined to open the door more than a few inches.

"I'm looking for Captain Ezra Pargeter," I said.

She shook her head and would have closed the door, but a voice from the hallway said, "Captain Pargeter, is it? See, Minna, someone knows about my ship. Show him in, girl, show him in!"

She looked over her shoulder and backed away from the door.

"He's not well, sir," she said quietly.

"Well? Well? I'm as fit as a flea, sir, and don't let anyone tell you any different. You've only just caught me. Due to sail on the tide, don'tcha know?"

"I didn't know, sir. I'll not keep you long."

I followed Pargeter into his tiny parlor crowded with the souvenirs of a lifetime on the ocean. He was eighty if he was a day, with a bush of snow-white whiskers and a black eyepatch. He had a fierce tremor in his left hand, but he was still turned out neatly in a blue sailing jacket now a little loose on his shrunken frame.

"Well, come in, boy, come in. What can I do for you? Have you found my ship yet? I have a cargo of mixed goods for our colony in Virginia, but I seem to have mislaid my ship."

I looked at Minna and she shook her head slightly.

"And you are, sir?" he asked.

"Goodliffe, sir, Philip Goodliffe." I bowed.

He returned my bow, if a little stiffly.

"My wife, Mrs. Pargeter, Mr. Goodliffe." He waved to the rowankind woman, who looked flustered. I noticed no ring on her finger, but there were many good partnerships not recognized by the church.

"Mrs. Pargeter." I bowed.

"Would you like some tea, Mr. Goodliffe?" she asked.

"Goodliffe? Goodliffe?" Pargeter stared out of the window, perhaps seeing the past rather than the street. "Used to have a first mate name of Goodliffe. Any relation?"

"My father, sir. You took him on when he came to Plymouth from . . ." I hoped he might fill in the blank if I left the sentence hanging, but he was off on a tack of his own.

"Good ship, the *Mary Anne*," he said and sat in a chair pulled right up to the meager fire. The varnish on the chair's front legs, blistered by the heat, testified to a fiercer fire in more prosperous times. I noticed the coal bucket was almost empty.

"It's about my father, sir."

"Good man, 'bout time he captained a ship of his own. Wasted as a first mate. Tell him to come and see me. I might be able to speak to a few people. Might have forgotten where I anchored my ship, but I never forget a good sailor." He leaned forward conspiratorially. "Minna says I'm a mad old man, but I have a long memory. Now if only I could remember where I put it, hey?" He laughed.

Minna came back in with a tray balancing a teapot, two china cups and saucers, a milk jug, and a bowl with the tiniest amount of sugar in the bottom.

"Are you not having a cup yourself, Mrs. Pargeter?" I asked.

"I'm . . . we're not . . . It wouldn't be proper."

"Of course it would. Let me pour for the captain while you get another cup."

Minna bustled out.

"I'm trying to contact family," I told Captain Pargeter as

I handed him his tea, making sure I put the cup handle into his right hand, as that seemed steadiest. "When my father first came into your employ, do you happen to know where he came from?"

"Simpler to ask him yourself, boy. Well, sit ye down. Don't make the cabin look untidy."

I sat on the only other chair. "He's not yet returned from his latest voyage," and never would, "and this is a matter of some urgency."

"Seem to recall he was from somewhere inland. Odd for a sailor, but seemed to make no difference to his quality. I can tell the quality of a man immediately, and your father is the best."

"My mother told me you stood witness at their wedding."

"I did, sir, and happy I was to do it. Have you seen my ship? She's taking on cargo for the colonies. We sail on the tide."

"I spoke to your first mate, sir."

"Bowers."

"Yes, Mr. Bowers, that's the fellow. He said to tell you that the cargo was still on the quay, sir, and not to worry, he would send a boy for you once it was loaded. I fancy it might be tomorrow's tide, now, sir, or even the day after."

"That's good news, Ezra." Minna returned with a third cup. "I would so like you to stay at home for a little longer."

"Of course, my dear, of course."

She came to stand behind him and put her hand on his shoulder. He reached up and patted it with his left hand, and she grasped his trembling fingers to steady them and shook her head at me.

I wasn't going to get what I'd come for, so I stood to take my leave and placed my cup and saucer back on the tray. "Thank you for seeing me, sir."

"It's always good to see old friends, Mr. Goodliffe. Chard."

"What, sir?"

"Chard. It's where your parents came from."

"Thank you, Captain."

"You're welcome, son, I'm sorry I can't offer you a position. Already have a damned good first mate, name of Teague Goodliffe. Do you know him?"

"I've had that honor. Good day to you, sir."

Minna followed me to the door. "Take no notice, sir, he mostly doesn't know what day it is and his mind drifts back thirty years or more. There's nothing improper goes on in this household. Nothing the church wouldn't like."

"Of course. But I see you take good care of the captain. He did my father a great service many years ago. Is there anything I can do for you?"

"We manage, sir."

"Of course." I resolved to have Dan send some bags of coal. "Good day, Mrs. Pargeter."

I almost skipped back to the Ratcatchers. Chard was one of the places Philip had mentioned. Coincidence? Maybe, but it was the best lead we had.

I had arranged to meet the *Heart*, fresh from her refit and repairs, off the Cornubian coast, so all we needed was passage on any vessel sailing west out of Plymouth on the evening tide. I'd called her, so the *Heart* would find us. Dan secured us passage on the *Troubadour*. With three hours to go before the tide turned, David and I sat in Dan's kitchen, drinking tea. I knew I'd lose enough fluid once our ship reached the open ocean, so I needed to coat my stomach now. I heard the outer door and then Dan's voice and another, slightly raised. A slight scuffling followed. By the time the kitchen door opened, I had one of my pistols out of my petticoat pocket with the doghead drawn back. As he barged through the door I was already pointing it at Mr. Corwen's chest. The look of surprise on his face was entirely gratifying.

"Mr. Corwen. If you'd be so kind as to sit down please. I don't want to hurt you, but I must protect my own interests."

Mr. Corwen took a step toward me. "I came to warn you that a party of gentlemen—not the watch—came looking for you at the Twisted Skein. They almost tore your room apart looking for something. Please, I'd hate for you to shoot me accidentally. I mean you no harm. Surely I've proven that already?"

"I'm not in the habit of shooting anyone accidentally, I can assure you." My hand was steady. "And all you've proven to me is that you know things about me which are dangerous. Dangerous to yourself, I mean. Right now I don't know whether to shoot you or thank you, Mr. Corwen, but you truly are the most annoying man I've ever met."

"I won't tell anyone where you are, if that's what you're worried about." He ignored the pistol pointing at his chest, stepped forward against the muzzle, narrowing the gap between us, close enough for me to feel the warmth radiating from him. "I would suggest that you leave the town as soon as possible if you have all the information you need."

"How do you know what I need?"

"I'll tell you later."

"There won't be a later."

"I'm not the one you need to fear."

Hookey would have shot him by now, as would Will, but I wasn't them.

I looked into Mr. Corwen's face, searching for any duplicity, and found none. I released the doghead of the pistol slowly and nodded. "Thank you. Please go before I change my mind."

I watched him walk out of the door, hoping I was a good judge of character.

20

The *Troubadour*

THE *TROUBADOUR* was an American barque, a real workhorse, three-masted, fore-and-aft rigged on the mizzenmast and square-rigged on the fore and main. Though built in Liverpool, she now sailed out of Baltimore. Her captain, Henry Foster, ran a tight ship. I liked him for it. His no-nonsense attitude reminded me of Mr. Sharpner.

There were eleven passengers altogether. David and I shared a cramped cabin with a graying widow and her three boys, impoverished gentlefolk traveling to relatives in the New World. Another cabin housed a merchant and his niece, and a third accommodated three gentlemen, all traveling separately, one of whom had not yet come on deck.

With no guns on board, I found myself thinking that the *Troubadour* would be a soft target for pirates.

"Ma'am." A pleasant looking American gentleman of late middle years strolled along the deck, tipped his hat to me, and passed by as I stood by the aft rail watching Sutton Pool, the pier, and the navy's Victualling Office slide past. We sailed beneath the Citadel's gun emplacements and the battery on the hill across the water. Boney would have a hard time of it if he tried to invade Plymouth from the sea.

"Do you miss Plymouth?" David came to my elbow.

"Not really, do you?"

"When Missis brought me here . . ." I noticed he rarely called her Mother, though he would sometimes refer to her as *our mother*. "I was homesick for Kent and my first family. Plymouth felt too big, too noisy, and it stank of fish, but after a while I found I liked it. Evy was kind to me, and I could always make a bit of time for myself between doing the missis's fetching and carrying. And Missis taught me more than just letters and numbers. When Evy and the stable-lad were sent to other places last year, I had the whole ordering of the household."

"You could have escaped then if you'd wanted to."

"I could, but who would have looked after the missis? She wasn't unkind to me, and it was plain I'd get my freedom sooner or later. I figured the closer I was to grown and educated, the more chance I had of keeping it. And besides, I was starting to come into my magic during those last few months, and being around other people would have been dangerous. Missis was too sick to notice."

"What do you remember about Philip? Did he have magic when he was at home?"

"Not that I knew of, but he wasn't around much. When Missis broke the news to him that the money was all gone and he'd have to be done with Eton College, he kicked up a real fuss and went up to London to stay with friends. I heard Missis say she disapproved of his sponging off people, and that caused another row. Soon afterward she received news of his death, and that was the beginning of the end for her."

David turned to stare as the Citadel slipped by off the starboard side, but I could tell he wasn't really watching the view. He lapsed into silence and we stood at the rail, both lost in memories.

As the harbor tugs let go of the hawsers and the *Troubadour* shook free and filled her sails, the last passenger emerged from the gentlemen's cabin, and I recognized his silver hair even before I saw his face.

"Mr. Corwen. Should I have used my pistol this morning?"

"Why, Mrs. Webster, what an unexpected but very pleasant surprise."

I was about to give him chapter and verse on surprises when the *Troubadour* crossed the harbor bar. The first wave from the turbulent waters of Plymouth Sound slapped into her flank, and she pitched and rolled. One minute I was spitting angry, the next I was miserably seasick. I barely made it to the rail in time. David was already there. We could resolve the question of Corwen when the *Heart* came. I put him out of my mind as I made my way down to our tiny, cramped cabin, squirmed into my hammock, no mean feat in a dress, and tried to sleep through the successive bouts of nausea.

David found it easier in the fresh air, but I liked the enclosed darkness of the cabin. The Widow Montague and her boys wisely gave me as much peace and privacy as they could. I can't have been a charming companion even after I got past the stage of dry-heaving.

By midafternoon on the second day my head was as clear as it was going to get, so I sponged down what bits of me could be sponged with half a pint of cold water and felt much better for it. We felt to be running calm with a steady breeze, and the *Troubadour* cut through the gentle swell without yawing. I decided to go up on deck. Maybe I'd tackle Mr. Corwen if he was about.

He wasn't, so I settled myself on a raised hatch by the mainmast and closed my eyes, breathing in the salt tang of the air and listening to the sounds of a well-run ship. The *Troubadour* handled beautifully, and Captain Foster, a fine seaman, had full measure of her.

"Sail off the starboard bow!"

I heard the lookout and stared across the water, but from deck height I couldn't see anything.

"Ship in distress, Cap'n," the lookout called from the tops.

The captain swept the horizon with his glass to one eye and ordered a change of course. No sailor left another in distress upon the sea.

David trotted down the deck. He still looked faintly green from the sickness, but the news had begun to put color in his cheeks. "Do you think it's the *Heart*?" he asked.

"Possibly. There's no way Mr. Sharpner will take risks with us on board the *Troubadour*. He could be running a rig, playing the bird with the broken wing to get the *Troubadour* close enough to hail."

But it wasn't the *Heart*. It was a schooner with her sails in tatters listing several degrees to starboard. There was no sign of life aboard, but her spars and timbers were undamaged.

Our passengers crowded to the starboard rail to view the stricken vessel, two of the gentlemen admiring her clean lines and guessing at her salvage value. I hovered by the head of the companionway where I could see everything Captain Foster did because, just as when you fight a man you should look at his eyes, not his hands, aboard a well-run ship you should always watch the captain. He remained cool and professional and sent two more lads up aloft to look in all directions for survivors or boats.

I had a bad feeling about this.

"Captain Foster, may I borrow your glass?"

He looked surprised. "Mrs. Webster, I'm somewhat preoccupied at the moment."

I held out my hand, palm up, and rather than argue he slapped the glass into it.

I gave it a little magical boost and my blood ran cold when I saw, at four points along the port deck rail of the distressed schooner, piles of canvas that had no need to be there.

Patting the pistol in my pocket I said, "Captain, she's carrying eight guns. See there—the crumpled canvas." I handed Foster the enhanced spyglass. "She's a pirate running a rig and we're already precious close."

He raised the glass. "By God, you're right. Mr. Ramsden, bring her around."

As the *Troubadour* wheeled away I heard a shout from one of the gentlemen passengers. Pirates erupted onto the schooner's deck and they began clearing canvas from four six-pound culverins on the port side—aiming to fire a broadside at us. They swiftly chopped away the tattered sails and hoisted a clean mainsail—gaff rigged, fore and aft—into place.

We were five hundred yards away and already had the wind in our sails, but if she brought her guns to bear quickly she'd rake us from behind without a by-your-leave.

I yelled at Mr. Corwen, "Get the passengers for'ard belowdecks and keep them down."

I heard Mrs. Montague's voice rise to a shriek, but Mr. Corwen had the smaller of the boys in one arm and was already shepherding the others away from the vulnerable stern. Their mother followed, flapping like a seagull. The merchant and his niece bolted for the for'ard companionway, as did one of the gentlemen, but the pleasant American was slow to move, and when the broadside came he was caught with a long splinter of timber in his thigh as a lucky shot struck below the aft rail. Another ball ripped through the top rigging, but two fell short.

Mr. Corwen and a sailor dragged the American to safety and delivered him to a man who came running with a bag of what I hoped were clean bandages.

I started counting. "Three minutes, Captain Foster, and then you can expect another one of those, but better aimed."

Will's ghost appeared on deck.

Where's the Heart, *Will?*

Just over the horizon. She's on her way up from the south. The pirate's one of Gentleman Jim's fleet. The Bitter Bird. *Captain's a sly bugger called Jackson.*

"Useful, isn't he?" Mr. Corwen had sent his charges below and was now staring at Will.

So Mr. Corwen could see ghosts, and hear them, too. I didn't have time to follow up on the information, but I stored it away. I had an idea, now, where I'd seen those eyes before. Though my rational mind told me it was an impossibility, the magical world was stranger, more wonderful, and possibly more terrifying than I had ever dreamed. I yanked my thoughts back to the job at hand, away from Mr. Corwen and my suspicions.

"Captain Foster. That schooner's one of James Mayo's fleet."

"You seem to know a lot about this, Mrs. Webster."

"Let's say I'm in the shipping business. Two and a half minutes."

"What?"

"Since the broadside."

Foster gave his orders and lengthened the gap between the two ships with deft seamanship. At three and a half minutes a second broadside thundered out. Two balls went wide and long, but one clipped the mizzenmast and another ploughed into the stern, dangerously close to the water line.

"Count three minutes, Mr. Corwen." I put my hand on Foster's arm. "Turn south, Captain. And I'll give you a fair wind."

"What are you talking about?"

"This."

A fresh breeze filled his sails and I heard him yelling orders to trim canvas. My stomach lurched but I pushed the seasickness away.

"Two minutes," Mr. Corwen called.

But with every minute we were leaving the schooner behind.

"Three minutes."

At three and a half minutes another broadside boomed out, but we had more of a safety margin now.

"Sail, ho!" The lookout cried.

"That will be the *Heart*," I heard David say, but I was still too wrapped up in giving the *Troubadour* wind and water.

The *Heart* put a single shot across our bow, more of a question than a warning. And I let the breeze die back.

The Widow Montague and her sons had come up on deck, and she set to screaming again until the merchant put his hand on her arm.

"What's this?" Foster, roared. "Another one?"

"No, Captain, she's a friend."

"We're holed, Cap'n." The first mate sprang up from the aft companionway. "Just above the water line."

"Is she shipping water?"

"Aye."

"Get below and plug the leak, Mr. Ramsden. Hands to the pumps." He turned to me. "I hope you're right about yon ship, Mrs. Webster."

"I am, sir. She's the *Heart of Oak* sailing under letters of marque from the British Crown. Let her get within hailing distance and you'll have your proof."

"And if this is another trap, I have a pistol with a ball in it for you."

I reached into my petticoat pocket and pulled out one of the pair of gold-burnished pistols. "As indeed do I, Captain. You may hold this for me as a sign of my good faith."

"Don't they come in twos?" I heard Mr. Corwen ask David quietly.

The *Heart of Oak* eased to within a hundred yards of us. I pointed aft to where the schooner, the *Bitter Bird*, was on the horizon.

Hookey signaled that he'd understood, and Mr. Sharpner brought the *Heart* around between the *Troubadour* and the *Bitter Bird* and hoisted the parley flag, but at the same time ran out his guns.

"What's happening?" Captain Foster asked.

"My crew is politely asking their crew to turn and go on their way."

"Just like that?"

"Not quite." I smiled. "The *Heart* will be laying prior claim to the *Troubadour*, and by the treaty forged between Will Tremayne and Gentleman Jim Mayo, the *Bitter Bird* will have to give way or start a war between Bacalao and the Dark Islands."

"How can she lay prior claim?"

"Because, Captain Foster, I'm already aboard and I have a pistol pointing right at your belly. As Mr. Corwen so cleverly spotted, Mr. Bunney of London makes this particular model of pistol by the brace." I pulled the doghead back on the second pistol. "Just for the record, consider yourself taken."

Before he could begin to bluster I eased the doghead back down. "But I want nothing from you except your co-operation and my spare pistol back. David and I will be transferring to the *Heart.* If you would be so good as to have my bags brought up and a boat lowered, I'd be obliged."

"And mine, too," Mr. Corwen said. "I'm going with them."

I ignored him. "Captain, do you need any assistance with the damage to your vessel?"

"Mr. Ramsden?" Captain Foster had a bellow that would cut through all but the strongest of gales.

Mr. Ramsden stuck his head above the companionway.

"Damage?"

"Nothing we can't deal with, Cap'n."

I nodded. "Then, if you'll excuse me, Captain." I turned to Mr. Corwen. "You and I need to talk." I beckoned him to the ship's rail. "I want to know why you've been following me and who sent you."

He nodded. "A fair question. I'll tell you when we're safe on board your boat."

"I certainly can't promise *you'll* be safe on board, and she's *not* a boat!"

He raised one eyebrow.

"Who are you, Mr. Corwen?"

"When we're on your boat." He pronounced boat very clearly, just to be annoying.

I could get rid of him instantly by leaving him on the *Troubadour*, bound for Boston, but if I did I'd never know for sure who he was, and whoever sent him could send someone else, someone I might not identify so easily.

I nodded. "All right. Get your things."

"Permission to come aboard, Captain?" I kept my face straight as the *Troubadour*'s boat pulled up to the *Heart.*

"Permission granted, Cap'n." Hookey's face split into a big grin.

I wasn't used to climbing in a skirt, but I managed. David and Mr. Corwen followed, and the lads manhandled our luggage.

There was a low whistle from one of the crew. Hookey turned and glared at Lazy Billy, who looked somewhere in the region of his feet.

"Sorry, Cap'n," Billy said, slightly bashful. "It's just that you makes a nice woman, I mean."

"It's all right, Billy. I'll take it as a compliment, just don't get any big ideas. I still carry a brace of pistols."

"No, Cap'n. Course not, Cap'n."

I couldn't help it, I cracked out laughing, and Hookey gave a great hoot and slapped his thigh.

I was too absorbed by the accounts of the *Heart*'s refit and the schooner they'd recently taken just off the port of Brest to worry about Mr. Corwen at first, but once the *Troubadour*'s sails were over the horizon I turned to him.

He was still staring around him, taking in details of the *Heart* and her crew.

"Now, Mr. Corwen. Tell all. Who are you? Where are you from and who sent you?"

He gestured down the length of the deck. "It's a fine boat. I can feel there's winterwood in her making. No wonder you're not seasick on her."

"Who sent you, Mr. Corwen?"

"Just Corwen will do. The Lady. She feels the tide of magic moving. She sent me to be her eyes and ears and also her mouth should the need arise. She told you she would be sending me as your guide."

That clinched my suspicions. I remembered the silver wolf in the forest and how familiar Corwen's eyes had been, without being able to connect him with any memory of a human.

"You're a werewolf!"

"Please. A shapechanger."

I laughed at the hierarchy of magic. Those ruled by the

moon would always be at the bottom. "Why didn't you tell me in Plymouth?"

"I thought you'd have guessed. Did you not feel this?" He brushed his fingers against the back of my hand and suddenly it was as if I was in the Okewood. Magic leaped up within me to meet Corwen's. I shuddered and drew in a long breath.

"I always have trouble with my magic on land." I stepped back a pace hurriedly. "I don't need it at sea as well."

He inclined his head. "My apologies."

"Why should she want to help me? And why you?"

"The Lady—"

"Interferes in my life, but it's you we're talking about now."

"I am her loyal servant."

"So what now? I don't need a watchdog, or even a watch-wolf."

The grin that had been close to the surface blossomed fully now. Had I noticed how clean and sharp his teeth were before? "All the same, I am commanded."

"I'm not."

I turned to Hookey, who was hovering nearby. "Mr. Corwen will be our honored guest for a while."

"Ah, right you are. I got a nice little berth belowdecks."

"That sounds perfect." I winked at Hookey, and light as you like, he and Sim snapped a set of irons onto Corwen's wrists. Using the word *honored* when I said Corwen would be our guest had been their clue to have them ready.

"Put an iron collar on him, too," I said. "About the size of a very large dog collar."

Corwen stiffened and turned. "You can't—"

"Actually, Mr. Corwen, I can. You're lucky I don't have you thrown overboard. I don't take lightly to people meddling in my affairs—even with the best of intentions."

I let Corwen off with that, giving him into Sim's charge instead of Hookey's, knowing that Hookey tended to guard me jealously and Corwen's interest disturbed him. Though I no longer feared that the shapechanger meant me immediate harm, I certainly didn't want him getting involved in my business.

The Lady of the Forests wasn't human, and her concerns were not for the affairs of humans. I didn't doubt that, in order to preserve whatever magical balance she saw fit, that she would sacrifice me or David or both of us together with no more regret than stepping on a twig. I was going inland without Corwen Silverwolf.

But first things first. I needed to get rid of the extra magical energy that I'd picked up from Corwen—and from my time on land—and let it dissipate safely. Aboard ship there were limited ways I could do that. I changed into breeches and jacket and went up on deck to where Mr. Sharpner had the watch as the sun sank low on the western horizon.

"How many knots are we making Mr. Sharpner?"

"Seven, Cap'n."

"I have some energy to burn, how do you fancy a fast run to Lyme Regis?"

"As long as she doesn't go arse over head."

"I'll not pitchpole her, don't worry. Trim your sail, let's see if we can double that speed."

That's my girl, Will said, perched up on a tops'l spar.

We topped fifteen knots and, by keeping the delicate balance between the action of wind on the sails and water on the keel, I was magically exhausted and yet at the same time strangely exhilarated by the time we stood off the bay.

Hookey was torn between his new position as temporary captain of the *Heart* and his desire to come with us, but this was family business, and I had no call dragging a seaman away from the ocean. He readily agreed to meet me with the *Heart* in London, where I thought I might need help to flush out Walsingham and get my brother back.

21

The Young Gentleman

IT WAS EARLY IN THE FORENOON when the *Heart*'s boat deposited us on the beach, me holding up my green skirt out of the shallow water. With my breeches and shirt tucked away in the bottom of a battered portmanteau that had belonged to Will, David and I took an uncomfortable and overcrowded coach ride to Axminster for the first leg of our journey. Not granted space on the bench, David was crammed in at my feet. I was staring out of the window when someone muttered something about how, in his day, their rowankind used to run behind. I wasn't sure which of the three gentleman sitting opposite me had said that, but I looked around and glared at them all, wishing for Corwen's easy attitude toward the rowankind. But Corwen was sailing fast toward the Lizard, where I'd asked Hookey to put him ashore. That should keep him out of my hair.

As we traveled away from the sea, a burning ache built up in my gut and my magic swelled inside me. I concentrated on keeping it at manageable levels as the road took us inland across rolling hills.

In Axminster we found the coach that had been due to

take us on to Chard had cracked an axle. With the holdup, the regular coaching inn was full, and so David and I were directed to a very small establishment around the corner and down a narrow alley.

We were welcomed by Mr. Emery, but it soon became clear that he had outside work to do and we retired early to clean rooms, one each, a luxury.

The following morning, it fell to his mother to prepare breakfast. She insisted on making us a pot of hot tea thickened with goats' milk and honey. She kept staring at David.

"Is he one o' the Fae, missis?" she said to me in hushed, almost reverent tones.

"I'm rowankind."

When David spoke for himself she almost jumped back a pace.

"Sorry, master." She bobbed her head to him as she had not to me. "Is the tea to your liking?"

I was going to say that I preferred it without milk—many years at sea had trained me out of wanting or needing to soften my drinks—but I realized she wasn't talking to me.

"It's very fine," David reassured her. "Just how I like it."

"You don't have any rowankind here?" I asked. I certainly hadn't seen any.

"Oh, missis, of course not. I'm an Axminster girl, born and bred, and we were allus taught that having the likes of they doing our bidding wouldn't be seemly."

"They?"

"Magic folks, missis. The Shining Ones. Fae. Like in the old stories."

"I don't know the old stories."

"Oh, yes, missis, you know: *The Fae and the Shoemaker*, *The Swan Princess*. You know the one, where the princess saves her brothers by going as a tithe to the Fae so the crops won't fail and the kingdom won't split asunder." She looked at me sideways. "You know, missis. Old stories."

"I remember *The Elves and the Shoemaker*. The elves help a poor shoemaker by leaving new-made boots and shoes on his workbench every morning."

"Oh, no, missis. That's not the real version. That's the one they tell the kiddies. There ain't no such thing as elves—leastways not that I've ever seen—though my ma said she'd seen a liddle ol' pixie or two when she were a girl in Cornwall. In the real version it's the Fae. They're the most powerful, though the rowankind is magic folkses, too."

Her eyes took on a dreamy expression as she launched into her tale while we drank tea. "The shoemaker sees the Fae dancing in the moonlight and he thinks that if he can but steal a pair of their shoes and take a pattern from them that he'll be able to fashion shoes that will make the finest dancer out of anyone who wears 'em. So the shoemaker leaves his wife and three liddle sons at home and follows the Fae back through the veil to Iaru when their dancing's finished—and that's the last anyone sees of him for seven years. When he comes out again he thinks he's only been gone for seven hours, but he finds his sons grown to young men and all taken up the cobbling trade and his wife three years in her grave. But he shows his sons the magical shoes, and there's celebrating and shoemaking.

"And so for seven years the shoemaker and his sons grow rich. His sons marry and have seven liddle sons between 'em in seven years. At the end of seven years the Fae show up, as bold as you please, and say they've come for payment. And they claim his seven liddle grandsons and spirit them away through the veil to make their dancing shoes. And once in seven years the shoemaker and his sons are allowed to visit the children who never age though they become master cobblers. The shoemaker, whose shoes are no longer the best in the land, ages and dies. His sons try to carry on the family business, but they don't prosper, and one by one they sicken and pass before their time.

"And when the last son withers and dies of grief and drink, his coffin is carried to the churchyard gate—but no further—by seven infants with eyes as old as the hills and shoemaker's aprons round their waists."

I shuddered. "That's a terrible story."

"Aye, it is. Fae are terrible and beautiful, and their magic is from the old time, like the master's here." She bobbed her head toward David again.

"Are you at your old tricks again, Mother?" Mr. Emery came into the parlor, wiping his hands on a cloth.

"I remember the old ways by my mother's memories, and her mother's and her mother's before her," she said vehemently, and glared at her son. "The memories of ten generations—nay, twenty or more—are in my head, and if I'd had a liddle daughter instead of a girt lump of a nonbelieving son, I'd'a passed 'em on. You mark my words, Jonty Emery, the old stories'll be proved right in the end."

The son laughed and turned away and his mother scowled at him.

"Mark my words, there'll come a day when the Fae will come again and the rowankind will be restored to glory. When that happens, folks will find that the tabby in the barn has turned into a full-growed tiger."

"Take no notice of my old mum." Jonty Emery whirled his finger around by his temple.

Behind the son's back, David held up his right index finger, conjured a flame from the tip of it, blew it out and winked at Mrs. Emery, putting his finger to his lips. She cackled once then clamped her lips together and pressed her finger there, nodding.

As we settled into the newly arrived coach for our onward journey at eight of the clock, David cracked a smile. "Did you see her face?" he asked softly.

"That was cruel, showing her the magic, but not letting her tell."

"Do you think so? I thought she needed something to hold onto. Besides, if she tells, no one will believe her." He suddenly looked serious. "Do you suppose she was right—about there still being such a thing as Fae? It seems like an odd thing to make up."

"Mad as a bag of beetles I'd say."

"There was something in it, I'm sure. It may not have been the whole truth or quite the right story, but the part about the Fae rang true."

A young couple with a baby climbed aboard and ended our conversation.

As our coach rattled along the quiet road and clouds rolled across the horizon, dark as a bruise, I had the opportunity to study David. Why should Mrs. Emery mistake him for Fae when he was clearly rowankind? I looked at him again and blinked twice. His skin was clear of any of the graininess of rowankind skin and had lightened from the slightly grayish weathered-wood color to an almost alabaster hue. When had that happened? Had it been such a gradual change that I'd hardly noticed it? Had David noticed it? If he had, he'd never said anything, but gazing into mirrors, even to set their appearance straight, was hardly the province of boys of his age.

The sky cracked apart and we drove on through persistent rain at a much slower pace. The green fields turned to gray haze occasionally broken by trees or a farmhouse or a way-marker. I gave up watching the land roll past and closed my eyes.

I almost felt lonely, until a presence made me smile.

Hello, Will.

Hello, yourself, Ross. You're a long way from home.

So are you.

He nodded, his ghostly form disturbing the air slightly. *You're caught in something that's bigger than you are. Have a care.*

What can you tell me, Will? Will? But he'd gone.

We arrived in Chard in the early evening. The rain had ceased, and the last rays of the autumn sun lit up the east faces of the cottages, made mellow by the preponderance of creamy hamstone and thatch. Along either side of Fore Street ran two narrow streams, little more than open drainage ditches. In front of the Phoenix Hotel, they had been bridged by enough flagstones to turn them into culverts, and I could see that before long they would be covered entirely and disappear underground.

The landlord at the Phoenix told me all his rooms were

taken. I caught his sideways glance at David, so when I crossed to the Red Lion I thought it prudent for David to wait outside until I secured a room. Once money had changed hands and I had the room key in my hand, I casually mentioned that I'd need an extra pallet making up for my rowankind. Though the landlord, Mr. Pratten, paled a little when he saw David, he still told the maid to see to it. We moved in to a plain room at the top of the main stair. The sight of a real bed, one that wasn't rumbling to the rhythm of horses, drew me to lie in it. I must have slept deeply, because David had to shake me awake at dinnertime, and we went down to the dining room to find it empty.

"I'm Dimity, miss. Can I bring you dinner?" The serving girl, human, not rowankind, greeted us pleasantly enough.

"What is there?" David asked, and Dimity looked at his face for the first time, staring at him as though dumbstruck.

"He asked what's for dinner," I repeated, beginning to get annoyed by the town's attitude toward rowankind.

"Oh, sorry, miss." She pulled herself together. "We don't get many . . ."

"Rowankind?"

She swallowed hard. "Yes, miss. R-rowankind. This is a quiet town, and godly."

"Why should rowankind be considered ungodly?"

"We're only twelve miles from the Old Maizy, miss," she said, as if that explained everything. "There's 'umble pie tonight, miss, and a sheep's tongue, and buttered parsnips."

She must have seen the look on my face at the mention of 'umble pie. "Or I can get you tripes?"

"Pie will be fine." I looked at David and he nodded. "For me, too."

The pie was surprisingly tasty, as long as you avoided the suspicious rubbery bits inside it. It had a rich, dark gravy under a dense, suety crust, crisp on the top and spongy on the underside. David cleared his plate quickly with obvious relish. I was a bit more picky and left various unidentifiable scraps of animal on the side of my plate, but I enjoyed the buttered parsnips and a slab of the tongue, which had been salted in brine.

"That was good pie, Dimity," David said as the girl cleared our plates away.

She said nothing, but watched him suspiciously out of the corner of her eye.

"I've come here looking for the Sumner family," I said, and saw her start at the name. "Are there any Sumners in town?"

She paused a little too long before she said, "No, miss."

"Well then, tell me about the Old Maizy Forest, if you would."

She looked at me as though I'd asked her to tell me why we breathe air.

"I'm not from around here," I said apologetically.

"Reverend Cleveleys says we're not to speak of it or even think of it, lest we draw down things from the old world."

"Things?"

"Things." She looked at David. "And suchlike." Then she scurried out of the room so fast that she almost ran.

"This is going to be an interesting visit," David said.

After the maid's reaction, I decided not to antagonize Mr. Pratten and ask about the Sumner family here at the inn. Instead I called him over and asked if there was a Mysterium office in town.

"No!" By the look of his face he realized that his answer was too sharp. He gave me an ingratiating smile. "Witchkind aren't well liked in these parts, ma'am, so the Mysterium leaves us alone, and that's the way we like it."

There was no public record office either, so it seemed that the only register of births, marriages, and deaths was in the church.

"That wouldn't happen to be Reverend Cleveleys, would it?" I asked.

I looked at David and saw him pull a face behind the innkeeper's back. My feelings precisely.

"Would you be leaving tomorrow, ma'am?" Mr. Pratten asked with unmistakable hope in his voice.

"We'll be staying for as long as it takes to conclude our business. I wasn't aware when you took my coin that there was a time limit on our stay."

"I'm sorry, ma'am. I thought you only wanted the room for one night, else I'd have mentioned it." He cleared his throat and looked uncomfortable. "Only the coach from Axminster to Bridgwater stops here on a Thursday night and all our rooms are gen'rally taken." His eyes flicked to David.

So that's what it's all about.

"So do you plan to evict us forcibly from our room, Mr. Pratten? Or would it be prudent to see if your colleague across the road could manage to find a few vacant rooms for coach passengers who are not accompanied by rowan-kind?"

"Err, yes, of course."

"Good. Thank you."

"What's wrong with this town?" David kept hold of his temper until we reached the safety of our room, then he slammed the door and kicked it hard. "I might as well have dragon wings the way folks are treating me. And did you hear that girl, Dimity Dimwit? Does she think I'm dangerous or something?" David's voice had risen.

"Shh! These walls are thin. I know it's hard, and I know I don't really understand what you've been through, but you wanted to follow the mystery of the box. It was never going to be easy."

I heard feet on the stairs. "Is everything all right in there?" Mr. Pratten bellowed through the door paneling.

"Yes, fine," I called back.

"Are you sure?"

"Yes, perfectly sure."

"Only I heard a disturbance. Is the young gentleman all right?"

I sighed and opened the door wide enough to show myself and David behind me. "Thank you for your concern. We are both truly fine."

"Oh, right, only I heard shouting and I didn't want the young gentleman to get upset, not with him being, you know."

"I do know." I started to shut the door in his face, but David grabbed the edge of it.

"Just what do you think I might do if I get upset?"

"N-n-nothing, your worship, sir." Pratten turned and almost ran down the stairs.

"Interesting reaction," David said. He folded his arms across his chest and frowned.

"Look, David, I know you must itch for action, but I have to go and see Reverend Cleveleys, and you have to stay here and keep out of sight."

He glared at me and took a deep breath. "You're right. This town has something strange going on, and it involves the rowankind."

Pratten's words came back to me: *"I didn't want the young gentleman to get upset."* Pratten had been truly worried about what David might do. He didn't think that rowankind were socially inferior; he thought they were dangerous.

Reverend Cleveleys' study was in the front room of his modest house, the whole edifice built next to the church out of plain, undecorated stone. His housekeeper, a hatchet-nosed woman wearing a dress twenty years out of date and corseted to within an inch of her life, showed me in and asked me to wait.

Cleveleys strode into the room, tall and somber, dressed in simple gray and black with not a hint of extra decoration. The natural state of his face was a deep frown with furrows between his eyebrows. His mouth was pursed in permanent compression. He might have been anywhere between sixty and seventy, and still wore a periwig.

He inclined his upper body, not exactly a bow, but a polite acknowledgment. I could tell from his attitude that, though we'd never met, he'd already heard of me.

"Mrs. Webster, how can I be of assistance?"

"I'm new to town, Reverend Cleveleys, here on a brief visit to search for any members of my late husband's family. There's a will that needs resolving, and I need to establish the existence—or otherwise—of any family members. He wasn't a man for keeping in touch with family, but he did once tell me that he had cousins inland in Chard, or maybe near Chard."

"Webster, you say? There are a few Websters in these parts."

"Actually, no. His mother was a Sumner."

Reverend Cleveleys' face glazed over. "I don't believe I can be of any help. Good day, madam." He began to turn away.

"I've come a long way, Reverend!" I snapped out the words in an effort to stop him in his tracks. It worked, and I softened my voice. "I'd be grateful if I could check your register of baptisms, marriages, and burials for the parish."

He took a deep breath.

"You'll not find any Sumner there, nor any Sumner living in this parish."

"You're sure? What about before you came to Chard?"

"None in my congregation, nor any in the church record books. Not now, not ever."

I wasn't sure I could have memorized over two hundred years of parish records, but I didn't argue any further. It looked like I'd need to do a little light burglary to get what I wanted.

"Well, thank you for your time, Reverend Cleveleys. I shall return disappointed."

"I'm sorry for that, and sorry for the loss of your husband."

"Thank you."

As I left the vicarage, I walked through the churchyard, checking for accessible doors and windows in the church itself.

22

Mischief

"ARE YOU SURE ABOUT THIS?" David whispered as we crept up to the church in the dead of night. "The last time we tried breaking and entering we nearly got roasted alive."

"I know. I feel bad about burgling a House of God, I really do, but it's either that or go home again and learn nothing."

He shrugged. "It's not my god. I've never been able to understand a god who's supposed to be good, but allows such injustices as happen in the world."

"You're not supposed to be able to understand God. He's ineffable."

David sniggered. "Don't you think that the clergy made that up to cover all those questions they can't answer?"

"I can't believe we're standing outside a church, ready to rob it, while debating the existence of the Almighty. I was brought up to say my prayers and it's a hard habit to break, even though I've seen such things as the Church would deny existed."

"The Church would deny you in an eyeblink."

I sighed. "True enough, I'm sorry to say."

"Look!" David put out one arm to stop me and pointed to a small window. Inside the church, in the vestry, a single lantern burned.

"Quick, this way. If that's what I think it is, we need to hurry." With a cold dread filling my belly I crouched low and ran for the narrow vestry door. Finding it unbolted, I flung it wide. I'd been correct. Outlined against the flickering flame of his own light, Reverend Cleveleys hunched over a table ripping pages from a heavy parish register.

He looked up at me and froze as the oak door smashed back on its hinges. Recognition didn't light his features immediately, probably because I was dressed as a man.

"I see you've saved me a job, Reverend. I presume you've presented me with all the entries for Sumner from your church records. I should thank you. How far back have you gone?"

He recovered his voice and began to bluster, backing away from me, and reaching sideways for whatever came to hand first. He gripped the shaft of a hefty brass cross, holding it up as if I might flinch from it.

"Don't come any closer! What do you want?"

"Exactly the same as I did this afternoon, the records of the Sumners of this parish. Only I would have taken the information in a less destructive manner."

"The Sumners are all dead. The whole Devil's brood of them. Dead!"

"Not all of them." David stepped out from my shadow.

The reverend's grip failed him and the cross clattered to the ground. "Fae!"

His knees gave way and he sank to the floor. By the stink, his bowels had let him down as well. What could terrify this stern man of God in his own church? Wrinkling my nose against the stench, I sat at the table and looked at the torn pages in the flickering lantern light.

"Keep an eye on him, David. Let me see what he's given us."

David dragged the reverend out into the corridor, leaving a wet smear on the stone floor and a lingering smell.

Once he was out of the door, I put up a witchlight to give a cool steady light to read by.

The first page I held was the oldest, and so I quickly rearranged them to start with the most recently dated. It was hardly recent, dating back to before I was born.

September thirteenth, 1771. I skimmed the page noting a list of burials. A lot of burials for one day, but no Sumners amongst them: William Dando of Chard; James Dando of Chard; Robert Lockyer of Draybridge; Daniel Latchem of Lopen; Simon Catley of Chard; Frederick Hancock of Chard. All men and no women. I looked at a small note scratched in the margin: *Unlawfully killed by Devilry in the explosion at Summoner's Well.*

Summoner's Well? Summoner? Sumner?

I looked at the reverend through the open doorway, but he wasn't watching me. He continued to stare at David as though the Devil himself had come to call.

I picked up the second sheet and glanced down it. Banns for the wedding of Rossalinde Sumner and someone whose name had been obliterated by the tearing of the sheet of paper. The date was also 1771, but in August, a few weeks before the explosion.

Rossalinde Sumner. Had I been named for a family member? Could this be my mother's sister, Rosie?

On the next torn-out sheet, back in 1765, I found a Sumner baptism and a burial within a few days of each other, the same child, John, the son of Francis and Emma Sumner, dead before he'd had the chance to live. It was a common enough theme. Children died all too easily, were buried and mourned, but life went on. I found earlier baptisms and burials. Francis and Emma had lost more than one child. Before John, there had been Mary in 1762, Annie in 1760 and Mark in 1758. What sadness. My own little lost soul who had been born on the rolling ocean with only Will for a midwife had had neither baptism nor burial. He rested with the fishes, now, stitched neatly into a tiny, weighted shroud, but mourned no less than a child lying in a churchyard. Would I find any living children for this couple? I hoped so.

In 1757 there was a John Sumner buried, aged seventy-seven years. After all the children it was a relief to find a Sumner who had lived out his allotted three score years and ten, plus a little more besides.

Finally, in 1751, I found a baptism that was not accompanied by an immediate burial—a twin baptism for—I guessed—my mother and her twin sister. Margery and Rossalinde Sumner, daughters of Francis Sumner and Emma, of Summoner's Well.

"David, I've found something."

David stepped into the doorway, and I kept my voice low so as not to let the reverend hear. "Our mother's baptism, I think, and her twin. The Sumners lived at Summoner's Well. I wonder if they're there still? Their parents, our grandparents, are Francis and Emma Sumner. We have family."

"If they still live."

"Indeed, but the reverend seems to have done a very thorough job of tearing out all references to the Sumners, and I've found no records of burials for either Francis, Emma or Rossalinde."

"How about we ask the Reverend?"

I hastily snuffed the witchlight as David dragged Cleveleys back into the room and hoisted him into a sitting position by his coat lapels. The smell was no better. The man whimpered and shrank away despite being almost twice David's weight.

"I'm not sure you'll get anything coherent from him," I said. "He seems to have lost his wits. I've heard tell fear can do that to a man, but I've never seen it before, though maybe it's something to do with . . ." I snuffed out the lantern. A definite soft light came from David's exposed skin. "You're glowing."

"What?"

"Whatever we're seeing now is by David-light. Can you stop doing that? I think it may be difficult for us to vanish into the night with you illuminated."

He held out his hands, turned them over and back again. "Ha, look, I'm a Shining One!"

Cleveleys whimpered again.

"He certainly thinks so."

David concentrated hard on his hands and the glow began to fade.

"Good, but we need to keep him quiet so we can get away." I thought for a moment, then stepped outside the door. *Will, are you here?*

No answer. There was never a ghost around when you needed one. I never normally had to do this, but I could if I had to.

William Tremayne, I call you to appear.

Will's ghostly form, much brighter than usual and dripping ectoplasm, popped into being.

"You call and I must obey." Will spoke audibly, which was unusual.

No need to be formal, Will. I replied in my head.

"You summoned me formally. It's obligatory."

How is this different from usual?

"It's stronger. Even normal mortals will be able to see and hear me."

Good. I was hoping to persuade you to that. I didn't know I could cause it.

"Ah, Ross, one day you and I will have a talk on the proper summoning of spirits. For now, what do you command me to do?"

Can you keep Cleveleys pinned down for us until morning?

Will nodded solemnly. I stepped back into the vestry and Will ghosted in through the wall. The reverend whimpered again, obviously able to see the specter.

Pshaw. He's shitten himself. Will wrinkled his nose.

Sorry about that. You've suffered worse aromas at sea.

What about the morning? Would the good reverend rush out and tell anyone who would listen that a Shining One visited him in the night and a ghost kept him company until morning? If so he'd likely end up in Bedlam. As long as he didn't set a hue and cry on us I didn't much care. We could have found all the information peacefully this afternoon without anyone getting hurt. Why did this whole town have a flea in its ear about rowankind, and why did the reverend want to cover up whatever had happened to the Sumners? It must be all connected, especially taking his reaction to David into account.

I didn't want anyone following us and weighed the potential results of Will's haunting against what Hookey would advise, which would be to make sure Reverend Cleveleys was silenced permanently. *Do whatever you need to do to keep him silent, Will, but no more than that. He obviously has his own beliefs and can't be blamed for that, however much I disagree with them.*

"You command and I obey."

Again there was that odd formality, but I didn't have time to think about it now. I gathered up the torn sheets from the parish register and folded them into my satchel along with the box. I was much relieved to see that David had stopped glowing like a will o' the wisp.

I nodded. "We're finished here. Let's go."

We hurried back to the inn and retrieved all our possessions. I contemplated taking a couple of horses from the inn's stables, but the stone mile-marker on the road indicated that Summoner's Well wasn't too far to walk in a night, and missing horses might cause Mr. Patten to call for a magistrate to have us apprehended. If we simply disappeared, leaving a fat gold coin in our room, he would just pocket the money and be glad we were gone.

With magical energy to spare, I worked a cloaking to make sure no one in the town saw two people heading toward Summoner's Well. Once we were out on the open road, I made a small witchlight so that we could see our way in the moonless night.

"I wonder what happened." I patted the satchel with the papers in.

"I'm glad to be away from that place." David checked his hands for glow and pulled his cloak closer around him.

"Let's see what the residents of Summoner's Well have to say."

"Maybe they'll be even worse."

"We'll have to deal with that when we get there." My

voice trailed off as I looked at David's face. All the blood had drained from it and he looked like an alabaster statue. "What's wrong?" I reached over and gently nudged his arm. "David! What's wrong?"

"Didn't you work it out? Dark magic. That's where it comes from. It's in my blood."

"No."

I grabbed him by the forearm and shook him hard. "David, listen to me. If you've got bad blood so have I."

He didn't respond, but by his thousand-yard stare I hadn't got through to him.

"David!" I shook him again and saw him come back into himself. "No more talk about bad blood. Your blood and my blood are both the same. Darkness is something that you can either embrace or turn away from. There's nothing evil inside you. Believe me."

He took a deep breath, but I didn't know whether I'd really convinced him or not. "Are you all right?"

He nodded.

"Let's put a few miles between us and that hateful place."

We stepped out and lost ourselves in the rhythm of our stride.

It was barely eight miles to Summoner's Well, a walk of less than three hours even carrying our bags, so we had to stop and take shelter in a copse of trees and doze for a few hours or we would have reached the village well before dawn. The rutted dirt road twisted through rolling farmland dotted with clumps of trees and finally dropped us into the main street of Summoner's Well early in the morning. The whole place was barely more than a single street with an additional clump of houses set back from the road. There wasn't even a church, only a few thatch-roofed cottages, a bakery, a general store, and a tavern with a blacksmith's forge attached to the side. I wondered if the Sumner home might be in the village, but with no way of knowing, the tavern seemed to be the obvious place to start.

It was a cozy affair with just a single public room. A small fire burned in the hearth to dispel the October chill. For sixpence the tavern keeper, who introduced himself as Albert, willingly arranged for us to sleep the night in his taproom with a blanket each. For an extra shilling he agreed to bank the fire up and provide supper and breakfast both today and tomorrow morning. He didn't seem at all worried about David being rowankind and treated him with as much civility as he gave to me. David visibly relaxed.

As we finished an excellent breakfast of bread and cheeses washed down with a local cider, I took a deep breath and said to Albert "We're searching for a family called Sumner."

It was as if I'd been looking through a lighted window and someone slammed the shutters closed. Albert's round face lost its cheerful grin and he straightened up warily without picking up the plates he'd been retrieving. I caught David's glance as if to say, "Oh no, here we go again."

This time I decided to take the bull by the horns. "Albert, I need to know why that name causes people to suddenly react as if we'd grown a Devil's tail. We had a very strange interview with an austere cleric in Chard and had to take matters into our own hands in order to find our way here." I reached into my satchel and pulled out the pages of the parish register. "Reverend Cleveleys was prepared to destroy portions of his own church records to deny the fact that there had ever been any Sumners in his parish."

"And why might you be interested, young sir?"

I'd forgotten for the moment that I was still wearing breeches from the burglary expedition. I pulled the ribbon out of my hair and let it fall around my shoulders. "Because I'm Margery Sumner's daughter."

"Bless us all!"

He took a step back. His mouth dropped open and then twitched up at the corners into a grin. "I should have recognized you. You look like your mother. Of course, she never went around in breeches. Well, bless my soul, and me only offering you a blanket by the fire."

"A blanket by the fire will be fine."

"Well, well! The girls survived!" He shook his head. "I can hardly believe it, Miss . . ."

"It's Mrs., Mrs. Tremayne, Rossalinde."

"She called you after your Aunt Rosie." His face turned somber. "Does that mean that Rosie didn't . . . that she . . . ?"

I spread my hands palm upward. "I didn't even know I had an Aunt Rosie until a few days ago."

He sat down heavily on a stool across the table and leaned on his elbows. "Oh, no. Poor Leo."

"Leo?"

"Rosie's betrothed. Didn't your mother tell you?"

I shook my head. "We weren't on the best of terms. I didn't even know her family name was Sumner until recently, but when she died there was a legacy, and I need to find the rest of the Sumners."

"She married?"

"In Plymouth."

Albert looked at David properly for the first time.

"She was my mother, too," David said. "Though obviously Ross and I had different fathers. I'm only half-rowankind."

"Well!" Albert stared into the fire for a few moments as if gathering his thoughts. He stared at David.

"Rowankind, you say?"

David nodded.

"If you say so." Albert shook his head. "You know that the rowankind are related to the Fae, don't you?"

"I didn't even know of the Fae until recently, but I'm beginning to hear more of them."

He nodded. "You're nearly thirty years too late to meet the Sumners. It was a very sorry business—the way they came to an end. Very sorry indeed. They always did well by us, and we were too late to help."

His eyes glazed over at memories. I reached out and touched his hand.

"We don't know anything. Start from the beginning, please."

"Aye, all right." He drew breath and gathered himself together like a storyteller searching for his starting point. "They built this village, or at least dug the well, some two hundred years ago. They were people of quality; built a fine house, Bullcrest, out on the Old Maizy Road. Used to have a lot of rowankind, but always treated them fair, you know. Paid 'em wages and wouldn't countenance anyone in the village doing any less. When I was a lad we had seven rowankind families living here, independent, like, though if anyone asked they all belonged to the Sumners, so no one else could lay claim to them. Good neighbors they were, too.

"As for the Sumners, they kept apart a bit. Not standoffish, you understand, but private. Thing is, we all knew they used magic, but it was subtle and no one ever spoke of it. We all benefited from time to time.

"They never registered with the Mysterium like they were supposed to do, but no one here would ever have reported them. If anyone went to them for help of any kind, magical or otherwise, they'd give it if they could. Eileen Sumner was a grand midwife. Her brother, Francis, your grandfather, had the weather magic like his father, John. Emma, your grandmother, didn't have magic, of course. She married in. She was a Wood from over Donyatt way. Even so, she had a fair knack with growing things."

Albert ran his hand through fading fair hair. "As Francis and Emma's twin daughters—your mother, Margery, and her sister Rosie—grew, it was obvious that the girls had power beyond either their father or their aunt. Unfortunately they gave themselves away in Chard when they were not much more than toddling babies. After that the townsfolk watched the whole family.

"There was no getting out of it, so on their eighteenth birthday Margi and Rosie registered with the Mysterium, just like the law says."

Albert sniffed and rubbed his face. "Maybe that's what brought the out-of-towner to Chard. It certainly wasn't locals that started the fuss, though some of them from Chard signed up for the militia, led by a man called Walsingham. Only he wasn't a regular Kingsman. He stank of magic.

"Things turned ugly very quickly, and a mob came marching for the Sumners. We didn't know until it was too late. We heard an almighty explosion from here, and though we rushed up to Bullcrest, the house was already a burning shell."

I shuddered.

"I'll lend you a couple of ponies. Go and see the Sumner place for yourself, and when you get back we'll talk again. There's other people you need to meet."

"Will they want to meet us?"

"Oh, aye. The Sumners might have been witches, but they were our witches, and they always did right by us."

He saddled a couple of sturdy ponies, gave us directions to Bullcrest, and we left the village.

23

Summoner's Well

THE BURNT-OUT MANOR HOUSE, yellow sandstone, fire-blackened with what remained of square bay windows, could clearly be seen from the roadside, standing stark against the skyline on a slight rise. Dense scrub grass, thistles, poppies, and a mixture of wheat and barley gone wild had grown up in the surrounding fields, but the ground around the house's footings was still scorched bare. Both our ponies balked, and no amount of urging would get them to move past the gateway, so we tethered them and continued up the overgrown track on foot. After a few yards of pushing through sticky goosegrass, I was glad to be wearing breeches and boots.

Once we got to within a few hundred yards of the house, we stepped out onto bare earth. David and I both looked at each other, feeling a strangeness about the place. Whatever had happened here had left a magical scar on the land. I wondered if the Guildhall would have looked like this if David had unleashed his pent-up fire magic on it and shuddered involuntarily. I heard David draw a deep breath beside me. When we both walked on, I realized I'd reached for his hand.

The roof of the house had long since gone. No one had picked over these ruins like they had with the remains of our mother's house, so we had to clamber over fallen rubble to get to the front door, now a gaping hole.

I would have thought that the soot from such an old fire might have been scoured away by the weather, but the stones still looked freshly scorched. We couldn't enter the ruin because the inside was open from cellar to eaves, with only charred stumps of timbers and jutting stone fireplaces to mark where the floors had been. Crazily crisscrossed timber and stone debris still lay haphazardly where the roof had fallen into the cellar.

I shook my head. "It hardly looks touched, does it? I can almost still smell the burning."

David's face was a mask, but I knew him pretty well by now. "What's the matter?"

"I thought . . ." He shrugged.

"What?"

"I thought, I hoped, that we'd get here and something would click into place for me. That I'd understand the people who'd lived here, and through that have more of an understanding of me."

I stepped back. "We're not going to find anything here."

Time to go back to Summoner's Well and see if Albert could add any more information.

Albert had prepared a meal for us that was fit for a returning prodigal. There was mutton pie, pease pottage, belly pork, crunchy on the outside and dripping with its own juices, potatoes roasted in the fat, and fresh-baked bread. We'd hardly finished eating before the tavern began to fill up with what seemed to be the whole village.

"They're always curious about strangers." Albert winked at me as I pushed my way through the locals to the trestle to get a couple of mugs of his hot, spiced cider. "I knew you'd be good for business. I should be paying you." He laughed and patted his pocket. "But of course, a bargain's a bargain."

"I don't begrudge you the extra business."

"It's a good village. Nice people."

"Have you been here long?"

"I was born here, and my ma and pa before me and their ma and pa before them. There's always been a Poppleton in Summoner's Well. My old gran said we came here with the first Sumner."

"As did the Seniors." An elderly gent with a liver-spotted balding head smacked his tankard on to the trestle.

"Aye, and the Seniors, too, Reuben, I'll grant you that," Albert said.

Reuben nodded and chuckled. "Albert's right. The apple doesn't fall far from the tree. You've got more than a look of Eileen about you."

"Eileen? My great aunt?"

"Most around here knew her as Gran'ma Sumner. She brought a good deal of 'em into the world, but I remember her when she was not much older than you are now. Good lookin' woman she was, but she never married. There was talk of a baby, though, but I don't know what happened to it. Hey, Albert, you were right." He proffered his pot for a refill. "Look at this 'un."

A loud silence descended on the whole room and suddenly every face was turned toward me.

"Oh, fox me!" A woman about my mother's age came right up to me. "I'm going to fetch Leo." She ran off without another word, and suddenly the whole room was buzzing with questions. Where had I come from? Who was my father? How had my mother escaped? How old was I? Where was Margi now?

They all seemed to be ignoring David, and I cast a glance across the room. He was standing with his back to the wall by the inglenook, frowning—a casual position, but knowing David's propensity for fire magic, also a defensive one.

Albert's voice cut through the rest. "Don't forget the boy. He's Margery's son as well. Half-rowankind."

"Eh?" Reuben walked over to David and the whole room fell silent. Reuben took hold of David's hand and said, “Come on, son, pay no heed to this lot. They mean you no harm.” He led David back to where I was standing. “Half-rowankind you say?”

He looked at me and I nodded. Then he studied David. “He’s not half-rowankind. He’s Fae. Look at the way he carries hisself. Beggin’ your Lordship’s pardon.” He bowed to David.

Now the questions were all mine and David’s, but before we’d had the opportunity to get any of them answered, the front door opened and a tall, distinguished-looking man in his fifties burst in and cut through the crowd like a hot knife through butter. “Where is she?” he demanded. “Where’s my Rosie?” He looked at me and his eyes held such loss and such hunger that I wanted to grab him and hold him tight.

“Steady on, Leo,” Reuben, half a head smaller and twenty years his senior, put a firm hand on Leo’s arm. “Give the lass a chance. She doesn’t know.”

I shook my head and raised my voice so that everyone could hear. “Until today I didn’t know anything about my family. My mother, Margery Goodliffe, never told me where she came from. I didn’t even know she had a sister.” I dropped my voice and turned to Leo. “I’m truly sorry. I can’t help you.”

I heard someone say, “Goodliffe, eh? So she married that sailor chap after all.”

Leo slumped. Suddenly he seemed no taller than Reuben. “Can we talk?” I asked him. I led him to the inglenook and we sat on the bench, leaving David to ask and answer questions at the bar.

“You loved her, didn’t you?” I asked.

He nodded. “Rosie was my life. When we didn’t find her or Margi in the ruins we all thought—all hoped—they’d escaped.”

“Were there bodies?”

He shook his head. “No Sumners. Anyone inside the house vanished in the conflagration. It was magical, you see, anyone could see that. But there were bodies outside. I have no sympathy. They got what was coming to them. They let themselves be driven to madness."

"Who started it? Was it Cleveleys?"

"He was there, new to the area and not so set in his ways. It wasn't him leading the mob. It was a stern fellow by the name of Walsingham. He stirred up trouble over a few dry wells—in the thirteenth week of a drought, so that was hardly unexpected. He came riding to Bullcrest with a mob behind him, saying the girls had diverted water to Summoner's Well, even though everyone knows our well is good and deep and has never run dry in two hundred years."

"So what happened?"

"Militia they called themselves, though they were mostly locals save for Walsingham, who said he had a warrant from the king. A hanging warrant, as I understand."

He sniffed and wiped his nose on a large white handkerchief. "Me and Rosie were betrothed. Another week and we'd have been to church, and she wouldn't have even been at home. I couldn't believe a lady like her would love a blacksmith like me, but she did, and her parents didn't naysay us."

"Walsingham doesn't look old enough to have been involved in events nearly thirty years ago. He's no more than forty or forty-five. He has dark hair and a pockmarked face, else he might be considered handsome."

"The Walsingham I'm talking about was killed in the explosion, so it wasn't the same man, but definitely the same name," Leo said. "He was fifty at least, gray-haired and paunchy. He lay in a sealed coffin in the church in Chard for nearly a fortnight before a young government man from London came to claim the body. There was one of Walsingham's men, a youngster, knocked senseless by the explosion. I don't recall his name, but I do recall his face was all cut about. It might have left scars. He'd be about forty-five now. You know a Walsingham? Not a common name. Father and son, do you think?"

"That would make it stranger than I would like to

contemplate. Why would two generations of Walsinghams want to kill all the Sumners?"

"Walsingham's trying to kill you?"

"Me, and possibly David as well. He already has my brother, Philip, though he's not in a rush to kill him because he thinks Philip will lead him to me. Maybe he's also trying to find Rosie, if she's still alive."

Leo blew his nose again and his hands shook. "Until today we weren't sure whether the girls were dead or alive, but if Margi survived, it's possible my Rosie did as well. We have to do something. If my Rosie's alive she's going to stay that way."

"Rosie's got magic?"

"Oh, aye, she's got magic, all right."

"Are you sure it wasn't Rosie that had all the magic?" Maybe the Lady of the Forests had been wrong.

"Nay, lass, Rosie and Margi were well matched, though I admit their magic was stronger when they were together, they still had plenty when they were apart."

"Are we talking about the same Margery Sumner?"

"We are. You're too like her not to be either her daughter or Rosie's. And that boy has a look of Frank despite being Fae. There's a story there, I'll warrant."

I stared at Leo. Another instant assessment of David as Fae, rather than half-rowankind. I had so many questions.

"But my mother hated magic."

"She might have hated it for what it did to her family, but she had it, and I'm guessing that you've got it as well."

I nodded.

He smiled. "We might be able to find Rosie yet." He pulled a gold locket on a long leather thong out from down the front of his shirt. "This was Rosie's. Is either of you a seeker?"

It wasn't until everyone had gone and Albert had closed the bar and climbed the narrow stair to his bed that David and I had the opportunity to exchange information as we sat on the bench in the inglenook, our faces lit by the glow from the burning logs, the smell of applewood smoke in our nostrils.

"I don't know how I feel," David responded to my obvious first question. "Two months ago I had no history to speak of, and now I've got more than I can cope with. What about you?"

"I keep thinking about our mother. I thought I knew her but I didn't. I thought she hated me using magic because she was scared of something she didn't understand, and now I find she understood it all too well."

I leaned forward and rubbed my knees to dissipate the intensity of the fire. "But she never used it. I never had any indication that she was doing anything to bleed off the power. She must have bottled it up. Maybe that's what soured her. Maybe it's what killed her in the end."

"Perhaps she was frightened, not of what the magic could do, but of what people do because of the magic." David stood and picked another log off the woodpile and threw it into the heart of the fire, where it settled with a small shower of sparks. New flames licked the fresh bark, and a small twig sticking out of one side exploded with a hiss of burning resin and was consumed.

"Maybe." My voice sounded dubious even to my own ears.

David knew when to leave a subject alone, so he said, "Do you think we'll be able to use the locket to find Rosie?"

"If Leo's been wearing it next to his heart for a long time I could find him with it more easily."

"You realize that if we do get any idea of where Rosie might be that Leo will want to come with us?"

"Well, he can't."

"I'll leave it up to you to tell him." David yawned and stretched. "I never thought I'd be tired enough to sleep tonight, but I'm glad I am."

"You sleep. I'm probably going to be lying awake most of the night."

I was wrong about that. I lay down in front of the fire with my blanket and heard David's breathing fall into a steady rhythm. That was the last thing I recall, until a cock crowing outside woke me with a start in the lean hours of the autumn morning.

⁂

Leo arrived before we'd finished eating breakfast. He seemed renewed, optimistic. I only hoped we didn't disappoint him. He came and sat with us and Albert brought him a large mug of tea, still nodding deferentially to David.

"I wish he wouldn't keep doing that," David said.

"Oh, Albert knows his manners, young man. Your sister told me something of your story last night, and I know you two have never had anything to do with the Fae, but if you had, you'd be respectful, too. They can be capricious b—" He suddenly remembered who he was talking to and looked dismayed.

David laughed. "You don't need to watch your manners around me. I'm not even sure you're right about me being half-Fae."

"Once you've seen them, you recognize the look instantly."

I interrupted. "Leo, no one I know has ever seen a Fae. How come everyone in this village has?"

"The Sumners, of course. Once a year the Fae came calling. They paraded right through the middle of the village, coming from the Old Maizy to Bullcrest. We never asked why, but we used to watch them pass from behind cracks in our curtains. They used to sing all the way up the road. Always the same song. I can't sing it—the notes are too difficult for mortal voices—but the words are about restoring magic to the realm and righting an ancient wrong."

Something I hadn't eaten stuck in my throat.

I had several questions at once, most of which I suspected Leo couldn't answer. I settled for one I thought he could. "Do the Fae live in the Old Maizy Forest?"

He looked at me as though I was an idiot child. "Yes, and no. Fae can be in any forest, copse, wood or dell. Fae are wherever they need to be. They have their own land. Scholars like your grandpa called it Orbisalius, but the Fae's song called it Iaru."

"Iaru." David's eyes had gone as round as saucers, and he breathed the word as if he were trying it for size and found it fitted.

"Aye, Iaru. That was one of the lines in their song. *'The rowankind will return to Iaru and wonder will flow once more into the world.'*"

"The rowankind come from Iaru?" I asked.

"Where else?" Leo looked surprised at my ignorance. "A long time ago, of course. How quickly such things are forgotten. The Fae come and go through the forests. Rosie told me. There are cracks between their world and ours. The Old Maizy is the heart of where they can cross over. It's old, you see. I mean, really old. Most of the woodland in this country has been cleared and wooded, cleared and wooded I don't know how many times, but the Old Maizy is different. It's never had a woodsman with an ax in it—at least—not for long." He shrugged. "Folks have tried to tame it, but foresters and hunters have run screaming from the trees."

Albert came over and took up the tale. "Yet travelers meaning no harm can pass right through it."

"And neither of you knows why the Fae visited the Sumners?"

Leo said, "Rosie told me something once. She said there was a doom laid on her family and it would come to her because she was firstborn, but I wasn't to worry because in eight generations the box had never spoken to anyone and there was no reason for it to start now."

"Box. This box? Has either of you seen it before?" I took the winterwood box out of the pouch and unwrapped a corner of it, feeling the familiar tingle of magic.

"Could this be what the Fae were after?"

Leo gazed at it. "I don't think so. It looks like the one Rosie's pa used to keep on the mantel. It was never guarded, though, not like something precious. Is it? Precious, I mean."

"I have no idea." I wrapped it again quickly. "But I do know that someone wants it very badly. And I'm supposed to find my family so that I can open it."

"So let's get on with the finding," Leo said.

"Do you have the locket with you?" I asked. Bleeding off some of my built-up power would be welcome this morning.

"Always." Leo took the locket from around his neck and dropped it into my hand.

I held the locket and tried to visualize its former owner. This kind of searching magic didn't come to me readily. My best workings were with weather and the ocean. I had only a passing affinity with metals.

David joined in with me. We clasped our hands together, his around mine, the locket in the middle. David's power was strengthening, I was sure of it. The heat in his hands built until I winced.

"I'm sorry, Ross." He released me and rubbed his hands together, flicking his fingers as if to diffuse the heat. "Let me hold the locket."

I handed it over. "Should I hold your hands?"

He shook his head. "Put a hand on my arm so we're connected, but don't get too close."

I pushed down my own unease as David took the locket. He'd said very little, but the revelations—correct or not—about him being Fae, plus what the Lady had said about a dark power, must have been churning in his gut.

"It's all right, Ross." He spoke very quietly.

I met his eyes.

"Really. It's all right. I won't lose control."

"I know you won't."

He clenched the locket in his right hand and wrapped his left around it. I rolled up my shirtsleeve and placed Leo's hand on my forearm, then I touched my fingers lightly to David's bare arm. His skin was fever hot, but not hotter than I could bear. I could feel blood pulsing through his veins with an unnatural strength.

He bent his head to stare at his hands. At least we had a fair idea of what Rosie looked like, since she and my mother were twins, and having Leo connected to us was almost more important than the locket.

I concentrated on the task. A picture formed in my

mind, drawn from my knowledge of my mother and from Leo's description of Rosie as a girl. I knew David could see it as well, and I hoped Leo might, too. Gradually it came into my mind as if a fog were rolling back. I saw a cottage, surrounded by trees. A woman who might have been my mother, except she was a little rounder, carried a basket of autumn berries through the door. She paused and came back to the doorstep looking outwards, as though she could sense someone watching.

"Identify." She only spoke the one word, but suddenly it was as if everything had been reversed, and instead of us seeking her, she was seeking us, and not necessarily with the best of intent. She sensed us as a threat.

I gathered myself to ward against whatever might follow, but all of a sudden she stopped and mouthed, "Leo?"

I didn't know whether she could hear me. "Rosie. Aunt Rosie. We need to find you. We need your help."

She stooped quickly and in the dry dirt at her feet etched a pattern and trailed her fingers along it. A map. I recognized the river Esa and the Ax. The road she drew led into the Old Maizy Forest, and her cottage seemed to be close to where the river and forest met.

That's where we were going next.

When David opened his fingers, what rested in the palm of his hand was a nugget of gold that had been melted and re-formed by his clenched fist. The locket had not given up its secret lightly.

"I'm sorry, Leo."

"No matter, lad, if it helps us find her." Leo took the nugget of warm gold and slipped it into his pocket.

24

Rosie

LEO WANTED TO COME WITH US, of course. My first reaction was to say no, but when I thought about it again, there was no real reason why he shouldn't. He was hardly a doddery octogenarian. He was fit and trim, with a good knowledge of local roads. Ah, who was I kidding? If Rosie's face had been anything to go by when she saw him standing with us, I owed it to both of them to do a bit of very belated matchmaking.

Within an hour, Leo had packed and was ready at the tavern. He'd borrowed a red-bay mare for me and a gray gelding for David. His own horse was a solid-looking brown cob. We had a two-day ride, and Rosie's hasty drawing had been rough at best, but Leo seemed to know where we were heading. He'd recognized the confluence of rivers and the bridge on Rosie's map.

David drew up his hood and kept his face out of sight after the few people we passed on the road all bowed to him. Each time it happened, he became more moody and withdrawn. Once or twice I caught a glance from Leo and realized that he was worried for the boy.

I was beginning to get beyond worried.

We spent the first night in a tumbledown barn, chilly and damp. For most of the second day we turned up our collars against the thin drizzle. Even the horses were miserable. On the second night, we chose a sheltered spot by a small clump of trees close to the river Esa. Leo started to build a fire, but the tinder wouldn't catch. David tethered the horses and mixed up the barley and bran feed we'd brought with us while I sorted out the smoked meats, dried fruit, and oats in our food pack.

"Come on, you little beauty. Ach! Thought I had it." Leo talked to the fire as if coaxing it would help.

"Here, let me." David almost pulled him out of the way and Leo, who'd been hunkered down on his heels, rocked back and overbalanced. It was a good thing he did. David pointed at the damp logs and a fireball five feet across whooshed up.

I think I cried out as flames wrapped themselves around my brother for an instant before they disappeared. In the couple of seconds that followed I was light-blind. I stumbled forward, expecting to find a smoldering corpse.

Flinging a witchlight upward I saw David still standing there, stunned but completely untouched by his own magic. The logs crackled merrily. Thankfully the fireball had gone over Leo's head. If he'd been any closer he might have been a pile of ash.

"David!"

He looked at me wide-eyed. Not since his very first lessons in magic had I seen such a look of fear on his face. He turned to Leo and saw that he was unhurt. "Leo, I'm so sorry."

Leo sat up and dusted himself down, ran his fingers along his eyebrows and his almost white hair as if to check for scorching. "Well!" he said, eyes wide. "That was an experience."

"Are you all right?" I reached down to give him a hand up, and his fingers trembled slightly as he grasped mine.

"I'm fine. Really, I'm fine." The second time was to reassure David. "What they say about the Maizy is true. Young

Master David is coming close to his source of power for the first time. There's no going back from that." He piled on a few more logs, settled a teakettle into the middle of them, and hunkered down again.

The following morning, the mist had lifted, though the sharpness in the air promised frost by nightfall. We saddled up and followed the track along the river. Rosie's cottage should be close by. As we got closer to the trees, my own magic strengthened, too, as it always did in the Okewood. I had no power surge like David's, but for once the proximity of so much living wood heartened rather than intimidated me.

The Old Maizy smacked of power, but rather than being oppressive, it was invigorating. The trees blazed with autumn colors, greens turned to a riot of orange, gold, and red. One good storm would strip the branches bare, but for now the effect was magical.

"Rosie must be somewhere close." Leo sounded hopeful.

I recalled the map Rosie had sketched. "It's this side of the river, I think."

David looked at the dark expanse of the wood and his throat worked as he swallowed hard. He nodded. We turned our horses into the trees on no recognizable path, pushing through dense undergrowth. Further in, where the light didn't touch at all, we had clear passage through the tall trees. Whichever way we turned, the forest looked the same.

"I think we're close." David pulled up his horse and dismounted. "Can you feel it?"

I could feel nothing and said so.

"There's a glamour."

A glamour! That was beyond my magic.

David swept his gaze right and left, eventually settling on a direction. As he walked forward there was a shimmer, and where there had been nothing but tree trunks I could see a well-worn track. Ahead of us in a small clearing stood a neatly laid-out garden and a timber and mud cottage with its front door swinging open.

"Rosie!" Leo called eagerly. "Rosie!"

He dismounted at the garden gate and rushed to the cottage door. As he reached it he paused.

"Rosie!" This time his cry was full of shock and horror and he almost fell over the doorsill in his rush. I heard his howl of anguish and ran forward, beating David to the door by a shoulder.

Huddled on the cottage floor, Leo sat crouched over the body of a woman. He held her cradled in his arms, and his shoulders shook with sobs. The cottage had been wrecked by someone or something. Blood pooled across the floor.

Leo looked up, tears streaming down his face. "My Rosie's dead."

"Let me see." I touched Leo's shoulder, but Leo didn't move. "David, get him back, let me see to Rosie."

David grabbed Leo and pulled him away. "Leo, let Ross take a look. She's been in a dangerous profession and has some knowledge of injuries and how to deal with them."

I stepped up close and searched for some small spark of life in Rosie. I don't know how long it was before I found a weak pulse and a whisper of breath.

Alive was a start, but Rosie's catalogue of injuries was frightening, any one of which could have killed her on its own. The worst was a very bloody head injury that looked as though her forehead had met with a heavy object. Her left arm had been twisted into an unnatural shape, and there were scorch marks radiating out from her chest above her heart. The fingers on her right hand had all been broken, systematically.

We lifted her on to a blanket and carried her to the kitchen table, hastily set straight amidst the chaos of the one-room cottage. I gently cut away most of her clothes around the burn and around her broken arm and bruised shoulder.

Leo pulled himself together after his initial shock and

proved that his blacksmith's skills extended not only to horse-doctoring but to bonesetting as well.

A quick glance at the debris in the cottage showed that Rosie was a well set-up witch with all the expected herbs, poultices, and potions, plus clean linen strips for bandages. I dressed the burn with oil of lavender. It wasn't as serious as I'd first feared—possibly she'd been protected by several layers of sensible woolen garments.

"You're a stubborn woman, Rosie Sumner," Leo whispered as he strapped her broken arm. "Don't die on me now."

By suppertime we had done what we could for Rosie and had restored the cottage to the best possible order. Other than not having enough unbroken chairs to go around, we were fairly comfortable. There was food in the larder and a fire to keep us warm. Rosie had not stirred since we found her, but her breathing remained even and her pulse steady. We couldn't do any more except wait. Leo, predictably, would not leave her side, and when David and I settled down to sleep on the rug in front of the fire, we made him take the chair.

"How could she?" Leo asked as I draped a blanket around his shoulders.

"How could she what?"

"Be so close and not contact me?"

"I don't know."

"I'll wait until I know she's all right and then I'll be on my way."

"Leo, why would you come this far and not stay?"

"Don't you see? It's been more than twenty-five years. If she wanted me she had only to send a message. I'd have come running."

"So you think she doesn't want you?"

He nodded. "Stands to reason."

"Well, damnation to reason. I saw her face when she recognized you in the seeking. You'd best stay around, because I'm not going to be the one to tell her you left."

"What if . . . ?"

"Give her a chance. If you leave you'll never know." I dropped a second blanket across his lap. "Get some sleep."

There was nothing to do but wait.

"Was this Walsingham?" David asked.

"I don't know. If it was, wouldn't she be dead?"

"He hasn't found the box yet. Maybe he thought she had it."

"How could she have it? He knew where the box was when we attacked the *Lydia*. Even if his witch drowned when Mayo sank the navy ship, he'd likely have found another to track it once news reached home. Corwen said the Twisted Skein was searched. Walsingham could have tracked the box to Plymouth and then lost it when we paid the witch to hide it with magic. Maybe he found a link to the Twisted Skein if the Watch reported on you." I talked it through, working it out for myself at the same time. "Unless he doesn't know that I had no knowledge of Aunt Rosie and thinks I might have taken refuge here, or sent it for safekeeping."

"I suppose it's logical to assume the two sisters kept in touch, but wouldn't Philip have told him otherwise?"

"Mother never told Philip about the box. He might think that when she gave me the box she told me where to find Rosie. Oh, if only she had, this might have gone very differently."

It was the afternoon of the second day when a small cry from Leo brought both of us running. Rosie's eyes were open, and she was gazing into Leo's face as if she couldn't believe what she was seeing.

"Am I dreaming?" Her voice wavered. If Leo was still in any doubt about his decision to stay, I wasn't.

"No, Rosie, love. It's me." Leo wiped a tear away with one hand and touched her face with the other. "And your niece and nephew. Margi's children."

She seemed to hear him, but she had no eyes for us, only for Leo, until she drifted off to sleep again.

David turned to me. "Is that it? Will she be all right?"

"If you're asking me if she'll live, I think so. If you're asking me whether she'll recover completely, I don't know. I'm not a surgeon."

"I'll be here to look after her," Leo said. "She'll not get away from me so easily again."

By the middle of the following day, Rosie had recovered enough to sit up. Seeing her pale and drawn like this reminded me of my mother on her deathbed. When I'd seen her in my seeking she'd seemed well-rounded, but now any plumpness had disappeared beneath unnatural swellings. Leo managed to get her to take a little broth, but her face was a mess of interconnected bruises, purple and claret, yellowing around the edges, and her lips were swollen and scabbed. Her words came out slurred.

"Hello, Aunt Rosie." I sat down carefully on the edge of the bed, and David came to stand by me. "I'm Ross—Rossalinde—Margi's girl, and this is David. He's Margi's as well—different dads."

"He's Fae." Rosie let her head flop back on to the pillow and it took a minute or two before she opened her eyes again. "Has Margi still got it?"

"What?"

"The box."

"This box?" I took the winterwood box from my pouch, peeled back a corner of the parchment concealing spell, and let Rosie peek in.

She gasped. "My sister is dead, then. It wouldn't leave her else."

"She never touched it, never claimed it, but yes, she's dead. She died last April." I wrapped it again quickly.

"Never claimed it?"

"She never told us she had magic. She gave me this on her deathbed. I don't know what it is, or what to do with it. That's why we came to find you."

Her eyes opened wide. "He wants it. He'll come back."

"Who?"

"The pockmarked man and the boy. They wanted to know where it was. I wouldn't tell them." She closed her eyes and choked back a sob. "I didn't want to lead them to Margi. We stayed apart all these years to keep each other safe."

"That's enough," Leo said, and pulled the covers up

around her so she could rest, but Rosie was tougher than she looked. She fixed her gaze on me.

"After we left Bullcrest I never saw Margi again."

A tear trickled down her cheek. "Margi and I agreed that we'd be safer apart, because together we were so strong that we couldn't help but drip magic into our daily lives, and people would notice us.

"Margi had settled in Plymouth, and so when I failed with the box—failed to open it—I knew where it must go." She rested for three slow breaths. "We were twins, but we all believed I was firstborn, so I took the box. When our father died the task to open it became mine."

"Why?"

She sighed. "Because it's the doom laid upon all the descendants of Martyn the Summoner." She took a deep breath. "The Fae wanted me to open it, too. I tried and tried, but I wasn't strong enough, and so I thought they might have been wrong. Two identical babies, we'd have been easy to mix up. Maybe Margi was firstborn.

"So I asked the Fae."

David and I both exchanged looks, but Rosie didn't seem to notice.

"They agreed to carry it to Margi, with a book to remind her of how we used to be, but there was a price for their help and their protection."

She tried to lift her hand toward Leo and winced. "I'm sorry, so sorry. I'd not planned to leave you, Leo, but soon after the box went to Margi, Dantin came wooing. I've never heard tell of a human woman that could resist a Fae. I certainly couldn't. They have a way about them. I bore his child, a Fae child, Margann. I loved her. I still love her. I raised her until she was called back to Iaru by the Fae Council. She still visits, and she still calls me Mother. How could I come back to you after that?"

Leo touched her face. "Ten Fae children would not have been enough to keep me away."

She smiled sadly and closed her eyes, letting her head fall back on the pillow, her breathing calm and even.

"I don't understand." Leo looked up at me, and I could

see a world of hurt in his face despite what he'd said to Rosie. "Why a Fae child?"

"I can explain."

I spun around so fast I almost fell. Corwen stood in the doorway, looking gaunt and tired.

25

Watch-wolf

DAVID GATHERED HIS MAGIC to strike. Part of me wanted him to do it and the other part of me, the part whose pulse was racing, wanted to leap between them. Good sense saved the day. Corwen didn't try anything fancy. He raised both arms.

"Friend! I come as a friend."

"It's all right, David." I put out my arm to stop whatever was building.

David pulled back, breathing heavily, relief written all over his face.

I scowled at Corwen, my own relief coming out in irritation. "I'd ask what you were doing here, but you seem to make a habit of following us."

"Just doing my job."

"Who's he?" Leo asked.

"A very annoying werewolf," I said. "The Lady's pet."

"Please. Shapechanger. I am not moon-called."

I knew he resented being called a pet as well, but I wasn't inclined to be nice to Corwen. He may think he was helping us, but his loyalty lay with the Lady, and I wasn't sure that our welfare entered into it. Besides, whenever I looked at him I had a feeling that getting too close would be dangerous, for me and my sanity. He was altogether too easy on the eye.

"So explain," I said.

"Iron collars can't hold me. I escaped the *Heart* the day after you left and—"

"Explain about the Fae child."

"Oh that. That's easy. Fae women don't readily carry children. They made the rowankind to be their servants and to carry their children, but human women can bear their brood, too."

"Halfbloods, like David?"

"In a way. A Fae child may have a human mother and some of her traits, but he, or she, inherits all of their father's power." He looked at David.

"We said you weren't half-rowankind." Leo looked at David.

"He's not half-anything," Corwen said. "He's all Fae—by power if not by birth—but he's got Sumner magic, too. Different magics all twisted up inside him, sometimes working together, sometimes fighting each other. I'm sorry. The Lady thought you'd both be better off not knowing, at least not yet, but here in this woodland I can see the Fae magic shining out of him."

He was right. David did look different. That he was wholly Fae, that Larien must have been Fae, had never entered my head, even after what Reuben had said in Summoner's Well.

"Does that mean we need to find the Fae?" I asked.

"Yes!" said David.

"No!" said Corwen.

I looked at Corwen. "If the Fae want the box opening, doesn't it make sense to ask them why?"

"They don't . . . They aren't human." Corwen seemed to be searching for the right word.

"And you are?"

"Almost. I'm as close as makes no difference. I have emotions like a human, I think like a human. I care like a human. Even when I am wolf I retain that human awareness. Fae think only like Fae. What concerns them is what's best for them. If it was in their best interest to wipe every human from the face of the earth, and if it was in their power, they wouldn't hesitate."

"Isn't it in their power?"

"Not entirely."

"Do they have an interest in opening the box?"

"It seems that they do."

"I should go." David stepped forward. "If I'm Fae what can they do to me?"

"Is that a question that needs an answer?" Corwen said. "At the moment you're independent. The minute you bend a knee to the Council, you're theirs for the rest of your very long life."

"Is that so bad?" David asked. "Don't you bend a knee to the Lady of the Forests?"

Corwen shrugged. "It's not the same."

Leo said. "Give Rosie a further hearing."

Corwen seemed to relax. "Good idea."

"And then we'll go and find the Fae," David said.

Having Corwen around wasn't as annoying as I'd feared. He fixed some of Rosie's broken furniture—a very useful magical skill that, try as I might, I couldn't emulate. He took a splintered chair, carefully aligned the broken sections of the leg, and bound it with magic to make it whole again. It was a slow, painstaking process; turning a new chair leg might almost have been as easy. I watched, fascinated, and then, aware that I'd gone from watching the magic to watching Corwen, I forced myself to turn away and busy myself with cleaning up. By evening, we had four usable chairs around the table and were able to sit together to eat a simple meal of ham with potatoes, parsnips, and cabbage from Rosie's garden.

Rosie awoke again as the rest of us were starting to feel sleepy. She managed some of Leo's broth, then said she wanted to talk.

She looked at Corwen as if getting the measure of him. "White bear, are you?" she asked.

"Wolf."

"Ah, that makes sense. You've got something of the canine about you." She turned to me. "Yours, is he? They're faithful once they've given their pledge."

"He belongs to the Lady of the Forests."

"It's not the same thing. Show me the winterwood box."

The abrupt change of subject caught me unawares, but I brought the box from the table and unwrapped it. She nodded.

"That's it. Wrap it again quickly."

"What do you know of its history?" I asked.

"It's a family legend. Two hundred and fifty years ago, Martyn of Cirencester, our many-times great-grandfather, was a student of Doctor John Dee. You may have heard of him."

I shook my head.

"No matter, from what you tell me it's hardly likely your mother would have directed you to read about him. He was a noted mathematician, astrologer, and occultist, an expert in alchemy and divination, and also advisor at the court of Good Queen Bess—Gloriana."

"Mother did say our family companied with royalty; I think those were her words. To be honest I took little notice at the time. She was far more intent on my clothes and on taking me to task for being a hoyden."

Rosie shrugged. "By the time Martyn came to court as an adept in his own right, Dee's star was fading and the Spanish were hammering at the door."

She sighed and took a moment to catch her breath. "In those days, the lines between science and magic had hardly been drawn. Dee was a pious man who became more intent on communicating with angels than with other magics. He suddenly accepted an invitation to visit Poland. Maybe he was about the queen's business, I don't know, but I do know that when the Spanish Armada came, he was absent.

"Naturally the queen turned to Martyn, whose proven abilities to summon spirits for divination purposes was well known to her. He became Summoner to Good Queen Bess."

"Summoner?"

"Summoner, Sumner. Where did you think the name came from, child?"

"Are we all summoners? And if so what can we summon?"

"To a greater or lesser degree we all have the talent, though it's said amongst the family that to the firstborn is the Great Talent. I've never been sure quite what that means. Margi and I seemed no different when we were growing up. Perhaps because we were twins it was diluted."

"My mother was a summoner?"

"Margi? Of course."

"Oh." I had a sudden moment of clarity. That was why, after seven years of estrangement, I had suddenly been compelled to visit her on her deathbed. Her last summoning. And that was why I was able to think of the *Heart*, know where she was and make her come to me. And the last time I had actually summoned Will he'd been forced to obey me, even so far inland, away from his beloved ocean.

A frown flickered across Rosie's battered face. "She never told you, did she?"

I shook my head. "She hated magic. She tried to beat it out of me, and then she tried to pray it out of me."

Rosie shook her head. "As if that ever worked."

"So what happened to Martyn the Summoner?"

"That's where things become a little confused and confusing. The story as it's been passed down may have been mistold or misunderstood. King Philip of Spain sent his Armada to invade England. We know Martyn was called upon to foil the invasion with magic, but we don't know what he did or how he did it. It's a matter of record, however, that the Spanish ships were delayed by storms as well as destroyed by fireships. Finally the remnants of Philip's fleet were driven up the East Coast of England, right around Scotland and then back down the West Coast. Many of the Spanish ships were wrecked on the rocky shores of Scotland and Ireland by a great gale."

"That was caused by Martyn Summoner?"

Aunt Rosie shrugged and winced. "It seems superbly fortuitous if it wasn't."

"You're tiring her out," Leo said.

Rosie smiled at him. "There's not much more to tell, or not much more that I know. When Queen Bess sent her own Armada to Spain, it failed too, and Martyn Summoner caught the blame. My gran'pa surmised that Martyn fled the court in fear of his life. There was a man, you see, a man who did whatever the queen needed done. A man you should never turn your back on. That's why we were so afraid when all the trouble started at the farm. It couldn't have been coincidence. It's not a common name. The queen's man was Sir Francis Walsingham.

"Martyn gathered his family and fled. I believe there were some years spent traveling. The only certainty is that eventually, after the death of the queen, the Sumners settled close to Chard and lived a very quiet life.

"Martyn never spoke of his time at court until he lay dying. Then he summoned the Fae, the Council of Seven. With them as witnesses, he pressed the winterwood box into the hand of his eldest son and confessed to doing a great and terrible wrong for the best of all reasons. He said a full account of his wrongs—and the way to right them—was in the box and that his children should take up his burden. But his son was already nearly sixty and four, and it very soon passed to the next generation, and the next."

Rosie paused and Leo held a cup of water for her to sip. "Ah, Leo, you always did know my mind better than I did. Don't go away, will you?"

"Never. I'm staying with you. If you want rid of me you'll have to beat me off with a big stick."

"Then you'd look as pretty as me. Ouch!" Smiling caused the scab on her lip to crack.

"So what's in the box, Aunt Rosie?"

"I don't know." She shook her head. "No one has ever been able to open it. It seems that Martyn was the greatest of us all. Whatever it is—whatever it does—it holds powerful magic, and that's a fearful thing."

"Fearful enough to kill for?"

"Both then and now." She closed her eyes and took a deep breath. "There were two men came for me. One was like walking darkness, the other looked much like you."

"Philip?"

"I never heard them use names, but it can't be coincidence."

"There are too many coincidences. Did the man—the one you say was like walking darkness—did he have a pockmarked face?"

"He did."

"Walsingham."

"What?"

"It's another Walsingham, Aunt Rosie. This one is making it his business to try and kill us all. He nearly succeeded with you. What can have happened to turn the Walsingham family against the Sumners?"

She shook her head and winced. "Philip, you say?"

"Walsingham has Philip captive. He has a poppet, and through it he can hurt or even kill him. Philip is bound to do his bidding. Even so, though I could believe much of Philip, I can't believe he would kill his own family."

"I'm not dead. Is that by accident or design? If by design, the lad's a powerful actor. He has Walsingham believing that he's entirely on his side."

"Philip was always a good liar. I never thought there would come a time that I might be grateful for it."

The short conversation exhausted Rosie again, and I let her sleep.

Could I believe there was good in my little brother? I so wanted to.

"David, what can you remember about Philip?"

"He had precious little natural kindness, but there's a huge gulf between being unkind and being a killer."

"You two need to talk," Corwen said. "I'm going hunting."

He stood up and went to the door, took off his jacket, and pulled off his shirt.

"Corwen?"

He grinned at me as he slung the shirt carelessly aside. If displaying his well-muscled and very manly torso was for my benefit, he needn't think . . . Ah, who was I fooling, it worked—at least insofar as my heartbeat quickened and I found myself wondering how much more he was going to strip off.

He shrugged apologetically. "Shirts are hard to deal with when you've only got paws. Don't worry about the breeches, I can run out of them." He opened the door and with one flash of smooth skin grew a pelt, shrank down, and vanished into the forest, loping like the silver wolf that he was.

The flash of skin disturbed me. I wondered, briefly, how he'd managed to arrive here clothed when his garments obviously didn't change with him.

"He trusts you," Leo said. "His kind don't change in front of just anybody."

"I don't want his trust." It was another complication.

Quite right, too. Will's ghost murmured in the back of my mind as his cold lips nuzzled my earlobe.

Corwen returned at dawn, naked and bloody. I know this because I only pretended to be asleep when he stepped in through the front door, sculpted silver in the moonlight. He collected his clothes and crept quietly away again, leaving me feeling . . . what? Discomfited? Aroused? Maybe somewhere between the two.

By the time the household stirred there was a neatly skinned and paunched young buck hanging from a low branch of the elm tree at the bottom of Rosie's garden, and the gore had been cleaned away.

I surveyed the buck. "Good hunting?" I asked him, wiping a speck of still-fresh blood from his chin with my finger and presenting it to him.

"Good enough." He clasped my hand firmly in his,

raised it to his lips, and slowly and deliberately licked the blood with one sweep of his warm, pink, and wholly human tongue. I think I gasped. The intimate action quite took my breath away. I flushed and turned my head, but not before I'd caught a glimpse of his wicked grin.

"Sorry, I sluiced down without the aid of a mirror."

I searched for a barbed comment to slow my pounding heart. "Do you even *have* a reflection?"

Baiting Corwen gave me something else to think about besides revenant brothers, injured aunts, and intimate touches. I smirked as I turned my back on him.

"I told you I'm . . ."

"Not moon-called, I know. Does it make a difference?"

"It will at the next full moon. It means you'll still be alive the following morning rather than a pile of cracked bones and torn flesh."

"Fair enough." I turned back to him. "Corwen, I need you to help me find the Fae, and quickly."

"No."

"David will go—with or without me—and I'd rather not see him go on his own."

"Even if he's more Fae than human?"

"He'll always be my brother."

"If you go to the Fae there's no guarantee you'll come home again."

"I have to come back. I need to free Philip from Walsingham."

"What if he was the one who hurt Rosie?"

"Especially then. Whatever Walsingham has done to him has to be undone. Philip used to be a wretch, yes, but he was never cut out to be a murderer."

"Remember what Rosie said about Fae lords being difficult to resist."

"I should be safe. I haven't been drawn to another man that way since Will died." I pushed thoughts of Gentleman James Mayo away, but then a sudden flash of Corwen's body as he crept quietly through the early morning shadows, of his tongue on my finger, sprang into my mind. I tried to ignore it. "Fae or not, I'm hardly likely to start now."

"And that's one of your problems, isn't it?" Corwen asked.

"Problems?"

"Widowed at twenty-two and still in love with a ghost."

And why not? I felt Will's ghost rather than saw him.

"You go too far, Mr. Corwen. I loved Will!"

"There! You said it in the past tense. Well done!"

"I still love him."

"But does he love you?"

Of course. Will's ghost reassured me. *I'll always love you.*

"Then let her have a life, Tremayne," Corwen said, looking straight at where Will's ghostly voice had come from. "Don't let the fruit wither on the vine."

She's not for your plucking, Wolf!

Will roused himself, a little ectoplasmic whirlwind, tough enough to move things in the real world like a poltergeist might. Corwen faced him, fists balled.

Men!

"Stop it, both of you!" I turned and stomped off into the house.

I think it was not mentioning the Fae again that made Corwen relent. He finished the last of his dinner that night and wiped his greasy fingers on a napkin and threw it on the table. "All right," he said, "we'll go. But you'll both agree to do as I say."

My relief at having an experienced guide evaporated with his first suggestion.

"Absolutely not!" I stood up so quickly that my chair smashed over backward and disturbed Rosie in her sleep. "Outside!" I inclined my head to the door so as not to wake her. Once through the door I turned on him. "I will not say I'm your wife."

"Would you rather be seduced by a Fae?" Corwen's teeth shone in the gathering gloom.

"It won't come to that."

"You're a good-looking woman, Ross."

"Am I supposed to take that as a compliment?"

"If you wish."

"I don't wish."

"We need not say the words, but if we jump the bonfire together I can contest any claim, unless, of course, you want to forget about Philip and waste the rest of your youth bearing Fae children. I'm told that being bedded by a Fae is quite an experience if—"

He didn't get any further. I slapped him hard, and Will's ghost chuckled.

Leo appeared in the doorway. "Not wishing to interrupt, but Rosie would like to see you, Ross. She says to come right away. No, not you," I heard him say when Corwen started to follow me.

26

Wolf Magic

"I'M SORRY IF CORWEN AND I disturbed you, Aunt Rosie. That man can be so infuriating."

Her eyes were brighter than yesterday. She waved me forward with her bandaged hand.

"Come sit."

I sat on the edge of her bed.

"You had a man and lost him."

"Will, yes. He's still here."

"I know. I can feel him. In fact—leave us!" She addressed Will's spirit. Surprisingly, he dissipated and was gone.

"I never intended to abandon Leo. That night the mob came for us . . ." She took a deep breath. "Things happened so fast. One minute it was just talk and intimidation and the next minute it was threats and fear and anger. And then the first torch came smashing through the window, setting fire to the furnishings.

"Ma collapsed from the smoke. She'd always had fragile lungs. We begged for mercy for her, but they wouldn't let her out. Pa wouldn't leave Ma. It was like a desperate madness was on him when she stopped breathing. Aunt Eileen tried to talk some sense into the mob. She'd birthed most of them, and their children, too. But Walsingham must have fired them up with wicked stories. They were past listening to reason. Someone threw a rock and it caught her clean on the temple, killed her in an instant.

"It was all happening too quickly, the smoke, the heat, the roaring of flames inside and angry voices outside. Pa rose from Ma's side and stood astride Aunt Eileen and cursed the mob. He blasted them with a huge explosion of power that must have drained him in an instant. Drained him beyond his limits. It flattened everything outside the house within a radius of . . ."

"I know. I saw the circle. Nothing grows there, even now."

She nodded and gulped. "We didn't know then that men had died. Maybe Pa did. Maybe he'd intended that they should. I think by that time he wasn't quite in his right mind. His wife and his sister gone.

"I thought we should all run, but Pa clutched at his chest and said he was dying. He wanted us away safe without a hue and cry following. He pushed the winterwood box into my hand. Separate and make a new life, he said. Then he told us what to do and wouldn't be persuaded that there was any other way. In truth, I'm not sure we could have carried him far, but by all that's holy we'd have tried.

"So we did as he told us. We stood beneath the solid lintel of the back doorway and blasted our home and all that was in it. A fireball so huge they must have seen it in Chard. And us at the very center unharmed." Tears ran down her face freely. "Margi was always a daddy's girl. I'll always wonder if we could have saved him. We sundered our magical connection like Pa told us to do, then split up and ran. I think I was mad with grief and shock for a while. I didn't think of anything, not even food or shelter, and especially not Leo. I daren't think of Leo. I didn't know Walsingham was dead. I thought if he knew about me and Leo then Leo would be in danger, too. So I just ran. I ended up here, and the Fae found me.

"They let me live under their protection, but I always knew there would be a price. After the box went to Margi I was going to go back and find Leo, but the Fae came for me, to collect their payment.

"I told you before that I couldn't remember the time I spent with them, but I can." She sighed. "I remember every glorious second of it. I forgot Leo altogether and I was totally besotted with my Fae lord, lying in his bed, carrying his child."

Rosie's face tinged pink. "And don't think me a maid with nothing to compare it to. Leo and I were well suited between the sheets. Does that shock you? I hope we might be again if he can forgive me."

"I don't think you have any need to fear about that, and no, it doesn't shock me."

"And you, girl, need to wake up to the real world. Find yourself a flesh and blood man. Will's gone. Move on and let his ghost move on, too."

"I've never—"

"What about Corwen? Fine figure of a man even if he is a werewolf."

"He's not moon-called!"

Was I defending Corwen? I shrugged. "Besides, he's only here because he's obeying the Lady's orders."

"I've seen the way he looks at you."

"That's one more good reason for not playing out a ridiculous charade when we go to the Fae."

"No. Exactly the opposite. It may only be a charade. No one is saying you have to say the words and abide by it afterward, but it will protect you. He'll be possessive, aggressive. That's what you need, unless you want to lose yourself to them."

"Of course not." I shook my head. "I've got too much to do, and somewhere back on the ocean there's my ship and my crew." I took a deep breath. "All right. I'll do as Corwen suggests—but it doesn't mean anything."

"If it doesn't mean anything, why are you worrying about it so much?"

Good question, Aunt Rosie.

I leaned forward and kissed her left cheek, the only part of her face that didn't look as though it hurt like hell.

We left the following morning after Corwen insisted that he and I actually jump the bonfire together in the time-honored tradition of country weddings. No one said the words, so it wasn't real, but David still applauded as we leaped the small fire he'd created. The sham enabled us all to lie by telling the truth. It would have more power if we consummated it, but there was no way I was going that far. Every time I looked closely at Corwen I felt nothing but confusion. He was a handsome man, tall and well-favored, but I didn't trust him. A little worm at the back of my mind reminded me that I hadn't trusted Gentleman Jim either and that hadn't worried me in the slightest. In fact it had added a certain spice to the experience.

We packed what provisions Rosie and Leo could spare into our saddlebags, and Corwen took Leo's horse, having arrived on foot, or four feet.

"So where are we going to?" I asked Corwen as he picked a path into the deep woods.

"It's not geographical," he said. "There are many worlds overlaid on this one, and the Fae inhabit more than one. They are here and in every patch of woodland you've ever seen, but their true home is Iaru."

"So how do we find them?"

"We don't unless they want to be found."

"That's comforting."

"Trust me, wife."

I heard David snort softly as if suppressing laughter, and somewhere overhead in the branches of a birch tree, Will's ghost dislodged a shower of autumn leaves.

"Haven't you got anything better to do?" I shouted upward.

We spent the first night huddled in a hollow beneath the roots of an old oak with an almost-full moon filtering through the branches overhead. We didn't set a watch, since we wanted the Fae to find us. In case the Fae were observing, Corwen insisted he and I sleep together, fully dressed, of course, but wrapped in both cloaks. I couldn't fault his logic, but I sincerely doubted his motive. Despite my reservations, however, I had to admit it was warmer than sleeping alone.

Halfway through the night, I awoke to find Corwen snuggled up tight behind me, his arm around me and his hand resting comfortably on my breast. Comfortable for him, that was. I bent his fingers back and pushed his hand away. He mumbled and turned over. I wasn't sure whether he'd really been asleep or whether he was acting. So I turned over with him and, pretending to be asleep, wrapped myself around him, letting my arm drape over his hip to his groin. See how he liked being embarrassed. But when my fingers trailed over the front of his breeches I felt him ramrod stiff. Hastily I turned over again and feigned a snore, feeling heat prickle my face even in the chill of the night.

I swear the bastard was laughing.

On the second day we rode deeper into the forest. Against all my expectations, I relaxed more the further we went. The upswell of magic that beleaguered me when I left the sea seemed almost normal, now.

"You're a woodland creature," Corwen said. "You should never be on the ocean, it's not your natural habitat."

"Of course it is. I'm a privateer captain, remember."

"I'll bet you're seasick on every other ship but the *Heart*."

"We both are," David chipped in.

"I spent time chained up belowdecks in the *Heart*," Corwen said. "I could feel her. There's winterwood built into her. She's a floating forest, a distillation of all this." He waved one arm toward the canopy of autumn leaves. "Admit you're not a child of the sea."

I wasn't going to admit anything. Will's ghost agreed with me.

We camped the second night on the bank of a small

stream, our horses hobbled to allow them to graze. We still had food in our packs: smoked venison, hard cheese, cold potatoes cooked in their jackets in the roasting pit two days ago, and apples, so we didn't need a fire, but it was pleasant to make one anyway.

David built our fire on the sandy bank of the stream and fed it on chunks of an old fallen branch. We sat companionably in the light of the round moon and the flickering flames until it was time to sleep. Corwen and I curled together again, but thankfully without the inappropriate touching. As I settled down, I was surprised to find that it felt good to have a warm body at my back.

In the darkness before dawn I woke with my scalp prickling. By his breathing Corwen was truly asleep. I gripped his arm and squeezed. He awoke instantly and touched my hand in return to tell me he was fully alert. I could hear David's regular breathing on my other side and small sounds from our horses.

Very gently, Corwen turned over, and I could tell he'd got his knees under him so that he could spring up quickly.

"Fae?" I asked under my breath.

"Don't think so."

And that's when the first fireball hit and I had no time to wonder about who it was. I barely had time to sense it coming and parry it with a burst of air to deflect it into the trees without thinking consciously how to do it. David sprang to full wakefulness. We stood back-to-back, staring out at the darkness.

For a moment I saw a dark figure, arms raised as if in an incantation, outlined in a flare from one of his own fireballs, then he was gone. Walsingham? I didn't think it had been Philip.

"Split up," David said. "Make three targets instead of one."

"No, he'll take us one at a time and think it a gift," Corwen said.

Another strike came out of the night and David and I sent out our own power to block it—mine air, David's fire—but we still staggered beneath the force.

"He's testing us," Corwen said.

Corwen was right. Hard on the heels of that thrust came a hammering, burning sensation that cracked the back of my head and drove me to my knees. Corwen hauled me upright and dragged me to safety between himself and David where the pressure subsided. Blow after blow smacked down onto our shield, one after the other, coming at regular intervals—too regular.

"Watch out," I gasped between hammer strikes. "Something's coming."

And something was.

The dark figure appeared again, his mouth moving as if chanting an incantation. Walsingham. At his feet huddled another figure, Philip. Walsingham had one hand on Philip's head and my little brother's back arched as if in agony. Walsingham was drawing power, feeding on Philip, working some kind of spell.

"Philip!"

I started forward, but Corwen pulled me back. "That's what he wants. Stay together. Ach!" The last exclamation forced itself from his lips and he pushed me away violently.

Corwen, not moon-called as he'd always insisted, began to change, but instead of the instant, smooth change into the silver-pelted wolf, this was an agonizing, bone-cracking, joint-grinding transmogrification into something completely different. His gray eyes rolled upward and his mouth drew back into a snarl. Huge, fierce canine teeth grew down over his bottom jaw as it elongated into a drooling black snout. Without him, power drained from our shield. I watched in horror as his spine twisted, forcing him to his knees. His clothes split and rough fur sprouted, spiky and unkempt. Corwen's wolf form appeared to have the same mass as his human form, but this creature, all werewolf, was much bigger than Corwen. Even on all fours he was my shoulder height.

Corwen's eyes rolled wild with fear, but not for himself. He managed just one word from tortured, elongating jaws. "Run!"

"Fight it, Corwen! Fight it!" I yelled, despairing as his

well-shaped hands extended into sharp, hooked claws, more feline than lupine. He snarled at me like a rabid dog and my insides turned to water. What kind of power did Walsingham have to be able to change Corwen's essential nature?

Without Corwen our shield should have broken. I'm sure that's what Walsingham believed would happen, and that's why he'd moved in close, but when I looked up, David was glowing. I understood what people said about Fae being instantly recognizable. His power swelled to plug the gap in the shield.

"Stop Corwen," David shouted. "Only you can do it. Don't let him draw blood or you'll lose him."

Lose him. Christ on a pig! If he drew blood it would be mine. Blood and bone and flesh. Mine and then David's. Though I thought David might just have enough power to kill a werewolf if it ate his sister.

The beast was almost on his feet, saliva dripping from teeth that would have done justice to a tiger. I shrank back. He probably smelled my fear. He took a step toward me, drawing himself up to his full height and shaking his head as if easing out spinal knots. There was nothing of Corwen left.

"I . . . I can't." My voice dried in my throat.

David's power surged. "He loves you. Don't let the beast win!"

He what? I didn't even have time to take that in, but as the slavering werewolf took another step forward I saw something behind its eyes, a spark of silver, and I ran toward him and flung my arms around his coarse, mangy fur and buried my face in the side of his neck. "Corwen. It's me. Corwen, come back."

He twisted and snapped at me. This wasn't a fairy tale where the beast is overcome by the power of love. I'd made a stupid mistake. I let go, pushed him away and smacked my fist down on his nose, hard, then grabbed his scruff one hand either side of his neck, hoping he couldn't get enough of a twist to get a hold of my flesh. I kept my fingers locked on his fur and my arms stiff, feeling his teeth rake the side of my sleeve, tearing cloth but not skin.

If he drew blood would I turn into a werewolf, too?

"Corwen!"

As he writhed I began to lose my grip. In desperation I let go, leaped half across his back and grabbed for both his ears, pulling them cruelly to stop him turning his head. I hooked my right knee around his side and pulled myself astride, where I hoped he could reach me with neither tooth nor claw. That didn't stop him trying though. He was as flexible as a dog. His head snaked around and snapped close to my left knee. He would have sunk his teeth into it, but I kicked him in the eye.

His head twisted to the other side, but he couldn't quite reach to bite, so he bounded forward and smashed me into the nearest tree. It cracked me across my left shoulder and scraped down my side to my hip and knee. It should have hurt, but in the heat of the moment it didn't.

"Corwen!" I kept repeating his name.

He spun around and I toppled sideways. I tried to keep my hold on his ruff, but the shoulder that had hit the tree seemed to have lost both strength and feeling, and I slid to the floor on my back with the werewolf poised above my throat.

"Corwen." It came out as a whisper. I shut my eyes and expected tearing teeth to meet in the gristle of my throat.

But nothing came.

I felt smooth silky fur under my hand, and when I opened my eyes a silver wolf lay prostrate, belly and head as low to the ground as he could get. He whined once.

I sat up. My left arm stabbed like hell if I tried to move it, and though I could move my fingers, my whole side felt wrong. I reached out with my right hand and grabbed the fur on the side of Corwen's head, wanting to kiss him out of pure relief, but not knowing where to start. I settled for pulling his head close to mine. "Well done! Now change back to human. We need you."

And we did. David had held the shield while I fought with Corwen. I looked for any sign of his Fae-glow diminishing, but if anything it seemed stronger.

Dizziness flooded through me. I couldn't remember how

to stand up. Corwen sprang to his feet, nature-naked, and offered me his hand. I couldn't reach for it without pain shooting through my left arm and my shoulder stabbing fit to make me scream. David glanced down at me, his face set in a mask. "Enough of this."

While Corwen and I held the shield, David lashed out with fire, north, south, east and, as Corwen sheltered me with his altogether too naked body, west. A blast of power scythed over our heads, across the ground. We all heard a cry and felt the pressure on the shield vanish. All around us we had a clearing of gray ash, and the starry sky shone brightly above.

Something moved in the darkness. Walsingham, dragging Philip with him.

"I'll get him." Corwen dropped to all fours and streaked away in silver-wolf form, teeth bared, but perfectly in control of himself. David began to run after, but when I stayed down he came back to me.

"You're injured."

"My arm."

"Broken?" He ran his hand from shoulder to elbow.

"I can make a fist. Shoulder dislocated I think." I probed with my right hand. The shoulder joint itself sagged as if the top of my arm and the point of my shoulder were no longer married to each other. I tried to move my elbow and winced as a blinding pain stabbed through my upper arm and left the whole side of my body feeling feeble.

It took me a few moments before I trusted my voice not to quaver. "You'll have to put the joint back."

"What? I can't." David looked horrified.

I'd once had to fix Hookey's shoulder, but I didn't think I could do my own. I knew the principles, though.

"Yes, you can. You need to straighten the arm and pull it steadily until it pops back in."

"That's going to hurt."

He was right about that. I could feel sweat beading on my brow in anticipation. Every little movement felt as though someone was driving a hot knife into my bicep.

"It'll hurt more and for longer if you don't do it."

He blew out a breath, hissing between his teeth. It was acceptance of a sort. "Lie down." David supported me as I leaned back. I think I whimpered.

Just straightening my arm was agony. I tensed for what was to come.

He pulled.

I screamed.

He stopped pulling.

"I'm sorry. I'm sorry."

It took me a few moments before I could speak again. "You mustn't stop once you start, no matter how much noise I make. Put your foot up high against my ribs, just under the armpit to give yourself some leverage. Pull gently and don't stop until you feel the joint pop back in."

He nodded. "I think you need to relax your arm. Let it go slack."

Easier said than done. I tried to slow down my breathing, to think about anything other than what was going to happen next.

David slipped off his boot and put his stockinged foot high against my ribcage as he took my left hand in his right and put his left on my upper arm. Pain slammed into me.

A steady pull, a grinding and a pop, and mercifully the agony subsided to an almost bearable ache that left me gasping for breath. David knelt by my side.

"I'm sorry. I'm sorry," he whispered.

I balled my hand into a fist and moved my elbow experimentally. "You keep saying that. Don't be. It worked. That's much better."

"I suggest you don't try and swing hand over hand up a rope for a week or two."

"I'll try and remember that."

David helped me back to the middle of our camp. Every step I took hurt. My left side, from shoulder to ankle, felt battered. I didn't know which joint to favor as I walked, but I could cope with it, and I didn't think there was any permanent damage.

"How do you feel? Have you any hurts?" I felt almost guilty. I'd been so wrapped up in my own misfortune that I hadn't asked David. I expected him to be exhausted, but instead, he looked invigorated.

"Strange. I feel strong. I can't explain it. As if the power I used didn't drain out of me at all."

I took my own weight again. "I can see the power. Rosie and Leo are right, you know, about the Fae thing."

"How can you be so sure?"

"The moon's behind a cloud and we're sitting in David-light."

He nodded. "This isn't going to be easy to explain to Mr. Sharpner."

Despite my aching side and despite Corwen still being out there, somewhere, for some reason we both found that very funny. David rekindled the remains of the fire and we sat by it, not speaking, but the silence was punctuated by one or the other of us starting to giggle again.

27

The Fae

IN THE COLD EARLY LIGHT before the sun breasted the horizon, Corwen came creeping back to camp in wolf form. He crawled the last few yards low to the ground and rolled over submissively, baring his throat to me. I could barely resist rubbing his belly as if he were a big dog, but that would be completely inappropriate in so many ways.

"It's all right, Corwen, it wasn't your fault."

He whined.

"You can change back, now."

I reached out and touched his head between his ears. He squirmed over and pushed against my hand, licking my fingers.

He whined again and David laughed. "Here!" he said, and threw a cloak over the wolf.

The shape beneath that rough wool changed, and Corwen stood holding the garment around him. "I . . . err . . . don't appear to have any clothes."

If a wolf could look sheepish, he did.

"It wasn't the Fae," he said.

David said, "I didn't think it was."

"I couldn't find them," Corwen said. "There was a scent, but it led me nowhere."

"Walsingham?" David asked.

"Two tracks. One of them was strangely redolent of Ross and Rosie. Family, I'd say."

"Philip?"

"Unless you have another brother."

"Dear Lord, I hope not. Did Philip try to kill us or was it just Walsingham?" I asked.

"I don't know. My nose is good, but not that good."

I'd killed hand-to-hand in the heat of a fight, but I'd always justified it to myself by saying that my victims had done something to deserve it, but in reality, mostly what they'd done was resist a privateer—me.

There's a defining moment in every person's life. This was mine. I'd never captain the *Heart* again. The revelation came to me as suddenly and as simply as that. No fuss, no agonizing over the rights and wrongs of it. The decision had been made and that was it. David would understand, but Will . . . what would my poor Will think?

Disappointment. Of course Will's ghost knew as soon as I did. He stood in front of me, hugging his arms to his chest and seemed somehow diminished.

"Perhaps Walsingham is forcing Philip," David said. "Using his magical strength. Perhaps that poppet is more than a threat. What if it truly makes Philip into a puppet?"

"I've never heard of any witch who can do that." Corwen, wrapped in his cloak, started hunting through the undergrowth for his clothes.

"You didn't see the markings on the floor of Skinner's Warehouse," David said, poking about with Corwen. "Walsingham is no mere witch."

"Damn!" But Corwen's exclamation was only for his shirt, found in tatters.

"Well, that's not going to be much use." Corwen looked despairingly at the rag. "I can fix some things, but that's more tear than cloth. I liked that shirt, too. We'd been together a long time."

"These might be repairable." David handed Corwen his

breeches, still recognizable, if a little ripped. Corwen, his lower half shrouded in blanket, bonded the fabric together magically and pulled them on. In the meantime we'd found his boots more or less undamaged. Neither of us had clothes to spare, but David gave Corwen his waistcoat, and though it didn't meet around Corwen's much broader frame it at least gave the appearance of having him clothed again. The cloak would help to keep him warm.

"Pity you can't grow a pelt while you're in human form."

He didn't laugh, and I felt mean.

David went downstream to see if he could find the horses.

While he was pulling the waistcoat this way and that, trying to mold it into a better fit, Corwen said, "I'm sorry."

"What for?"

"Isn't it obvious?"

"We fought a dangerous enemy and if we didn't win, we certainly didn't lose. You've got nothing to be sorry for."

He started to protest.

"Enough."

We heard horses coming through the trees and David called out. "It's all right. They're friends."

Turning to look in the direction of his voice, we saw an unearthly glow, and David walked into camp leading our horses, followed by seven Fae riding in a line, and at their head was Larien.

It was Larien, yet not as I remembered him. He was taller than I recalled, and I'm sure I would have noticed if he'd glowed with power, and if his skin had been smooth and translucent instead of the color and grain of weathered rowan wood. I immediately did what all humans seem to do when faced with Fae. I bowed. I noticed Corwen followed suit. So the Lady's creatures acknowledged the Shining Ones, too, did they? Interesting.

To describe a Fae in words would make them sound human, but they were as far removed from human as gold is from base metal. Each human-shaped face exhibited an unearthly quality, unmarked by life, but all knowing. If I'd had to use one word to describe the whole group I would have picked *graceful*, for indeed they were full of grace, not just in the way they moved, but also in the way they embodied an inner stillness born of utter confidence in themselves.

Their clothes were woven of the finest thread, which shone with the luster of precious metals while remaining as soft as silk. Any dirt that tried to splash them would shrink away in fear.

Their horses would put any in a king's stable to shame.

"Miss Rossalinde." Larien's tone was formal as he stressed the honorific he'd used when he'd been masquerading as my mother's rowankind. Masquerade it must have been, though he'd worn that mantle well enough at the time. I wondered whether he hated all humans. I wouldn't blame him if he did.

"Lord Larien. I see you've met your son."

David turned his head so quickly I thought he might spin right around. So Larien hadn't introduced himself. I'd thought that might be the case.

"Is that why you brought him to me?" His mouth quirked up at the corners.

"David's heritage is something we hadn't suspected until recently, but it explains a lot."

"Your beast knew it all along." Larien barely acknowledged Corwen's presence, and I bristled at his offhand dismissal, though Corwen, wisely, didn't let himself be goaded.

I concentrated on Larien, wondering if our past relationship would help or hinder. Larien had stayed with my family for his own reasons, but he'd been a bondsman, treated like nothing, taken for granted. Old Mrs. Emery's words came back to me. Something about: *I wonder what will happen when folks find that instead of a tame mouser they have a tiger in their barn.*

"Come with me." Larien looked at David and then at me. "Not the beast."

Corwen stepped forward and his voice remained calm

and steady. "Ross and I have jumped fire together. Where she goes, I go."

It wasn't exactly a lie.

Larien turned to look at him, and I held my breath, but he merely nodded once and said, "Have a care Silverwolf. We know where your allegiance lies. You play a dangerous game, and you are a world away from the Okewood."

"My Lord." Corwen bowed.

We mounted our horses and rode in the column, David with Larien, Corwen and I close behind, and the rest of the Fae following us like an escort, or guard.

I thought we rode through the same Old Maizy Forest, but subtle things had changed. The further we traveled the less autumnal it became. The season ran backward until the green leaves were more like high summer. I spotted creatures in the woodland that I couldn't identify, brightly colored birds and—only glimpsed for a moment through the trees—one small roan pony with a horn in the center of its forehead.

Iaru, I thought. We were no longer in our own safe world, but somewhere else that existed outside of geography, yet we'd crossed without passing any noticeable border. I glanced at Corwen, and he nodded as if reassuring me that he'd noticed, too.

Larien and David were deep in conversation, David more animated than I'd seen him in weeks.

I'm going to lose him. Finding a family member I could love was a novelty for me, and losing him would hurt. In recognizing that, I knew I'd already accepted the possibility that David's path may run in a very different direction from mine, but it didn't make it any easier.

We neared our destination after a journey that may have lasted minutes or days. I heard the sounds first, instruments and voices in perfect harmony. The notes carried my heart away with them. Yet when I saw where we had come to I almost forgot the music as my eyes tried to take it all in. Encampment? Village? City? Palace? It was all and more. All and less.

A woodland glade became a lofty, fan-vaulted hall of

tree trunk and arched branch. Indoors, yet also outdoors, it glowed softly with diffuse and dappled light from a totally alien sun. I think I stopped breathing. At any rate I realized I was going dizzy and forced my lungs to suck in a breath of air, inhaling strange spicy perfumes and a hint of tangy smoke.

Six younger Fae came forward, all bearing a look of the Sumners. One dark-haired, fair-skinned female came to me. "I'm Rosie's daughter, I thank you for caring for her."

"Margann? That makes us cousins, I believe?"

Was it wise to claim kinship? I held my breath.

She smiled and inclined her head. "It does." I saw a strong family resemblance to both Rosie and my mother. I supposed that meant to me as well.

"Couldn't you go to her?"

"I am still counted as a child amongst the Fae, and not allowed to cross over into the world of men without dispensation."

"And do you always do as you are told?"

"Of course." Her eyes held humor. "I was given no specific instructions, however, regarding the glamour around her cottage. Did you think one of my father's workings would be so easy to see through without a little help?"

"Your father? Are you Larien's as well?"

She laughed and shook her head. "Dantin is my father. Don't judge him too harshly. He has little liking for your kind, but it's with good reason."

I wanted to ask why, but she bowed and left me.

Corwen spoke softly. "I told you they are not like us. Keep your wits about you."

A young Fae boy took our horses and another brought me a goblet. I didn't know whether it was more rude to refuse the cup or to take it and leave it full. Out of the corner of my eye I saw Corwen take the cup offered to him, raise it to his lips, but not drink, so I did the same.

More Fae, some single, some arm-linked couples, drifted into the hall to listen to the music or, more likely, to see the newcomers. A fair couple stepped up to us, ignored Corwen, and bowed politely to me. The man touched my cheek and I swayed toward him, fascinated, before Corwen's hand clamped down on my arm with bruising strength and his lips curled back in a snarl even though the wolf was nowhere to be seen.

"She jumped the flames with me." He looked straight across me into the eyes of the male Fae.

"And why would I worry about that, beast?"

For a moment their gazes locked and it was as though both men had invisible hackles rising, but the Fae's gaze dropped before Corwen's did. The Fae woman put her hand on her partner's arm and broke his concentration. "There will be others when the rowankind return," she said, drawing him away.

For a fleeting moment I was angry with Corwen; then I realized how easily I would have slipped into the couple's thrall.

"Thanks."

"I told you to keep your wits about you." He sounded angry.

Margann walked back into the circle hand in hand with a young Fae lord. I had to look twice to see that it was David. He was the same but different. Why hadn't I noticed how beautiful he was? I'd never seen his hair brushed back from his face, except when wind-lashed, so to suddenly see a perfect widow's peak accentuating a broad intelligent forehead made me wonder if I'd ever looked at my little brother before.

My guts twisted. I *had* lost him.

Larien clapped his hands once. It was as if he'd signaled the start of a business meeting. All the Fae who had no reason to be there melted away and only the council of seven Fae lords remained, plus David and the six young Fae. Seven tall chairs stood in a circle where there had been no chairs before. The lords sat, a young Fae standing behind each chair. David moved to stand behind Larien. Corwen and I filled the only spare space in the circle's circumference, standing like supplicants. Corwen's knuckles brushed against mine, and I took strength from the touch.

I managed to lock glances with David and mouth, “Are you all right?”

I got a tight nod in return. He looked like a beggar who’s been invited to sup at a king’s table, slightly bemused and not quite sure which spoon to pick up first.

“What do you want of us?” Larien asked.

“I ask the same question.” I took the winterwood box from my pouch, unwrapped it and held it out. Some magical force lifted it gently from my fingers and suspended it in midair.

The oldest Fae cleared his throat and in doing so had complete attention. His dark hair had gray wings and the skin around his eyes had developed folds. I wondered how old he might be. “The time is approaching,” he said.

“We have waited long.” The next Fae in the circle spoke.

“That which your family took from Iaru . . .”

“May soon be restored.”

“Yours is the task . . .”

“If balance is to be maintained.”

Each Fae spoke in turn, finally coming around to Larien. “The box must be opened and an end put to the Summoner curse.”

My heart lurched.

“I don’t understand. What curse? What’s in the box? Why must it be opened?”

Larien focused on me. I suddenly remembered him with my mother, in her bed, and my face heated. I’d been too young to understand then. Now I wondered if he’d made her happy for a time. I hoped so.

The Fae elder said, “More than two centuries ago as you reckon time, a Summoner called us from the forests to ask for our help. He said England faced its greatest danger in five hundred years, an invasion force from Spain.”

“You helped Martyn the Summoner to defeat the Armada?”

The lord to Larien’s left, the one in the chair attended by Margann, leaned forward swiftly, his weight almost on his feet as if he would leap up at any moment. “The affairs of humans are not the affairs of the Fae!”

"Dantin." Larien put one arm sideways to still his neighbor and turned back to us. "It is as my brother says. Our concerns are not for the world of men. We refused him and returned to the forest, but before we did, we gave him our word not to interfere in his task, however he chose to complete it. You must understand that our word, once given, is binding, for the Fae do not lie."

The lord to Larien's right spoke. "Though the Summoner's power . . ."

"Was greater than we thought." The lord to *his* right finished off his sentence.

"The mistake was mine," Larien said. "I judged him of little consequence and I was wrong. When we refused our help, he summoned our servants. They were less able to resist. Those woodland sprites whom our forefathers had drawn forth from the living rowan trees to mingle their seed with ours. Those children became the rowankind, children of our own flesh, who lived alongside us for many thousands of your years. They had their own wild magic, a magic of growing things and natural forces. They became our servants, yes, but also our friends and often the mothers of our children. A gentle people, yet with a deep power of their own. Martyn summoned them across the borders of Iaru into the land of men."

"A whole race," Dantin added.

"Found their power . . ."

"Sucked away . . ."

"Like mother's milk from a tit."

"But unlike mother's milk . . ."

"There was no replenishment."

The sentence went around the lords again, and Larien took up the explanation once more. "The Summoner drew thousands of our rowankind to him, fastened upon their power of weather-working, called it forth, and left them empty, like eggshells."

Dantin scowled. "And we had sworn not to interfere, though there were those of us who would have willingly broken our oaths."

"The elders forbade it," Larien said.

Dantin exhaled sharply. I had no doubt that he was one of the rebels. "Martyn promised to restore them, but he could not. The time came and passed. We could do nothing to ease their torment except erase the memory of what they had once been, in their minds and also in the minds of men. My own leman amongst them."

He'd lost his lover. Was that the reason for Dantin's bitterness?

"A kindness to prevent the rowankind from going mad," Larien added. "Soon after we made an agreement. England's queen decreed that they would be provided for in the households of her subjects."

The older Fae spoke up again. "Within a few generations they became chattels, their sacrifice forgotten and the Summoner himself withered and gone from the world, beyond our reach, his evil unpunished."

I knew little enough of magic beyond what I'd needed for myself over the years. I couldn't claim to be learned, but I did know that magic didn't simply vanish without consequence. Whatever Martyn the Summoner had taken from the rowankind had to have gone somewhere.

A cold knot filled my belly. I reached for Corwen's hand and found it waiting for me, warm and reassuring against my icy fingers.

"I've got it, haven't I?"

Dantin snorted, a half-laugh. "Don't flatter yourself."

"You have some of it," Larien said. "As do all the Sumners, down the generations."

"How do you mean?"

The young Fae behind the chairs stepped forward and knelt before them, each facing the center. David followed suit.

"These are all Fae children of a Sumner mother," Larien said. "David you know about, and Margann who is daughter of Dantin and Rosie Sumner." Margann inclined her head. "And here are the other Sumner children. Alder is the son of Eileen, your grandfather's sister."

A dark boy nodded but didn't smile. Alder had to be at least as old as my mother and Rosie, but he looked about twenty. The villagers in Summoner's Well had said there were rumors that Eileen had carried a child, though she'd never married.

Then Larien introduced Bronn, Elva, and Nerea—children of earlier Sumner generations. Again they still looked to be barely more than children. Though there had to be at least twenty years between each of them, they looked the same age as each other. At last he held out his hand to a fair-skinned, golden-haired one who appeared only a few years older than me. The young man bowed stiffly but managed a smile with his eyes.

"And I am Galan, son of Jane Summoner, who was the youngest daughter of Martyn the Summoner himself."

That would make Galan almost two hundred years old. I hastily revised my estimate of the lifespan of the Fae.

"We each have a part of it, Ross," David said. He waved a hand to the Sumner-Fae. "What they believe is that you have the Summoner talent, the Great Talent of the first-born, that can draw the power out of us and transfer it back to the rowankind who rightfully own it. You can release their magic back into the world. Right the wrong done by Martyn the Summoner."

"And does the box contain the means to do it?"

There was a silence.

"They don't know," David said. "They think so. Summoning isn't a part of Fae magic, but Martyn left it for a purpose, and they think it's a way to undo what he couldn't do in his lifetime."

"We still don't know how to open it."

"Your mother had the power, but not without her sister, and once they were sundered, that was impossible," Larien said. "Now we think her children, yourself and David together, may succeed."

"You mean we could have opened it at any time?"

"We think that the box is sensitive to the power-holders, and that it can only be opened when the right people are gathered together to complete the transfer of power. The rest of the Sumners—your Aunt Rosie, Margann, and the other Fae-children—must be present to willingly yield their power."

"Or have it ripped from them," Dantin spoke.

"All of them?" I asked. My fingers tightened on Corwen's hand.

He nodded.

I glanced at David. He'd gone a shade or two paler.

"And what happens to us all when we relinquish the stolen magic?" I asked.

Larien shrugged, a curiously human gesture, and I wondered if his time in Plymouth might have made him a little more understanding of humankind than most Fae. "I don't know. Each of you has a different magical inheritance."

"I don't mean magic. Will we live through it?"

Dantin cut in. "Expendable."

I saw the surprise in David's eyes. The other Fae youngsters seemed to know, even though Margann licked her lips and swallowed hard.

"Expendable how?"

"When the rowankind power is sucked away, we don't know what will be left."

"What happens to me if I'm the one doing the sucking?"

"We don't know that either," Larien said. "The Sumners have a strand of magic that's purely their own. You'll be using that. If you're strong enough, you may survive."

Thanks, Larien. What a comfort.

The full realization of what might happen if we succeeded hit me. Wild magic, such as had not been seen for centuries, would suddenly be loosed. The rowankind tabbies would turn into tigers. I dropped Corwen's hand. What part would the Green Man, his Lady, and all of their creatures play in this?

"Think it through, Ross," Corwen muttered.

"I am. That's the trouble."

We had come so far in just the last thirty years and now science and industry, our very society, would be overturned if magic came back into the world. Would that be good or bad? Reason could so easily become unreasonable, chaotic, disordered. Dangerous.

I began to see what Walsingham's mission was. Why he intended to purge the Sumner family from the face of the earth.

And I wasn't entirely sure that he was wrong.

It might be the end of the world as we knew it and the start of a new era for humankind, one dominated by magic. But if I didn't open the box, a whole race would continue living in unjust servitude.

It all hinged on the Fae. What would their part be in all this? What did they intend for my kind? I couldn't trust that they'd be humane. I'd already seen that they didn't care about our life or death. What did they intend for the rowankind? Would they go from one servitude to another under the Fae, their creators and masters?

I needed time to think.

"There's a Sumner child missing," I said. "My brother Philip."

"He's dead," Larien said.

"No, he isn't. He's been taken by a man called Walsingham. He's in London."

I didn't think it possible to surprise a Fae, but Larien's eyes registered shock before he regained his composure.

"I have to free Philip," I said. "If you're right we can't do this without him."

Dantin leaned forward. "It will take all the Summoner's offspring, Larien, and we cannot travel to the city without—"

"I know." Larien sounded irritated. He turned to me. "How do you propose to go about this task?"

I shrugged. "I don't know. Walsingham has magic. He's more than just witchkind, he's a sorcerer. He works with darkness and spellcraft. He works with blood."

"You intend to do this alone?"

"She won't be alone." Corwen spoke up.

"I'll go. Philip's my brother, too," David said.

"No, you will not," Larien said. "The beast is expendable, you are not."

"Ross isn't expendable."

Larien silenced David's protest with a look.

"But I'm also the only one who can find Philip. Right, Larien?"

I caught a watch-your-step glance from Corwen.

"The city is poison to us," Larien said. "My time in

Plymouth would have killed me without frequent trips back to Iaru. London would be even more dangerous for any Fae. It's much more densely populated and polluted with humankind. For any one of us to travel to the city would take many months of purification both before and after. We can find Philip—and we will if we have to—but not without cost."

So the Fae power was not unlimited.

"I can walk you between worlds and take you to the outskirts of London," Larien said. "You must find Philip and bring him back. All three of Margery Sumner's children must wield the power together."

"But if you can't free him, you should kill him," Dantin said. "So that Philip's power passes to you and David."

"You're asking me to kill my own brother?"

Larien glared at Dantin and then turned back to me. "It's true that it works equally well as a solution, but I know you too well, Rossalinde. We will give you a chance to bring your brother to us alive. If we have to go in search of him, he may not be so lucky."

They would step on Philip and think no more of it than they would if they stepped upon an ant. Hot acid burned the back of my throat. I swallowed hard and tried to squash my anger down to manageable proportions. "Why not just kill me as well, so David can open the box alone?"

"You are the firstborn," Larien said. "You have inherited the Great Power to summon the wild magic and return it to its rightful owners."

"And if I refuse?"

Dantin jumped to his feet. "The Fae do not ask."

Corwen stepped forward between us, a snarl on his lips.

"Dantin!" Larien's use of his name was a warning. "You have said too much." He turned to me. "Rossalinde, we must go swiftly."

"And take your dog with you," Dantin said.

28

Larien and Margery

THE GROVE DISAPPEARED around us and Corwen and I stood with Larien beneath the branches of a two-hundred-year-old oak on the edge of heathland. This certainly wasn't Iaru or even the Old Maizy. Autumn leaves covered the ground. One good breeze and the trees would be winter skeletons. I shivered at the sudden drop in temperature. There was no sign of David. Was he a hostage for my good behavior?

Our horses were tethered nearby, looking totally unconcerned despite their adventure.

"Where are we?" I looked around, pretty certain that I'd never been here before.

"Richmond Park," Larien said. "The city of London is ten miles that way." He pointed. "Stay south of the river by Wimbleton and Southwark. There you'll find London Bridge. There's all you need in your saddle bags, gold and some clothes for your wolf."

"And David?"

"I will keep him safe."

"Until it's time for me to rip the power out of him."

"Until then, yes."

"And what if I don't come back?"

"You will."

"If I don't?"

"We have David."

"He's your son."

He cocked his head slightly to one side as if he didn't understand why that should make a difference. He was right, dammit. I would go back.

"May I ask one question?" I'd saved this one up for when Larien was away from the other Fae.

"One."

"It's a question of two parts."

"Ah, nothing is ever simple with you mortals."

I took that for assent. "When you brought the box to Plymouth, why didn't you force Mother and Rosie back together to open the box between them?"

"It is an answer in two parts. Firstly, your mother was terrified of seeing her sister again after what had happened at Bullcrest. An endeavor of this magnitude cannot be undertaken by someone who is not fully committed to its success. I could force them together, but I could not force them to try the box. And secondly, by the time I arrived in Plymouth you had been born, the first of a new generation. Small as you were, I sensed in you that power which maybe your mother lacked."

"So do I still get my second question?"

He nodded.

"Instead of forcing Margery and Rosie back together, you decided to seduce my mother and make another Sumner-Fae child. But, having succeeded, why did you stay?"

"Your mother was a complex woman." There was something in his voice.

"Don't tell me you loved her?"

"Is that a third question?"

"No, go on, tell it your own way."

He inclined his head and continued. "A complex woman full of deep emotion which she imprisoned inside because she thought that was the only way to stay strong. You talk of love, but there is also care. To the Fae, mortals are a mayfly race. They come and go so swiftly that loving them will never be more than a brief flare of passion. I did care for her, however. I saw how she let her past shape her future, and I saw how it affected the way she dealt with you. She recognized your magic when you were still a tiny baby, and it terrified her. She feared that her relationship with you would bring out your power, just as the closeness between herself and Rosie had intensified their abilities. She made herself distant, leaving you to Ruth's care and a succession of governesses and tutors, never keeping one for too long lest they notice something odd about you and identify you as a potential witch."

"She never cared—"

He looked at me and I shut up. I felt Corwen's warm hand seek mine and I twined my cold fingers with his.

"I wasn't there all the time. I came and went as it pleased me, though no one in the household ever realized it, as I was able to alter their perceptions—even yours." He smiled. "I kept an eye on your development. Philip's, too. This was before your mother and I became close. Philip showed no magic potential as a small child, and that's why he became your mother's favorite. He was not only her son and heir, he was safe.

"When it became obvious that your mother was not going to be the one to open the box, I knew I would have to wait for you to grow up."

"So you thought you'd while away the time by seducing my mother. That wasn't a question, by the way."

He smiled. "There was certainly some seduction involved. As I said, your mother's passions ran deep. David was a consequence, a welcome one—on my part anyway. You asked me if I loved Margery, and I ask you whether it is not a good thing to care for the mother of your child? I had seen David's foster home and knew he was well looked after, but your mother was still troubled. When your magic manifested in front of her and I saw her reaction, I knew that I had tried my best and failed. Her complexities became difficulties. I thought of revealing myself to you, but you were still growing. Then you ran away with your pirate. Once on the sea you were lost to me. And without you, the box could not be opened, no matter what your mother did. When your mother lay dying I visited her one last time and put it into her mind that she needed to summon you and give you the box."

"So you planned this?"

"That is your third question, and I'm not obliged to answer."

Corwen's throat rumbled in a soft growl as Larien stepped back and faded into Iaru between one breath and the next.

"We should go," he said. "Flee. I have family in Yorkshire. They would welcome us, or we could go back to the *Heart*. You heard what he said. Once you ran away to sea, he lost track of you."

When had Corwen begun to include himself in my future plans? Damn that bloody bonfire!

"I can't leave David without being absolutely sure he's all right," I said.

"I know, I know. He gives you no choice." Corwen put his arms around me, and I relented and allowed myself a moment of comfort, my head resting on his chest, still naked save for the too-small waistcoat.

"Brothers, huh! Life was much simpler when I thought myself alone."

"David told me a little about Philip. It doesn't sound as though there was much love between you. If he were my brother I might leave him to stew."

"What do you know about brothers?" I pulled away from Corwen's embrace.

"Enough."

Did Corwen have brothers in Yorkshire? I knew nothing about him, yet, annoying as he was, I'd started to put my trust in him. When had that happened?

I shrugged. "I might not like Philip very much, but he is

my brother. If only he were more like David." In just a few short months I'd grown to love my new little brother. If his way lay permanently with the Fae, I'd miss him.

The crew would miss him.

With a guilty start I realized that I'd barely thought of the *Heart* and her crew since finding Rosie. I stretched out my awareness of her and found her already anchored downriver by Gravesend. We'd arranged to meet by Wapping Old Stairs—the only bit of London I knew—and I summoned the *Heart* to our agreed destination.

"I've found the *Heart*," I said. "She'll come upriver on the tide and be in Wapping by tomorrow in the afternoon."

I had a sudden awful thought and checked my pouch. The box was inside, safely wrapped, though I'd last seen it hovering in the air in the center of the circle. I didn't know whether I was relieved or angry. I leaned my back against the oak and blinked back tears.

Corwen busied himself checking the contents of the saddlebags and wisely didn't try to comfort me again. I think I might have bitten his head off if he had.

"Even if I can do what they ask, why should I? I don't want to destroy their *expendable* children, and I especially don't want to hurt David or Rosie's Margann. The rowankind don't know any better. It was their many-times great-grandparents who lost their magic. These rowankind are . . ."

All those phrases came back to me. *They're like children. It's for their own good. They can't look after themselves. It's a kindness, really,* and then I thought of those flashes of anger I'd seen when they'd thought no one was watching, and little Annie's admission that some of her friends spoke of rebellion. Not all rowankind were happy with their lot. Besides, happy or not, it wasn't *right!*

"How did I let myself get caught up in all this in the first place?" I banged the back of my head against the tree trunk twice and then stood upright, one hand on the bark for support as my brain caught up with itself.

"I'm in an impossible situation. If this foolish and totally impractical plan somehow succeeds and I manage to deliver Philip to Iaru and if we manage to open the box and somehow miraculously restore power to the rowankind, what happens then?"

"What do you mean?" Corwen's brows drew together in a puzzled frown.

"Well, say you know your place, and that place is below stairs, and suddenly you find yourself infused with magical power and burning with the knowledge that you and generations of your race before you have been kept only to obey and to serve. What would you do?"

"Rowankind are peaceful people. Why would you suppose—"

"You've never lived in the real world. I've seen the way some of the rowankind look at us when they think we can't see."

"I have lived in the real world, Ross, I just choose not to at the moment. I've seen rowankind under pressure. Yes there are some hotheads, but that's true of every race. Give them the benefit of the doubt. Local difficulties are a small price to pay."

He turned away and busied himself by drawing a shirt and cravat from the saddle bag, followed by a green silk waistcoat and a darker green cutaway frock coat and then, to my amazement, ivory breeches and leather knee boots which on their own looked twice as big as the bag in which they'd been stored. More Fae magic.

"Here, look." He drew out a cream day dress and burgundy pelisse.

"How on earth does so much fit into such a small bag?"

"The same way that, if I need to carry my clothes with me in wolf form I can pack them into a bag so compact that I can strap it to my body before I change and have it still there when I change back. Not my magic, by the way, but borrowed from the Lady."

"The Lady has Fae magic?"

"The Lady and the Fae have different origins, but magic is magic."

He tossed the dress to me. "Larien's got good taste," he said. "Let's hope they fit."

I tossed it back to him. "Save that for later. I'll stick with what I'm wearing while we ride. Perhaps people will assume I'm your unkempt servant." I dropped my voice into a low gutter accent. "You being such a smart ge'man, an' all."

He laughed and packed the dress back into the bag.

Corwen took off David's too-small waistcoat and shook out the folds from the clean linen shirt. I gazed mesmerized at the muscles of his back as he raised his arms and pulled the shirt over his head. The fabric slipped down to cover bare skin and I realized I was staring. I deliberately turned away as he dressed in breeches and boots. By the time he was fully clothed, I had regained my composure.

"Ah, perfect fit." Corwen flexed his shoulders and stretched his arms. He grinned. "I must get the name of Larien's tailor."

My mind darted hither and yon. Was Corwen right or would freeing the rowankind and restoring them to what they once were generate a massive retaliation? Would there be blood in the streets or just a few of what Corwen called local difficulties? What were the rowankind capable of when at full power? If they had no sympathy for either human or witchkind, who could blame them? Their release could return elemental magic back into the world, the likes of which had not been seen in over two centuries.

And what did the Fae want? Was their desire to see the rowankind free wholly altruistic? They'd said themselves that they'd made the rowankind, so the rowankind power was a mix of tree spirit and Fae. Did the Fae want it back? They could probably rule us, even turn us into their slaves, if that's what they wanted. That they could didn't mean that they would, of course. They could have done it long ago and then the course of history would have been very different, but we'd set an example by keeping bonded rowankind for two hundred years. What if the Fae thought it was time to turn the tables?

Or what if the Fae wanted me to free the rowankind so they could enslave them again?

"These are yours, I believe." Corwen held out my pistols, Mr. Bunney's finest. Corwen packed away the Fae bag and handed me my horse's reins. I mounted and nudged him into a steady walk.

My brain whirled. There were too many possibilities. What would the Mysterium do if wild magic were released? Would there be witch hunts, riots, and mobs? The world was not ready for such magic. In the two hundred years since Gloriana's time, we English had grown up. We had warred amongst ourselves, killed a king and restored his heir while giving much of his power to Parliament, fought off two Scottish rebellions, and invited the Hanovers to become our Protestant monarchs rather than return to Catholicism. Common men ruled now. Reason prevailed. Science was in the ascendant.

We lived in a practical, modern world, with its steam engines to provide unlimited power for the use of the new breed of manufactory owners and captains of industry. Just before I ran away with Will, news had come to Plymouth that a man in Cornwall had used spirits of coal, a kind of flammable air, to illuminate his own home, and I had recently read an article in the Gentleman's Magazine about a plan to light up the streets of the capital.

"What are you thinking?" Corwen asked as he rode alongside me.

"That magic is being squeezed out."

"How so?"

"Science can now do so many of the things that magic does that there's no longer a need for witchkind." I put up a small witchlight. "What need of this when the streets of cities will soon be lit by lamps that anyone without magic can make? Magic is going out of fashion. It will fade."

And maybe that was no bad thing.

Corwen scowled. "Magic isn't subject to fashion. It just exists. I'm not a shapechanger because it's fashionable. I have no choice."

"The Mysterium—"

He cut across me. "A bloody end to the lot of 'em! The Mysterium knows nothing of magic. They're a bunch of pettifogging clerks led by frightened men."

"So what do you want me to do, Corwen? Or should I ask what the Lady of the Forests wants, for surely it's one and the same? Are you here to ensure one outcome or the other?"

He shook his head. "The Lady sent me to watch and report back."

"To be my watch-wolf?"

"If you like, yes."

"She didn't send you to jump the fire with me."

He grinned. "I have a certain amount of autonomy."

"And how do you report back?"

"Like this." He held out his left hand and a crow flapped down and alighted on his wrist, causing his horse to skitter sideways until he brought it under control, one-handed. He stared at the bird, and the bird stared back until he released it into the air and it flew high over the trees. "It doesn't have to be a crow. Weasels make good messengers, as do rats, but never trust a fox."

I saw a glint in his eye, a promise of what might be if wild magic returned to the land, and was reminded that he was not a tame wolf, no matter how well he controlled himself.

If I opened the box and returned the power to the rowankind I could bring on disaster, change the course of human history. Yet a great wrong had been done and was still being done. It was true that it was a subtle slavery and that they were in many ways more comfortable than some of the poor wretches begging on our city streets, but they were still not free.

On a personal level, to right this wrong might cost the lives of seven magical children, and all of the remaining Sumner family. I was under no illusion; the Fae would probably not be unhappy to see the Sumners wiped out after what we'd . . . after what Martyn had done. This was truly a case of the sins of the fathers, or in this case, the seven or eight-times great-grandfather, coming down to rest upon the shoulders of the children.

"Why now?" I muttered.

Corwen gave me a sidelong glance.

"If I die, does Philip inherit the Great Power?" I asked him.

"I don't think it works like that, otherwise Rosie would have inherited it when your mother died. Always to the firstborn."

"My firstborn is dead."

There was a long pause while he took in the new information. I wondered if it made any difference to the way he felt about me, to know that I'd carried another man's child.

"I'm sorry. I didn't know." His sincerity was evident in the tone of his voice. "That explains why the Fae are suddenly keen for this to happen now. Your firstborn—a boy or a girl?"

"A boy."

"Your son would have had the Great Power, which means you're the last of your kind."

"The last hope for the rowankind?"

"Yes."

I nodded. It was a minor miracle that the Sumner firstborns had all survived to breed a next generation—until now.

"I feel as if I am being pulled and pushed, and all I want to do is live my own life. I never wanted any of this magic. I tried to leave it behind. Why can't I have a few more years to be me?"

Corwen didn't answer. There was nothing he could say.

"This isn't your fight, Corwen. Go home." I suddenly felt very tired.

"I'm not leaving you."

"I told you it's not your fight."

"I jumped the fire with you."

"That was for the Fae's benefit. It wasn't real. We didn't say the words."

"I wouldn't have done it if I hadn't been prepared to stand by it."

He nudged his horse in close to mine, reached across and took my hand. I couldn't bring myself to look him in the eye, but I studied his strong, capable hand, the palm free of calluses, the fingers long and well shaped, the nails clean and neat.

Will's ghost, curiously absent during our time in Iaru, shifted behind me on the horse. *Can you trust him?* he asked.

"Yes," I said, and then realized that Corwen would take that the wrong way.

Let's go back to sea, Will's ghost whispered in my ear. *I really don't like him.*

Would you like anyone who took an interest in me? I kept my response to Will internal.

There was a long silence, and I thought he'd gone, but eventually he shuddered as if sucking in breath. *James Mayo. I like him. Yes.*

You only say that because you know Gentleman Jim was a mistake I won't repeat.

There was a long silence and then he asked, *Do you love Corwen?*

I didn't answer him.

29

Corwen

WE TOOK ROOMS AT the White Hart on the edge of St. George's Fields, or at least I thought we'd taken rooms. I shouldn't have let Corwen see to it while I checked on the horses. When he led me from the supper room up the stairs I found we'd taken a room—singular—and it was sparsely furnished with only one bed.

"What's this?" I asked suspiciously.

"It's a bed."

"I know. It's my bed. Where's yours?"

He held index finger and thumb a whisker apart. "We've been sleeping this close together for the last—"

"That's different. Out in the forest. Fully dressed."

"Keep your clothes on if you prefer. It's near freezing in here, anyway."

He was right, the small fire barely took the chill off the room.

He raised one eyebrow. "Do you want me to sleep on the floor when there's room for two under the covers?" He sat on the edge of the bed and it dipped obligingly, looking soft, comfortable and surprisingly clean. He began to pull off his shirt.

"Corwen—"

"Relax. Do you feel safer like this?" He took off his shirt, dropped down on to all fours and jumped up onto the bed as a silver wolf, pointedly putting his paws over his eyes.

I was almost disappointed.

I turned down the oil lamp to the softest glimmer and shrugged out of my clothes by feel. I was grateful to unfasten my breast binding and slip on a shift.

"Have you got fleas?" I asked, feeling Corwen's weight, comfortably heavy on top of the blankets next to me.

His tongue licked my ear. A kiss of sorts. I reached out, feeling his ruff, soft under my hand. Comfortable. I let my hand stroke his fur. I know I shouldn't have, but it was hard to resist. Then it wasn't fur under my hand any more, it was warm skin, a well-muscled shoulder. He raised himself up on one elbow and pushed my hair back off my face.

"I don't think you know what an effect you've had on me." His kiss left no doubt about his desire.

I swear my arm wrapped around his neck all by itself. I had absolutely no intention of twining my fingers in his hair, so like, yet unlike, his wolf fur, and rising up to meet his kiss. I certainly hadn't intended to enjoy those warm lips on mine moving so slowly and sensuously. Giddiness swept through me, and I could hear my own heartbeat pounding in my ears.

This was not part of my plan. I groaned and started to pull away.

"Ross, I . . ." He rolled back a little, just enough to give me a breathing space. "Only if it's right for you."

"Shh." I leaned into him again and pulled him close, fastening my lips on to his. Heat spread from the pit of my belly.

The coverlet was still between us, and Corwen's weight held it down, but a wriggle and a twist freed me from its confines, and also from my shift. Though the chill of the room gave me goose bumps down my back I stretched myself against Corwen's nakedness, feeling that delicious contact, flesh to flesh, from breast to toe. Now it was his turn to groan as I thrust my hips forward, rubbing my belly against him and feeling him hard against my softness.

He massaged the goose bumps out of my back, taking his time, exploring every inch before stroking my side and gradually working his way up to my breast. I gasped as he kissed my mouth again before moving down slowly from chin to throat and then down again, until his tongue found my nipple.

I traced the smooth curve of his flank, feeling a shock run through his muscles at my touch. My fingers marveled at the shape of him as they traveled from back to front, chest, belly, and that little line of hair that leads downward to the point of no return.

I was ready.

So ready.

Will's ghost towered above us, luminous in the blackness. *Ross. Ross!*

"Will!" If someone had thrown a bucket of seawater over me they couldn't have brought me back to reality more suddenly.

I jerked away from Corwen, hearing him curse softly as he rolled over.

"Away, Tremayne." Corwen sprang off the bed and squared up to Will. I put a witchlight up into the rafters, seeing its golden glow reflected off Corwen's powerful back muscles.

Will's face was a mask of fury. If he could have struck Corwen down, he would have.

She's my wife, Wolfman.

"Until death did you part, ghost. She's mine now!"

Will looked to me. *Call me, Ross. Summon me! Make me solid. I'll fight for your honor.*

"My honor's not at stake, Will."

Then I'll fight for my honor!

I could see the tension running through Corwen's body, but he'd adopted the ready pose of a natural fighter, weight forward, arms loose, knees slightly flexed. "If that's what it takes, Tremayne, let's get it over with."

I rolled across the bed and stepped between them. "I

will not be fought over. Will, I'm no longer yours. When you died, I grieved so long and so deep that it nearly killed me. I tried to keep you with me. I tried so hard—but I was wrong. The living and the dead don't belong together.

"Corwen, let's get possession out of the way. I'll come to you, be with you, love you, but I won't belong to you. I belong only to me."

I pushed Corwen back a pace with my hand against his bare chest. My hand passed right through Will, but he backed off as if he could feel it.

Ross. I love you.

"And I love you, Will. I'll never love anyone in quite the same way, but we're not in the world together any more. I used to think it didn't matter. I used to think I could make it not matter, that we could still love each other, but I was wrong. I want this with Corwen."

Like you wanted your night with James Mayo? He looked past me at Corwen. *What's the matter, Wolfman, didn't you know she'd fucked that whoreson pirate?*

"That's my business, Will. You've no right to be so downright mean."

Corwen's expression never changed. "You heard the lady. She's her own woman. You say you love her. If you do, give her your blessing to move on and make a new life."

Will's ghost gave a strangled sob and vanished with an audible pop. There was a lingering aroma of ozone and rum, and I thought I heard, *It's not over yet.*

I stared at the space where Will had been until Corwen's voice, low and gentle, brought me back to the present.

"Come away under the covers, you'll catch your death of cold."

We were both standing there naked, and I realized I was shivering.

Corwen pulled the covers back and drew me to the mattress.

He didn't rush.

"I've been wanting to do this for the longest time."

I let the witchlight soften to barely brighter than a single candle flame. Corwen tutted over the livid bruises left from my fight with his werewolf and rubbed them gently with his fingertips.

"They may look bad, but they don't hurt much now."

"And this?" His fingers drew the line of the scar across my ribs.

"It's old. Will stitched that one up."

"Was he a good man? Good to you, I mean?"

"Yes, he was."

"I'm glad. If you're not ready to move on, I can wait."

"I'm ready."

Was I really?

Corwen's readiness was obvious.

I let my fingers return to the muscles of his chest and back, surprisingly unmarked by scars or bruises, waiting for the hot liquid fire to reclaim my body, but it was taking its time. Will had well and truly doused it. "You seem to take good care of yourself."

"Not always, but I heal fast. The change helps. As bones and flesh undergo their metamorphosis they heal. I couldn't grow back a missing limb or cure a mortal disease, but I can deal with a gash or a bite or a broken bone."

"There's so much I don't know. Have you always been a wolf?"

"I first changed when I was seven. Scared my parents half to death. It came as a shock to my mother as no one had told her about my great-grandfather who died before she was born. My grandmother had to explain it to the family. Can't say they were very happy about it."

"Will you age seven times faster than I do?"

"Uh-uh." He shook his head. "I'll age normally."

"It was you in the forest, wasn't it? Leading us a merry dance for the Lady?"

"Of course. Even then you stirred up such feelings in me. I wanted to ravish you and protect you and eat you all at the same time." He sighed and ran his hands down my body. "Wolf emotions are complicated. I wouldn't have eaten you, of course. You've seen the difference between my wolf and the beast."

I shivered.

"You're cold."

"No."

But I was.

He sighed. "I understand. Will just doused your passion. Come here. We've got time."

He pulled the sheet and blankets around us both and drew me to him. Folds of linen separated my skin from his, but his warmth seeped through into my bones. He kissed my cheek and I snuggled close.

"Corwen, I . . ."

"Shh, just go to sleep."

I was too wound up to sleep. Long after Corwen's breathing steadied and deepened, I lay awake. It was as if I stood on the edge of a cliff, and Corwen had just asked me to step over with him.

I dreamed I stepped over, plummeted to the breaking ocean and at the last minute arched my body back, back and back, skimmed broken rocks and roiling waves, swooping down and upward again in flight, and then I realized Corwen's hand was in mine and we flew together up into the blue sky, supported on the air, my element.

I awoke, my heart pounding. Corwen curled around my back, sound asleep. The sheet was no longer between us, and his hand rested low on my hipbone, his fingers pointing into that ticklish spot between belly and groin. Though his hand never moved, I knew the moment he woke. Intent crackled between us.

He nuzzled my neck just below my ear, his breath inflaming my skin. I curved my back against the length of him. What had been soft against my buttocks now became hard, and I pressed against it, hearing a groan escape his lips. I took the hand, still resting against my hip, and massaged it with my own. A flotilla of butterflies circled in my belly. I didn't know this man, not in this way. It was like being a virgin again. A whole world of discovery waited for me. I hadn't felt like this with James Mayo.

That delicious ripple of heat that I'd lost when Will interrupted us started in my belly and flushed through me. I heard my own groan sigh out to meet Corwen's.

I put up a witchlight, so I could see his eyes.

"Ah, Ross." He nibbled my ear and kissed the hollow at the base of my throat, his fingers on my flesh drawing goose bumps.

I giggled. "Ticklish."

"Where? No, don't tell me. Finding out is half the fun."

He rolled me on to my back and positioned himself between my legs without settling his weight, then dipped his hips toward mine, touching briefly, tantalizingly. I drew my knees up and ran my hands along his arms.

"No preamble, Mr. Corwen? I'm not sure I'm ready."

"Oh, I think you are." He kissed my lips lightly. "And instead of preamble we'll try some afteramble—" He laughed. "Is that even a word? Anyhow, whatever you want to call it, it will be preamble for the next time. I promise you won't be disappointed." He paused above me. Time stretched. "Tell me how you feel."

"Excited. Afraid. I feel . . . empty. I want you inside me."

I did. I wanted him to fill up my loneliness as I had not wanted anyone since Will. I didn't only want him to thread the needle beneath the sheets, I needed him to be more than meat and muscle and blood.

"Say it again." His voice was husky now.

"I want you."

With an unerring sense of direction he obliged and I thrust my hips up to meet him.

Dawn crept into our room and found us lying in a tangle of sheets, Corwen's hand comfortably on my breast and my head tucked into his shoulder. Without even opening my eyes I knew Will was standing at the foot of the bed.

"Do you want me to apologize?" I asked him softly, but instead of answering he faded away, silent and sad.

Corwen's hand tightened on my breast. He was awake again. I was going to ask if he'd seen Will, but what followed next drove the question out of my head and meant that we didn't get down to breakfast at all that morning.

We were now close enough to London for me to try searching for Philip. I knew him as well as anyone, or I had known him up until seven years ago, when our pathways had parted so suddenly.

Corwen stood and watched me while I arranged myself cross-legged on the bed. I sent out my thoughts on the breeze in search of the older Philip whom I'd seen so briefly in Bideford. I had to be careful that I didn't *summon* him. I didn't want to give away our presence to Walsingham on his home ground.

I concentrated on Philip as I'd last seen him. I thought of the boy that I'd known, mischievous with a sly streak a mile wide. It hadn't always been cold between us. When his mischief hadn't been directed at me I'd even found it endearing. We had been allies while Mother was traveling, and our relationship had remained affable for a while even after she returned.

Mother had employed a tutor for Philip, Mr. Burroughs, a gentleman who had fallen on hard times, which had lowered his expectations of employment. On Mondays, Wednesdays, and Fridays he came to the house to teach us. His primary task was to stuff Philip's head with Greek and Latin, philosophy, mathematics, and natural sciences, all in preparation for him being sent away to school. I was only supposed to learn music, drawing, and as much French as would give me an air of sophistication, but in truth I liked Philip's curriculum better, and our tutor obliged me with further reading.

That had suited Philip, too, for while Mr. Burroughs was discussing the finer points of geometry with me, he was entirely failing to notice that my little brother was doing as little as possible in the schoolroom. He was, however, doing it charmingly.

I put Philip to the forefront of my mind and concentrated hard. I had loved him once.

My head began to ache, and still there was nothing but a blank where Philip should be. At length I looked up at Corwen and shook my head.

"Anything at all?" he asked.

"Nothing. It's a blank."

"Do you think he's not in London?"

"I can't sense him anywhere. It's like he's never existed."

"Do you think he's concealed by magic?"

I nodded. "Could be. We concealed the box." I rubbed my forehead with my fingers. "If only I knew how to do that—conceal us magically, I mean." I unfolded my legs and swung them off the edge of the bed to pull on my boots. "For far too long I've ignored my magic, not studied its full potential. I never thought to need it in this way, to work against, or even protect against, someone like Walsingham."

"When this is over . . ." Corwen began.

"I'm not sure it will ever be over unless I open the box. Even then, it may be the beginning of a whole new set of troubles." I blinked away tears. There was no time for self-pity. I didn't start all this, but somehow I had to find a way through this mess. I considered that the world would be much better off without me in it. Walsingham was a national hero.

Corwen held out a hand. "Come on. You can only do what you can do. No use brooding about it."

30

London

WE HEADED TOWARD LONDON at a fair clip, our horses fully rested, and covered the open ground to the edge of the city in less than an hour, paying our turnpike toll at Kennington Gate. On the outskirts of the city we could see gardens and green fields behind a single line of dwellings, but they soon gave way to row upon row of tall, narrow houses with shops, manufactories, and businesses crowding in on each other. Ripe scents of tanneries, breweries, and the all-pervading stink of sewage assailed our senses. Corwen looked over his shoulder once or twice. The city didn't suit either his nature or his keen sense of smell.

I heard the river before I saw it. The clamor of the city folk going about their business was drowned out by the sound of rushing water as we came upon the many-arched London Bridge. I'd seen an engraving in the Gentleman's Magazine of how it used to be when it had been covered from end to end in a fantastic jumble of buildings.

"This bridge has stood for close on six hundred years," Corwen said. "Though it was altered half a century ago."

"You've been here before?" I knew nothing of Corwen's past.

"A few times—under duress—on business for my father or with my mother and sister."

This was a side to Corwen that I hadn't suspected. He'd barely mentioned his family before. I'd almost supposed he'd been raised in the forest, but he was too much at ease with people for that. I was about to ask more, but it would have to wait. He pointed to the middle of the bridge. "See, they made a larger arch in the middle to make it safer for shipping."

The bridge's narrow arches and broad starlings around the piers still formed a substantial barrage. The river spurted through the arches like a millrace on both the flowing and ebbing tide.

"I was here with Will about five years ago," I said. "He took me to Vauxhall Gardens by boat, but we went at slack water. When the tide's on the turn it's quite safe."

Hundreds of people swarmed across the bridge, some on foot, others balanced precariously on loaded wagons or tucked safely in their carriages. Barouches and phaetons rolled wheel to wheel with costermonger's carts. Only the convention of keeping to the left prevented the most hideous of accidents. The roadway was crowded with all manner of people, rich and poor, on foot, on horseback, pushing barrows, carrying children. A pair of leather-waistcoated rowankind carried a tottering stack of boxes on a four-handled stretcher despite the hazards of the pitted roadway. A carriage rattled past with a rowankind coachman and two rowankind footmen dressed in fine livery to match the vehicle. The closer I looked, the more rowankind I saw. Some were smart but not fashionably dressed, most likely servants of prosperous households, others were decked out in working garb and were fetching, carrying, pushing or pulling. A few were close to ragged, flesh clinging too tightly to their skulls and limbs stick-thin, reflecting the station of their masters, I suspected, or their ignorance.

I had read that the locals said the bridge was for wise

men to pass over, and for fools to pass under. My attention was captured by the gush of water beneath us as we pushed into the crowd and began our crossing. The ebb tide had all the force of the mighty Thames behind it.

Corwen shuddered. "They take boats under there. It's called shooting the bridge. Every so often some fool gets it wrong."

A cutter had just disgorged passengers on the south bank above the bridge and as the passengers, four of them, set off to walk down the bank on the Southwark side, the four oarsmen in the cutter began to pull out into the current, for a while running parallel to the bridge. Then, as the water took them, they turned the cutter's nose and steered for the wider center arch.

The cutter disappeared into the shadow of the bridge, and a few moments later it was spewed out of the other side to whoops and hollers from a gang of urchins who'd raced from one side of the bridge to the other to watch for either success or catastrophic failure. The crew pulled for the shore again and picked up the family who had chosen to walk around in safety rather than shoot the bridge.

Corwen shuddered. "I suppose you'd take something like that in your stride."

"Not me. I'll stick to the oceans."

The view across the bridge was of an impressive church spire and a tall columnar monument. We turned right before the monument along Lower Thames Street.

"You do know where you're going, don't you?" Corwen asked. "I don't know this part of the city at all."

"I've arranged for the *Heart* to anchor close to Wapping Old Stairs." It was a place I knew from my previous visit with Will.

"Aren't we getting a bit too close to that?" He nodded toward the looming fortress ahead.

"It's the Tower of London."

"That much I know, but do we have business there? I appreciate that you think Walsingham could be somewhere in a royal building, but if that's it, we're howling at the wrong moon."

"Christ on a pig, Corwen, I hope he's not in there. Don't even think about it. Don't worry, we're only going past it."

And skirt the wall is exactly what we did, then headed back toward the river rather than get lost in the press of mean streets.

We followed St. Catherine's Street, got turned around in the jumble of alleyways by the church itself because of a muddy creek that blocked our way, and backtracked via New Street. A beggar boy hobbled alongside us for part of the way until Corwen gave him a penny and he ran off with no sign of a limp.

"There's every kind of fake and fraudster on the streets," I said, averting my eyes as a young man with both legs lopped at the knee looked up at me imploringly.

"Spare a copper for a sailor, sir," he called. I pulled up my horse and leaned down to press a sixpence into his hand. "Navy?" I asked.

He nodded. "Both legs took off with a cannonball at Cape St. Vincent in ninety-seven."

"You'd have done better on a pirate ship. At least they retire their injured with a payoff."

"Are you a seafaring gent? I sailed with Horatio Nelson, sir, there ain't many pirates can say that."

"There aren't indeed." I pressed a second sixpence into his hand. "Good luck to you."

"God bless you and keep you, sir."

"And you, sailor."

I rode on, aware that Corwen was staring at me.

"What?"

"I didn't know you were such a soft touch for a sob story."

"What of it?"

"Nothing. Just observing. You warn me about fakes and fraudsters and then give a shilling to a man with two good legs bound beneath him. But he was good, I'll give him that."

"He didn't . . ."

Corwen raised an eyebrow. "Admit it, you were taken in."

We argued about my putative amputee until I realized I'd been paying more attention to proving Corwen wrong than to the streets. I stopped to get my bearings.

"You said you knew this area," Corwen frowned.

"I've been here once before. The river's still on our right. If you can do any better, lead the way! No? I thought not."

We continued along St. Catherine's by a huge brewhouse reeking of hops and yeast. He wrinkled his nose at it, but I was pleased enough to see that it was Godwin, Skinner, and Thornton's. I knew exactly where we were now.

"It's enough to put a man off ale for life," Corwen said. "How do the people here stand it?"

"They probably think this is normal and that the countryside stinks of pig shit."

"Give me pig shit any day. How much further to the *Heart*?"

"Not far now."

We were driven away from the Thames by another creek, but this time there was a bridge, and we quickly found our way back to Wapping Street. I recognized a narrow passageway leading to Hermitage Stairs and pulled up. Dismounting, I threw my reins to Corwen and made my way along the alley to the head of the steps leading down to the river. At low tide there would be a shoreline of stones and stinking mud, but now the river lapped and sucked at the steps. Below the high-water mark everything was liberally coated in green slime and feathery weed.

Out in the river, away to my left, sails reefed, the *Heart* bobbed at anchor just west of Wapping Old Stairs. I grinned at the sight of her.

"She's there," I told Corwen as I took my reins. "We need to find stabling for the horses."

There were several inns, but Corwen's nose drew him to the Red Lion on the north side of Wapping Street. Satisfied that the ostler knew his business, we paid for stabling, and Corwen shouldered the Fae's magic bag. The alley to Wapping Old Stairs squeezed alongside the narrow-fronted Town of Ramsgate public house. Hookey sat in the doorway, leaning back against his chair and sucking on an evil-smelling pipe. An empty plate was on the table in front of him, and he had the satisfied expression of a man who has just put himself on the outside of a plate of, if I knew Hookey, rump steak.

"Cap'n!" He jumped up when he saw me, and his face split into a grin. "Well, you're a sight for sore eyes."

"Hello, Hookey. How are things?"

"Fine and dandy." His eyes flickered to Corwen. "I see he caught up with you."

I sighed. "Yes."

"Sorry, Cap'n. We should 'ave kept him longer, I suppose." He dropped his voice. "Want me to take care of him once and for all?"

"No!" Maybe I was a little more emphatic than I intended, for Hookey gave me a raised eyebrow. "I'm getting used to having him around."

Corwen's mouth twitched in a suppressed smile, which earned him a speculative look from Hookey.

"Where's Davy?" Hookey asked.

"With family. Long story. If you don't mind, I'll wait until we're aboard so I don't have to tell it twice."

Hookey stepped over to pay his bill.

Hookey, now there's a man I could accept. Not as suave as James Mayo, but faithful.

Will's ghost sat on Hookey's table, smack in the middle of the empty plate, idly swinging his legs.

"Will! Stop it. Hookey's nearly old enough to be my father."

Well, I'm seven years your senior.

"Not anymore."

Will would now be forever twenty-nine. Seven years had been a considerable age gap when I was thirteen, but it seemed less by the time I was eighteen. I shivered. "Will you still be here, saying you love me, when I'm sixty and wrinkled and you're still twenty-nine?"

I'll always love you.

"And I'll always love you, Will."

And Corwen? Will's ghost faded away as I thought about how to answer that question.

Hookey rousted out four sailors from the far end of the long, narrow bar. One was Lazy Billy, who greeted me with his lopsided smile, but the other three were newcomers to the crew, taken on to replace our dead from the battle with the *Lydia*.

"This is Dickie." He nodded to the first one. "And Stingo. We took them on afore we sailed from Bacalao. And this bracket-faced hulk of a creature is Bone. Took him on while we was anchored off Gravesend an' he piloted us upriver. He might look powerful ugly, but he used to be a Thames waterman before he fell foul of the guild. Knows the river better than his own wife."

"Aye, and like her better, too, since she ran off with an Eye-talian." Bone's voice was almost a growl, and when he spoke I saw that he had several front teeth missing. "And fish ain't the only thing I can fillet." He tapped the long knife at his hip.

A useful man in a brawl, then. I'd remember that.

The *Heart*'s boat was tied up at the side of the stone stairs that led down into the choppy waters of the Thames. Hookey tossed a coin to the urchin who'd been left guarding it.

This is where you belong. Will's ghost drifted up out of the water and reclined in midair along the line of the steps, waving his arm toward the vista of oceangoing vessels anchored for loading and unloading by the Thames lightermen.

Not until this thing's finished. I'm a danger to the Heart *and all her crew.*

There's no danger now that the box is wrapped up all nice and quiet. He can't see it any more.

"How do you know that, Will?"

He faded away to nothing.

"Will?" I glanced at Corwen. "Did you hear that?"

"It seems that he's been spying on your man, Walsingham."

"What does he think he's playing at? If he could do that why didn't he tell me?"

"He's a ghost, Ross, an echo of what was. He's not your

Will any more. He's got his own concerns, and helping you may not be part of it. He wants you. If he could take you to be with him, he would."

"Will would never harm me."

"The old Will wouldn't, but Will's ghost probably doesn't think that enticing you to *be* a ghost is harmful. He is one himself."

"You're wrong."

"Suit yourself, but have a care."

Corwen and I stepped into the bow of the boat. Billy, Bone, Dickie, and Stingo took up oars and pulled away into the current with Hookey at the tiller. I could feel the outgoing tide tugging at the boat and see Bone and Stingo's muscles working beneath their shirts as they pulled us across to the *Heart*.

Mr. Sharpner leaned over the side and greeted me as I climbed aboard. The lads mostly found something to be doing on deck so they were there to watch us come over the rail.

"Good to have you back, Captain," Mr. Rafiq said.

"Good to be back, Mr. Rafiq."

There was a chorus of ayes from the ones that I knew, but I noticed more strange faces and suddenly felt as though I was standing alongside myself, watching. It had only been a few weeks, but already there were sufficient changes that I no longer felt totally at home. I was a guest here.

"It's all right, Mr. Sharpner. He's with me," I said as my sailing master's heavy hand fell on Corwen's shoulder.

The term "with me" was about to get a little complicated. I should have thought it through. "Would you have one of the lads make up Mr. Corwen's old berth, but without the chains and padlocks?"

I glanced sideways at Corwen and could tell immediately that he understood the way of it. He half-bowed to me formally. "Ma'am."

"Mr. Corwen, please join me in my cabin."

"There's a nice salmagundi on the boil, Cap'n," Mr. Sharpner said. "Shall I send some down to you both?"

"Thank you, yes, I'm famished. I'd like to call a war council. I'd be obliged if you, Mr. Rafiq, and Hookey would join us."

"Is there trouble?"

"There might be."

As the cabin door closed between us and the outside world, Corwen grabbed me and kissed me. Lips, cheek, ear, throat.

"I'm sorry about the separate berth."

"I know. You have to keep up appearances."

Did I? Or was bringing Corwen into Will's bed the last taboo?

I pressed myself against him, feeling heat rising between us. My fingers were already reaching to untie the cravat about his throat when I heard heavy boots outside the door. I jumped back as if caught in some misdemeanor and we both laughed. Corwen straightened his cravat and ran one hand over his silver hair as I opened the door and took delivery of the bowls of hot food.

The salmagundi filled a hole where dinner should have been, though Corwen ate it cautiously—the combination of meat and fish being unusual for him. The church bells in the city had rung five before we all assembled, sitting or standing around the map table in my tiny cabin.

In their turn, Hookey, Mr. Sharpner, and Mr. Rafiq all took sideways glances at Corwen. Maybe it was the Fae clothing, but he looked as clean and elegant as if he was newly bathed and dressed. In comparison I felt sure I looked as though I'd been on the road for days.

"Gentlemen, Mr. Corwen and I have made our peace." I hesitated over how to explain it. *He's done me a great service,* could so easily be misinterpreted, or more likely interpreted all too correctly. I bit my tongue before I said anything unwise and settled for, "He's my guest, and I'd be grateful if you would extend every courtesy."

Hookey cleared his throat but said nothing. Mr. Rafiq

half-bowed. Mr. Sharpner mumbled an apology for the manacles on Corwen's last visit.

"I probably deserved them," Corwen replied graciously.

"To business." I took out the box and placed it on the chart table, still wrapped in its precious concealing spell. "Take my word for it that the bespelled parchment wrapped around this little box is all that's preventing real trouble from dropping on our heads. I didn't know it at the time, but this is what brought the *Lydia* and His Majesty's ships of the line to trap us. There's a man called Walsingham who wants all the Sumner family—my mother's family—dead and the box laid to rest unopened."

I had their undivided attention and began my story, telling them of my mother's parting gift, Martyn the Summoner, the rowankind, and what had been done to them. "To cut a long story short, I'm the last of Martyn's descendants with the ability to open the box and free the rowankind."

"That's good, gal, ain't it?" Hookey spoke up. "I don't hold with no one being kept where they don't want to be."

Mr. Sharpner nodded.

"I agree," I said, "but there's a chance that freeing the rowankind will also bring back wild magic to the land, and that could be bad for all kinds of reasons."

"Ain't that what you got? It don't seem so bad," Hookey said.

I turned to Corwen for an answer.

He cleared his throat. "What if creatures of legend—tree spirits, water spirits, shapechangers, boggarts and bogles, good creatures and bad—were real? What if the kraken roamed the seas again?"

Hookey shuddered and then turned to me. "Has he got magic, too?"

I nodded, but didn't elaborate.

"A grave moral dilemma." Mr. Rafiq understood at once. "A heavy decision for one person to make."

"What should I do? What would you do, Mr. Rafiq, if by one single but dangerous act you could end the Africa trade?" By the look on his face he would take the risk in an instant.

"Though the decision has fallen to me, there are vested interests. The Fae—" I had to stop as everyone spoke at once, but as soon as I could make myself heard again, I continued. "Yes they still exist, and yes they are powerful, but since the rowankind were taken and stripped of their power, they've shunned mankind completely. They know that I'm their last chance to open the box, and they have David in their home, Iaru, a world between worlds." I held my hand up to forestall another outburst. "He's fine, they're not going to hurt him, but he's the reason I have to go back there."

"Your other vested interest would be this Walsingham," Mr. Rafiq said.

"Yes. The Walsinghams have taken a blood feud against the Sumners. It was a Walsingham that hunted my ancestor after the Armada. Almost thirty years ago, a Walsingham destroyed my mother's family, but was himself destroyed in the process. My mother and her twin sister survived, and thought themselves safe as long as they stayed separate, hiding their magic away from the world, but now there's another Walsingham."

"He's trying to kill you?" Hookey's eyes held cold murder.

"He's got magic, Hookey. Big, nasty powerful magic."

"More than you got?"

I nodded, my mouth dry.

"I think so. Different, anyway, and much more deadly in the way he uses it." I glanced at Corwen. His mouth was compressed in a thin line. "And since he's got my brother, Philip, I can't just run away, much as I'd like to."

"You're not made for running away, gal—sorry—Cap'n."

"You're the captain now, Hookey. No need to stand on ceremony."

He cleared his throat and rubbed his hand up and down his face to cover up an unseamanlike blush. "So what do you want us to do?"

"I need to find Walsingham before he finds me. I have to free Philip."

"I'll send the lads out on to the streets to ask around," Hookey said.

"I suppose that means they'll be asking tavern keepers and whores." I raised one eyebrow.

"No better folks to ask."

"Well, give 'em a shilling or two for ale and a supply of Mrs. Phillips' prophylactics if they're going to be asking those kind of questions. Your new crewman, Bone, ask him to talk to some of the watermen, see if they've rowed Walsingham on the river. And better be ready for trouble if all these questions stir any up."

"Aye, Cap'n."

I tried not to smile at his automatic use of my former rank.

31

Walsingham

I SPENT THE AFTERNOON on deck waiting for any news to come in from the scattered crew. Mostly I paced up and down, passing Corwen, who sat against the deck rail. I expected him to be restless, like a caged beast, but he had an amazing capacity for stillness. Sometimes I thought him asleep, head propped on arms, supported on bent knees, but if I hesitated in my pacing he would raise his head and look at me with barely concealed hunger on his face.

Once as I passed I reached out and took his hand, feeling his grip, warm and dry, around my cold fingers. For a brief moment our hands did what our bodies couldn't, fingers twining and exploring knuckle, nail, and fingertip. His thumb caressed the center of my palm while I folded my fist around it and squeezed.

On what felt like the hundredth turn around the deck I could stand it no longer. I stopped by him and touched my fingers to his silver hair. He raised his head, and shivers ran through me as his eyes locked with mine.

My voice caught in my throat. "Mr. Corwen, I have a

private matter to discuss, would you mind joining me in my cabin in five minutes."

"Of course, Captain." He inclined his head.

I'm not sure if we fooled Lazy Billy, who sat on a nearby hatch mending a tear in a pair of canvas trousers, but I didn't care. I made myself walk steadily down to my cabin and, once down there, shrugged out of my jacket and waited for Corwen, heart pounding.

It was a long five minutes.

The instant he closed the door behind him and turned the iron key in the lock I flew into his arms, fastening my lips to his, feeling a pang deep in my belly. His hands ran up and down my back, hot through the linen of my shirt. He undid my buttons, pulled my shirttail loose, and ran his hands over the outside of my breast binding.

Corwen soon worked out the fastening, and he leaned me against the stout oak door while he pulled it loose, slowly, and then kissed what it had been covering until I moaned and squirmed.

"Shhh," Corwen whispered. "Or your crew will wonder if I'm murdering you."

I kissed him thoroughly and that put an end to my moans for a time. He carried me to the bed, Will's bed. Small as it was, it served us well, and afterward we dozed together until late afternoon, passion spent, the last taboo broken.

With a start I realized that Will had not put in an appearance, and neither had I thought of him once during our lovemaking.

I drew a deep breath. "I feel guilty lazing here like this," I said, "with the crew all out working on my behalf."

"They're probably working in just the same way, with added ale and rum." He laughed softly. "Besides, they'll be back soon."

He dipped his lips to my breasts again, and I felt him rise to the occasion.

We eventually disentangled ourselves and dressed to await the return of the crew.

The first few back had little to report except for a good

time. Hookey returned with a self-satisfied smile but no news. Mr. Rafiq, however, had dressed himself in fine gentleman's clothes and gone in search of a higher class of Covent Garden lady. It had paid off. His lady had a gentleman friend named Dominic who was prone to pillow talk and boasted of his connections via his employer, Mr. Walsingham, to Sir George Shee, Baronet.

"Shee?" I asked.

"I believe," Mr. Rafiq said, "Sir George Shee has recently succeeded Mr. Wickham as Under-Secretary of State for the Home Department."

"A scribbler?" Corwen asked

"More than that, Mr. Wickham was to King George as Sir Francis Walsingham was to Good Queen Bess—spymaster—so one must assume that Sir George has now taken on that role."

I waited until Mr. Rafiq had retreated and then gave a low whistle. "Coincidence or what?"

"You don't think this Walsingham could be the same one, do you?" Corwen asked. "I do know there are those who might look wholly human who nevertheless have enough Fae blood to live for many—"

I shook my head. "Leo was sure that the Walsingham who was responsible for my grandparents' death was killed in the explosion. Besides, he seems to have been an older man than the present Walsingham. While Fae blood might extend a person's natural lifespan, I doubt even the Fae could turn time backward and have someone cheat death and grow younger with the passing years."

He nodded. "So let's presume Walsingham is working for Sir George Shee. Shall we find him at Westminster?"

"Or Whitehall, or any number of properties in this city belonging to the Crown, or maybe some dark little hideout in a tenement. Oh, this is hopeless without resorting to magic."

"As soon as you try any kind of seeking, he'll be able to follow it right back to you."

He was right, but hearing him say it didn't help.

The rest of the men returned before full dark and were ferried back to the *Heart* in groups of five and six. None had anything to report. It seemed that Walsingham and his kind didn't frequent the kind of places my sailors did. Bone was the last to return, arriving on a Thames cutter rowed by a crew of two watermen. Hookey brought him to my cabin.

"You found something?" I asked.

"I think so, ma'am—Cap'n." He looked at Hookey, not knowing which of us to call captain.

I gestured for him to continue.

"Mate o' mine, name of Doff, regularly plies his trade around Westminster. Often ferries them toffs from Parliament and their flunkies. Gets slipped the odd shilling extra to keep his mouth shut sometimes, but ain't against making two shillings to open it again. Says he knows Mr. Walsingham and that new young man of his. Always together he says."

"Does he recall where he takes them?"

"Vauxhall Stairs, ma'am."

"Is that the man who rowed you here?"

"It is. He's waiting for his money."

"Thank you, Bone." I gave him the two shillings he'd promised to pay his friend and three more. "Ask him to wait, please."

I looked at Corwen when Bone had closed the door behind him. "How's your nose?"

He grinned. "Good as ever. I'll go tracking."

Corwen's wolf nose could pick up scents from miles away in the country. I was less certain of it with all the city smells to cover up Philip and Walsingham.

"I'm coming with you. Trot at my side like a dog and most people will take you for one in the dark. Slink around like a wolf on your own and you're likely to find someone pointing something dangerous at your ribs."

He nodded. "Deal!"

I strapped on my sword and loaded a pair of serviceable pistols, not the small ones by Mr. Bunney, but a brace of sturdy British sea-service pistols I had used many times in action. Corwen didn't need armaments. As an afterthought, I grabbed the leather bag that the Fae had given us.

I called Mr. Sharpner and Hookey before we left the *Heart* and told them that Corwen and I were going to go and nose around. I was pretty sure they didn't think I meant it literally, but I didn't explain.

We climbed down into the waiting cutter, crewed by two watermen who looked enough alike to be brothers. Bone's friend Doff nodded to us and asked where to. I told him Vauxhall Stairs. We settled ourselves in front of our two rowers, who took up the oars, their strokes harmonized by many years of experience.

The high tide was almost on the turn, so we passed under London Bridge at slack water. Seeing it from below, at night, shadow upon shadow, I could appreciate how truly ancient it was. In the light from the lantern on the cutter's prow, the stonework showed its age. Huge starlings, great bulwarks of stone and wood, had been built to protect the piers of the old bridge, but they only served to restrict the flow between the arches even more. Collisions with boats and debris had gouged and scarred them, and even without the tide churning up rapids between the arches, our watermen negotiated the narrow passage carefully, there being not enough width for the boat and her oars at full stretch.

Blackfriars Bridge, by contrast, was a much easier passage, with wider arches of Portland stone showing pale in the moonlight. Corwen's nose twitched at a sudden stench of sewage.

"That'll be the River Fleet," Doff said. "Empties into the Thames at the north end of the bridge. It's not much more than a drain now. Ripe, innit?"

"Ripe indeed," Corwen replied.

As we passed under Westminster Bridge and slid past the palace, I asked Doff about Walsingham.

"Don't rightly know much about him, sir," Doff said. "Just ferry him from place to place."

"But frequently to Vauxhall Stairs?"

"Aye."

"And not just during the season at Vauxhall Gardens?"

"All year round, though sometimes not for weeks at a time, when I guess he may be out of town."

"And lately he's had a young man with him, one who looks somewhat like me?"

"I wasn't going to comment on the resemblance, sir, but now you mention it, there is a likeness."

"How does he seem, the young gentleman? Is he easy or fretful?"

"He's just a young ge'man, sir. Not over talkative, but not uneasy in his manner. He seems well, sir, if that's what you're asking. Never bosky like many of the young ge'men we rows after dark. But Mr. Walsingham is never bosky neither. A very sober and serious ge'man. Gracious with his money, though."

"Do you believe Mr. Walsingham lives on the Vauxhall side of the river?"

"It's often a journey he makes late at night. And in the mornings he's most likely setting off from Vauxhall Stairs. We've picked him up many a time and rowed him to Westminster, or Whitehall. Sometimes to the Tower, though he's not one to shoot the bridge. We drop him upstream of the waterworks and pick him up again at Billingsgate. The young ge'man shot it with us once, though, just to say he'd done it."

I tried to imagine Walsingham indulging his prisoner, but he'd proven in Bideford that he could give Philip enough rope to hang himself, knowing that he had the poppet with which he could kill or maim at any time. If Philip drowned in the Thames it would just save Walsingham the bother of finishing him off eventually. I suspected that at the moment Philip was only alive as bait to trap me.

"Do you want us to wait?" Doff asked.

"No. Go about your business or get yourself some sleep."

"Aye, sir. Good luck to ye, sir."

"Thank you."

Corwen bounded up the steps ahead of me, not such a long climb with the tide so high. A row of houses to our left offered no dark corners in which he could change, but a series of sheds on our right, a warehouse or a small manufactory, offered shelter from view. Corwen quickly shrugged out of his clothes and handed them to me before changing smoothly.

I stuffed them into the Fae bag, which held everything, even the boots. The bag itself weighed next to nothing when I slung it diagonally over my shoulder. Two men walked up from Vauxhall Stairs and Corwen pressed himself close to my leg. I ran a hand across his silky fur as we waited for them to pass out of sight and he nuzzled my fingers. Once they'd gone he was off, nose to the ground, casting around for a scent. I could tell by the way he reacted that he'd found something, and I walked briskly alongside him, trying not to make it obvious that he was leading the way.

We followed the route that thousands of revelers took during the season when they crossed the river by boat to take delight in the lavish enticements offered by Vauxhall Gardens with its flowerbeds, gardens, and musical entertainment, whole orchestras enjoyed from the open air or from the luxury of private supper-boxes.

Will had brought me here once, on our only trip to London, and I'd thought it a wondrous place, well worth the two-shilling entrance fee and the exorbitant price for a cold collation served to us on a table in front of the orchestra building. We'd eaten Vauxhall ham, sliced so thin it was claimed you could read a newspaper through it, along with salads and cheeses, all washed down with a good Bordeaux. But the startling thing was the illumination. The whole garden was ablaze with over a thousand oil lamps that came on simultaneously at dusk. I'd thought it magic at first, but later discovered the lamps were lit by a series of cleverly laid fuses.

Now there was no such glow of light. The season ended at the beginning of September, the autumn being no time for outdoor entertainment. Instead of taking the road around to the Gardens, Corwen followed his nose straight to the biggest source of light in the neighborhood, the White Lion pub, sitting on the roadside across from what smelled like a vinegar distillery. I could see through the bowed front window that the landlord was doing excellent trade. The public bar was full of drinkers and pleasantly hazy with smoke from tobacco and from the wood fire that burned in the hearth.

Corwen sat on his haunches. I ruffled his soft fur, delighting in the feel of it beneath my hand.

"You think he's in there?"

A very restrained yip from Corwen.

"Philip?"

Yip!

He stood up and waved his tail, leaning heavily against my thigh.

"Walsingham?"

A low growl that I took for an affirmative.

"How shall we tackle this?"

I didn't expect an answer, but Corwen immediately trotted away from the inn and up a narrow alley that led into the inn yard, where deep shadows and quiet corners abounded. Facing the inn, across the yard, a range of buildings looked like stabling. I opened the door, and the gentle smell of horse dung cleared the sharp tang of vinegar out of my nostrils. I could hear a quiet munching of hay, and one of the horses shifted in its stall and stamped a hoof.

Corwen changed back into himself and took the bag from my hand. He seemed not at all worried that he was naked, but even in the dark, when, apart from the outline of his shoulder, everything else was imagination and memory, my heart beat faster.

"A little light wouldn't come amiss," he said, fishing around for his breeches.

"Can't you make light?"

"I don't do light, or fire. I can manage a little illusion, some shielding, and a few small magics courtesy of lessons from the Lady, but they should be used sparingly."

I was going to ask for specifics, but it seemed more important to let him get dressed, so I gave him a low witchlight in the far corner of the stable and reluctantly turned away from his neat buttocks, setting myself to watch the yard in case someone noticed and came to investigate. I needn't have worried. Apart from one very drunk gentleman weaving his way from the back door of the inn over toward the privy, not finding it, and pissing against a wall, no one entered or left the yard.

The stable housed six horses. I wasn't sure, but one could have been the bay Philip was riding on the day I met him in Bideford.

"I have an idea," Corwen said as he finished pulling on his boots and ran his hand down the front of his shirt to smooth it into place. "We're so close now, can you summon Philip to come and check on his horse? It would hardly take a thought and might be such a small working that Walsingham wouldn't notice."

"I don't know anything about Walsingham's magic, or how much control he has over Philip." I chewed my lower lip.

But even as I voiced my doubts I was reaching for Philip, the brother I barely knew.

"Done." I nodded to Corwen and let my witchlight fade to nothing.

We only had to wait.

We slipped out of the stable and crammed ourselves into a narrow passage between the privy and the wall, so recently pissed upon. The miasma was putrid, as if something had died in there and no one had bothered to bury it, but it had the advantage of running clear through to the street, an escape from the yard should we need it. I tried shallow breathing, but the stench clawed up the inside of my nose and lodged in the back of my throat. Corwen huffed out a breath and buried his face in the back of my hair. With his heightened sense of smell, even when not in wolf form, he must be finding this intolerable. I reached back and tapped him on the thigh, a mute enquiry. He touched my shoulder reassuringly, but then tensed.

The inn door opened, and a single figure emerged and headed toward the stable. I felt Corwen's magic at work, and then stared slack-jawed as I saw myself standing by the stable door, wearing my traveling dress and redingote as I had when I'd first become acquainted with Corwen in Plymouth. This version of me looked prettier than the image that I usually saw in a mirror. Was that how I appeared to Corwen? This image was the Rossalinde that Corwen loved, and my heart sank. How long would it be before my silverwolf realized the reality could never live up to what was in his head?

I swallowed my thoughts, in danger of getting distracted.

Philip saw Corwen's illusion and glanced back over his shoulder. I held my breath, waiting to see what he would do. I didn't know what hold Walsingham might have. If Philip was going to raise a hue and cry we'd be out of the yard via this noisome alley in a flash, and sisterly obligations could go to the devil.

But there was no cry for help. Philip stepped forward eagerly. "Ross. I had almost given up on you."

I sucked in air again, only then realizing that I'd been holding my breath.

Corwen's illusion was convincing, but I doubted he could put words in its mouth. Philip would see through the magic soon, and then what? But my Corwen was clever. The image beckoned Philip toward where we hid in shadow then, as she got to the mouth of our tiny alley, she held out a gloved hand one last time before slipping into the shadow where she popped out of existence.

"Ross?" Philip called, a little too loudly for my comfort.

"Hush, Philip. Want to wake the world?"

"Ross, I can't see you. Where are you?"

"I can see you just fine," I said. "Where's Walsingham?"

"Inside. He lodges here. Me too. He keeps me close."

"Are you treated well?"

"Yes, quite well, thank you, though my days are not my own. Did you find the box?"

"Yes, but it's not here." I wasn't going to admit that it was in my pocket. "Does Walsingham know what it does?"

"Opens a door to let old magic back into the world."

"And sets the rowankind free." When he didn't reply I wasn't sure whether he already knew or whether he was digesting the information. "Did you know that?"

"Yes, but at what price?"

A question I had asked myself. Maybe Philip and I were not so far apart after all.

"Has he still got the poppet, Philip?"

"Yes."

"Can you get it?"

"He keeps it on his person at all times."

"Damn! Can you get him out here, just you and him alone? Tell him his horse looks sick. He has got a horse in there, hasn't he?"

"A gray, Bessie."

"Tell him you think Bessie has colic. Just get him into the yard alone. I'll do the rest." I nearly said *we*, but for now I wanted to keep Corwen's presence a secret.

"Wait here. I'll see what I can do." He turned, then said over his shoulder, "I didn't think you'd come back."

"Go get Walsingham. We're not in the clear yet."

He gave a quick nod and made his way back to the inn door.

"What do you think?" I asked Corwen.

"He sounded sincere."

"Philip always does. Let's move to be on the safe side."

We ran back to the stable, leaving the door pushed into place but not latched, so a good shove would open it from the inside. We loosed all the horses and turned them to face the door, then scrambled into the hayloft via a wooden ladder built up the side of the wall. I'd glanced in here earlier, so I knew there was a back way out through a full-height loading door that opened directly on to the street behind the yard. Vauxhall Gardens was directly beyond. From this height the shapes of the trees stood out black against the night sky. A window with small square panes, three of which were broken, overlooked the yard. A mat of hay beneath our boots muffled our footsteps. Corwen loosened his shirt in readiness in case he needed to change quickly into wolf form. I drew my pistols, pulled back both dogheads, and took up position where I could see but not be seen.

I had cold-blooded murder in mind.

When you're dealing with someone who has unknown magic, possibly superior to your own, better to finish it quickly. I was a good shot, and even in the darkness I could put a significant hole in Walsingham before he even realized he was walking into a trap. I took deep breaths to steady myself. This wasn't the same as facing an enemy in a skirmish, and I didn't relish it, but I hadn't started this. With Walsingham down, Philip could get the poppet, and all three of us would be out of the yard before anyone knew what had happened. The horses, driven into the yard, would be a diversion to help us escape into the city before the law arrived. On this side of the river, we were a long way from the Bow Street Runners.

Two men left the inn separately, one turning right and the other left, and were quickly lost in the darkness. When the inn door opened again, two figures emerged together. My heart began to pound. One was definitely Philip, the other must be Walsingham, though he was wearing a long, caped coat which hid his form.

I aimed my pistol at the center of his chest and followed his progress across the yard until he was close enough so that I couldn't miss.

"I didn't start this!" I muttered to myself as my finger closed on the trigger.

As if he knew, Walsingham suddenly threw back the coat and raised a stubby weapon. I stared down the fat barrel.

Blunderbuss!

I recognized the shape and threw myself to the floor, knocking Corwen sideways at the same time, but not before creatures from nightmare boiled out of every crevice and nook into the yard, including the narrow passage we'd briefly sheltered in.

The window above me shattered under the onslaught of lead shot. Debris stung my cheekbone. Once discharged, Walsingham's blunderbuss was useless—unless he had another, which I daren't risk. Corwen crawled over to the top of the ladder and stuck his head through. I heard his wolf snarl and thought he was changing, but he came back up as himself. His intent had been to spook the loose horses. The lead horse barged against the door and the six of them charged into the yard, thoroughly panicked. I popped my head up above the windowsill and saw a scene of utter chaos.

The horses had run, kicking and plunging, into the waiting jaws of nightmare creatures that looked like unholy crosses between big cats and wild dogs, with maybe a bit of giant rat thrown in for good measure. In a slavering frenzy, three of them set upon Walsingham's gray mare. One was on her back with its jaws clamped around her spine just above her withers, another had her haunch, and the third had gone for her windpipe from below. She screamed in terror and pain, stomping and whirling, but failing to dislodge them. Walsingham tried to call them off, genuinely distressed about the horse's plight. I was sure he wouldn't have been so sorry if it were me being torn to shreds.

I didn't waste a second. I aimed and fired, feeling the pistol kick and seeing Walsingham jerk as the ball hit.

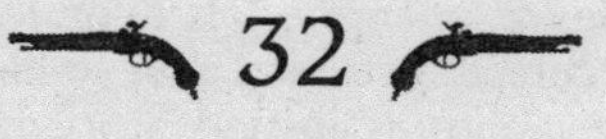

32

Hellhounds

PHILIP STOOD FOR A SECOND as if transfixed.

"Get the damn poppet!" I yelled, hoping my voice would carry through the chaos.

Philip came to life. He knelt swiftly by Walsingham and looked to be searching the body, jumping to his feet clutching something in each hand. Though none of the creatures threatened either him or Walsingham he backed away carefully to the stable door, stepped inside and pulled it closed after him.

"Up here," I called.

I heard footsteps on the ladder and a loaded blunderbuss pistol emerged, pointed at my chest, followed by Philip's head. He flung the blunderbuss on the floor and pulled himself up into the loft.

Corwen grabbed it.

"Walsingham?" I asked Philip.

He just shook his head.

Dead, then. One problem resolved.

"Are you hurt?" I asked, seeing Corwen in a shaft of moonlight.

"No. You?"

"No." I shook my head and felt something trickle down my cheek.

"What's this then?" Corwen touched my face. "Blood!"

"It doesn't signify. A graze." I shook him off. "Let's get out of here."

Corwen dragged open the loft door, looked down into the street, and cursed. I crossed over to him. A baying, slavering knot of creatures jostled around the corner and scrabbled at the wall below our door.

"What are they, Philip? Are they called or made?"

"I don't know."

Corwen fired the blunderbuss into the middle of the pack and was rewarded with yelps and at least two of the creatures dead. Several others turned on their dead companions and began to rend them. I fired my second pistol and killed another outright, but there were still four or five.

Corwen dropped to all fours. "I'll draw them off, you get back to the river."

"And then what? Swim for it?"

"If you have to. I doubt these will cross running water."

"And what about you?"

"I can outrun them. I'll see you back at the *Heart*."

My protest was cut short by a pistol shot from outside, and another of the creatures yelped.

A volley of fire followed. Creature bodies flew. Then a familiar voice yelled up from the road. "You should have told us what you were about. Then we wouldn't have had to follow you. Come on, Cap'n, jump!"

I didn't need another invitation. I wriggled my feet over the edge of the doorway and looked down to see Hookey, Mr. Rafiq, Lazy Billy, Nick Padder, Windward, the Greek, and Crayfish Jake.

"You're a sight for sore eyes," I said and dropped into their midst, steadied by Hookey's good hand.

Corwen and Philip jumped down after me, Corwen entirely on his own, surefooted, Philip stumbling and being yanked back on to his feet by Lazy Billy.

"I dunnamany more o' these devils there is," Hookey

said. "We'd better hoof it out of here smartish. Bone's got the boat just off Vauxhall Stairs. Tide's on the turn. It'll be a fast run downriver."

More baying, and another pack of the creatures rounded the corner of the inn yard. I heard the lads draw steel.

Hookey pulled his last pistol and took down the leading creature. Two more set on it and it slowed the pack down.

"Run!" I yelled.

Two more creatures hurtled out of an alleyway from the White Lion's yard and drove us across the road toward Vauxhall Gardens, fenced off and closed up in darkness. The grand gates of the main entrance were boarded with what looked like a set of old mismatched doors. I yanked at one and it gave slightly. A mighty hand pushed me aside and Windward took hold and heaved. I could almost hear his muscles straining. Then he let the door spring back and immediately heaved again. With a crack of splintering wood the boarding gave way, and we all poured into the gardens. Windward pulled the wood closed behind us.

I laughed, in truth more of a hysterical giggle. "That'll be two shillings each, lads. This way to the supper boxes and the orchestra."

"Can we come in for a shilling? I always preferred a good fiddle tune to all them fancy concertos," Hookey said, staring around the Grove at the silent buildings. If anyone lived here out of season, there was no sign of them tonight.

I heard the sound of pistols being reloaded and began to load mine, working in the dark. Half-cock it, black powder down the muzzle, tamp down. Ball in the patch, down the muzzle, tamp again. Prime the flash pan. Ready. Repeat for the second pistol.

I breathed, grateful that the baying had stopped. "A shilling it is. My shout!"

"What was them things, Cap'n?" Lazy Billy asked.

"I don't know. Nightmares."

"I ain't never had nightmares like that."

"You will from now on, Billy," Hookey said. "How many of them are there?"

"I don't know," I said. "Philip?"

"Fifty."

"God's ballocks!" Hookey said. "Then I don't suppose we've seen the last of 'em."

"I doubt it." Philip agreed. "They hunt by both scent and sight."

"Then we'll give them a scent to follow and nothing to see except me," Corwen said. "I'll meet you all by Vauxhall Stairs. Don't lose my boots."

"Corwen!" I called out to stop him and then swallowed my words.

He pulled off his boots and shrugged out of his coat and shirt. "Get up there." He pointed to the open balcony of a supper box above our head. "I'll lead them off into the garden, see if they want to sink their teeth into a statue or two. Can you give me light about halfway down there?" He pointed to the Grand Walk, some three hundred yards long. "As soon as I've distracted them, you all get out of here as fast as you can."

He didn't give us any chance to question him but dropped to all fours, changing before his front feet hit the ground, and immediately ran out of his breeches. He bolted back for the gate we'd come in by.

Mr. Rafiq raised one eyebrow but made no comment.

"Jesusmaryan'joseph!" Lazy Billy crossed himself.

He wasn't the only one. I saw the expressions on the faces around me, ranging from incredulity to outright terror. I mustn't let terror take hold.

I picked up Corwen's cast-off garments and shared them out, pushing his boots into Billy's hands. "Don't lose these."

"Wha . . . ?" Billy's eyes were wide with shock. I slapped his shoulder.

"There's worse following us, man. The wolf's on our side. Jump to!"

He blinked. "Aye, Cap'n."

Like a well-trained troupe of acrobats, the lads swarmed up Windward and over the balcony above into an open supper box. Windward boosted Philip from below, and the Greek hauled him the rest of the way. Hookey and Mr. Rafiq reached down and pulled me to safety. Then Windward made a lunge, caught the edge of the balcony, and swung upward.

The box was big enough to maybe seat six in comfort at a table, but all furniture had been removed for the winter, and the floor was carpeted with a layer of autumn leaves.

"Get back and keep down," I said, and immediately dropped to my belly to watch the walkway through the balcony railings. Corwen wanted light, and light he would have. Instead of putting up a single witchlight, I concentrated on the gardens as I'd seen them when I came here with Will. There had been so much light it had looked like some vision of Heaven. Thousands of lanterns dangling from the trees had turned night into day.

Lanterns.

I directed my thoughts to the lanterns in the trees, and halfway down the Grand Walk the night began to glow. I poured energy into it until it looked like Vauxhall Gardens was open for business once more, a golden pathway between two carefully planted wilderness areas.

I heard baying again, and a silver-gray wolf streaked through Vauxhall's famous Grove with almost twenty of the creatures at his heels. Corwen! I almost shouted his name out loud, but I clamped my teeth tight and swallowed the lump that was threatening to rise in my throat and choke me.

"I reckon it's time." Hookey jerked his head at the balcony. Mr. Rafiq went over the edge and steadied the first lads down. They, in turn, steadied the rest on the ten-foot drop to the floor.

I couldn't take my eyes off the chase. As Corwen got to the center of the pool of light he stood up as a man again, naked and golden in the lamplight. A procession of woodland animals emerged from the trees on either side of the path, led by a magnificent stag bearing an enormous rack of antlers. Foxes, deer, badgers, hares, rabbits, and squirrels followed. They looked like the ones I had seen in the forest with the Green Lady. I wondered how Corwen had called them. The walls between worlds must be thin here, it was such a theatrically magical place during the season that some of it must have rubbed off. Corwen had said he held small magics courtesy of the Lady—this must be part of that bounty.

The stag nosed Corwen's shoulder. Corwen said something to him, though from this distance I couldn't tell what, and sank back down to wolf form. As the nightmare things reached the pool of light, the woodland animals exploded into action, splitting up and offering a choice of trails, drawing the creatures after them. The light pool emptied in a few seconds.

Corwen! I wanted to run after him and drag him to safety.

"Over you go, Cap'n." Hookey nudged me as soon as Philip dropped to the floor.

I forced myself to climb over the balcony, stiff-limbed. Hookey grabbed my hand and lowered me to Windward, then followed me down. Pistol drawn, I headed back to the gate, knowing I couldn't help Corwen now. It was up to him.

We met no resistance as we jog-trotted back toward the river. The front of the White Lion looked the same as ever, giving no clue as to what might be happening in the yard. Had they found Walsingham's bloody corpse? Were they even now sending for the Bow Street Runners?

The river still lapped near the top of Vauxhall Stairs. It hadn't been all that long since we'd arrived, maybe less than an hour. Bone brought the *Heart*'s boat in at our hail, and one by one, we gained the safety of wood on water.

"We need to go now, Cap'n ma'am," Bone said. "Else we'll be shooting the bridge at the wrong time and none of your lads, beggin' their pardon, is used to this kind of oar-work."

"We can't go yet. We have to wait for Corwen."

"I got his boots safe, Cap'n," Lazy Billy said.

"Good lad, Billy."

Ten minutes passed, then fifteen. Then I heard a distant bell strike the half hour.

"Cap'n ma'am, we need to go. Now," Bone said again. "Otherwise we should wait upriver until slack water again to get the boat through. She's not built for river work. She's wider than a cutter."

"I hear you, Mr. Bone, but we're waiting for Corwen."

What if he didn't come? What if my Silverwolf had cut it too fine and was even now being ripped to shreds and weighting down the guts of those nightmare creatures? Damn Walsingham. I wanted him alive so I could kill him all over again, but this time slowly, if any harm had come to Corwen.

A baying in the distance, coming closer now, alerted me. "Pull into the stair, quickly, and then get ready to row for your lives."

A silver-gray streak shot down the steps and leaped for the boat before her bow had kissed the steps. Corwen changed back instantly to naked man. "Go! Quickly!"

Eight men pulled in unison. My lads may not be used to river work, but they knew how to bend their backs to an oar. The gap between the steps and the boat widened, ten feet, twelve, fourteen. Half a dozen of the nightmare creatures poured along the quay and down the steps, two abreast. I fired my pistol and the leader fell into the water with a howl. The second leaped at the boat. Its claws scrabbled at the stern and with great presence of mind Bone took an oar and cracked it over the snout. It fell back limp, but that didn't stop the remaining four. They plunged into the water and began swimming.

"I thought you said they couldn't cross running water," I said to Corwen as I reloaded.

He cursed as he dragged on his breeches. "Walsingham must have made them from creatures that can swim. I fancy there's a bit of otter in them."

"Only four. Is that all that's left?"

He nodded. "I used up one of my favors from the Lady. You saw the stag?"

I nodded.

"Hartington drew a lot of them back into the woodland realm. The Lady will deal with them there, if they manage to cross the barrier without reverting to what they were."

"You think Walsingham made them from real animals?"

"That would be my guess, but it's twisted magic."

"Philip, what do you know?"

"Nothing." My baby brother's voice was barely more than a whisper. He'd hardly said anything unless asked since plucking his own poppet from Walsingham's coat pocket.

"Have you got the poppet?" I asked him.

He took it from his pocket, a tiny thing no longer than six inches.

I held out my hand. "Should we destroy it?"

"No!" His voice almost squeaked and he snatched it away protectively. "I have to keep it safe. Always. It's still me. I'm still it." He tucked it inside his shirt.

"We'll find a way to render it harmless, I promise," I said. "The Fa . . . There are people who can help."

"Cap'n, they're gaining on us." Lazy Billy warned as we slid under Westminster Bridge.

I turned and looked. Sure enough, in the phosphorescent moonlight on the river, four vee-shaped wakes marked the creatures' heads. Their bodies submerged, they made a small target in the darkness. Even, so I had to try. I discharged my pistol at the nearest head. Though it bobbed under, it resurfaced, this time slightly closer to the boat. I tried my luck with the second one with much the same result. The flow of the river, the ebbing tide, and the muscles behind our oars carried us swiftly, but the creatures also had the tide and the river with them, and they swam like otters.

Hookey passed me his pistol and I tried again with no success. I reloaded. A fourth attempt also failed, but on the fifth try I hit another, and it yelped and went limp in the water, still being washed along. That left three as Blackfriars Bridge flew over our heads and the stench of the Fleet drain hit our noses.

"We should wait here for slack water," Bone called. "The bridge is lethal at night with such a river running."

"Lethal enough to drown those things?" I asked.

"Lethal enough to drown us all."

"We can't stay here. We can't go ashore. Shoot the bridge, Bone. We're in your hands."

"You're all mad. If I get out of this in one piece, I'm leaving this crew. You can have your guinea back. I didn't sign up for magic and mayhem."

"You signed on for money, Bone, and a share of the prize," Hookey said. "We'll see you right. Now can you shoot the bridge or do we have to do it without you?"

"Just make damn well sure you all do as you're told." He looked at Corwen. "Can those paws of yours hold an oar?"

Corwen, fully dressed now, held up both hands.

"Trade places, then, and careful how you go. I don't want pitching in the river."

The boat barely rocked as Corwen and Bone changed places and Corwen took an oar.

"You, Cap'n Ma'am, since you're so all-fired keen on this, get for'ard and fend us off the starlings if we get too close." He handed me the boathook. "Once she's under the bridge, grab onto something and hold tight, she's going to buck like a poxed whore when her nose hits the slide."

I stepped through the pairs of rowers into the bow of the boat, squeezing Corwen's shoulder as I passed. He returned my touch by twisting his head so his cheek brushed my hand. Only Philip didn't have a job to do, but I figured he was pretty useless as he was.

Though we bore down on London Bridge, carried by the flow of the river and the ebb tide, it seemed the other way around, that it bore down on us. In the moonlight the water looked deceptively calm, but ahead of us I could hear rushing like a waterfall.

I expected Bone to aim for the wider central arch, but he didn't. Instead he aimed for one of the narrower arches.

"Isn't that one safest?" I pointed and shouted.

He nodded and yelled back. "Do you want to drown these bastards or not?"

I did.

I vowed that if Bone got us under the bridge safely I'd bribe him handsomely to stay on the crew.

I stood in the bow, ready to fend us off the starlings, but I needn't have worried, Bone steered straight through the center of the narrow arch. I heard him yelling for the rowers to boat their oars and then I crouched and clutched a stanchion.

The river dropped away from beneath us as water gushed through the narrow opening. The flood was so backed up above the bridge that it created a natural waterfall, a four- or five-foot drop to the seaward side. It felt like ten. For the longest moment, the bow of the boat hung in midair, and then everything tipped as we plunged down, ploughing through a standing wave at the bottom where the rush of water drove under itself in a foaming swirl.

My stomach went with it.

The bow axed through the spume and the living river drenched us all. I feared we'd gone under and would never surface again. The force of water lifted me bodily until I was anchored only by my desperately clutching fingers.

Then the boat's nose broke the surface, she yawed and righted herself, and I crashed back down onto sopping timbers, bruised but still breathing air.

A cheer went up.

I shook my head, but didn't risk standing again. "What about the creatures?" I yelled.

"Can't see nothin', Cap'n," Lazy Billy shouted. "I think we drownded 'em."

"Row, you bastards, else we'll get sucked back in." Bone cut through, and four pairs of oars dipped back into the icy Thames, pulling for the *Heart* with good will.

As soon as we came alongside my lovely schooner, even as I was pushing Philip up a rope ladder, Hookey was calling for Mr. Sharpner to make sail and get us underway on the tide.

I put up a witchlight for the crew to work by and turned to find Bone. He was standing, looking uncertain.

"Ten guineas for tonight's work, Bone, whether you stay or go, but I hope you'll stay. Captain Garrity's fair, the *Heart*'s a good vessel, and she's got a good crew."

"Thank you kindly, Cap'n Ma'am, but I—"

His eyes widened and he made a lunge for me and

pushed me down. Something solid and heavy rushed overhead. Bone's body jerked backward. I rolled and came to my feet, crouching, ready, knowing instinctively what I'd find. One of the nightmare creatures was a better swimmer than the rest. It stood on the deck, dripping river water, front legs splayed, snarling, ready to spring, its maw coated in blood from Bone's throat. Tiger, dog, otter, rat, whatever it had been made from, it was all malice and on a mission to kill.

I stared at it, hardly daring to blink. It stared back, eyes diamond-hard. I was aware of Bone lying in a pool of blood like some cast-off doll. I only had a knife; both pistols were empty. Any loaded pistols from the boat crew would be soaked.

Slowly, still holding the creature's gaze, I reached behind my waist for my knife, holding it point upward. If I could get the point into the creature's throat as it leaped, I could try to drive the blade up into its brain. Whether I could do that before its teeth ripped my throat out and its back claws disemboweled me was a question I didn't want to answer right now. I gathered my magic and hurled a light into its face, and another one. It had little effect. The creature crouched to spring.

A silver-gray shape leaped past me and I felt the impact through my feet. Everything happened too quickly for me to follow, but the two animals slid, twisting and snarling, into the deck rail with such a crack I thought they'd surely break the wood and fall in the river. If that happened, Corwen was dead. Wolves swim, but they are ungainly in water, and this thing was part otter.

Mr. Sharpner pushed a pistol into my hand and Hookey came up with one from somewhere. He leveled it at the clawing, squirming pair, but I put my hand out to hold him back. Any shot had just as much chance of killing Corwen as the creature.

"Corwen, back off," I yelled, but either he couldn't or he didn't want to.

"Get the water pump!" I snapped, and heard several people jump to, but it seemed an achingly long time before

I heard the end of the leather hose dropped down into the river and the creak-creak of two men manning the pump. The first jet of water had no effect, but the men found their rhythm and the water spurted out under pressure, driving a wedge between Corwen and the creature.

I fired. So did Hookey. Both shots cracked out almost simultaneously. The creature jerked back, twitched and was still.

"Corwen!"

He flopped to his side, panting, his fur matted with blood, seemingly without even the strength to change back to human.

"Quick, a length of canvas. Use it as a sling. Carry him down to my cabin," I said, to anyone who'd listen. "Billy, bring bandages, brandy, and boiled water."

I followed them down the companionway, and though I know they didn't mean to bump and jolt him, I heard lupine yelps from inside the sling as Sim and Nick tried to stop it from swinging. Windward lowered it down as gently as he could, and Hookey took the weight from below.

"Get him on the bunk," I directed the lads. Billy scuttled in with bandages, water, a pouch of salves and nostrums and a flagon of brandy. He barely glanced in Corwen's direction, then scuttled out again.

"Do you want any help?" Hookey asked.

"I'll call if I need anything."

"Aye, Cap'n."

"You're still captain, Hookey. I can't stay. This thing's not finished yet. Will you see to Bone?"

I'd hardly known the man, yet his loss stung my eyes and burned the back of my throat.

"Course, lass. We'll bury him at sea as soon as we're out into the Channel."

"I promised him ten guineas. Did he have family?"

"Not since his wife ran off."

"He was worth every penny, ten times over."

"He was."

"Will you say the words for him, Captain Garrity?"

"I will."

Corwen groaned, almost a human sound coming from his wolf lips. I turned to see to him, and heard the cabin door snick shut behind Hookey.

My wolf needed me.

⁂

"Look what a mess you're in, wolf." I bent over him to assess the damage.

He growled low in his throat, a warning not to touch him.

"I know it hurts. You need to change back and take care of some of those hurts then let me salve the rest."

I put my hand out to his face and he growled again, this time his lips wrinkling back into a snarl. He meant it, but at least he was giving me warning.

"All right. It's up to you. Change if you can."

He did, but it wasn't his usual smooth change. First his feet changed, and then his hands, but the instant his hands changed, his feet slipped back to paws. I grabbed both his hands in mine.

"Come on. It's a start. Keep going."

Gradually and painfully, Corwen changed from wolf to man.

He was covered in blood.

"Don't worry, 's not all mine," he said, slurring his words. "You should have seen the other fellow."

"I did."

As I washed off the blood, the water bowl turned red, and Corwen turned pink. When he was clean I called for more water. He was right, much of the blood had been from the creature, and some superficial cuts had begun to heal with the metamorphosis, but there was a worrying fourfold claw gash down his flank and thigh, which began high under his rib cage and ended just above his knee. It hadn't gone deep into vital organs, but the edges of the parallel cuts were already puffy and inflamed. I sluiced it with the brandy, causing Corwen to grit his teeth and curse, but since the bleeding had already stopped I left the wound uncovered to scab over if it would. I can't deny I was worried. Who knew what kind of contagion those things carried? Maybe it was even a poison of some sort, to make them doubly deadly.

Philip might know.

With a guilty start I realized that I hadn't thought of my brother since arriving back on the *Heart*. In the back of my mind, I'd thought *mission completed* and hadn't worried how he might be feeling, supposing him to be relieved to be free of Walsingham.

I draped a sheet across Corwen. He muttered something I didn't catch.

"I'm going to find Philip. I must see how he is. Will you be all right for a few minutes?"

"Mmm. Yes. Let me sleep," he said, and managed to blink his eyes open and look somewhere in my direction, though his unfocused gaze made his gray eyes abnormally dark.

I dropped a kiss on his forehead. "Back soon."

33

Brotherly Love

I FOUND MR. SHARPNER ON DECK. We were already on the move, drifting steadily down the Thames on the tide, with minimal sail and a light wind in our favor.

"Do you need me to give you a breeze, Mr. Sharpner?"

"No, Cap'n, she's doing just fine. We'll be in open water in no time. What's our course?"

I needed more time, so I gambled the Fae wouldn't hurt David. While we were at sea we were safe from them.

"Round the coast to the West Country for now. Corwen's bad. I'll know by tomorrow just how bad—whether he's improving or not. Where's Philip?"

"Up by the for'ard mast. He hasn't said much. Generally a quiet one, is he?"

"Not to my best recollection, but seven years can change a person."

"Aye, they can."

"Hookey?" I asked.

"Sleeping below. Snoring fit to wake the dead."

"I'm sorry I've brought my troubles to the *Heart*, Mr. Sharpner. None of you deserves this mess, especially Bone."

"He was come and gone so fast none of us really knew him, but he seemed like a stout feller."

"Yes, he did, and I'm truly sorry for his loss."

I found Philip sitting on the deck with his back to the mast, just like David used to do. He clutched his blanket around his shoulders, but I could see he was shivering.

"Intending to stay there all night?"

He jumped, startled. "I tried the hammock. It's a little strange. Surrounded by so many people." He shrugged. "I dare say I'll get used to it, if I have to." There was a long pause. "Do I have to? Am I your prisoner, now?"

David had asked me almost the same question. I squatted down beside him.

"Prisoner? Philip, you're my brother. We might not always have been kind to each other as children, but we're family."

"Sumners."

"Yes. How much do you know?"

"I know we represent the greatest threat to this nation that it has ever faced."

"You make it sound dramatic."

"It is. Can you imagine what it would do to this land if old magic was released into it again? If the Fae regained power?"

I shuddered, and not just with the cold.

"The Fae already have power, but they've not used it outside of their own realm in centuries. Why would you think they would want to use it now?" I found myself arguing counter to the fears I already harbored. "Our ancestor, Martyn the Summoner, took power not from the Fae, but from the rowankind. It's to them the power must be returned, otherwise they'll never be free."

And what then? I asked myself.

"Is that what they told you?" Philip's face twisted in a wry smile. "Walsingham tells it differently, and I'm inclined to believe him. He's no reason to lie, no family or wife or wide circle of friends to impress. The Fae made the rowankind for their own use. They made them from dryads, tree spirits, willing or not, mated with them, and begot a whole new race. The power of the rowankind came from the Fae, and to the Fae it will return. Don't you see, Ross? The Fae only want to free the rowankind from human bondage so they can enslave them again."

"You're wrong." But this echoed my own fears, and part of me believed him.

He put a hand on my arm. "You say we haven't always been kind to each other, Ross, and that's true. More especially there were times when I was mean to you, and I'm sorry for it. I was a child, then. I'm a man grown now, and I would set things right between us."

Philip's eyes held an earnestness I had not expected. His regret tugged at my heartstrings. I found myself truly wanting to believe that this was Philip written anew, another brother I could love. "I'm listening."

I settled down to sit on the cold deck and crossed my legs, putting up a small witchlight so I could see his face, pinched and pale.

"Walsingham—yes, he was my captor, but he taught me a lot. He was not unkind. He was a dedicated man, to be sure. You might even call him driven, but he was true in his purpose."

"And that purpose was to kill me."

"I know this is hard to believe, but he held no malice against you, not personally, I mean. It was only what you stood for that put you on opposite sides. He could have killed me, but he didn't. I believe he felt sorry for me. He told me many times over that I was deluded. Explained carefully what had happened all those years ago at the time of the Armada, even showed me the records left by all the Walsinghams. He's not . . . he wasn't a monster. All his magic was used in the service of the Crown, not for himself."

"You admired the man."

"I'm not ashamed to admit it."

I thought about Aunt Rosie's injuries and wondered where admiration stopped and cooperation started, but before I could ask the question I didn't want to hear the answer to, he continued.

"He took me to see the king, late one night, in his private apartments at St. James. We were admitted privately. They say King George is mad, but if that's so he showed no sign of it that night. He's a very great man. He has a keen understanding of magic. The only oddity was that he called me Mr. Summoner, but he asked me if I knew what might happen to Britain if the realm lost the labor and the goodwill of the rowankind, or what the repercussions might be if that race were freed and magic restored."

I felt myself going a little light-headed. These were fears I'd had myself.

"And then the king asked if I would swear allegiance to him. To the king, direct. Of course I said yes, and promptly dropped to my knees and did so. He thanked me for my vow and shook my hand." Philip raised his right hand and looked at it. "So I ask you to consider, Ross, your duty to the realm."

I swallowed hard. "I will consider it, Philip. Believe me, I have been considering it already, but right now I need to know whether Walsingham's hellhounds carried any sort of poison in their claws. Corwen is sick and it's more than just the wounds."

He shook his head and examined his own fingernails. "I don't know. Walsingham used spell-craft, but I wasn't privy to the workings."

I disliked the way he avoided my eye when he said that, after what had seemed like refreshing honesty when he'd spoken about the king.

Corwen slept restlessly while I dozed in my threadbare old armchair. As dawn crept sluggishly through the thick glass of my window, I woke and rose to see if I could get him to take some water. As soon as I put my hand on his forehead I knew I'd slept too long. He burned with fever, and when I drew back the sheet his claw marks almost glowed with heat. The inflammation had spread outwards from the edges of the wound.

"Corwen!" I tried to wake him, but though I think he

heard me he didn't react coherently. "Corwen, you've got to change. Change to wolf and then back again."

Holding a cup to his lips only soaked both of us as he shook his head violently. I doubt he swallowed any of the bitter liquid containing willow bark and feverfew. I dripped water laced with brandy and sweet cordial between his lips, anything to get liquid inside him.

I flung open the window as far as it would go to reduce the temperature in the cabin and left wet cloths on his forehead and around his wrists at pulse points. Pulling back the sheets I sponged him down—face, arms, chest, belly, legs—too worried to dwell on his nakedness.

"Corwen, change." I rolled him on to his side, facing me, and dropped a light kiss onto his brow. He managed to draw his knees up to his belly. "Yes, that's it." I stroked his arm from shoulder to fingertip. "Change! Change! Change!"

I repeated it, still stroking, until it became a chant and gradually his breathing deepened and silver-gray fur appeared beneath my hand, like down at first, but then thicker, stronger.

"Yes, that's it. Change. Heal yourself."

It happened so slowly that I feared he might stick halfway between man and wolf, but eventually the transition was complete. He wouldn't have the strength to return to human straightaway.

He blinked at me, eyes glazed, and I sponged him down again, soaking his fur. His tongue lolled out of his mouth and he panted, but there was no snarl this time.

"Rest a while, then we'll try again. I love you, Corwen." I kissed the top of his furred head, between his ears. "Don't give up on me."

He managed to thump his tail twice on the bed, and I left him to sleep.

I took breakfast on deck: yesterday's bread and a milky oat porridge, sweetened with honey and served up with crisp apples, a luxury for sailors who spent long months at sea out of sight of cows and orchards.

Philip poked at his bowl listlessly.

I sat down beside him and started to spoon mine. "You'd be grateful for that if you were used to a seagoing diet."

"I could never be a sailor."

"You once said you wanted to be a pirate."

"Did I? Childish fancies."

I smiled.

"And look at you," he said. "You practically are a pirate. What happened to you, Ross?"

"Mother happened. Magic happened. Will happened."

"Where is Will? Who's this Corwen?"

"Will died."

"But Tremayne's reputation . . ."

"That's me. Captain Ross Tremayne."

"So why come inland and get mixed up with magic? Don't you like life here on the ocean?"

Another question David had asked, but with the opposite intent.

"I didn't intend to get mixed up in anything. Mother *summoned* me. She thought you were dead and knew she was dying, so she passed the box on. Maybe it was one last gesture to the life she might have had if it hadn't been for the Walsingham family."

"Walsingham family?"

"It was an older Walsingham who killed our grandparents, and was, in turn, killed by them. I assume your Walsingham was out for revenge. I hope he has no son to follow him."

"There is no Walsingham family."

"What?"

"Walsingham's not a name, it's a title. He's a government man who reports to Sir George Shee, the king's spymaster. Walsingham and his agents deal with magic. And they dabble in magic themselves."

I shuddered at his use of the word. Those creatures had been made by more than dabbling.

"They're not part of the Mysterium?" I asked.

"You'd think they should be, wouldn't you, but no. The Mysterium deals with small magic, the licensing of hedge-witches, many of them charlatans. Walsingham's men are so secret that their organization doesn't even have a name. It was set up over two hundred years ago, when Queen Bess realized what Martyn the Summoner and his like could do if they were against her rather than with her. Grateful as she was for the defeat of the Armada, she believed Martyn to be responsible for the failure of her expedition to Spain. When he disappeared so suddenly, Sir Francis Walsingham, her spymaster, was sent to hunt him down, but Martyn proved elusive, and by that time Walsingham was old. When Walsingham died, a man called Nicholas Fellows took his place and his name. He believed—they all believe—that giving your real name to a witch is dangerous. There's always a Walsingham, but they're never related, and their real name is never Walsingham. When one falls, another takes his place. The organization has the support of the Crown, financially and in every other way. In turn Walsingham reports back, though never to Parliament, only to the spymaster and His Majesty."

"Government agents, just for us." I blinked twice. "It seems excessive."

"Not if we can truly do what Walsingham believes we can."

"The Fae believe we can, too," I said.

Philip was silent.

"Mother never told you anything about it, did she?" I asked. "I thought she might have, you being her favorite."

He shook his head. "I realized when I was still at school that I had magic, but I'd already seen her anger when she saw your magic manifest for the first time."

"She was scared." I didn't tell him what Larien had told me. Even now I couldn't think of it without trembling.

"Scared?" He gave me a look of frank astonishment. "Of course she was scared. Were you so wrapped up in your own head that you didn't see it at the time? Scared for you and for the whole family."

"I never . . ."

"That's exactly right, Ross, you never thought of anyone but yourself. It was all about you."

I felt my jaw drop. Was he right? I'd been young and had

possibly handled the whole thing badly. I thought Mother hated me for my witchcraft. If I'd known about her and about the family maybe I'd have seen how terrified she was that my magic would lead Walsingham to her—to all of us. Walsingham had destroyed the Sumners, had caused her to lose Rosie, the only family member she had left. Yes, she'd been harsh with me. Had I deserved it? Couldn't she just have told me? Was it her silence that led to our estrangement, or my intransigence?

Philip continued. "When I saw you could do magic, I wanted that for myself. Oh, how I wanted it. I tried and tried to stir up the wind. But that wasn't to be my power. My magic didn't come to me until I was away at school. By that time, I was prepared. I decided I wouldn't give her the opportunity to do to me what she'd done to you. I never told her, of course. Even when I registered with the Mysterium, I never brought my magic home."

"What's your ready-magic?"

"Divination. I see spirits, ghosts, whatever you want to call them. It's easier to hide. Not as obvious as creating a whirlwind in the hallway. Mine's a pretty useless talent, really, except for gleaning money from the pockets of the recently bereaved. There's quite a decent living to be made once word gets around, mediating in conversations between the living and the departed."

"And Walsingham found you?"

He shrugged. "I got careless. And in my own defense, I was ignorant of all that I know now. He taught me a lot. I'd never considered that magic could truly be evil, but I began to see, under his tutelage, that in the wrong hands magic could destroy the realm."

"And did you never doubt him? Wonder if he was trying to indoctrinate you? You know I'm a loyal subject of the Crown. Why should Walsingham believe me a threat?"

"I was wary of him, of course. He had the poppet, and that ensured my compliance, but I never doubted that he believed absolutely in everything he said. He wanted the box. He said it was dangerous. I didn't even know what he was talking about at first. Do you have it, Ross?"

"Yes." I took it out of my pocket and unwrapped it, knowing Walsingham was gone.

"Ah." He hissed out a breath, reached for it and then drew his hand back. "May I?"

I nodded.

He turned it this way and that, looking at it from all angles and running his fingers over the winterwood to feel for any openings. "Such a small thing. How does it work?"

"I don't know. The Fae believe it will take all of our mother's children together to open it."

He tossed it back to me quickly. "Then we could open it now?"

"Not without David." I wrapped it again.

He gave me a puzzled look. "The scrawny houseboy with the big eyes?"

"Our half-brother," I said. "David is our mother's son, Larien's his father. Remember that time Mother went traveling? Well, she had a good reason to vacate Plymouth for half a year."

"He was there one time when I came home for the summer. I never knew where he came from, never cared enough to ask to be honest. Mixed blood?" His mouth turned down. "How could she? With a bond servant?" He shook his head as if to clear it. "I have a half-rowankind brother. That's unnatural."

I thought of David as I'd last seen him in all his Fae glory.

"Even if that were true, it would have been no one's business but Mother's, but as it turns out there was more. David's not half-rowankind, he's all Fae. Larien is Fae. You'd better hear all the rest."

I told him the bare bones of what had happened to me since that last visit to my mother. I watched his face carefully as I spoke, wondering if he'd give anything away by his expression, but he remained impassive until I spoke of Aunt Rosie's injuries.

"Walsingham made me," he said. "When it was obvious she couldn't tell us anything he told me to kill her and left me to do it. It was like looking at Mother, Ross. A rounder, softer, kinder version of Mother. I couldn't do what he wanted me to do, but I told him I had. Is she . . . Does she live?"

"She does."

I so wanted to believe that he wasn't responsible for her torture that I didn't press him further. I went on with my story.

He listened without interrupting and then said, "The Fae have only their own interests at heart, Ross. I don't want anything to do with this. Put me ashore, please. Let me take the box and disappear quietly."

I shook my head. "The box always comes back to me. I tried to throw it into the ocean and it washed up on an island beach halfway across the Atlantic Ocean. Besides, the Fae will always be able to find you. Dantin left me in no doubt that they'd be willing to kill you so that David and I could open the box alone. Better to face them together." I put my hand out and touched his arm. "I've only just found you again, Philip. I don't want to lose you. There's been too much estrangement in this family. If you'd seen the devastation at the Sumner house, you might have more sympathy. Even now the ground is barren. Our grandparents, our great aunt, all of them killed except for the girls." I felt tears welling up. "Can't we forget our childhood differences and make a new beginning? I still don't know what to do for the best. If we all decide not to open the box, there's not much they can do about it."

"I guess David wants to open it."

I nodded. "More than anyone. He's lived as a rowankind. He knows what it's like."

"And I don't want to open it. So that leaves you with the final decision. Think on it, Ross. You're not stupid. I know you can make the right choice."

I headed back to check on Corwen. I had hoped that sharing the information with Philip would give me some insight into what should be done, but I was no nearer to knowing whether it was right to free the rowankind and risk the consequences for humanity or whether I should refuse.

Corwen was no better. He might even be worse.

I knelt by the bunk and whispered, "Change, now. Come back to me."

He opened his eyes, cool gray, but there wasn't much behind them.

"Come on, Corwen. Change and heal." I ran my fingers through his ruff. "You can do it."

As before, the change was a long time coming, and even then it was slow. The claw marks were even more livid against pale skin. I went to the door and shouted for Lazy Billy to bring more boiled water—hot this time—and the kaolin powder. I mixed the powder to a muddy paste and smeared it on linen strips then pressed it hot on to Corwen's claw marks in sections, building up a poultice that I hoped would draw out the infection. He moaned slightly and then settled.

"How does that feel?"

I didn't expect an answer, and I didn't really get one, but he seemed to be more comfortable.

I changed the poultice twice more throughout the day, alarmed by the dark bloody pus the first time, but relieved that the second round seemed cleaner. By evening Corwen's fever seemed lower, and he had downed a cup of my herbal brew, albeit in single swallows over the course of the afternoon. Finally, as dusk closed in and the wind freshened, he opened his eyes and they were clear.

"Rough sea?" he asked.

"Moderate."

"Where are we heading?"

"Good question. Away."

"Sounds sensible."

"We're beating to weather along the English Channel. Right now we should be somewhere off the Dorset coast."

"We lost the horses—Leo's horses."

"Yes we did. And since he borrowed them for us in good faith I guess we owe someone in Summoner's Well for them. Are you hungry?"

"Famished."

Thank God!

He downed a cawdle of ale, oats, cinnamon, and eggs and then looked around for more. Being a wolf, he needed meat. Luckily Mr. Cruikshanks had restocked in London and there was fresh beefsteak. It was only when Corwen was heartily tucking in to a whole plate of it, barely seared over the galley stove, that I relaxed, acknowledging for the first time that, for a while, I had feared I might lose him, and that thought had terrified me.

Were you ever afraid of losing me? Will's ghost asked in the back of my mind.

I never thought I would. You were always so strong, so confident. I thought you indestructible. And then the unthinkable happened and opened up the possibility that it might happen to anyone I love, at any time.

Corwen looked at me sideways as if he sensed something, then put down his knife. "I thought he'd decided to leave us alone when he didn't show up in London."

I shrugged. "He's Will. He comes and goes in his own time. Does he worry you?"

Corwen shook his head. "If I'd lost you I might want to hang on for as long as I could, too. I don't blame him." He flashed me a grin. "But I haven't lost you. Come lie beside me and sleep for a while. You look tired. Have I been such a bad patient?"

"Terrible. I hope I shall never have to nurse you again." I leaned over to kiss him.

He reached up and touched the side of my face. "You're cut."

"Flying glass. It could have been worse. Does it mar my beauty?"

I asked him tongue in cheek, never thinking I had much beauty to mar, but he answered me seriously. "Nothing could mar your beauty for me."

I shuffled out of my clothes and, taking care not to catch his wounds, slid into the narrow bed beside him, pulling the blankets up to cover our nakedness. He cradled me to his good side, and I let my hand slide down his chest to rest lightly on his flat belly. We fell asleep.

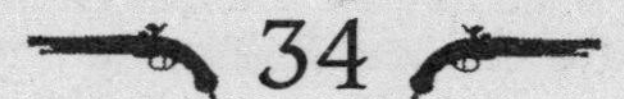

34

Here Be Pirates

SOMETHING FELT WRONG! I awoke, breathless, my heart racing, deep in the middle of the night. Rather than the steady rise and fall of the *Heart* breasting a brisk sea, she felt dead in the water. It was the stillness of a ship unnaturally and totally becalmed.

I rolled out of bed and into my breeches and boots, dragging on a warm jacket, then I sat down suddenly, fighting my instincts and bumping against Corwen, who had been disturbed by my sudden flurry.

"What's wrong?" he asked, touching my back.

"Can't you feel it? It's not natural. Too still."

"Are you going on deck?"

"I should leave this to Hookey. I'm not captain anymore."

"You're still the shipowner. Doesn't that count for something?"

Right then, there was a knock on the door and Lazy Billy called out, "Cap'n asks if you'll come up on deck, Cap'n."

"Hah!" I leaped to my feet. "Be right there, Billy." I

turned to Corwen. "You rest a while longer. I'll let you know if it's anything to worry about."

I expected to come on deck into a thick fog and find us drifting gently with extra lookouts fore and aft, but it was a sparkling, clear night, bright stars overhead and the English Channel turned to glass. Our sails hung slack without a breath of wind to stir them. I wasn't the only one spooked; the men were stumbling out onto the deck one at a time, some only half-dressed.

Corwen followed me up the companionway, still limping a little, his shirttails outside his breeches, his face pale. "What's wrong?"

I shrugged and shook my head. "Captain Garrity? Mr. Sharpner?"

"Been like this for about ten minutes, Cap'n," Mr. Sharpner said. "Not natural. Leastways, not natural in my experience."

I turned to look at Hookey, stifling my desire to take charge, but he was already doing everything I would have done. He sent the men back to their hammocks and went aloft with my ensorcelled spyglass, but could see nothing. He offered me the glass back, but I told him to keep it.

"Can you find out what's causing this?" he asked me. "Or who?"

"I'll try. Corwen, will you come for'ard with me?"

Corwen nodded and followed me, tucking in his shirttail as we went.

"How do you feel?" I asked him softly.

"Much better than I did."

"There's magic at work. We need to pinpoint it."

"Of course."

Philip sat by the foremast as before. He'd learned the trick of wrapping his hammock around him over the top of his blanket to keep in body heat, but I was surprised to see him still asleep.

"Philip!" I nudged him with my foot.

He didn't move.

"Philip!" I bent to shake him but found him stiff and unresponsive, bolt upright but insensible.

The pulse at his throat was light but steady, and though his skin was doughy, he wasn't cold beneath his blanket.

"Looks like some kind of spell." Corwen confirmed my suspicions. "It can't be the poppet, though. He's still got that, hasn't he?"

I checked his pockets. Yes, the poppet was there and undamaged in the pocket next to his heart. I left it where it was.

"Captain Garrity!" I called Hookey over.

"He's been magicked, just like the ship." Hookey stepped back from checking the pulse in Philip's throat. "Your trouble's following you, Gal. You sort out the magic and leave the *Heart* to me an' Mr. Sharpner." He called over his shoulder, "Billy, Nick, take Master Philip below and sit with him. Let me know if there's any change."

"Aye, Cap'n." Billy and Nick carried an unresponsive Philip away, followed by Hookey.

"Can you call the wind?" Corwen asked.

I tried, but I couldn't grasp anything tangible. So I felt beneath the keel for the roll and pitch of the waves, the slither of the ocean currents, sometimes close to the surface and at other times buried deep.

Nothing.

I shook my head. "Neither wind nor water is answering."

I reached out to try and find what magic was causing this, but it was as if the currents of magic had fallen dead as well. All I succeeded in doing was giving myself a headache.

"Anything?" I asked Corwen, but he just shook his head.

"Another Walsingham?" I suggested. "Who else would attack Philip?"

"Maybe it's not a deliberate attack on Philip. Maybe he's just susceptible to the forces causing the calm."

"Maybe." I shivered.

We stayed on deck throughout the rest of the night, wrapped in blankets, unsure as to what we could do, but feeling the need to be ready. Though we didn't even hold hands, Corwen and I sat close enough to touch: shoulder, elbow, hip and thigh, sharing warmth and comfort. Some of the men on duty joined us in our eerie, silent vigil. Eventually the inky blackness lightened to a deep royal blue, then lighter still, until dawn's first blush illuminated an empty sea—empty, that is, save for us and miles and miles of flat, dead-calm water all the way to the horizon in every direction.

No seabirds. No fish. No clouds in the clear October sky. No swell in the glassy surface of the water. Though it was still well above freezing, I could look out on it and imagine it turned to ice.

Hookey sent out the boat and eight strong oarsmen. He gave orders in a hushed voice, as if the monstrous calm had ears. They dipped and pulled . . . and stopped. Two fell over backward, completely shocked by the lack of water resistance. Their blades sliced the unnaturally still water as if it were air, and the boat didn't even bob on the surface. Though they were only a few feet from the ship, carried by the momentum of pushing off with oars, they couldn't even get back until Hookey threw a rope.

Philip continued unresponsive, as if frozen in time.

The rest of us watched and waited through a full day.

Eventually Hookey told everyone not on watch to get some sleep. Grateful for the prompt, Corwen and I threaded our way through the maze of hammocks slung belowdecks, unconcerned about giving away our relationship. We fell on the bed, fully dressed, and slept in each other's arms until daybreak.

On the second day, on Captain's orders, Mr. Rafiq took an inventory of our stores and rationed them. We had plenty, but this stillness was so ominous that it seemed like a sensible precaution. No one grumbled.

On the third day we were all thinking too much about our bellies, so Hookey called a gun drill as a distraction, only to find that the crew worked up an even bigger appetite, all but Philip, who slept through everything. I sat with him myself for a while, but though his pulse remained strong and his breathing even, he was as becalmed as the *Heart*.

On the fourth day the sea was still empty.

And then, suddenly, it wasn't.

Between one blink and the next the sea was filled with four pirate ships flying James Mayo's fleet flag and sitting, one to port and one to starboard of us, not five hundred yards distant, with one more at our bow and another at our stern. They were all broadsides on, with gunports open. No small schooners, these were full-rigged, three-masted ships carrying eight-pounders and long twelves plus stern and bow chasers. Mayo's flagship, the *Black Hawk*, a six-hundred-ton, French-built frigate of the Magicienne class, carried at least thirty-two guns. She was twice our length, with a draft of twenty-two feet.

The *Heart* almost rocked with the force of sixty men jumping all at once, but it was too late, we couldn't run out our guns in time. Even if we could, any one of the big ship-rigged vessels was more than our match. The *Black Hawk* alone could blow us out of the water with a single broadside.

Corwen stared at Mayo's ship. "Even a landlubber like me can tell this isn't good."

I almost laughed. I'd been so worried that it might be Walsingham that I hadn't even considered the possibility that Gentleman Jim was behind all this. I felt guilty. My actions had contributed greatly to his current disaffection. I'd ignored what I now realized were his deeper feelings for me. Even so, I hadn't thought him so petty as to put all this effort into seeking revenge, though in hindsight I'd probably given him reason. Any one of my actions could have turned him into an enemy: running so quickly from his bed, the attack on Ravenscraig, stealing back the box, or even the incident with the *Bitter Bird*. I'd been so fixed on one enemy that I'd completely ignored the other. One entirely of my own making.

"Well if that don't tear the bumhole out of a baboon." Hookey spat over the side. "Even with a score to settle, this is a bit rich."

Hookey was right. Mayo might be sensitive to magic, but he wasn't a witch. He could never run a rig like this. He'd obviously hired someone incredibly powerful both to cause the calm and to mask four ships approaching.

"He's hoisted the parley flag." Hookey scowled. "What's he want to talk for? He's got us dead in his sights."

"He wants the box," I said, half to myself. "And probably parts of my anatomy nailed to his mast." I shivered. Nailed wasn't a word I liked in this context. "He might even want David, but at least he's out of luck there."

A puff of white smoke appeared from the *Black Hawk*'s for'ard gun a split second before the boom and a splash as he put a ball neatly across our bows.

"I think that meant hurry up," Hookey said.

I took a deep breath. "All right, lower the boat. Hookey, I'd be obliged if you'd be at the tiller yourself with your eight best men at the oars."

"The oars don't work."

"I bet they will now," I said as a light breeze kissed my cheek.

"Armed?"

"What do you think?"

"I'm coming too," Corwen said.

"No, you're not!" Hookey and I spoke together.

I put my hand out to touch Corwen's arm, feeling the tension in his muscles. "Mayo would kill you for fun as soon as he realized you weren't one of the lads."

"Which would be as soon as he saw you." Hookey growled. "Likely you'd get us killed, too."

I pulled Corwen down the companionway, grabbed him by the shirtfront and kissed him, swift and fierce. He squeezed me tight to him, belly to belly. I held on. *Please don't let this be good-bye.* When he let me go, we were both breathing heavily.

"Keep this for me." I pushed the box, still in its wrapping, into his hands and nudged him toward the cabin.

"Stay safe!" he growled. It wasn't a request, it was an order. "If the bastard harms one hair of your head he'll pay for it."

I hoped that was a promise he wouldn't have to make good on.

"Aye-aye." I touched my forehead with my fingers in a salute.

The lads lowered the boat and rowed me toward Jim's flagship. I could see Jim on the quarterdeck, hands clasped behind him, watching our progress. I wondered what he wanted most, revenge or the box.

"My dear Captain Tremayne, welcome aboard." Mayo sprang down to the main deck and called down over the side. "Still making good use of my castoffs, I see."

Hookey bridled.

"Come up alone and send your boat back. And don't try anything, I've got a dozen crack-shot riflemen in the top rigging with their sights trained on your oarsmen. They can't miss at this distance." He grinned. "Not in such calm weather."

I felt sick. "Do as he says, Captain Garrity." I lowered my voice. "Do me a favor, keep the *Heart* afloat and stay alive for long enough to get the bastard for me if this all goes wrong. And stop Corwen from doing anything stupid."

"Aye, Cap'n." Not one to waste words, my Hookey, but there was a wealth of feeling in that response.

I love you, old friend, stay safe.

I climbed the rope ladder, trying to get my breathing under control. Gentleman Jim himself held his hand out to help me over the rail. I ignored it and hopped neatly onto the *Black Hawk*'s deck, balanced with my weight on the balls of my feet, ready—for what?

"Nicely done. I've always admired the way you handle yourself aboard ship. Always so trim and elegant. I'm surprised no one sees through that mannish disguise of yours. You always look like a woman to me." His words were light, Jim's usual banter, sometimes dangerous, sometimes not, but his voice sounded strained.

"Is that a compliment, Captain Mayo?"

I searched his face, but he was tight mouthed, giving little away. Sweat beaded his temples despite the chill autumn air.

"I always pay you compliments, Captain Tremayne. You don't always appreciate them. I thought we'd made some progress last time we met." He lowered his voice to a throaty whisper and leaned in close to me. "I thought we'd made a lot of progress."

I held myself ready, not knowing whether to dodge a kiss or a kick, but suddenly his eyes held something I didn't expect to see—fear.

"The man who wanted the box. He's here on board, Ross, I'm sorry. I was told you'd left Garrity in charge of the *Heart*. I didn't know it was you he wanted or I'd never have agreed to this. For pity's sake, help me."

"Walsingham?" Had I failed to kill him after all or could this be his successor, the new Walsingham, already running me down?

Jim looked out to sea so no one else but me could see his lips moving. "He offered a fat bounty. Joined us yesterday. Told us where to find the *Heart*."

So he hadn't turned against me despite what I'd done to him. I felt a pang of guilt. "I've treated you badly, James Mayo, and I'm sorry for it. This business is dangerous. Watch your back."

He blinked and nodded, a world of understanding passing between us in a split second. Then Jim raised his voice for the benefit of onlookers. "Where's the rowankind boy?"

"Gone. Safe."

Jim turned and glanced at someone in the bows.

I whirled around. Walsingham!

Surely I'd killed him. Philip had said he was dead—or had he? I thought back to the fight in the stable yard. Philip had grabbed the poppet after I'd shot Walsingham, and had simply shaken his head when I'd asked after the man. I'd jumped to conclusions. I should have known. The creatures wouldn't have kept coming after us so long and so hard if he'd been dead.

"Mr. Walsingham!" I had the satisfaction of seeing that

he looked gray and tired; either my pistol ball or his magic use had taken its toll.

"Mrs. Tremayne. I didn't tell you to bring *him*."

Will's ghost shuffled his feet. I hadn't even noticed him materialize.

"Will didn't obey me when he was alive, why should he start now?"

"Begone!" Walsingham gestured.

Surprisingly, Will's ghost disappeared, sinking down through the deck. A frisson of fear ran through me. If Walsingham could banish a determined ghost so easily what else might he be able to do?

"You've got something that belongs to me." Walsingham kept his voice level. He even managed to sound reasonable. Did he mean the box or Philip?

"I might have something that you want, but I don't have anything that belongs to you."

"Hold her!" Walsingham said. "Search her—thoroughly."

Two burly seamen sprang to, one at each elbow and a third began to run his hands over my body, pinching and poking my breasts and sliding his hands between my legs. He began to tug at the buttons on my breeches.

"Enough, Ned!" Jim's sharp command caused the man's hand to fall away. "Have some respect. Mrs. Tremayne is here at my invitation. She's under my protection."

"Oh, for Heaven's sake!" Walsingham stepped past Jim and completed the search impersonally and efficiently, then stepped back. "Where's the box, Mrs. Tremayne? I mean to have it, and it will go badly for you if you don't surrender it."

"As you can tell, it's not here."

"So it's on your ship. You wouldn't have left it anywhere else. Very well, it will go badly for them if you don't hand it over. You may have noticed that there are four ships arrayed against you. Four broadsides. How will that go for your little *Heart of Oak*? She's bonny, but I think her strength lies in her speed and maneuverability, not the toughness of her planking. I have no interest in your ship or the lives of your crew. No interest at all, one way or the other. In fact, sinking her with all hands might achieve the end I desire. You can hardly use the box if it's at the bottom of the ocean, can you?"

I didn't tell him that whatever he did, the box would come back to me whilst I lived. There was no use suggesting the obvious solution to his problem.

"Mr. Walsingham." The strain was evident in Jim's voice. "We agreed that the *Heart* would be mine, and her captain also mine to do with as I pleased. I thought that would be Garrity, but I can wait to settle with him. If Captain Tremayne is returned, that doesn't alter our agreement. The captain is mine." He glanced at me. "And she's the captain."

I didn't set him right on that score. James Mayo was an infinitely better proposition than Walsingham.

"If I may—"

That was as far as Jim got.

Walsingham reached into his pocket and pulled out a twist of paper and yanked it straight.

Jim gasped out a strangled sound as his words were choked off in his throat. He clawed at his neck as if trying to loosen an invisible rope, face deepening to red and then with a sucking, shuddering sound, like a child with the whooping cough, he sucked air into tortured lungs.

I sought the breeze above me for enough energy to make a vortex, but though the wind kissed my cheek it still didn't answer my call. Walsingham produced another twist of paper. Even from here I could see writing on it. Letters the color of dried blood writhed around as if possessed. He opened it out fully and said a word that my ears heard but my brain did not translate into speech.

Whomp!

It felt like an unseen hand, strong as a bull, had swatted me to the deck. One second I was standing, the next it was as if someone had yanked the ground away from behind me, and I crashed flat on my belly with the breath knocked out of me and my cheek pressed into the planking.

"I didn't agree to this, Mr. Walsingham." I saw boots as Jim stepped between me and Walsingham. "You said you wanted the *Heart*, you said nothing about Captain Tremayne." I heard him loosen his saber in its scabbard.

A foolhardy moment of gallantry, or maybe the bravest thing he'd ever done, but he paid dearly for it. Walsingham didn't even reply. All I could see of him was his ankles, which flexed as he thrust his weight forward. Jim's feet left the deck completely and I heard him thump down somewhere behind me. The twist of paper fluttered down, the letters already fading away. Walsingham had prepared his spells in advance. What kind of magic did this man have? Whatever it was, it was more powerful than anything I could muster.

Jim's crew gasped in unison, but no one uttered a word of protest, not even Tarpot Robbie, who'd sailed with Jim for as long as anyone could remember.

"I'm not here to play games." Walsingham bent down low over me. "Give me the box, the halfbreed, and Philip, and I'll spare your life."

"No, you won't." With my mouth pressed against the deck and my head feeling as though it was being forced through the ship's timbers, I could barely get the words out.

He sighed. "All right, I won't spare your life. Thou shalt not suffer a witch to live, especially one who can overturn the order of Britain. You are a dangerous woman, Mrs. Tremayne. I've dedicated my life to finding the box before it could be used, and there have been others before me. Do you know what that kind of dedication does to a man? No family, no children. My mission is my wife, my little troop is my family, my apprentices my children.

"I was an apprentice once, myself, standing beside my master outside a house called Bullcrest. Ah, I see the name means something to you. You didn't know I was there? Well, there's no reason you should. I was the older of two apprentices. Geoffrey was the other one, Geoffrey Meadows—not his real name, but real to us. He saved my life that day by being directly between me and the blast your family caused. I got these scars." He knelt and put his face close to mine. "You thought it was the smallpox? My face looked like ground meat. Geoffrey wasn't so lucky, and neither was our master. I didn't want a promotion to Walsingham. I was too young. I still had too much to learn. I believed your family all dead, and I celebrated even in the depths of my misery. I thought it was over. For more than two decades, I went about my business, overseeing the prevention of magical threats to the realm. Imagine my dismay when your brother came to my attention and I discovered there was another generation. It's time to end it. Your family has been a threat to the Crown for too long."

If I hadn't been properly terrified before, that pronouncement sucked the courage out of me.

"I can't spare you, Mrs. Tremayne. Even with the box gone, the Fae could use you as a catalyst. But please believe me, I'll spare your ship and your crew if you give me the boy, the box, and your brother."

"Go to Hell." It was all I could manage to say.

He released the pressure and rolled me over. Cautiously I sat up, seeing Jim slumped either unconscious or dead, a spreading stain of blood beneath his head. I swallowed down rising sickness, not at the blood, but at the hollowness of a life thrown away. Jim and I had had our differences, but his last words had redeemed him in my eyes. I'd never loved him, but I had liked him.

Walsingham didn't slap me down again. Glancing sideways to the rest of the crew, I saw they were all very busy minding their own business.

"You!" Walsingham pointed at Tarpot Robbie. "And you. Get rid of that." He jerked his chin toward Jim. "Over the side." He didn't even watch them. I heard a splash, and the most fearsome pirate of his day was gone without ceremony. I'm not saying James Mayo didn't deserve to die for any number of good reasons, but not like that, carelessly, swatted like a bug.

35

Fire Down Below

WALSINGHAM PACED THE DECK. As he turned away, Will's ghost appeared, or at least his head popped up through the timbers. He looked at me and hummed a chantey. Will only sang when he was drunk, and even then he couldn't hold a tune in a bucket, but I recognized what passed for his discordant version of *Fire Down Below*. He vanished before Walsingham turned and strode back toward me. What did Will mean? *Fire down below* was a common sailor's term for the pox, unless . . . Did he mean it literally?

Walsingham stopped in front of me and took a small pouch from his pocket. He delved inside it and tossed a pinch of brownish powder into my face. I'd breathed some of it in before I realized what was happening, then he repeated the gesture and breathed in the powder himself. A spell of some kind, but I just didn't know enough about his kind of magic.

"We'll fetch them together," he said. "I'm not much of a summoner, but you are."

At first I didn't take his meaning. I thought he meant

fetch them literally, which would be foolish, even for someone as powerful as him. My lads wouldn't stand by like Jim's had. But then I realized that he intended to force me to use my power. The bullish pressure returned, monstrous, crushing, but this time, instead of squashing my body, it was inside my head, trying to burst out.

Walsingham invaded my thoughts, that very center of self, his touch more intimate than any lover's.

"Get out!" I gasped.

"I think not." He spoke between gritted teeth. All I could do was take comfort in the fact that, even with prepared spells, this wasn't coming easy to Walsingham.

I tried to push him out of my head. Anything I could do to make this more difficult for him might give me some insight into how I could free myself. He flinched, but then he blew another pinch of the brown powder into my face and took another pinch himself.

He breathed deep. "That's better. You're stronger than I expected. I won't make that mistake again."

In less time than it took to blink, Walsingham's magic stripped the whereabouts of the box from my thoughts. He took my summoning power and wore it like a hand puppet, causing me to do his bidding, making me focus on the box.

Come! I summoned it.

It slid across the chart table in my cabin. In my head—or maybe even through Walsingham's eyes—I saw Corwen make a lunge for it, miss, and slam the door shut instead. I might be able to levitate the box, but I couldn't move it through a closed door. Well done, Corwen.

I tried to fight Walsingham's invasion, but his magic was powerful. This was a prepared spell that I couldn't begin to comprehend. My heart raced, and I panted as though I'd run five miles. Walsingham's power pounded through my head. I touched a trickle on my top lip and my hand came away bloody.

Again through Walsingham's eyes, I saw Philip struggling to break free from Lazy Billy, Sim, and Nick Padder while they called for help and other sailors piled in to restrain him. He was struggling like one possessed.

Summon them! Walsingham's voice was inside my head.

The box smashed itself against the closed window. The thick glass chipped, but it didn't shatter. The box flew at the glass again and Corwen took another lunge, netting it in the Fae's magical leather bag. He folded the flap closed and hugged it tight to him.

Walsingham turned against Corwen, using my summoning power as if it were his own. Corwen sank to his knees, pushing against the door even as he fell, making sure that his body trapped the door closed.

Corwen!

With a jolt I realized that my concern for Corwen had given Walsingham a hold over me. He began to force Corwen hard onto the floor. Through our link I could see it all, feel it all. It was as though it was me doing those things, building pressure inside Corwen's head, waiting for the first precious blood vessel to pop.

No!

I couldn't best Walsingham in a straight fight, so I did the only thing I could do. I flung a witchlight at his eyes.

Walsingham dodged and grimaced. "You won't distract me so easily."

Good!

I stopped trying to fight him, gave my power to him entirely, trusting that Corwen would keep the box safe a while longer and that no one would let Philip get away from them. I tried to wall off the terror of being used, and turned my attention to the witchlight now floating behind Walsingham. I sent it up, across, over, down the hatch, into the ship's hold. Will moved to the head of the companionway, ducking his head to watch the light and bobbing back up guiding, pointing. I dropped the witchlight down to where he pointed, making it hot, hot, hotter still, nurturing a thin wisp of smoke, darker now, more dense. Finally, a tongue of flame. Though I couldn't draw a whirlwind, I managed a light breeze, enough to fan the flames.

In our cabin, Corwen was now pressed flat to the floor, his lips almost blue. I couldn't tell if he was alive or dead. *Hang on, Corwen.*

A cry went up from somewhere aft. I was dimly aware of the sound of running and of bodies hurtling over rails and hitting water, but I was concentrating on creating a little breeze to push my flames toward where Will pointed—the ship's powder magazine. I had to stop Walsingham somehow, even if it meant my own life.

Will's ghost sprang up through the timbers. "Now, Ross!"

Walsingham turned his head and couldn't fail to see the smoke billowing from the companionway. For an instant it distracted him, and, suddenly released, I scrambled forward and flung myself over the ship's rail, scraping my ribs, not so much a clean dive as a desperate leap. The icy water took my breath away, but I surfaced, swimming for my life until common sense forced me to tread water to get my bearings. I was lucky: my instincts had taken me almost on a straight path toward the *Heart*, and I saw her boat already gliding out toward me, oars dipping together. But I was still way too close to the *Black Hawk*.

The *Hawk* gave a shudder. The deck bucked and splintered beneath Walsingham's feet. Flames blossomed around his body. An immense roar; a scorching blast. The ship erupted into matchwood and fire. The explosion sucked the air right out of me. Something solid struck me a glancing blow on the side of the head. Something else hit my arm. Water closed above me.

"Ross?"

Ross!

Two voices calling me, one toward the day, the other toward a different kind of light. Corwen beckoning me to life, and Will to somewhere else entirely. I stood between life and death, between the love of my past and the love of my future. In my left hand, Corwen's warm hand. In my right hand, Will's cool, shadowy fingers.

Corwen; Will. Will; Corwen.

If at any time in the last three years I'd been offered an afterlife with Will I would have taken it without hesitation, but now, at last, I'd begun to give myself permission to be whole again, and I liked it.

Ross. Will's warm breath kissed my neck. *Together. Forever.* He cupped my cheek with one hand. I leaned in toward him. Corwen's grip tightened on my other hand in desperation, pulling me back.

It wasn't only a choice between two lovers.

Life; death. Death; life.

Should I even hesitate about a choice like that?

Life!

"I'll always love you, Will." Slowly, oh so slowly, I let him go.

"Corwen?" He was in the water beside me.

"Ross? Oh, love, I thought I'd lost you."

His lips moved, and I guessed the words from their shape, but I couldn't hear anything for the roaring of the sea in my head. I let go of my spar and lay my head back on his chest, letting Corwen support me in the water. Willing hands lifted me up, and soon I was wrapped in a blanket, huddled in Corwen's embrace.

I managed to put my hand on his arm. "I think Will's gone."

"He's dead, Ross." Again, I guessed the words from the shaping of his lips.

"No, I mean really gone."

"Rest now."

They lifted me onto the *Heart* by making a sling from my blanket. I tried not to cry out, but I don't think I succeeded, if the number of times Corwen touched me was anything to go by. Finally, I remember the cabin and my little bed, and Corwen dripping some kind of bitter draft between my lips. After that I slept.

More crashing waves in my head. Dressings being changed. My arm, my head. Salve on my ribs. More pain. Another bitter draft, and another.

When I came to my senses, the *Heart* was moving steadily beneath me like a quiet mare afraid of throwing a nervous rider, the gentleness of her action at odds with the rushing wind and crashing waves inside my head.

"Hello," Corwen said, his gray eyes bright with concern. "What do you need? What do you want?"

"Where are we?" I asked, raising my voice. "I have such a noise in my head I can hardly hear you."

"Sailing for Bideford with all possible speed."

"Why?"

"You're injured. I'm taking you to the Lady of the Forests." He kept his face turned toward me as he spoke so that I could see his lips move.

I would have protested, but just trying to raise my head told me he was right, though I wasn't sure what the Lady could do.

"Philip?" I asked.

"Recovered. Says he remembers nothing."

"Thank God he's safe. Gentleman Jim?"

"We don't know. The *Rhodes* turned and ran even though she was in no danger. She certainly picked up some survivors. We don't know who."

"He tried to help me. Walsingham had him heaved overboard. His crew stood by and did nothing."

"Walsingham's a scary bastard."

"Was, not is. He can't have survived the explosion. Please God, he hadn't." I put my hand up to my ear, but met with a thick bandage.

"Don't mess with it." Corwen pulled my hand away gently and kissed my fingertips. "I did the best I could, and Lazy Billy stitched your arm."

"How did we get away? Even with the *Hawk* and the *Rhodes* gone, the other two ships had us cold."

"Hookey asked for a parley with the captains. With Walsingham and Mayo gone they didn't see any profit in taking the *Heart* for no reward and also buying a whole heap of trouble from Bacalao for breaking the treaty."

I nodded and then wished I hadn't as the roaring crescendoed.

"Rest now while you can."

"Stay with me."

"Of course."

Tears flooded my eyes, and I squeezed them shut and turned to the wall.

We reached Bideford in two days. I slept most of the time away, helped by more of the bitter draft. I asked to see Philip, but when he came he was distant and quickly excused himself on the grounds that I wasn't well enough for visitors. I tried to tell him that he wasn't just a visitor, he was family, but I feared that ship had sailed a long time ago.

By the time we anchored off the north coast of Devon, the last dose of medicine had worn off. My head wasn't exactly clear with the roaring in my ears, but it was as good as it was going to get. Philip, Corwen, and I went ashore in the *Heart*'s boat, rowed up the estuary at the dead of night. Hookey offered to come to the forest with us, but I refused. I was never going to captain the *Heart* again. She was Hookey's responsibility now, and I couldn't take him away from that.

I even left my man's clothing behind in my sea chest. Corwen obligingly helped me into the green traveling dress, using the opportunity for some wholly appropriate touching and a little light teasing as he worked out the mechanics of stays and petticoat. I topped the outfit with a heavy cloak, since the sleeves of my redingote were too slender for the thick bandage on my arm.

Knowing how nervous I was that Walsingham's successor might already be on our trail, Corwen loaded my small pistols, the pair made by Mr. Bunney of London, and slipped them into my hidden pockets. They hung comfortingly at my waist, though whether I had the strength to use them was debatable.

I've never liked long good-byes, unless you count the years I've been saying good-bye to Will, so when the *Heart*'s boat docked quietly in Bideford I walked along the quay with Corwen and Philip without looking back. I tried to stay straight and tall for as long as it took Hookey to lose sight of me, but in truth my head still roared, my arm throbbed, my ear burned like hell, and my ribs hurt whenever I breathed in deeply. If Walsingham had survived and if he caught up with us now, I was dead.

Corwen woke the landlord of the T'gallant Inn by Bideford Long Bridge. The man's grumpiness subsided in the face of Corwen's easy charm, helped, no doubt, by the generous sum of money he offered for the purchase of three horses, once it was established that he wouldn't hire them to us. Corwen lifted me astride a very broad-backed gray, slipped my booted feet into the stirrups, and arranged my skirts as well as he could. Despite the lack of breeches, I was grateful not to have to cope with a sidesaddle.

His hand remained warm on my knee. "This mare's an old plodder, but we must make haste. Do you think you can manage?"

I heard him through the rushing in my ears and nodded, curling my fingers under the saddle as I'd been taught never to do in case the horse threw up its head and broke my bones. My knuckles on the gray's neck served to remind me which way was up as we set off at a walk.

I remember little of the journey to the Okewood except for the steady, four-beat plod of the mare. We stopped to rest several times, but all I could do was sit. I had no energy, and my arm burned where the stitches pulled.

A couple of times Corwen tried to draw Philip out with conversation, but after a string of monosyllabic answers, he gave up. I confess I was too wrapped up in my own misery to make any effort to communicate. I had to be looking at someone directly to make out words properly. My arm continued to worsen. I'd been lucky so far. My ear seemed to be healing cleanly—though Corwen had not allowed me a mirror—but infection could still kill.

Eventually I became aware that the open road had been replaced by dense trees. Corwen led us further in before stopping. I think I may have started to topple from the saddle, but he was by my side before I fell. He lifted me from the horse and set me down on the ground to sit with my back against an oak.

I shivered. Corwen knelt by my side with a worried expression. "You're feverish."

"No."

He put a hand on my forehead. "Yes, you are. I was afraid of this."

He reached to check the bandage on my ear, but I shook my head, setting the waves swishing inside my ears again.

"It's my arm."

He unwrapped the bandage and hissed. "Why didn't you tell me?" he asked.

My flesh had swollen around the stitches. Tendrils of red spread out from the wound.

"It worsened on the journey. I didn't want to worry you. There's nothing we can do."

"Irish moss, or honey. Garlic, even. A moldy bread poultice to draw the infection. Alcohol to clean the wound again."

"All things we don't have."

"You think I couldn't find a bee-tree in the Okewood?"

"I'm sorry. I'm not thinking straight." My brain felt numb from cold, yet a fire burned inside.

"The Lady will be here soon. Can you hold on?"

I nodded. Did I really look that bad?

"Ross!" Corwen snapped at me. He was worried. Really worried.

"I'm all right," I managed, obviously not. "I just need to sleep."

"Try to stay awake."

But it was too much effort. I closed my eyes. "Just a short nap."

Eventually Corwen's worried face solidified out of a jumble of shadows and sounds.

"How are you?"

Horizontal, lying on something soft. Light filtering from above. Scents of resin and vegetation heavy in my nostrils.

I worked my tongue against the roof of my mouth to try and find enough spit for speech. "I don't know. Sore. Tired. Confused and . . ."

"What?"

"I can't hear the sea." Oh, the relief. "I can hear you perfectly, the roaring has gone."

Corwen breathed out a long sigh and ran his fingers through his silver hair. "Good. The Lady healed you." I reached up to touch the worry lines around his mouth and smooth them away. He took my hand and kissed it.

"She's here?"

"Actually, we're there."

I glanced around. I was lying in some kind of bower, draped all around with ivy.

"Can I sit up?"

"Of course." He put one arm around my shoulders to help me. "Oh!" He touched the side of my head. My bandage had come off at some point.

"Is it horrible?" I asked. "It must be bad, or you'd have let me see it by now."

"It's not horrible. It will hardly show beneath your hair."

I put my hand up to the side of my face, scared at what I was going to find. My fingers met with a normal earlobe, but above it the cartilage along the top of my ear ended abruptly. There was no scabbing, however, just fresh scar tissue. And it didn't hurt.

"It's healed," he said. "As good as it's ever going to be. The Lady took care of more than the blood poisoning."

"I've lost half my ear!" The second I said it, I despised myself for whining. It was a small price to pay. I was lucky I still had a head. I swallowed down my reaction. I'd seen blood poisoning kill strong men before. "The Lady saved my life."

"She did."

"Did you know she would?"

"I hoped."

"What is she to you? You're not only a child of the forest, you know too much about how to go on in the real world."

"I told you I have a family, parents, older brothers, two

sisters, a place in the real world. It's just that I chose not to inflict myself upon them. They don't need me, and they don't need my strangeness."

"They aren't a family of shapechangers?"

He laughed. "Good God in Heaven, no! Well, only my little sister. The rest of them are totally unremarkable. Minor landowners, local gentry in Yorkshire with responsibilities: tenant farmers, financial interests in a coal mine, and a modest woolen mill. They have a well-regulated, ordinary life. My father is proud of his horses. My mother worries about keeping up with fashion, embroiders kneelers for the church, and does whatever good works she can without getting her hands dirty. I left. Probably the best thing I ever did for them."

"You aren't totally estranged, though?"

"Not really. Merely a third son, and an embarrassing one at that. I couldn't be what they wanted. A younger son should go into the church, you know, or maybe purchase a commission in the army." He laughed. "While the army might benefit from my talents if they had the imagination to put them to good use, I thought Wellesley might balk at a wolf in the ranks. I ducked out on my obligation, escaped, you might say. The Lady offered me a better alternative in return for pledging her my loyalty. I haven't been back to Yorkshire in six years."

"Don't you want to know how they are? A lot can happen in six years."

"They can get a message to me if I'm needed—an address at a totally unremarkable inn. The innkeeper's daughter is a vixen. They don't know that, of course. The less they know, the better."

"But they do know you're a wolf?"

"Ah, sadly, yes. When I was fourteen—ah, well, let's just say I had a few wild years, in both senses of the word. Enough about me." Corwen ran his hand down my ribs, much in the way a horseman checks a new mare. "How does that feel?"

My strength surged. "Good enough that I'd like you to do it again."

He choked off a laugh and turned it into a snort. "Later."

"Promise?"

"Promise. Let's see your arm."

I let him unwind the dressing to reveal only a long ragged scar already fading to white. He nodded, satisfied, with that, but he still frowned.

"What's the matter? Isn't it good?"

"It's good that you're healed, but . . ." He shrugged. "I expected herbs and poultices, not a miracle. The Lady doesn't often do these kind of favors for humans. It's a sign that you're going to need your strength. It's not over, yet."

"I think we knew that."

"I was hoping . . ."

"Even if I killed this Walsingham, there will be another."

He shrugged. "Please promise me you won't try and blow yourself up again."

I came to my knees close in front of him and pulled him toward me so that our bodies pressed together from shoulder to kneecap. "I will make you one promise, Corwen Silverwolf. When this is all over, if I still have breath, I will stay with you in the forest for as long as you want me."

His lips found mine and I lost myself in the feel and the spicy scent of him. His hands played along my spine, releasing little shivers of expectation and a delicious heat.

"Uh, damn stays. Why did I let you talk me into helping to lace you into them?"

"Because it's a lot of fun getting me out of them?"

"Or working around them."

He bunched up my skirts and shift, stroked the outside of my thigh and cupped my buttock through the fine muslin of my drawers, then ran his thumb around the bottom edge of the stays until I giggled.

"I told you I'd find all your ticklish spots," he whispered.

"Ahh." I sighed and arched against him as he slid knowing fingers inside my drawers and between my legs. "There's one."

I began to quiver, and he steadied me with his other hand in the small of my back.

He kissed my half-ear. "It's still beautiful. You're beautiful. I was so afraid I'd lose you, Ross. I'm still afraid. This is all new for me. I never expected to fall in love."

I sighed. "Me neither. I thought, after Will, I'd turn into a dried-up old widow, but look at me, I'm alive again. Whatever happens now, Corwen, you've given me a great gift, and I don't intend to let it go."

I pulled him down sideways on to the springy, bracken-filled mattress, feeling a new strength and energy, and reached for the buttons on his breeches.

It was a long time before we surfaced from what followed.

36

The Winterwood Box

CORWEN AND I EMERGED from our bower into a woodland glade, holding hands. My brother sat in silence next to a tall man with hair the color of a red deer, dressed all in buckskins. Hartington, the stag shapechanger, I guessed. Corwen nodded an easy greeting to him, and Hartington nodded back.

Our horses, freed of their saddles and bridles, nibbled on the few blades of grass growing in patches where the sunlight kissed the shaded earth. They looked refreshed.

Philip raised his head.

I would have hugged my brother, but his blank expression stopped me dead.

Still warm from Corwen's love, I felt snubbed by Philip's coldness. I didn't know why I should, except that David had taught me about brotherly kindness.

Hartington smiled. "The Lady will see you now." He took in Philip with his glance. "Both of you."

"All three of us," Corwen said.

Hartington inclined his head in acquiescence and pointed to where we should go.

The Lady waited for us by a huge grandfather oak. This time she was clothed in simple greens and browns. Corwen dropped to one knee and bowed his head. She put out her hand to touch her fingertips to his hair.

"See, Silverwolf," she said, glancing at me. "She is healed. I've done as you asked."

"More than I asked, My Lady. Thank you."

"You've done well. Your duty is over, you may return to the forest."

"No, My Lady." He stood up and reached for my hand. "My duty is not over."

She looked at him as if assessing all that he had been and all that he might be. "Very well. I release you from my service—for now. Though know that you will always have a home with us and the places of power will always open to you. Do what you have to do."

"Thank you."

The first time I'd seen the Lady, I didn't even know the Fae existed. Once I knew about the Fae, I think I'd assumed that the Lady was one of them, but now that I was in her presence again, I knew that she was not. Though they might operate in the magical realm, the Green Man and his Lady were wholly of this land and not of Iaru. Comparing them to the Fae was like comparing the left hand to the right. They were the same and yet not, alike and opposite. Though they were both elementals, the Lady and her consort were born of, and tied to, the green places of the realm. Their magic was earth and water and growing things, while Fae magic was air and fire.

The realization stopped me in midstride. So what was my own magic? Had I ever really explored it beyond the weather-working which came easily to me? I vowed that I would learn all I could if I survived the next few days.

The Lady's gaze rested on Philip and me with a sweet, sad smile. I bobbed my head, unused to curtseying in a dress. Philip didn't respond.

"Come, take refreshment, we have much to talk about."

We sat on fallen logs and ate and drank such food as I couldn't afterward describe, but the smallest mouthful, if you allowed it to, would satisfy hunger. Corwen ate quickly but didn't look for more. Philip sniffed it but didn't take even one bite. I nibbled slowly, not wasting a single crumb. My stomach warmed, and I felt strengthened.

"So you found your family, Rossalinde," the Lady said.

"I did. More relatives than I would ever have thought possible, and stranger, too."

"And are you ready to right the wrong of your ancestor?"

I didn't reply.

"You are troubled," she said.

I nodded and glanced sideways at Philip, who suddenly seemed to be taking much more of an interest. "There was a man who worked for the king," I said. "Walsingham. I have no other name for him. He is dead now. He believed that releasing wild magic and freeing the rowankind would plunge Britain back into the dark times. Was he right? Who's to say that in correcting one mistake I won't be making another?"

"You've thought deeply about this."

"I have, Lady, and the more I think, the more confused I become, except, if I could have some assurance that neither you nor the Fae will take revenge on humans for what has happened, I would very much like to see the rowankind freed."

A slow smile filled her face with warmth. "As would I."

"But," I took a deep breath. "I don't want them to be released just to be given back into the control of the Fae. I want them to be totally free, to decide for themselves what to do with their lives."

This was the only way I could see that might free the rowankind without delivering them into another kind of servitude, one in which the Fae could use rowankind power for their own ends.

"That's impossible!" Dantin's voice came marginally before he appeared out of nowhere, followed by Larien and David.

The ethereal procession emerged from Iaru, bathed in translucent light.

"David!" I jumped up and hugged my little brother, who had no qualms about hugging me back heartily. It was only when I stepped back from him that I spotted Aunt Rosie and Leo. For good measure I hugged them, too. Rosie seemed well recovered from her ordeal, though her arm was still splinted in its sling. I noticed she glanced askance at Philip without greeting him. I couldn't blame her. In truth I didn't quite trust him, and I could see that Rosie didn't either.

"The rowankind are ours." Dantin paid no courtesies to the Lady of the Forests.

"Dantin!" Larien cut in. "Remember where you are. This is not Iaru." He bowed low. The Lady inclined her head in return before turning to Dantin.

"You would lay claim to a people you say should be freed?" the Lady asked.

"We made them," Dantin said.

"From the trees of our forest." She looked at me. "What Rossalinde asks for is not unreasonable. Let it be so and you may have free passage for them through the Okewood and all our green places to Iaru, should they wish to return there. But remember that many generations have passed, and these are no longer your rowankind. They belong only to themselves."

"And if we don't agree?" Dantin began to argue, but the Lady nodded as if all was agreed and faded away, taking with her Hartington, our poor horses, and all the attendant creatures who made up her retinue. Dantin stood, open-mouthed. I enjoyed a tiny frisson of pleasure to see him discomfited, and then felt mean for doing so.

I turned back to Larien. "You've known me all my life. I've never wanted this power, I'd be happy to give it all back and see the rowankind get their freedom, but what happens when they do? Will there be reprisals, riots, blood in the streets? Will the Fae return to the world and seek power over humankind?"

"And what if we do?" Dantin cut in.

Larien put out a hand to silence Dantin. "If we wanted power over humankind, we would have taken it centuries ago. Human concerns are not ours."

"But don't the rowankind hate us? What about you? Don't you hate us? You lived in our household as a rowankind. Not free."

Larien shook his head. "I was always free. I was there by choice."

"It won't be as simple as that, though, for the rowankind, will it?" I asked. "Britain has grown fat on their labor—domestic service, the new manufactories. There will be a vacuum that won't easily be filled."

Dantin sniffed. "Your politics are not our concern."

I sighed. Maybe they weren't my concern either. There was only so much I could take responsibility for. It wasn't my place to second-guess the future. Without the rowankind, maybe the wretches who begged on the streets would find honest employment at last, and all would be well.

"Tell me what needs doing and I'll do it," I said.

"No, Ross, you won't!" Philip stepped forward and put his left hand on my arm.

My first reaction was surprise, not just at the vehemence of his words but at his touch. He'd avoided all physical contact since our lives had come back together.

Then I heard the click of a doghead and felt the coolness of a pistol muzzle at the base of my skull. He'd used my body to shield what he was doing from the others.

"Everybody back away," he said. "Stay very still, Ross. Keep your hands where I can see them, and no witchlights." Philip pulled me back a couple of paces, still using me as a shield.

I froze, the flintlocks in my hidden pockets hanging heavy against my thighs.

Corwen started forward.

"Get back, Wolf," Philip said, "or I'll put a hole straight through Ross's head."

I heard the growl in Corwen's throat as he took a few paces back.

"I know I can't beat you all with magic, but you can't

argue with a bullet." Philip's voice caught in his throat. "Whatever magic any of you can do won't be fast enough to stop me from pulling this trigger."

"Philip, what's this about?" I managed to keep my voice steady. "You're free of Walsingham, now."

"I'll never be free. He was a hero. Freeing the rowankind will condemn this country to chaos. I'd rather see you and the bastard dead than let that happen."

He was my *brother*, for God's sake! How could he do this?

"Walsingham pushed himself too far," Philip said. "That night in the inn yard, you nearly killed him. He told me to stick close to you in case you escaped his hounds. Said it was up to me to finish this thing if he died."

"But you were his prisoner."

"At first. But then I saw that he was right. Freeing the rowankind and releasing wild magic back into the world will destroy all that we hold dear. I gave him my parole and then my loyalty."

"It was you becalmed the *Heart*!"

"I had to give Walsingham time to catch up. I've never had a cause before, Ross. It was novel to discover that I could really believe in this one. I told you I met the king, swore allegiance to him. He's mad, of course, like they say, but mad in a knowing way. Only the monarch and the spymaster know about the Walsinghams." He laughed and it came out high and cracked. "You killed a good man, possibly even a great man, when you blew up that ship. I hadn't looked for such promotion, but I'm Walsingham now. Though, I don't expect I will be for long. Can you see your wolf letting me live once I've blown your skull apart?"

Corwen growled again.

"See what I mean?" Philip breathed as if he'd run a hundred-yard dash. "But with the last of the Sumner summoners finally dead, the Walsinghams can all rest in peace."

I could feel Fae magic building, but I couldn't tell what they were doing.

I should have been terrified—just one twitch of Philip's

trigger finger could end me—but suddenly I was energized. The world slowed down and gave me more time to think.

Corwen stood very still, his expression a little too bland, his hair a little too neat, his shirt a little too crisp for one we'd thrown to one side hastily during our lovemaking. I had to look twice to see that his figure was an illusion. The real Corwen was on the move, hidden by Fae magic. Philip pulled a second pistol from his belt and pointed it at David.

Philip was going to try and kill David first while everyone was immobilized by the threat to me. After that, killing me would be easy.

"Philip, you don't need to harm David. I'm the firstborn, the only one who can summon the power out of the Sumners. David doesn't have it any more than you do."

Philip drew the second doghead back. I couldn't hit him with a whirlwind. If he fired the primed pistols anyone could be hit, Corwen, David, Rosie, Leo. Or me.

Philip focused on the pistol in his left hand. His right hand, the one aimed at my head, wavered slightly. I inched my hand toward my pocket. Corwen took his chance. A silver-gray shape streaked across the clearing and strong jaws chomped down on Philip's right arm. The first pistol fell from nerveless fingers. Philip staggered, swung the second pistol toward Corwen, and fired.

There were two almost-simultaneous shots.

Corwen howled and flew sideways, rolling into a snarling crouch. Philip dropped like a stone, heartshot through the poppet in his pocket.

The acrid smell of black powder filled my nostrils.

In my right hand was a small golden pistol made by Mr. Bunney of London.

I collapsed to my knees.

What have I done?

I don't know how long it took me to become aware of others, but by the time I noticed someone talking to me and looked up, the light had changed subtly. It was David.

"Come, sit, Ross. Let Rosie take Philip for laying out."

"I should do it."

"No, you shouldn't."

"Corwen? Where's Corwen?" I looked around, suddenly gripped by panic.

"He's going to be all right. Leo has taken a ball out of his arm and he's already changed three times. The wound is healing nicely."

All my breath whooshed out of me. I felt giddy with relief. And then the terrible ache returned.

"I've killed our brother."

He needed killing. A memory of Will's ghost sounded in the back of my mind.

I started to say no, but as I reexamined those last few fateful seconds in my mind I knew that it was him or me. He was bent on killing me, and David, too, and anyone else who stood in his way.

Maybe he had needed killing, but how I wish it had not been my fate to do the deed.

"I'm sorry, David." I turned my head into David's shoulder and sobbed. When did he get so tall?

We buried Philip in the grove. Leo said words over him. I can't even remember what they were. Better it was someone who didn't know him making up well-meaning platitudes. Those of us who did know him would have found nothing to say that flattered his memory.

Corwen had his left arm bound, but was neither excessively pale or pained. With his right hand he held my left during the burial, and I leaned into him. David stood at my other side, fingers twined in mine. I drew strength from both of them as, dry-eyed, I watched Philip being lowered into the ground, wrapped in a clean white shroud that the Fae had produced from nowhere.

When I had tossed a handful of earth over Philip's shroud and left the graveside, I walked through the maze of trees, hoping that the Lady would return. Hoping? Summoning, maybe. Whatever I was doing, it worked. She stood before me, those eyes sad as before.

"You knew Philip intended to betray us, didn't you?" I asked.

"I knew it was in him, but he always had a free choice."

"I'm not even sure he wasn't right to want us dead. Whichever path I choose, there's an element of good and an element of evil. I don't know whether I've made the right decision, but for better or worse I've made up my mind. I'm going to free the rowankind if I can."

"You have my blessing."

"Thank you for Corwen's freedom."

"He was always free. Free to go, free to return. As are you." She took my hands, leaned forward, and kissed me on the cheek. "Wes hael, Rossalinde. Be well."

And then she was gone, leaving nothing but the scent of a spring morning. I turned to find Corwen, David, and Larien waiting. Corwen took my hand in his good one, and we stepped through the barrier into Iaru.

Negotiations with the Fae council were long and tortuous. I spoke for myself, and Corwen spoke for the Lady. In the end it was agreed. If I could indeed restore the power to the rowankind, the Fae would have no automatic right to their service, but might offer friendship and assistance and accept what allegiance the rowankind freely gave.

"All we need to do is touch the box," I said as we Sumners all gathered in the Fae's great timber and leaf hall.

Now that Philip had gone, David and I could open it together, provided our mother didn't have any more secret children we didn't know about. We faced each other. Dappled sunlight streamed through the branches above us. The Fae children and their fathers stood a short distance away, watching intently, while Leo and Rosie waited uncertainly by the door. Larien beckoned them to join him.

I didn't know what would happen next. No one did. Was there some kind of magical artifact in the box, or would there be some great cataclysmic force unleashed that would instantly rip the Fae power out of the assembled Sumners and redistribute it to the rowankind? Would it be that easy? And if that were the case, what would happen to the Sumners? Were we all doomed?

Corwen leaned against the trunk of one of the great trees that formed the pillars of this cathedral-like space. He'd abandoned his jacket and waistcoat in the balmy air and wore only his breeches, boots, and linen shirt, open at the throat. I didn't mistake his casual stance for complacency. This could be the end of me, and he knew it.

I smiled at him, hoping to reassure him, but his expression remained serious. So I puckered my lips and sent a subtle kiss in his direction, and only then received a wry grin in return. "I love you," he mouthed back at me.

I squeezed back a tear. To have one love in my life was a blessing; to find I had a second was nothing short of a miracle. I tried to save this image of him in my mind forever: broad shoulders, silver hair tied loosely back, handsome face, nose just slightly too long to be pretty, serious gray eyes crinkled in a smile. A smile that was for me alone.

I love you, Corwen.

"Ready?" Larien's question wrenched my mind away from Corwen.

I turned and nodded.

" David?" Larien asked.

"Yes." His voice didn't waver as he reached his hand to the box that I held out.

I expected an explosion of energy, but there was only a tiny pop. The seam which had hitherto been closed so tight was now plainly cracked.

With the finger and thumb of my left hand I lifted the lid. Nothing happened.

"Huh?" I heard Corwen's puzzled grunt over my shoulder as he stepped forward to see.

Inside the box was a hank of wispy gray hair, a small bone, a glass vial with a waxed stopper, and a piece of yellowing paper. On it, written in old script, the ink now fading to brown, were five words: Martyn the Summoner. Summon me.

"I don't know what it means," I said.

"It means your many-times great-grandfather didn't

trust his secret to a box," Corwen said. "The only way you'll get it from him is by summoning his spirit."

"After two hundred years? That's impossible."

"Not for a Summoner, and not with these." Corwen pointed without touching. "Hair, bone, and blood."

"I've never tried to summon a ghost before," I said.

"You did it with Will all the time." David put an arm around me.

"Will was his own man, and he became his own ghost. I never knew when he was going to appear."

"Never?"

"Well, sometimes . . ."

"Summon Martyn," David said. "You've got the Great Power. You can do it."

37

The Great Summoning

WERE THERE FORMAL WORDS TO SAY? Probably not. With me it had always been the intention rather than the words.

"Martyn Summoner." I unstopped the vial and poured a thin trickle of dark red blood into the palm of my left hand. Surprisingly, it had neither congealed nor dried in two hundred years. I added the hair and the bone, and curled my fist around it all.

"Martyn Summoner."

And a third time: "Martyn Summoner."

In my mind, heavy gates opened on creaking hinges and time leaked through. I closed my eyes and *pulled*. When I opened them he stood there, looking as solid as any living human, though I didn't try to touch him. He had a long gray beard but only a few wisps of hair sticking out from under his embroidered cap. He wore what might have been an elaborate dressing gown or an old-fashioned robe of a deep red, now faded to the color of an ancient bloodstain. Had he died in it? A faint scent of dry linen and cloves wafted over me.

Rosie broke the silence. "You look just like Grandpa John."

"I rather think, young lady, that he looked just like me." Martyn examined the faces in the hall and the focus of his eyes showed me he could see everyone. "Who summoned me?"

I cleared my throat. "I did, sir. Rossalinde Tremayne, daughter of Margery Goodliffe, granddaughter of Frank Sumner."

"Rossalinde, what year is this?"

"The year of Our Lord 1800, sir."

He drew in a sharp breath. "Have I bred a family of numbskulls? Has it taken more than two hundred years to produce a child who could open a simple winterwood box?"

"You left them a bitter legacy, Martyn Summoner," Larien said.

"I know you, Fae. You denied me your help." Martyn pointed at Larien, and I noticed that he missed the little finger on his left hand. "If it weren't for you, all this would never have happened."

"No, old sorcerer." Dantin leaned forward. "If it weren't for you, all this would never have happened. You tricked us into a pledge and took from us what we would not give freely."

"Easy, Dantin. What matters now is that we set it right," Larien said. He turned to my ancestor. "Your first generation ran mad when your power poured into them. I think it had already made you a little mad yourself."

The ghost nodded. "Once I'd destroyed the Spanish fleet I intended to give back what I'd borrowed, but Queen Bess wanted more. She wanted to send her own Armada against the Spanish and thought I could give her victory. I'd made an agreement with the Fae, but Gloriana delayed and the agreement soured. No good ever comes of breaking an agreement with the Fae." That last sentence he said directly to me. "We passed beyond the time when I could return the power easily. Not that the power did any good. It's one thing to send wind and wave to destroy an invasion force, but only a good fleet, well captained, can secure victory."

He shook his head slowly from side to side. "I tried to return the power to the rowankind, but I could not. I sought out John Dee, but he shunned me for what I'd done and went back to his study of angels. Angels! When we were already surrounded by magical beings. I feared for my life when Sir Francis Walsingham, the queen's man, took an interest in my affairs, so I gathered my family and fled.

"France . . ." He wrinkled his nose. "It's foreign, you know. I didn't take to it. Eventually we returned in secret and settled near Chard."

He sighed. "But the knowledge of what I'd done wouldn't leave me alone. I had my own magic, but the rowankind's power boiled within me, eating me from the inside, stopping me from thinking straight. I had used up my own gift, you see. Worn it out. And so it was time for the next generation to take up the burden."

He looked at the Fae children. "And who might you all be?"

"I'm Galan. My mother was your daughter, Jane."

"You have more than a look of her. Tell me, did she have a good life?"

"She had a child before me."

"Robert. I remember him. She doted on the child, and on her husband, though I thought him rather boring. I can't even recall his name."

"She was widowed young. My father . . ." He indicated a tall Fae to whom I had not been introduced. "He brought my mother to live in Iaru. I believe she was happy, though she missed her other son."

One by one the remaining children introduced themselves.

"Nerea, your great-granddaughter. My mother was the daughter of your grandson, John."

"Elva, your great-great-granddaughter of the line of your third son, William."

"Bronn, your great-great-grandson, descended from your youngest son, Rupert."

"Rupert—he was still a child when I left the world. Tell me how he fared."

"I'm sorry, I don't know. He died before I was born. I do know he lived to be an old man."

"Ah, well I suppose it has been too many years to keep track."

"Alder. I'm your six-times great-grandson descended from your oldest son, Hugh."

"This one's mine." Rosie patted Margann's hand and inclined her head toward Dantin. "And his, I'm sorry to say, though I liked him well enough for a year or two, before I came to my senses."

"Margann," the young Fae said, bobbing a curtsey, the only one to politely acknowledge their ancestor so far.

"And I'm David, son of Larien and Margery Goodliffe." David followed suit and bowed his head respectfully. "Ross is my half-sister."

"Where's the rest of my clan?" Martyn asked.

"This is it, as far as I know." I stretched my arms to encompass those of us in the grove.

The Summoner gasped. "Is this all? I had nine children, and they had children of their own."

I remembered the parish registers from Chard. "I fear your line didn't prosper, sir. Many children died. This is all there is."

"I had thought to found a dynasty to bear the burden. How many?"

"Just nine, sir."

"Only nine? Nine then and nine now. I should not have waited. This will go very hard with you all. I'm sorry."

He explained how I could return the power to the rowankind. "By the time I understood what must be done," he said. "I was too feeble, and too afraid for my children. Do you think you can do it?"

"She will do it," Dantin said.

"That's all very well for you," Corwen growled at Dantin. "And for Larien. Neither of you are risking yourselves. What about Ross and Rosie? What about these children?"

"We knew when we made them that we made them for a purpose," Dantin said.

"You heartless bastard!"

I grabbed Corwen's hand to prevent him from calling Dantin out right there, but he wasn't strong enough in this place, and he knew it. He'd found his voice, though. "Is there nothing that can be done to save them?" he asked Martyn. "They're your family!"

"Maybe. There is Summoner magic besides the rowan-kind magic. If each one of them has a loved one to anchor their souls, they need not be entirely lost." He looked over his shoulder toward something I couldn't see. "My time is done here, Rossalinde. I'm sorry it's fallen to you. Do it well and bravely."

He faded away.

My mind swirled with dark thoughts. If there had been a hundred of us, the strain would not have been so great, but with only nine I doubted that any of us could survive, not even the Sumner-Fae children. If any did survive we would be stripped of most, if not all, of our magic. I'd never valued my magic, but now, suddenly, the thought of not having it disturbed me. I shook my head, feeling stupid. If by some miracle I survived, magic would be a small price to pay.

"Whatever comes next, I'll be right there with you." Corwen stepped up close. He put the palm of his hand between my shoulder blades and warmth spread from it.

"Thank you."

"You're welcome."

"I mean for not suggesting we run away from here right now."

He put his lips close to my ear. "If I thought we could get away with it, I'd be fleeing back to the Okewood with you over my shoulder, but Martyn Summoner hesitated until it was too late. If this thing has to be done—and I see why it has—now is the time."

Oh, why did I have to find Corwen right now? Why couldn't we have had more time together—time to build this passion into a lifetime of companionship and understanding? I pulled his face down to mine and kissed him very thoroughly, trying to put everything I couldn't verbalize into one desperate meeting of lips.

Time stood still. Fire blazed within me and heated my core to melting point.

He didn't want to let me go. He groaned as he released me and put his hands on my shoulders. "When we jumped the bonfire together, Ross, we didn't say those formal words, but even though you didn't swear to love, honor and obey, I want you to obey me now. Whatever happens . . . You. Will. Survive."

I nodded, not trusting my voice.

We nine remaining Sumners sat in a circle in the tree hall. The Fae children each had their respective fathers to support them. A set of grimmer expressions would be hard to find. These were not men sacrificing their children willingly or easily, but their faces said that they would do what they had to do.

Leo knelt behind Rosie, and Corwen behind me. His warmth gave me strength.

This would be my biggest summoning. And probably my last.

Larien touched David's shoulder, as if in reassurance, and said we should begin if I was ready. Ready? I supposed I was, but this next part was mine alone. Prepared or not, it was time. One by one, we Sumners all held hands in a circle. I took David's hand in my right and Rosie's in my left.

I looked around. "Ready?"

Corwen knelt behind me, his hands on my shoulders. "Don't worry, Ross, I won't let you go."

"I know you won't." It was all I could say. Should I have said good-bye? I couldn't. I didn't want him to think I didn't trust him, even though I knew this working was bigger than either of us could control.

I could feel the nervous anticipation in the group. Even Dantin, who had professed so many times that the Fae children were expendable, now knelt behind Margann, tension showing in every line of his body. He dipped his head and kissed her hair, and she glanced back up at him and smiled. I almost liked him in that moment.

How difficult was this going to be?

Impossible, a little worm in the back of my head told me. I ignored it and began the summoning, first identifying and then teasing out threads of magic stuff from each person and drawing them together. It was as if I was unraveling a great tapestry of interwoven lives over several generations. I picked at the weft and drew the warp threads together into plaited bundles that I held like reins between my thumbs and fingers. From the tapestry, through my hands, the threads converged on my heart.

The tapestry rose before me like a sail, billowing in some unearthly breeze. The strands started to pull against my fingers and drag against my core. I clenched my fists tight and hung on, pulling back with all my might.

Before a minute had gone past I was panting with effort. Two minutes and I could feel sweat rolling down from my hairline, dewing my cheeks and trickling down between my breasts. Like some celestial bout of tug-of-war, I gradually won ground and then lost some. Won more and lost a little. I leaned back against the threads and willed them to come to me, hoping I was winning more than I was losing.

Corwen pressed up against my back, pouring his energy into me.

Opposite me Elva began to whimper and then sob. Her father leaned forward and clasped her hands in his to make sure she didn't break the circle. He whispered encouragement, his face a twisted mask of fear that he might be killing his own daughter. So much for the Fae children being expendable. She clamped her teeth together and bit off the sound. I wanted to let her thread go, but if I did, all this would be for nothing.

If I was a praying person, I would be calling on Jesus Christ Our Lord right now, but I had spent too many years on the sea without a chaplain, and while I still believed in the Almighty, I had lost the habit of prayer somewhere on the ocean between Plymouth and Bacalao.

I don't know how long it went on. Time stretched. I drew more and more thread into my aching fists and felt my heart swell to accommodate all that I had won until it sat like a boulder within my chest.

Without warning, one of the threads snapped. The ends of the plait flew loose and began to unravel. I hastily grabbed them and bunched them together as well as I could. Even as I was trying to hold the working together I wondered who had left us so suddenly. To my right Alder slumped forward, drained. Dead? I didn't know, and I couldn't stop to find out.

I felt David falter, shocked to his core. *Stay with me, David.*

Margann gave a small cry and let go of Alder's hand. Dantin dragged her sideways, pushed Alder's father out of the way, and grabbed Bronn's hand, shoving Margann's into it to repair the breach in the shrunken circle. He wrapped his own hand around their bond. Rosie still had Margann's other hand, and she poured energy into her daughter as well as giving it to me. I wanted to scream at her to look after herself, but I daren't let my concentration drop. Dantin reached across and placed his hand over Rosie and Margann's clasp, and he fed Rosie, too. Something passed between them, warmth for a past not quite forgotten.

I had less to work with now, yet still I pulled, sweat running in rivulets. Losing one person from the ring increased the strain on the rest of us. The weight of it threatened to drag me down. My heart felt swollen to twice its size, pressing against my lungs.

Elva suddenly flung herself backward, convulsing. I yanked on her thread and quickly gathered in all she had left. *Pray that I wasn't killing her in the process.* It was almost like the reverse of falling from a great height into water. The higher the fall, the more solid the water feels. This felt as if the water was solid inside me, smashing me from the inside out. Elva's father caught her and dragged her away. Bronn was quick to grab Nerea's hand and complete the circle one more time.

Seven of us left.

Still I hauled on the rowankind magic, pulling it to me,

struggling to contain it all. The swelling in my chest became a fierce grab of steady pain radiating upward into my throat, making my jaw throb and shooting down my left arm. I was panting and couldn't draw enough air. My head whirled.

Something hit me on the inside, a noise, but silent. That didn't even make sense. Threads began to unravel. I drew them tighter. Six of us left now, but I couldn't tell who had dropped out. *Please, God, let it not be David.*

Maybe I was a praying person after all.

David was still there, still grasping my hand, but he was weaker. Fading.

Corwen held me upright, his right arm wrapped around my waist, the other across my breasts to my shoulder. "I've got you," he whispered. "Stay with me."

"I can't do it." My voice came out in wheezy gasps. "Too much. Too big." It was all going to be for nothing. I'd failed. Alder, Elva, dead for nothing, I'd let them down. Let the whole family down, all of those generations, passing on the box in the hope that one day it would give up its secret.

Corwen's breath was hot against my ear. "If you don't do it, no one else will."

Anger rose inside me. Had it all been a lie? Was Corwen only there to make sure I gave the Lady what she wanted? Had my seduction been part of his plan all along?

Bastard!

The anger drove me on.

I wasn't going to let it beat me. I wasn't going to let *him* beat me.

I felt huge and bloated, with sausages for fingers and toes. My head pounded as if my brain was about to burst from my skull, my heart thundered within my rib cage—fast and faster still. I would pop at any minute like a bottle of fermenting wine. Tighter and tighter.

The pressure building. Power like I had never known, and it all belonged to me. If I could keep it. I could—

I wanted to laugh like a maniac. This must have been what drove Martyn the Summoner out of his wits. Power that no human should ever hold swelled in me.

Corwen pressed his hand over my heart. "Christ, Ross, it's like a runaway horse. That's enough."

And still I pulled, drawing power into myself. Power and pain.

I knew it would be my death, but the more I had, the more I wanted.

David moaned and doubled over but didn't let go of the link. We'd forged a bond, physical as well as emotional. His pain was mine and, God help him, mine was his.

"Let me share it, Ross," he said between clenched teeth.

"It'll kill you! Larien, don't let him."

Besides, it was mine. Mine!

Larien reached forward and pulled David upright, whispering something in his ear, but the words were lost. He held him in a strong embrace, put one hand across his heart and the other over his forehead, and pressed his own forehead to the back of David's skull, eyes closed in concentration.

Thank you, Larien. Don't let him go.

At last, I had it all. I could hold no more. The power burned in me, but I didn't want to release it. What could I do with power such as this? My ancestor had smashed the Spanish fleet with it. I could shatter the government that had sent Walsingham to kill my family. I could show them.

Aunt Rosie broke the circle. I felt it like a hammerblow between the eyes, but it snapped me out of the trance that had been building. She touched my arm, a cool oasis of calm amidst the fire. "Now, Ross. Send it away. Do it now while you still can. Don't be like Martyn. The power's not for you."

David slumped back into Larien's embrace. I couldn't tell if he lived or not. There was nothing but a gaping emptiness where Alder, Elva and Bronn had been. I mustn't let them down. To falter now would mean that they had sacrificed themselves for nothing.

"Let it go, Ross." Corwen growled in my ear as if he knew what I was thinking. "You don't need it. It will destroy you. It will destroy us."

Ah, Corwen, you are my rock.

He was right. Rosie was right. This thing was only half-done.

Having gathered the magic, I now had to deliver it to its rightful owners.

Time to push it away before it crushed me.

I pictured all the strands shooting out like arrows to all points of the compass. Each plait unraveling into individual threads, finer and finer, shooting out to lodge in the hearts and minds of the rowankind. With it I sent a message: *Come to the forests. Don't be afraid, this is your birthright. Use it wisely.*

The power tore out of me as if my heart had exploded. I felt my skin shrivel and shred, my lungs deflate to nothing. There was a moment of equilibrium, of painless floating in a place that was not Iaru and not the world I knew. I had done it, but it wasn't enough. I tipped past that point and still I gave. When I had nothing left to give I gave myself. My heavy rock of a heart began to shrink to nothing in my chest. It felt light, fluttering like a butterfly wing. I gave and gave and gave, until I slid into a gray land somewhere between darkness and light.

Ross!

"Will? I thought you'd left me."

You shouldn't be here, Ross. Go back!

"I think I'm dead, Will."

All the times I've wanted you to cross over so that we could be together, but not this time. Go back. I love you, but go back.

A door closed in my face.

A club pounded into my chest. Once, twice, three times.

After all the pain this was too much to bear. I gasped, drawing in air to protest.

"Ross?" It was a different voice. Corwen. "Ross! Ross, hold tight." He gripped my icy hand, and I held on as tight as I could.

It was over.

I opened my eyes and saw in painful clarity. Corwen leaned over me, his eyes wet with tears.

"Corwen?"

"Right here."

"Don't leave me."

"I won't."

My breastbone ached. "Did you just hit me in the chest?"

"Your heart had stopped. I didn't know . . . I couldn't . . . Yes, I hit you." He put his hand to my breastbone. "Sorry."

I grasped his fingers. "Don't be. Help me up. Owww!" Moving hurt.

Our circle had shattered. Alder lay still, his father by his side closing his eyes, placing his lifeless hands across his breast. Elva lay in her father's lap, pale as death and unmoving. Bronn sat, head in his hands, his father next to him, relief limned on his face. Nerea, on hands and knees, was throwing up, and Margann had crawled to her mother's side, leaving Dantin sitting with eyes closed. I didn't know whether the Fae acknowledged any god, but if they did, Dantin looked as though he was thanking him.

To one side of me Leo knelt over Rosie, but she had weathered the trial well enough to grasp Margann's hand and to tell him to stop fussing and help her up. To the other side, David rubbed his eyes and stared about him, taking in the scene of chaos.

"Did we succeed?" I asked.

"At some cost, but yes, we did." His eyes flickered to Alder's still body and to Elva, pale and unmoving in her father's arms. Another loss. Larien sat back on his heels. "Can't you feel it?"

I shook my head. "I'll take your word for it. I can't feel anything beyond a lot of aches, and I'm grateful to have them."

Trying to get to my feet proved that my sense of balance had deserted me. I let Corwen carry me to a quiet corner, and with his arms around me, I slept.

38

Between Wind and Water

MARGANN CAME TO SEE ME on the second day. I still couldn't walk far without assistance and lay reclining on a soft bed of furs in a nook surrounded by a wall of greenery, close by a burbling stream. Corwen had not left my side except to bring me food, but now he tactfully slipped away. I watched him go, feeling a little uncomfortable under Margann's gaze. I had, after all, killed two of her siblings.

She sat cross-legged to bring her head down to my level. "My father doesn't have it in him to say thank you, so I will say it for both of us."

"I almost killed you."

"No, you kept us alive."

"Not all of you."

She shook her head. "We all knew what the Great Summoning would mean. We were brought up knowing it, expecting it would end us."

"You lived your entire lives under a threat like that? Couldn't your parents have protected you from it?"

"Then we wouldn't have been prepared."

"You might not have been willing."

She smiled. "You were willing. My mother was willing, and so was David. If all of us had died, it would still only have been nine lives against the freedom and birthright of so many. A small price to pay in one way, though the greatest price of all for us individually, and for our families. Alder and Elva have gone back to the earth and we have honored them."

"A funeral? I should have been there to pay my respects."

"Not quite a funeral. We don't do things the way you do, and your respects were taken for granted."

"Will you stay here?" I asked her. "Or will they let you go back with your mother?"

"My mother has Leo. They plan to return to Summoner's Well. I will visit, but for now my father needs me."

I couldn't envisage Dantin needing anyone. I think my thoughts must have shown on my face because she smiled. "He's hot tempered sometimes, but he cares for me, and sometimes I think he needs me to retain his balance."

"He's very different from his brother."

"Larien and he are half-brothers only, but my father's is a tale for another time, except that you should know that when Martyn the Summoner drew the rowankind from Iaru, my father lost both his rowankind foster mother and his wife. You see why he is the way he is with mortals?"

"Yet he and Rosie were together."

"He did his duty, and I think he became fond of her in his own way, but he was happy enough to let her go once he had me."

"Did the Fae think Rosie was the firstborn?"

"They hoped so. If she had been, then the Great Power of summoning would have passed to me. When they realized she wasn't, Larien took the box to Plymouth, only to find that Margery had a child already."

"And that she had rejected magic."

"Indeed. After the destruction of Bullcrest, my mother and Margery believed that because they were twins, their magic was amplified. They were bound together by close magical bonds, and those bonds would always lead them back to each other. It broke their hearts, but in one last working, hurriedly and in fear of their lives, they sundered their bond of kinship in order that each one of them would have a chance to escape alone. I think it may have driven my mother quite mad for a time. Whatever else he did, my father gave her back her sanity and allowed her to heal."

I reached out my hand and touched the back of hers. "Thank you for telling me that. It makes me want to kill Dantin slightly less."

She laughed. "He is infuriating at times, isn't he?"

"Yes, but he loves you."

"He really does."

Three days later I was strong enough to stand without wobbling. The first rowankind had already found their way to the Lady's forests, and some had, out of choice, passed through the barriers into Iaru. One of the first was Annie, from the Twisted Skein in Plymouth.

"I like her a lot, Ross, and she likes me," David said when he came to see how I fared.

"She's twelve, David and you're fourteen."

"She's thirteen. And we have no need to rush."

"You seem very sure of this."

He grinned at me. "I am, and so is she. We both have a lot to learn. I may have lost the stolen magic, but I still have my own Fae magic to master. Actually, I haven't lost all my Sumner magic either, though it feels different." He raised an index finger and produced a small steady flame. "The Sumners always had their own magic. It wasn't all stolen. I bet you still have some of yours."

Maybe I did. I wasn't trying it out yet, though.

"What will you do now, Ross?"

"I need to make one more trip to the ocean, to say my proper good-byes."

He nodded. "Give the crew of the *Heart* my good wishes."

"Has anyone heard how it goes in the cities?" I asked.

"Is there blood in the streets? Have the rowankind risen against their former masters?"

David beckoned Annie forward from where she'd been hovering. "Tell Ross what happened in Plymouth."

She started to bob a curtsey and then stopped herself and glanced sideways at David. He gave her a nod of encouragement.

"I was in the yard at the Skein, my hands in a tub of wash water going from cool to cold. I wished the water could warm itself again, and then I realized it was doing. Warmer and warmer until it was quite heated up and my fingers didn't hurt nearly as much. Then I realized they didn't hurt at all, and neither did my back from bending over the tub. I felt new again. Like I was hardly me anymore. And I thought to myself, what am I doing working for poor vittles and a worn blanket to sleep under?"

A little smile played on her lips. "And then cook walked out of the kitchen straight as a lady, screwing up her apron in her hands and dropping it on the floor. The master came into the yard all of a bluster and told us to get back to work, but John Ostler told him that working for nothing was a thing of the past and if he wanted our labor he must pay a fair wage for it. The master said—" She pressed her lips together. "I can't rightly say exactly what the master said, but it wasn't polite, so we all walked right out of the yard and didn't look back. There was a crowd of folks just like us, gathering in the market square, all laughing and talking and standing straighter than they'd ever stood before. I swear I felt as though I'd grown a handspan in just a few minutes."

She giggled. "The master followed us and threatened to send for the law, but we looked at each other and back at him and wondered what the law could do. There were plainly more of us than there were special constables in the whole town. Someone said the redcoats had been sent for, so John Ostler said we should march to meet them. Someone said we should arm ourselves, but John Ostler said that would be foolish and they listened to him."

She took a deep breath. "I didn't know what would happen, but I followed anyway. On Broad Street there was a wall of redcoats with muskets and a troop of Kingsmen with sabers drawn. The officer at their head had his hand on his sword, but he didn't draw it, and he didn't tell the redcoats to raise their muskets either, so we stood and looked at them, and they stood and looked at us. By this time there were hundreds of us. Maybe a thousand. I don't know what a thousand folks look like, but it was a lot. I think there were more of us than there were of them, though we didn't have muskets, of course. I can add up. Even if the Kingsmen had fired their muskets there would have been hundreds of us all over them before they could reload, and weapons or no, they couldn't stand against us.

"Anyhow, the captain stepped forward to have words with John Ostler and some of the other leaders, and they ended up shaking hands. The rowankind were allowed to march out of the city, all those who wanted to."

"Did they all want to?" I wondered about Captain Ezra Pargeter's wife Minna. There were those tied to humankind by bonds impossible to break by magic.

Annie shook her head. "John Ostler walked with us to the Tavistock Road and then shook my hand and Elsie Cook's hand and said he was going back to the Twisted Skein to negotiate a fair wage. He said if the master wouldn't agree to it, he'd try the Queen's Head over the road because surely every inn in Plymouth would be needing experienced ostlers, but he hoped the master would listen to sense because he liked working with the horses and didn't want anyone slapdash looking after Bonnie and Major and Grayboy."

"But you didn't want to stay?"

"There was nothing for me there, and I felt the pull of the Okewood. I didn't rightly know what was waiting, but it had to be better than skivvying."

David reached out and took her hand, and she smiled at him. She'd found something better at last.

We left Iaru, or Iaru left us, David promising that we should meet again soon, and we four mortals—three humans and a shapechanger—began to pick up the pieces of our lives as best we could. With Iaru's perpetual summer behind us, the autumn chill settled into our bones.

Rosie and Leo returned home to Summoner's Well with promises to visit exchanged on both sides, while Corwen and I, riding Fae-bred horses, traveled westward into Devon, staying in roadside inns whenever possible until we reached the Okewood on our way to the ocean.

Though our Fae horses could gallop for hours without tiring, we camped for the night on the edge of the Okewood, in a hollow close to a stream, where a woven bower provided some shelter from the breeze that shook the stark branches above our head, dislodging the last coppery leaves. The Lady and her entourage were absent, though the forest was still redolent with her presence.

Corwen gathered wood while I tethered and unsaddled the horses and gave them oats from the supply we carried in saddlebags, which seemed just as full after we'd taken out the day's supply. Corwen's dapple gray and my bright bay watched me with liquid brown eyes, following my every move. We had no names for them. I remembered something about it being unlucky to change a horse's name, but we couldn't keep calling them Gray and Bay, and Larien hadn't told us their names when he'd given them to us.

"So what do we call you?" I murmured as I rubbed the bay's saddle mark.

He stretched his neck and raised his head, opening his mouth and pulling back his lips to show two rows of tombstone-like teeth.

"Are you laughing at me?" I asked him.

He snorted and nodded.

"Coincidence," I said, and slapped him on the neck.

He shook his head and his mane rippled.

"Not coincidence?"

He shook his head again.

Corwen came back into the clearing with wood for a fire and began to build it.

"Did Larien say anything about these horses?" I asked. "Can they understand us? Communicate with us, even?"

Corwen laughed. "They're horses."

"When you're a wolf you understand human speech."

"I'm a shapechanger. They're horses."

"You don't suppose they're . . . ? No, that would be so embarrassing."

Corwen came to stand beside me. "If they were shapechangers I would know it. Besides, shapechanging isn't one of the Fae magics."

"And you know this because?"

"Because I learned my lessons well. When I first came to the Okewood, Hartington was my tutor."

"How old were you?"

"The first time? Fourteen or so."

"You came more than once?"

"It's complicated." He smiled. "Wolf shapechanger. Respectable Yorkshire family. We didn't always see eye to eye."

"Your parents didn't understand you?"

"On the contrary, they understood me all too well. The neighbors, however, were not fond of wolves."

"It seems I do have a lot to learn."

In the meantime both horses were behaving entirely normally, standing head to head in quiet companionship. No matter how many times I glanced in their direction, I couldn't catch them out in any unusual behavior.

Corwen laughed and pulled me to him, holding me close so that I was enveloped in his warm arms.

I shivered. "I wish this breeze would drop."

"You could do something about that."

I hadn't used my magic since the summoning, and wasn't sure I could.

"What's the matter?"

Until I tried and failed, or tried and succeeded, I didn't know how much of my magic I had lost. *All of it,* I suspected. And that was why I was afraid to try. I didn't want to know.

"Magic or no magic, I love you just the same, but if you don't try, you'll never know." Corwen echoed my thoughts and dropped a kiss on top of my head before carrying both saddles into the bower, leaving me to think.

I reached into the air with my imagination and tried to still the breeze, but it remained lively.

I tried again. No change.

I called rain, not really wanting it to rain, but needing affirmation.

Nothing happened.

Wind and water had always been my ready-magic.

Corwen emerged from the bower and could probably tell from my face that I was ready to burst into tears. Any number of times I'd wished for my magic to vanish, and now that it had I felt bereaved.

"What did you try?" Corwen asked.

I told him.

"Hmmm, well the weather-working was probably part of the rowankind magic. It was, after all, what Martyn the Summoner used to defeat the Armada. It had to have come from somewhere. Try light and fire."

I'd never been able to make fire, but I could make a light and heat it until the wood caught. I concentrated hard and felt a tiny echo of the old familiar tingle, but no witch-light came to my command.

"You're trying too hard," Corwen said.

"I don't think I'm trying hard enough."

He laughed and pulled me to him. "Don't worry, it will come."

"And if it doesn't?"

"I have a flint and steel. It's too cold to camp without a fire."

He kissed me and ran his hands up my body until his palms rested neatly against my breasts.

"Damn stays again," he said. "Well, it's too cold to strip off tonight." His thumbs massaged my breasts above the line of the stays. I could feel the warmth through the layers of my dress and chemise. "Ah, Ross, if it were warmer I would . . ." And he whispered in my ear, in thorough detail, exactly what he would do if only it were warmer.

Without thinking, I tossed a witchlight into the fire and heated it until, with a little pop, the dry sticks burst into flame.

"You see?" He laughed.

"You did that on purpose, you bastard."

"Of course."

"So my magic isn't all gone."

"It appears not."

"So I may still have my summoner magic."

"Can you tell where the *Heart* is?"

"She's off the coast of Bideford."

"Yes, but you know that. You arranged it with Hookey. I mean can you feel where she is?"

"Yes!" I grinned at him. "I can. She is off the coast of Bideford, just as we agreed."

He kissed me.

I didn't reply as the kiss deepened, and I pulled him down into the overhang of the bower, sheltered from the breeze I could no longer control, but warmed by the fire I'd built.

It was a long kiss, full of promises on both sides. Before the next one began I managed a throaty growl. "So now you have to do what you said. I'm not even sure it's physically possible without pulling a muscle or putting your back out."

"I always keep my promises."

Hours later, safe in Corwen's warm embrace, I used my magic again and called the *Heart*.

I was still a summoner.

The following afternoon we arrived in Bideford. While Corwen waited with our horses I strolled down by the quay. There was little difference to be seen here for the town's loss of their rowankind, except that those who toiled loading and unloading the clay boats were wholly human. It wasn't until I reached what had been the office of the Mysterium that I stopped, my jaw hanging slack. The office had gone, and the old merchant house that had housed it stood a burnt-out wreck. Was this a sign of things changing at last? I hoped so.

Beyond that, the *Heart* bobbed gently at the quayside,

her decks clean, her sails squared away. It seemed she'd been welcomed. I stood at the bottom of the gangplank, so tempted to step on board one last time, but my feet knew what my head didn't and refused to obey. Never strong on material comfort, this little vessel had been my home for many years, and she still tugged at me in ways I found difficult to comprehend. Maybe I'd never be able to sever all my ties. Just as I'd summoned her, she might still summon me in times of need, but right now we didn't have need of each other.

Lazy Billy waved from the deck and, when I asked for Captain Garrity, pointed to a street where every other establishment was a tavern. I should have guessed. I found Hookey on the second try in the Golden Pot. The alehouse was run by a pair of comely sisters who seemed to have taken a shine to him, as well they might, for he'd transformed himself. He wore a fitted velvet frock coat, black breeches and polished black boots, a shirt with ruffles, and a smart tricorn hat, all a little old-fashioned, but very dashing. He'd got a new hook of polished steel, but the biggest change of all was that he'd shaved off his beard. It made him look ten years younger and almost handsome.

"Hookey!" I couldn't help but hug him. Now I wasn't his captain it was allowed. He hugged me back and I swear his eyes moistened.

"How are you, lass?" He squeezed me tight. "Looking much better than the last time I saw you." He lifted my hair off my ear with the point of his hook and frowned.

I shrugged. "I reckon I got off lightly. How's everything on the *Heart*?"

"We're doin' all right, lass."

"Philip's dead."

Hookey sniffed and shrugged as if it didn't signify. "I know he was your brother, but sometimes blood ain't thicker than water, not saltwater anyways. Davy's all right, though, is he?"

"Yes, he's fine. He sends his good wishes."

Hookey nodded approvingly. "We've applied for our own letters of marque from the king. Mr. Rafiq wrote the words. Will Tremayne's no more. We reported him dead at sea, along with his wife, so you're in the clear as long as you leave the Tremayne name behind. Henry Garrity is the legitimate captain of the *Heart*." He sounded out every syllable: *lee-git-i-mate.*

"Well, don't let it go to your head, Hookey, legitimate cannonballs do as much damage as bastard ones."

"Aye, lass, I know it." He raised his hook.

"Where were you when the rowankind were freed?"

"Out at sea taking a very nice French merchantman. We missed it all. I heard tell there was a right ruckus in London. A riot. And some big house or other set aflame. There's talk that folks is right out of sorts with the Mysterium, though how that will turn out is anyone's guess." He jabbed his head in the direction of the burnt-out building. "If you're going to stay ashore from now on I wouldn't show your hand, if you know what I mean."

I nodded.

"That's *if* you're going to stay ashore." He glanced at me slightly sideways. "You can always come home. And you can bring that fancy silver-haired fellow even if he is a werewolf. Well, what do you say?"

That was such a loaded question. It said so many things, including: *I really like being captain and I don't want to give it up*, but at the same time it also said: *I love you and I miss you and you can have everything back if you want it.*

I smiled at him and touched his cheek. *My Hookey. I love you too.*

"No, I'll keep my owner's share, but I'm not coming back. I've had enough saltwater and blood to last me a lifetime. Stay safe and give old Boney's ships a drubbing for me."

"We will that, lass. And you take care of yourself. And tell that there werewolf of yours that if he don't look out for you he'll have me to answer to."

I laughed. "I will, Cap'n Garrity."

Corwen was waiting for me at the other end of the quay. It didn't take us long to get back on the road, heading for the

Old Maizy via the Okewood, clipping along at a smart pace on our Fae-bred horses. It felt good to be riding free with Corwen at my side. Whatever the future held, we'd face it together, but I fancied we'd both settle for a quiet life, at least for a while. Rosie's cottage was available, and Corwen and I deserved some time to ourselves.

As for Will, after he'd saved my life one last time he'd moved on without my help, and in a way almost without saying good-bye. Like dying all over again. Part of me would always miss him, but it was time to start over.

Corwen grinned at me as we rode. "All right?" he asked.

I nodded. "I think I am."

Jacey Bedford

The Psi-Tech Novels

"Space opera isn't dead; instead, delightfully, it has grown up." —Jaine Fenn, author of *Principles of Angels*

"A well-defined and intriguing tale set in the not-too-distant future.... Everything is undeniably creative and colorful, from the technology to foreign planets to the human (and humanoid) characters." —*RT Book Reviews*

"Bedford mixes romance and intrigue in this promising debut.... Readers who crave high adventure and tense plots will enjoy this voyage into the future." —*Publishers Weekly*

Empire of Dust
978-0-7564-1016-2

Crossways
978-0-7564-1017-9

DAW 198

Kari Sperring

Living with Ghosts

978-0-7564-0675-2

Finalist for the Crawford Award for First Novel

A Tiptree Award Honor Book

Locus Recommended First Novel

"This is an enthralling fantasy that contains horror elements interwoven into the story line. This reviewer predicts Kari Sperring will have quite a future as a renowned fantasist."
—*Midwest Book Review*

"A satisfying blend of well-developed characters and intriguing worldbuilding. The richly realized Renaissance style city is a perfect backdrop for the blend of ghostly magic and intrigue. The characters are wonderfully flawed, complex and multi-dimensional. Highly recommended!"
—*Patricia Bray, author of The Sword of Change Trilogy*

And now available:

The Grass King's Concubine

978-0-7564-0755-1

To Order Call: 1-800-788-6262
www.dawbooks.com

DAW 206